D0960971

Midnight
at the
Camposanto

A Taos Festival Mystery

Mari Ulmer

Poisoned Pen Press
Scottsdale, Arizona

Copyright © 2000 by Mari Ulmer
First Edition

10 9 8 7 6 5 4 3 2 1

Library of Congress Catalog Card Number: 99-068781

ISBN: 1-890208-30-2

All rights reserved. No part of this publication may be reproduced, stored in, or introduced into a retrieval system, or transmitted in any form, or by any means (electronic, mechanical, photocopying, recording, or otherwise) without the prior written permission of both the copyright owner and the publisher of this book.

Poisoned Pen Press
6962 E. First Ave. Ste 103
Scottsdale, AZ 85251
www.poisonedpenpress.com
sales@poisonedpenpress.com

Printed in the United States of America

With all the love in my heart for the people of Talpa,
Llano, Ranchos, and Taos
Toda la gente

And for Jim, my love,
who helped so much and so many with his life

This is a work of fiction. While Northern New Mexico and its communities are real places, they are used fictitiously in this novel and are the products of the author's creative imagination, as are the characters and events herein depicted. Any resemblance to actual persons, living or dead, or to actual events or locales, is purely coincidental except for a very few specific references to the Los Alamos historical record.

ACKNOWLEDGEMENTS

With thanks and grateful acknowledgement to:

The enthusiastic Louis Silverstein, who cheered; N. Scott Momaday, Bill Crider, and Rebecca Smith whose belief in my writing was important; my patient, persistent and creative editor, Barbara Peters, who with publisher Robert Rosenwald demanded my best, and then some; my dream group who were always, always there with love and support; young Sean Privette who took pictures and had an adventure; my beloved Jim Ulmer who helped plot, kept me going, and with whom I can only share in spirit, and *toda la gente* who gave—and give—so much and with such devotion. *Gracias a Dios.*

PROLOGUE

Swooping, gliding, sailing, the eagle rose and fell on the thermals over the valley, now and again beating his wings. An early spring morning provided few strong updrafts, the kind that might rise three miles. A blue haze drifted beneath the raptor, *piñon* smoke from cookstoves that combined wood with gas in the adobe homes huddled close together against the chill far below.

The mountains to the east kept the community of Talpa dawn-gray, but the eagle saw morning sunlight on the vast high mesa lands, strewn with sage, dramatically cut by the huge Rio Grande Gorge, a rift so deep that the Great River seemed just a trickle between its cliffs, so deep that the crevasse muffled the sound of snow-swollen waters hitting boulders and pluming up into white spray. That same snow-melt added moisture to open the gray leaves to hints of green.

Birds flew in that gorge, dark peregrine falcons and red-tailed hawks among them, some flying no farther up than the rim of the gorge but still seven thousand feet above sea level in this high north country of New Mexico.

The eagle watched those birds beneath him, showing a wash of gold when he wheeled to take in the mountains ringing the valley. Those mountains bore lilting names and snow-streaked peaks: Tres Orejos, Vallecitos, rocky Jicarita, wooded Picuris peak, Truchas, and San Antonio where the eagle knew elk lived. But the landscape was dominated by Taos Mountain, the Pueblo Indians' Sacred Mountain, the New Agers' Magic Mountain.

It rose abruptly from the valley floor, showing both rocky flanks and piñon and juniper clad slopes.

Nature made ridges and mesas, arroyos and streams. Man made *acequias*, the irrigation ditches which gave life to the narrow fenced and hedge-rowed fields set in the midst of vastness.

Roads, mostly dirt, wandered here and there across hundreds of square miles of dusty plains, but travelers on them could not see the desert abundance the eagle surveyed: the quick hop of horny toad, the tail flick of the gila monster, the slither of a rattler as the sun warmed and these creatures moved to life.

Because the great bird was a raptor, he watched more of this life on the valley floor: a coyote trotting home from a night's hunt, a prairie dog standing upright on its back paws taking guard duty for its town, a rabbit nibbling its early morning repast, a deer folding its fragile legs to nap during the day. He recognized flocks of sheep he might plunder, cattle soon to drop tasty calves, buffalo, people and their buildings. Of these, the ancient multi-storied pueblo was here first, its adobe bricks made from the surrounding earth. Centuries later, when they followed the Conquistadors, the Spanish settlers, too, built from the earth.

Now there was a town of Taos to which the soaring eagle gave little attention except when a downdraft took him. Of more interest were the little villages and communities of Llano Quemado, Ranchos, Talpa, Los Cordovas, Cañon, and Cordillera, where his prey stood corralled or gathered into herds.

The eagle saw all this by sunlight in a sky that was now turning a deeper blue while the sun cast shadows of sage and highlighted each fold and crevice on Taos Mountain. This day was no different than others. The sky was almost always blue. Only the shade varied: azure, cobalt, indigo, sapphire. When fires were needed with the cold spring twilight, the the piñon smoke rose, darkening into gray, spreading low between homes and the heavens.

The sky darkened even more and the eagle gave way to the night raptors in the owl family, the great horned owl couldn't fly high or far enough to view all the valley. And it was in the valley that groups of men, mostly Spanish, left the Holy Thursday vigils at Catholic churches and chapels to march in procession back to their prayer halls, the *moradas*. These men belonged to *La Hermandad de Nuestro Señor Jesus*, The Brotherhood of Our Lord Jesus, the centuries-old lay society known as the *penitentes*.

To the north, that night raptor, wings outstretched, eyed one such group, dark shapes on the moonlit road below it. The great owl made a long silent glide to eye this straggling line, bothered by the wailing noise of men singing ancient *alabados* for, as they marched, the Hermandad chanted their hymns, a wild and primitive sound.

When they reach the morada, they will hold vigil for Jesus for they know that his disciples had slept while he awaited his death on the cross. The penitentes will sing to mourn Jesus' crucifixion, and they will grieve for Mary's pain, and man's sins.

Losing interest in the marchers, the owl made no sound as he flew lower to the earth, intent now upon the business of the night.

Chapter I

At the graveyard some distance from the Sacred Heart Church in La Mesa, miles north of Taos, a secret uncomfortable watcher squatted in hiding near a morada. The death squeal of a mouse caused him to jump, then berate himself for reacting.

He didn't care that this morada, like all moradas, was the prayer hall of the Brotherhood of Our Lord Jesus. One member penitente was his target; studying the man, the watcher had discovered that the Brothers always spent Easter week in the morada situated in this *camposanto*. Tonight the devotions of this religious society had taken them to the Church and soon would bring them back here. That's when he would kill one. He was anxious about the stabbing. Too personal. Not antiseptic.

He had practiced on a dummy with his usual compulsive care, plunging the knife into a cross on the back, making sure it went through to the heart marked on the front.

He looked at the hand, white in the moonlight, that held the knife and thought of his own bones beneath the skin, articulated to grip. His bones, his skeleton, an obsession that was always with him. When he smiled he thought of the rictus of death, seeing behind it to the hideous grin of the skull.

The assassin stared at the windowless adobe building waiting silently in the moonlight, three large crosses guarding the only door. The graves of the camposanto reached close, some mounded high with bare dirt, most marked with smaller wooden crosses and decorated with plastic flowers, their bright colors taken by the darkness. Here and there a wandering shaft of moonlight reflected on the rare polished stone monument.

At long last, the dark air carried the barely audible sound of men's voices, chanting incomprehensible words. Night sounds paused expectantly and then this silence around the morada seemed heightened, not broken, by shouted song as the brothers came nearer. Their alabados were plaintive, stirring, but did not move the impatient killer. He forced himself to hunker motionless as the penitentes wailed of Jesus' death and their love of Him. The stalker heard only a gang of wild men crying out strange foreign chants. Cold, aching from inaction, apprehensive, agitated, he held the knife awkwardly. His hand sweated despite the cold. Stabbing was too chancy. He would have to move next to his target. Close. Force the knife through skin, tissue, muscle, careful to avoid the bones. His thrust must not be deflected. It was unfortunate that shooting didn't fit the plan.

The killer looked again at the morada absorbing the moon's rays into its adobe walls.

He strained to see down the road from which the eerie sounds came. The dirt appeared almost white in the moonlight. As he narrowed his eyes to peer into the distance, the watcher made out the first penitentes topping the hill. The dark figures carried three large, red-dressed figures of Jesus, each wearing a crown of thorns. More and more men topped the incline and their singing grew increasingly loud as the band trudging back from the chapel approached.

The ragged procession turned down the path leading through the camposanto to the morada. The killer tried desperately to distinguish faces, frightened that his target might not be last but farther up the line. The sacrifice had to be at the end for this to work. The stalker's concern switched to fear of being seen although he hid himself behind a new grave that rose up higher than the old ones. That made him stand in mud though all around him were tall grasses beaten down from the winter past. Here the earth had opened itself to insidiously melting snow. He imagined the mud smelled of rotted leaves, bird droppings, crushed tiny new grass, and, yes, seepage from the body liquefying in its coffin, the bugs, the bones surrendering their flesh—a horrible sweetness. Could he see the miasma, the vapors formed from decay, corruption? Was there a low ground fog? Nothing at all?

The moonlight shone too brightly. His breath came too fast. Panic filled his brain. He wiped the knife on his pants for a better grip.

The noise made by the penitentes' marching feet covered any sound the killer made as he slipped in a crouch from grave to grave. He brushed against stiff plastic flowers while the voices rose in devotion, then began to fade as slowly, too slowly, more and more brothers entered the windowless morada. The last of the line neared the low door. The hunter inhaled sharply as he raised the knife.

CHAPTER II

In Talpa, on the south side of Taos, some thirty miles from that La Mesa morada, Christina Garcia y Grant could faintly hear a different group of penitentes singing their hymns. Their prayer hall was fairly close to her *hacienda* and the night held an old silence beneath the alabados. Alone in her kitchen, Christy shivered in response. The sound thrummed in her blood, a fervent wailing that took her back in time. The ghosts of her Spanish ancestors stirred in the hacienda that once had been theirs. They had also marked Christy as one of them. The bloodline showed in her warm skin tones, the high cheek bones in her oval face, and the green eyes contributed by some northern Spaniard. Her thick short hair was black, shot through with gray.

Yes, she shared the hacienda with followers of the Conquistadors and when Grandmama left the property to her, Christy saw it as a way out of practicing law. She would make it into a bed and breakfast that would let her leave the courts to write instead. She was burned out from all the years of struggle, fighting for those who couldn't pay what her fellow attorneys demanded of them. The unending parade of people in need of legal help overwhelmed her. She could see them, a line stretching into infinity. And then there were the Rambos, those attorneys with attitudes and a slash-and-burn approach to the law. Life was too short and writing was her love.

Christy came home to Talpa, but "Anglo-cized" said some old friends. Bad enough to go away to college and then to law school, Christy had made it worse by marrying an Anglo. Then, when her beloved Jean Paul Grant died, she continued her career alone, away from Talpa and Taos and family. Now, Christy found the move home left her sometimes shaken, unbalanced between an uncertain place in the ancient Spanish culture and an Anglo world that she couldn't fully embrace.

Christy gave herself a shake. "Listen to those chants," she thought. They returned her to a sweeter past. and she smiled at the memory of one night when she and her sister Odelia were very young. Grandmama had called them to come quick to the window to see the penitentes pass by.

Count how many you see, m'hijas. Count them quickly.

Three, four, seven, thirteen. Fifteen, Grandmama.

Ah, my daughters. Only eleven living march. The graves have given up their dead this night. They march to repent their sins.

Christy glanced toward the kitchen window over the sink. Were the dead marching with their brothers tonight? Nothing moved in the darkness beyond the warm yellow light that spilled on the dirt road outside.

The windows across the kitchen looked out over the courtyard side. Their light pooled on the brick floor of the portal that ringed the inside of the hacienda. Traditionally the old adobe had few outside doors or windows, turning its back on the world, opening its heart to the courtyard in its center. There, sheltered by the U-shaped dwelling and its encircling high adobe walls, daffodils bloomed; the swamp willow by the gate in the wall showed reddish yellow with the thought of leaves; and the cherry trees were seriously considering putting out pink buds.

This cold spring night called for a fire. One burned in the rounded, beehive-shaped kiva fireplace, adding its share of piñon smoke to scent the night air.

Christy was late preparing tomorrow's breakfast because of participating in the Holy Thursday services that began the *triduum*, the three days of prayer before Easter. Tonight they had celebrated the ritual of the Last Supper when chosen parishioners represented the disciples. Her eyes had teared as Jesus told these ordinary people, "Do this in memory of me."

Humility came when Father Joe washed the feet of those disciples and recited more words of Jesus, the Master become servant.

At the end of the mass, Christy had joined other pilgrims taking the Blessed Sacrament on the two-mile walk from Ranchos to Talpa. The moon shone down on the long silent line of people whose procession repeated centuries-old tradition. The land, too, was still the same: narrow, stubbly fields separated by hedge rows that loomed darker than the fields lying in pale light. Everything moved, breathed, stood as it always had, allowing Christy to forget the modern world and her conflicts in it. She had willed her thoughts to the solemnity of the march.

Steps had shuffled a little more and breathing became audible as the long hill toward Talpa began to affect the marchers. Then, chanting, the penitente Brothers had arrived to lead the people to the chapel, their singing overpowering every other sound. Those responsible for the chapel, the *Mayordomos,* had thrown open the double doors to show the homely beauty of the little *capilla* lit only by candles. Christy had swallowed back tears when she saw the bare spot where the altar had been. The flowers and decorations had been removed, the saints draped in purple. The Church was in mourning for the approaching death of Jesus.

Easter would be the great celebration when Jesus rose from the dead, but midnight tonight would bring the depths of despair.

Night air, carrying the scent of wool and candles, had slipped inside with the marchers, and white lace curtains smelled freshly washed and starched.

Feeling the centuries of prayers that permeated the thick adobe walls, Christy had knelt to pray with the others who filled the little chapel with devotion and the anticipation of Good Friday.

When Christy had left, she knew others would take her place, parishioners coming and going until midnight. Then Father Joe and the Mayordomos would blow out the candles one-by-one, signifying the coming of darkness over the world at this darkest hour of night before Jesus was nailed to the cross. Because He was gone to be crucified, they would take the Host from the tabernacle, leave the door standing open, and put out the eternal light. That was always a terrible moment. The light meant God was present; the light extinguished, God was gone.

It had been a long night, but Christy was home now and she heard the Brothers returning to their morada, too. Her chores were almost done. The bread was ready, each loaf covered by a clean light towel, set to rise overnight, looking prim and tidy in a row. Christy would bake them in the morning, but she still had to stuff the oranges for breakfast.

"Nobody dies of tired," she muttered.

"What's that you say?" A sharp masculine voice broke the quiet.

Hard, irregular beats jolted Christy's heart. Well, certainly. There she was mumbling to herself all alone, then sudden chatter at midnight. The new guest, Duane Dobbs, had sneaked up on her. Registered from Oak Ridge, Tennessee, he represented the Department of Energy, checking over Los Alamos his secretary had said.

Duane Dobbs wore a blue silk turtleneck under a jacket, well-cut brown pants that matched one shade of the brown in its blue flecked tweed.

She forced a smile and hostess tone. "Oh, hello there, Mr. Dobbs. You must have found some late entertainment."

Tall and well-built, Mr. Dobbs smiled a charming smile. White teeth contrasted nicely with his graying dark hair. He appeared antiseptically white, in fact, while his flat brown eyes showed nothing. His face was thin, ascetic. "A very, uh, atmospheric place on the other side of town."

His condescending tone added to the irritation Christy still felt from the alarm he'd caused. She gave in to impulse: "You must have found Los Bailes. It has a reputation. Shootings— and the Devil's been seen there, you know."

This was obviously culture shock for Duane Dobbs. "Oh?" he said, looking blank.

Christy knew she shouldn't keep on but couldn't resist adding, "Wicked ways. They stay open Good Friday, for one thing. And I have an aunt who says she saw the Devil going out the door one day. He thought it was concealed, but she could see his tail sticking out from under his coat."

Mr. Dobbs decided to smile and change the subject. "Is that our breakfast you're preparing?"

"Stuffed oranges." Christy answered. "In the morning they go under the broiler."

Silence. Mr. Dobbs searched for conversation. "Nice kitchen."

Christy joined him in admiring the mellow old dark-red brick floor. It had worn down to a smooth finish and soft edges on the bricks, just like the round corners she loved on the adobe walls. Unfortunately, Dobbs broke the silence with, "So has my lovely, green-eyed hostess always run a bed and breakfast?" He gave her slender figure an appreciative look.

"Hardly," she answered shortly. His come-on was out of line. "I'm a widow-lady, a lawyer who's just recently given up her career." Reaching for the broom at the side of the refrigerator Christy added, "Now, if you'll please excuse me, I need to sweep the floor."

Duane Dobbs moved out of the way as Christy started up the step between the kitchen and dining room and cracked her head on the damned low *viga*! She always forgot that supporting beam.

"Are you hurt?" Mr. Dobbs moved toward her solicitously while the pain jolted tears out of her eyes. Damn! Damn! She kept doing this in front of guests, and they always asked if she was hurt. Embarrassed as usual, she lied as usual. "No. I'm fine. You just go on to bed."

Reluctantly, he eased past her through the dining room into the Middle Room and out of sight. Christy watched across the courtyard until she saw his light glow through the french doors. Duane Dobbs was in what had been the master's bedroom, the Don's Room.

The trouble was, Christy realized, that Duane Dobbs affected her as had some would-be jurors in her trial days. When her hackles rose at the first words, or just at the very sight of someone, she knew to excuse that person from the jury. Studies had shown that the potential juror would feel the same toward her.

The thought of juries gave Christy a familiar pang. I do miss it, she thought, my brain on over-drive, the excitement of the contest. She smiled remembering, And when that jury came in with a verdict for my client.... Now that's a high!

She finished sweeping and washed off the new *saltillo*-tiled counters above the friendly old wood cupboards. Then, after locking the courtyard door, she remembered to duck at the step-up this time and walked through the dark dining room. Although her money had run out before she could put electricity in here, Christy made charm out of necessity. The dining room was lit by chubby kerosene lamps on the walls and candles in the black wrought-iron chandelier. Guests were delighted with its ambiance.

Christy double-checked that Duane Dobbs had locked the outside door after himself in the Middle Room and then turned on the night light for her guests. She glanced at the heavy closed door to her left. The *curandera's* room behind it had been the healer's separate quarters in Grandmama's day. Right now a trio, Lisa, Lolly, Tama, occupied the curandera's space.

In the front part of that room, fine mattresses now covered *bancos*, wide benches made of adobe, which the curandera used for her sick patients. In the back, a low wall separated the new double bed from the healing bancos. Christy never mentioned to guests that the bed occupied the space where the curandera laid out the dead. They were seldom her dead. The curandera had been known for miraculous cures.

Christy stepped down from the Middle Room into the dark and quiet living room, *La Sala*. The large area was shadowy now, its vigas lost in the high ceiling, the fire down to lovely glowing red coals. A Liszt piano concerto played on the stereo hidden in the old Spanish chest. Too tired to listen, Christy left it on; the hacienda liked the music.

Searching out her favorite saints, the *santos* standing in their now dark *nichos* on the white walls, Christy watched stray flare-ups from the fire pick out one, then another carved figure. She spoke to St. Francis, ending with "Still have your little bird? No one's knocked it off?" Then she addressed Santo Niño, the Baby Jesus, "Thank you for calling me back to the old ways. Pray for us, bless this house and all who sleep in it. And, dear Lord, keep watch over all those who watch or wait or weep tonight."

Christy crossed the room to the long, many-paned window. She looked across the dark portal and moonlit courtyard toward the little guest house. Her friend Mac had created it from the old sheep shed. She remembered her prayer and added another line to it, one for Mac, that grieving, courtly Southern gentleman. She hoped he was sleeping, not lying awake brooding.

Up another step to the back hall where a curved wrought-iron stairway led to her room upstairs. Down here, Mr. Dobbs' door to the left was firmly shut as was that of the honeymooners to the right. Christy smiled remembering the struggle to find a bed frame and mattress she and her helpers could wrestle through the tiny door. She named this, her favorite room, *La Escondida*, meaning hidden, secret. Christy's Spanish ancestors built it about three hundred years ago after a lovely young woman, following the conquistadors, met a strong young Spanish colonist driving his oxen to Santa Fe. They fell in love, married, and then started their home by digging down next to the irrigation ditch. Chuckling, the acequia still ran happily all these many years later.

Everyone seemed safely bedded down. Now, if she could just make it up the stairs....

CHAPTER III

The phone rang at five forty-five. Christy was already awake behind her closed eyelids, aware of birds singing in the first morning light as they greeted the day from the high branches of the big old cottonwoods. She fumbled for the phone as reflex, honed in her law years, made her stomach a tight ball of apprehension. Too many calls in the dark hours. Murder. A wife broken and bloody. A kid in jail.

"Are you up?" came the familiar deep voice of Christy's tiny mother.

Relief and irritation mixed in her answer. "Mamacita! It's not even six yet!"

"*Verdad. Pero, solamente los enfermos y la gente mala duerman tarde,*" Perfecta Garcia rattled off in Spanish.

"Talk English, Mamacita. I was dumb to think it was cool to refuse to speak Spanish when I was little. Just remember how they punished us in school. So, what is it?"

"Christina, Christina," Perfecta sighed. "I *said* 'only the sick and wicked sleep late.'"

"Mama!" Christy remonstrated. Something bad was coming and she wanted to get it over with.

"And *si*, you are no longer little, but big now. Perhaps too big, but—"

"Big compared to your five-foot nothing. Five six is not too big. Only among the aunts and uncles, *tias* and *tios*." As usual she was being led off the subject.

"Hold your tongue, Christina. I call with the sad news. Did you hear?"

Christy sat up, reaching back to prop up three pillows. She tried to shake off the dregs of sleep. "Hear what, Mamacita? Did someone die?"

"It is on the first Hometown News. The one that comes at five," Mama began. No one could ever hurry her story telling. "It is the *primo*, the cousin of Patricio, el Hermano Eusebio Salazaar," she sorrowed.

"What, Mama? What?" Christy asked, although she knew her impatience would provoke Perfecta to drag it out even more. Usually she made appropriate noises, patiently, as every detail, every relationship unfolded, but not now, not with breakfast to be done. Still, trying to be tender with Mamacita's easily hurt feelings, Christy spoke gently, "Mama, please."

"Si, si. I know how you hurry. All the time with that bed and the breakfast I never wanted you to do. Especially a widow. It is not seemly alone with all those men. Why not be the lawyer as you fought me to be. Why not stay with that?"

Christy refused to react to this well-worn jab. "Not now, Mama. The story, go on with the story."

"So. Los Hermanos wake this morning on their mats in the morada. The one near La Mesa. You know that morada?"

Christy sighed, hoping to bring Mama to the point, but she did think of the morada at La Mesa. It was one of the many scattered over northern New Mexico and southern Colorado. Prayer halls and meeting places for the Penitente Brotherhood, the moradas were in constant use during this, Holy Week.

Mamacita continued, "Yes. Well, when Los Hermanos rise, one does not get up with the others." She paused dramatically. "A most terrible thing! Blasphemy! It is Eusebio, the cousin of Patricio, whose mother married the brother of Benny Martinez' wife."

"What happened to him? Is he sick?" Christy asked anxiously.

"Dead, dead. Blood all over. The early Hometown News says 'an apparent knife wound in the back.' Who did it? Who knows? I know only that no Hermano would do such a terrible thing." Mama's deep voice now growled, "Blasphemy, I say again! Satan probably. You know how *El Diablo* must try to harm each good thing."

Christy wanted to discount Mama's Devil talk, but a cold darkness lapped at her mind, the horror of murder, the evil made worse by killing at a morada, a sacred space. The blood of a devout man. Good Friday.

Suddenly remembering her guests, Christy forced aside her feelings. "Yes, Mamacita. I'm sure a Brother did not kill Eusebio, and I am very sorry. But now I must put on my robe and start breakfast."

"Your robe!" Perfecta was aghast. "You will show yourself? You, a woman reaching a certain age?"

"Mama!" A number flipped over on the digital clock. She swung her bare feet to the floor and rattled off, "It's a long robe. I'm completely covered up. Really, I have to hang up now."

"Today is Good Friday. When are you leaving?"

"I'll make the walk, Mama." Christy tried not to sound too impatient. "Then go to the services at San Francisco. But it's getting late."

"Late?" Mama struck with cunning. "What of Eusebio, eh? Too late for him, no?"

Christy felt a pang, but she had to be firm. "Good-bye, Mama. Talk to you soon."

"*Bueno* bye." Defeated, saying the Taos-style "good-bye" in a little squashed voice.

"Bueno bye," Christy answered, having no time for that guilt either, and then dashed for the bathroom. She took no time to study the attractive face in the mirror. Heavy sorrow weighed her down as she quickly washed and lightly made up.

Pressured by time, Christy tried to make no sound as she slipped quietly down the iron steps. She didn't want to wake the honeymooners or Duane Dobbs.

The fragrance of coffee already scented the kitchen. Thank God for automation. Christy whipped into action, turning on the oven, putting in the nicely risen bread, spooning the orange marinade mixture into the orange shells ready for broiling. Next, she started to make the blueberry muffins.

It didn't seem right to be doing these homely chores in the face of Mama's dark news. A good man was dead, his family grieving, the morada desecrated by his violent death. How could she turn away and produce smiles and chatter?

Soon the comforting aroma of baking bread mingled with the smell of coffee. Plan on eight guests for breakfast. Twelve were possible at the dark, softly shining carved table. She turned to Grandmother's wonderful old *trastero* and got out the deep blue place mats. Next, the classic Mexican blue-patterned crockery. She straightened the massive carved chairs. Their plump seats invited lingering conversation. Sometimes there was too much lingering on days when she was rushed.

Christy stretched to light the candles in the black iron chandelier over the table.

"Allow me." That voice again, startling her, and a hand reaching over her shoulder, the arm brushing her breast. Damn! Overbearing, too. Telling herself to take a deep breath, Christy managed a pleasant, "Good morning, Mr. Dobbs. Sleep well?"

"Like a baby."

Christy forgot to warn him to duck at the low viga. Crack! "Goddamn! All the doors are too short for me. Who lived here anyway? Pygmies?"

Christy clenched her teeth at this insult and answered, "My grandparents were the pygmies. My mother grew up here, too. And it wasn't only their size. Low doorways, small windows helped the adobe walls hold the heat in winter, the cool in summers."

Luckily, the three from the front room interrupted with their arrival. Lisa, tall and svelte; Lolly, round and red-haired; and pretty Tama, seeming somehow fuzzy around the edges. Each was attractive in her own way and all had somehow latched onto the Taos uniform of old jeans and nondescript top.

Introductions flew about as the guests sat down. The trio took one side of the table, their backs to the high, street-side windows. Duane Dobbs was alone on the other side, his back to the courtyard.

Christy quickly poured coffee at the little table by the middle room arch. Then she dashed for the broiler before the stuffed oranges burned. Bent over the oven, Christy heard, "Can I help?"

Startled again, Christy whirled around and then realized it was her friend Mac. Lanky and relaxed, he grinned. "At your service, ma'am."

Christy smiled in reply and Mac continued, "You seem a might busy. What can I do?"

"Serve these oranges. Introduce yourself to the guests. Start slicing the bread while I get these muffins out of the tins—" Hearing an echo of herself, Christy said, "Sorry. I'm sounding like a top sergeant."

"You always do until you get this show on the road," Mac answered mildly.

Mac's easy-going style went with his appearance: tall, solid and yet loose-limbed, rangy. His shock of white hair contrasted with his black eyebrows and the somewhat youthful look of his friendly, open face. He wore a faded flannel shirt and equally elderly jeans. Comfortable in his bones, Mac didn't look like the surgeon he was. He seemed made to stride the open range.

Christy needed to share the bad news. She moved near to murmur, "It's not my usual early morning tension, Mac. An Hermano—you know, a penitente—was killed at the morada up in La Mesa."

"What! Was he family? Someone close?"

"Shhh. I don't want to upset the guests," Christy whispered. "Not related, no, but yes, family in a way. They all are. I had to tell you. Maybe you'd have to be Spanish and a *Taoseño* to understand. Los Hermanos are part of our lives, guardians in a way...."

Mac squeezed her shoulder with one big hand.

"Oh, Lord! Mac," Christy sighed. "I used to go with Mama to take food to this morada during Holy Week. And my sister and I got to be the little girls dressed in black."

Mac's face showed his puzzlement.

"They represent the two Marys and lead Los Hermanos in one procession....No, I've probably only seen this Eusebio around, but he's part of the family." She mourned for a man she didn't know, because he was a Brother, because it was so unfair, because the old ways were dying, too.

"I understand." Mac gave her a quick hug. "And I'll surely do what I can with our Taos breakfast stories. Let you out of some hostessing."

Christy thanked Mac for his support but her mind quickly returned to the crime. She wondered who would handle the investigation and how they would treat the Brotherhood. La Mesa was out of the jurisdiction of her cousin, Taos Police Chief Barnabe Garcia. The situation could be explosive. Holy Week was already a highly charged time for the penitentes. Today was Good Friday, the solemn climax. The emulation of Jesus' crucifixion. Then add in the death, the murder, of a Brother! A dangerous mix if some ignorant cop came charging in.

Still fretting, Christy followed Mac into the dining room. The honeymooners were bashfully trying to slip unnoticed into seats next to Dobbs. Already rather fragile looking, their shorts and tank tops made Christy squirm with chilly empathy. When checking in, the couple explained that the trip to Casa Vieja and Taos was a wedding present. They thought it would be like the Arizona desert.

Christy began, "I want you all to meet Jack and—"

"This is Mrs. Ravioli," the groom added with pride. "*Mrs.* Jack Ravioli!"

The guests beamed at the couple and several voices said, "Honeymoon?"

Wide-eyed Jack asked, "How could you tell?"

"Stop it, Jack. You're embarrassing me," the bride complained. She was pretty in a pinched sort of way. "Hi, all. I'm Di. Uh. Diane Ravioli."

There was another exchange of greetings while Christy served. Then Duane Dobbs asked Mac abruptly, "You live here?"

Offering butter to Lisa on his left, Mac answered, "In a manner of speaking." He raised his voice for Christy who was back in the kitchen, "Shall I tell the story?"

Christy called back, "Please do, Mac." She heard him begin, "You see Christy's grandparents had a sheep shed in the courtyard for visiting guests' livestock. It was mighty fine, built up against the wall next to the cherry trees."

"Pass the jelly, please."

"Want more coffee?"

Christy took her place at the table as Mac continued his story: "Well, I was staying here, a guest at Christy's bed and breakfast when I came to Taos after my wife died."

Little murmurs of sympathy along with "Another muffin?" "Piece of toast?"

"She and I had planned to retire here—" Mac cleared his throat. "Yes, well...I thought early retirement...." Mac sat straighter, waved his hand dismissively. "Enough of that.

"So, anyway, I got to admiring that sheep shed same time I was trying to find a small rental. One thing led to another. The upshot? I needed some time to work without thinking, do a little physical labor. With our hostess' permission, I got busy digging out, rebuilding...Christy and I turned the sheep shed into what the English call a 'bed-sit.' End of story. Who has the cherry preserves?"

With her pretty, long blond hair swinging forward around her face, Tama leaned toward Christy, asking, "When you were showing us our room last night? Didn't you mention that there was a story about it, too? Some kind of a healer? I'm into healing, you know?"

Christy answered, "Yes, your room was part of my great aunt's separate quarters. She was a much-admired curandera. That's a healer, herbs and prayer, never to be confused with a *bruja*, a witch. They're very touchy about that."

Putting aside her other thoughts, Christy took a sip of coffee, and began, "Our curandera here had such a reputation for miraculous cures that gossip started. People said that she wasn't a curandera at all but in league with the Devil, a bruja. That was especially appropriate here in Talpa—"

The pause received the expected questions: "Why Talpa?" and "Witches?"

Christy looked at the faces around the table. "Because, in the old days before they were driven out, Talpa was known for its witches. Back then, when the people sat around evenings, telling stories, each community had a label. It was 'cabbage heads' for Llano Quemado, 'witches' for Talpa."

Plump, red-haired, Lolly pointed at the muffins. Christy paused to pass them to her, then continued her story. "Bruja.

Our curandera heard the gossip. So one day, when she saw a group of neighbors gathered, she marched up to them angrily. 'If you think I am a bruja,' she said, 'when you see me flying through the sky, run fast to get your guns and shoot me down! Then, ah then, *mis compadres*, see if that which lands at your feet is I!'"

Laughter and applause.

For the moments of the storytelling, Christy managed to forget the murder, but the words "shoot me down" brought back dark thoughts she tried to hide. One of the problems of having a bed and breakfast in her home was the need to conceal personal feelings for the sake of the guests. Now, since she still had to hostess, Christy turned to Tama and prompted, "You're involved in healing, you said? Mac is actually Dr. McCloud, a surgeon but semi-retired."

Head shake from Tama. "Oh, no, you know? The other kind?" Curling a long strand of blond hair around her forefinger, "Crystal healing?" Her soft voice trailed off.

Lisa's voice was both mocking and affectionate, "Tama's into astral projection, too. Flew all around before she found Taos."

"Lisa? You make it sound silly, but that's the reason we came, you know? I saw Taos in my astral travels. It had channeling and the crystal healing? The workshop for all that stuff?"

"More to do here than that, thank God," Lolly said with her mouth full of muffin.

The phone rang.

"Excuse me." Christy hurried into the middle room to her desk.

"Good morning. Casa Vieja Bed and Breakfast."

"Hey, Christy. This is Ignacio. ¿*Que pasa*?"

"Breakfast, of course." She wondered if he could have heard of the murder already. "What's going on? This is early for you, Iggy."

"It's Ignacio, Christy. I've asked you not to call me Iggy. Who can respect a lawyer named Iggy?"

"I can, for one. Remember, I'm teaching you how it's done." She paused, sat down on her desk, her mood lightening as she pictured Iggy's cherubic face attempting a scowl. "So why did you call? The man who's never in his office before ten?"

"Why are you still at breakfast? It's almost nine."

"Don't I know it! I have to be at the capilla at ten for the walk."

"You should be practicing law, not cooking breakfast for strangers," he scolded.

Now was the wrong time for that routine. "Don't start on me, Iggy," Christy answered sharply. "I already heard it from Mamacita this morning."

"Well, she's right." Iggy replied firmly. And he could be firm: baby-faced, head of curls, and all. They were good camouflage for his go-for-the-jugular legal mind. "Anyway, I called because I need your help. All hell's broken loose."

"The murder at the morada?" Christy asked with foreboding.

"Just had a call," Iggy answered. "Remember, I have the public defender contract?"

"Surely not an arrest already?" That jumpy feeling in her stomach increased while her thoughts raced ahead of the conversation.

"Big, screw-up, Christy. Seems someone called the cops when the penitentes—"

"Los Hermanos, Iggy," she corrected automatically.

"Whatever. We didn't have them over on the east side."

That comment recalled happier days and Christy was momentarily able to tease, "All you have on the east side of the state is Texans. You know, 'Poor New Mexico, too far from heaven—'"

"'And too close to Texas,'" Iggy finished for her. "Don't rub it in. Back to my ignorance. They sent up that brand new State Trooper, Brown's his name. Can't find his ass with both hands. A sergeant, transferred over from my poor old east side."

Christy could picture some hotshot cop, all creaking leather, growing frustrated with the Brotherhood. They would refuse to violate Good Friday, the most holy of days. The trooper would command, they would stare at him impassively. His anger would escalate....Christy brought herself back to her desk. "Iggy, please! You'd better cut to the chase. I'm late."

Unperturbed, Iggy continued, "So Brown tells all the Hermanos they're suspect—"

"I won't have it!" Christy surprised herself by exploding. Too much. The Hermandad subjected to the violent death of a Brother. Then to make them suspect!

Startled silence, then, "Why are you yelling at me, Christy? Won't have what, for God's sake?"

Too upset to remember a roomful of guests, Christy answered loudly, "I won't have some damned cop trying to involve Los Hermanos! Men of faith and dignity! There have been enough idiots in the past who twisted penitente worship into all sorts of lurid tales. People still hunt them with cameras, try to sneak up on their religious rituals!" Christy's voice shook with anger. "They're already grieving, shocked that someone murdered a brother. Murdered, Iggy! And on Good Friday. And at their holy space. Goddammit!"

Iggy's tone grew cold. "Look, *Miz Grant*, you have no reason to yell at me. Do you want to hear the rest of the story or not?"

Christy took a deep breath, exhaled. "I'm sorry, Iggy." But then her tone grew sharp again. "It just makes me so damn mad."

"That's apparent." Iggy paused to control his irritation. "Well, all right. Where was I? Oh, yeah. Super cop told the peni....Told Los Hermanos they all had to come in and give statements. They tell *him* this is Good Friday and they're not about to go anywhere."

"Good for them!" Christy jumped to her feet.

"Both sides more stubborn, madder...Brown can't stand it. Has a tantrum. Tells the Brothers that they're all under arrest. I get the public defender call. I phone you. You blow up." Iggy's voice grew more forceful. "So come on down and help sort this out. They know you and you can try to explain their ways to the asshole, if you'll pardon the description."

Christy saw her receptionist, Desire, drift in the front door. Time to get off the phone and deal with business. "Look, Iggy. Desire's here. I have to start her working so I can get ready and make it to the walk."

"You shout at me that you 'won't have it' and then you take off to walk?" Iggy's tone was caustic.

Christy refused to fight. She explained it was more important than ever for her to make the procession to Calvary now.

"Afterwards, well you know I've mostly sworn off defending, but I'm going to do my damnedest to get this thing stopped right here." Christy's voice rose again. She was frustrated that she couldn't deal with the Hermandad immediately. "No one's going to tie Los Hermanos into Eusebio's murder! But I can't do anything now. Now I have to—"

"Okay," Iggy interrupted. "But when can you make it? No telling what's happening to the crime scene while Brown and company are threatening to haul penitentes off to jail."

Commanding herself to breathe and stay calm, Christy told Iggy about the Good Friday procession followed by the church services. Then she'd go to his office and take on....

Iggy cut her thoughts short. "Okay. Just be sure you get here."

"I will, Iggy. Thanks." Christy hung up and turned to Desire. She realized that Desire was why Tama seemed familiar. Both were tall, blonde, pretty, and out-of-focus.

Today Desire went for the clown look in a white parachute silk jump suit dotted all over with large circles, colored pink, green, and yellow. "Isn't this a happy outfit?" she asked, pride in her voice.

Emotions still roiling, Christy answered, "Yes, yes, it...aah... certainly is happy....Look, Desire, I don't have Ellie to help clean today since it's Good Friday. You'll have to do the kitchen and dining room for me. I'm out of here as soon as possible."

Desire gazed at Christy sweetly, her lips curved in a gentle smile, with no indication of understanding. Christy explained again and then invited Desire to share a cup of coffee.

Mac apparently appreciated her will power. The others at the table looked at her, seeming to wait for an explanation. Damn! Christy swore to herself. She'd forgotten about yelling. No doubt they had all heard that and then tuned into the rest of her conversation with Iggy. She wasn't about to start telling them about a murder at the morada or correct all the penitente stories they might have heard.

Hell! Now, Duane Dobbs was speaking, "I couldn't help overhearing" the sentence took an unexpected turn, "about your Good Friday walk. Is that the procession to the...aah, moradas that I've read about?"

"Yes." Christy answered shortly. Here it comes, she thought crossly.

"If I promise to be most respectful, may I go along?"

Christy was shamed by this request and by echoes of the language she'd been using. "Uh, yes, Mr. Dobbs. That would be fine. Just let me run upstairs and get dressed."

"You do that," he approved. "I'll duck across the courtyard to my room, change into walking shoes. Then I'll get the car started. Meet you out there." He might be from Tennessee now, but that New York accent, spiking words of command, gave Christy a wicked urge to salute. She resisted.

The guests seemed reluctant to leave the table without an explanation of Christy's intriguing phone conversations, but could hardly ask. They scattered.

She dashed for her room, hoping to make the walk on time.

Chapter IV

Christy honked and pointed out the window for Duane Dobbs to leave his car where many people parked. He could easily return here at the end of the pilgrimage. He got into the Buick with her to ride to the chapel.

Going back down the one-lane dirt road, already late, Christy found two pick-ups blocking the way. One was headed east as they were, one squeezed into a wider spot pointing toward them. Stop and wait.

Peevishly, her passenger asked, "What are those fellows doing? Don't they know this is a public road?"

"Mating." Christy answered poker-faced.

"Say what?" He looked incredulous.

It was a bad day and this man brought out the worst in her. Christy couldn't resist continuing deadpan, "You asked what they were doing. I answered *mating*. Happens all over, in Talpa, Ranchos, Taos. Two pickups nose-to-nose while the drivers hang out the windows talking. Some of us call it mating."

"Well, why in hell don't you honk? Get them moving?" His voice became a little shrill.

"Honking wouldn't *move* them, just the opposite. They'd sit there longer, simply to show you."

Finally, conversation over, the pick-up heading east started moving and Christy followed until she found a wide spot to pass, then zipped around some curves and onto the highway. The number of cars close to the capilla clued her that most of the walkers were already here. Christy found a space to park on the grass verge.

A varied collection of adobe compounds surrounded the little plaza. The small and sturdy chapel nestled in the middle, bearing a name larger than the building: *La Capilla de Nuestra Señora de San Juan de los Largos.* Some of the homes belonged to people Christy had known all her life, one or two others to newcomers. Walled and gated, one was built long and low the old-fashioned way, the house enlarged as the family grew, simply adding one more room, building with adobe bricks. Over there, an adobe wall had melted through the decades of snow and rain, leaving soft irregular edges. Leaning against it was an aged peeling door, open to space.

The Good Friday March was a somber occasion, but a glow touched the people gathered in the small plaza in front of la capilla. Their faces absorbed the delicious early Spring sun, shone with joy at greeting one another.

A wave of people crested and broke, and Christy was engulfed with hugs and kisses from friends and family: tios, tias, *primos*, *primas*. They warmed that cold, shriveled part caused by the murder.

Mamacita was absent because her legs weren't that good now, but two of the tias still made the walk, surrounded by great grandchildren.

Friends from grade school were there, of course. Seeing their children, Christy felt a pang, perhaps jealousy springing from her childless state. But for her there had been law school, a demanding career, her marriage to Jean Paul, his life cut short so young. Somehow the time never came for children until too late. Enough of that! she told herself. And no more of the murder. Think about this wonderful crowd in the sunshine.

Over and over Christy exchanged the set Spanish greeting: loving, friendly, casual, but stylized as a minuet. One had to know *some* Spanish. She wished that she hadn't been so anxious to Anglo-cize as a kid. Why had she done it? Probably it was the combination she'd told Mama, a process continued by college and law school. But right now Christy was well aware that if she didn't ask the questions, they'd still answer "*Muy bien*," so she obliged.

"*¿Como 'sta?*"

"*Muy bien, gracias. ¿Y usted?*"

"*Muy bien, gracias. ¿Y su familia?*"

"*Bien, bien.*"

These greetings sang through the crowd, moving like a musical theme. Mostly the people were Spanish, but some Anglos were mixed in. A few tourists were there, Christy thought, to observe our quaint customs. Newcomers talked of being taken back in time. Why back? she wondered. This was the beginning of the procession to Calvary, the way one recognized Good Friday and its awful sorrow.

The other death on Christy's mind, Eusebio Salazaar's murder, had been mentioned among the people, but no one was closely connected to him. Although Eusebio had lived only thirty miles northwest in La Mesa, it stood apart from Taos, a tight community. Most born in La Mesa stayed there, and few Taoseños would have been related to—or would have even known—the man. However, momentary quiet spots in the crowd signaled that Eusebio was being mourned. So far, no one seemed to have heard of the wicked attempt to blame his death on the Hermandad.

Soon the crowd parted as Father Joe and two of the Mayordomos came out the chapel door. Each of the three men was dragging a huge wooden cross. People made a ragged line behind them, supposedly two-by-two. The lights of the hired protective police cars flashed, stopping traffic both ways on the highway as the long procession of walkers moved across. The Hermanos trotted up and down the line like sheep dogs moving their flocks along.

The formerly ebullient crowd was nearly silent now, the sound of their steps muffled on the dirt road leading up the hill. Christy felt at one with these pilgrims, the *peregrinos*. Her heart knew that all of this walk was the walk to Golgotha, the hill of skulls, where Jesus was nailed to the cross. Most of the people here would take turns carrying and dragging the heavy wood to offer up its weight to Jesus.

Down an embankment on the right, the pasture was bright green, its still bare, ancient fruit trees sturdy, twisted. This was usually the first place spring came.

Beside her, Duane kept his word and remained quiet.

On the soft dirt road, around the curves up the hill, the procession walked two-by-two past the homes of friends, family, acquaintances: small and large adobes, some well-kept, some melting back into the earth, some traditionally flat-roofed and some with bright new corrugated tin roofs.

The march was prayerful, Our Fathers and Hail Marys mostly. The hill left many of the peregrinos too breathless to recite them with their original vigor. Duane Dobbs seemed intent on trying to breathe.

The hill accomplished, the walk was easier now. Willows showed yellow and chamisa grew green. Wire fences next to cut-off gray wood barriers, high "coyote" fences made of irregular tall *latillas,* and simple impassable brush protected houses and trailers. The walkers passed the occasional pen of pigs or sheep, here and there a horse or two, chickens, ducks, geese honking, dogs barking.

The singing began again as they marched toward the first of the five morada where all the Hermanos were now. At the beginning, the peregrinos sang the Spanish hymns as they had for hundreds of years, the words rounded and polished into the music by time. This one was in English, its stark words reverberating in Christy's heart: "Were you there when they crucified My Lord? Were you there when they crucified My Lord? Ohhh, ohhh, it causes me to ponder, ponder, ponder. Were you there when they crucified My Lord?" As they marched, the singing went from the last wails to the next verse, "Were you there when they nailed him to the tree?"

Christy looked at those surging ahead of her; all the people seemed so beautiful. Some were very heavy, some thin. A seamed and lined face here, an arthritic hand clasping a cane there. Some painfully swollen ankles. Young ones had sweatshirts tied around their shoulders or waists, boys had modern odd haircuts, girls ponytails. A few more Anglos—that used to be called "Americans"—were there, but, in the main, the faces were the same as they had been for centuries and their songs rose up like incense to heaven the same way, whatever the language. "Were you there when they nailed him to the tree?"

Suddenly, the highest peak, Mount Wheeler, blazed white ahead of them, while Taos Mountain rose bright in the sun to the front. When a breeze came up, Christy smiled at Duane Dobbs, saying, "Oh-oh. It's been too nice to last. Usually I'm the coldest I ever get when we have the Good Friday march."

"Do you need my coat?" he asked solicitously.

"No thanks. I'm fine so far. And if I get chilly, I have my sweatshirt."

Having come into full view of Taos mountain, they could also see the crosses and headstones of the graveyard of the first morada on their walk. The morada itself would soon be visible. The camposanto was freshly tidied, the graves decorated with wreaths and bright flowers, some plastic, some real: red, pink, green. A bed of purple iris just budded accented a flock of yellow daffodils. They looked very brave there.

Finally, the ancient adobe morada appeared, huddled low to the ground. In front, a life-sized wooden *Cristo* bent forward to drag his cross. He was dressed in white draped with red.

Looking back Christy could see how long the line of marchers had been, while the people ahead of them at the front of the procession had already reached the morada. Father Joe and some others were out of sight inside as the rest of the peregrinos stopped. Christy knew those in the morada would be kneeling on the bare dirt floor of the *oratorio*, facing a platform crowded with the carved figures of the saints brought there by many families. The most dominant would be the red-robed figure of Christ belonging to that morada.

"What are we doing now?" Duane Dobbs asked, breaking her mood. Christy tried to share her feeling of peace by explaining softly, "The Mayordomos have already taken the blessed sacrament to the morada. At this time, they're sharing communion with La Hermandad."

People shuffled about, talked a little, waited. The crowd was more subdued as the death of Christ became more real and the tragic sacrilege of Eusebio's death was remembered.

Chanted alabados rose dark in the sunshine like cries of pain.

The sound visibly affected Duane Dobbs. It changed his clipped tones. "What's that? What are they doing in there?"

"Los Hermanos are singing prayerful songs. Today they also mourn the man who was killed."

The sun warmed the mud wall of the morada as Los Hermanos emerged and lined up against it. They, and the women of the auxiliary who had brought food to the morada during Holy Week, formed a receiving line to shake hands with the pilgrims.

Christy passed down the line, embraced by friends and neighbors, thinking, "You are my people. No one's going to hurt you if I can help it." She looked at the worn, warm faces of those who had labored and believed devoutly all their lives. And she was pleased to see that among the mostly elderly Spanish Hermanos, the group included some younger ones keeping to the old ways. The variety of the devout, from many walks of life and professions, included an elderly Anglo cardiologist, a young architect.

When Father Joe and two new volunteers again took up their crosses, the Hermanos from this morada led the way, chanting. Their ancient song vibrated within Christy.

Some time earlier, the Brothers had placed little pictures marking the Stations of the Cross around the reservoir. Now they led marchers up its steep slope to walk along the Stations. At the far end, a rough wooden cross stood alone on the rim—stark, silhouetted against light spring-blue sky.

"We venerate the cross here," Christy explained to her guest. "As we come to it, you can genuflect, touch it, kiss it, or whatever you feel comfortable with."

The Crucifixion was very close to the hearts of the people now. One by one they stood next to Christ's passion in the form of this empty cross. Knelt, kissed the wood, touched the wood. Veneration. The man who died on it.

Up here, the wind was cold, the water in the reservoir ruffled gray. Silently the marchers proceeded down the slope of the reservoir, heading toward the next morada. Then, all at once, a frightening noise broke the quiet: the sound of sirens, many sirens. Their eerie wailing pierced Christy.

Most of the pilgrims must have heard the sirens, too. Heads lifted the way dogs will sniff the air.

"Fire trucks?" Duane Dobbs asked.

"Yes, and police and ambulances, and a whole bunch of volunteer firemen. Sirens on their pickups. You can tell the different sounds."

"I wonder what's going on?"

Christy wondered, too. She sensed that more bad news was in the making, but said nothing.

Tiring, their steps not as quick now, the walkers reached the second morada, and again, paused where they stood. This time, after a number of people had passed along the receiving line, an excited muttering ran through the crowd.

A cluster formed not far from Christy and she joined them.

Prima Bea was speaking, "Someone heard on the radio. No one was there to call 911. It's the same morada in La Mesa where Eusebio Salazaar was killed. Burned to the ground! Ruined. Totally ruined! Destroyed after hundreds of years!"

News had flashed that the morada in La Mesa was on fire and all the fire trucks in the county had sped there, but they were too late. The roof, with its vigas, latillas, straw and adobe mud, had fallen in.

Christy stood in silent shock as others exclaimed, asked questions, crossed themselves, offered prayers. "Was anyone hurt?" "Did Los Hermanos all get out?" "What about los santos? Everyone brought their santos for Holy Week."

And then, someone must have remembered what had happened in Abiquiu years ago. A voice asked fearfully, "Is that why Eusebio was killed? Was it Devil worshipers?"

A cold chill ran through the crowd. Christy felt it.

Chapter V

Christy panted as she climbed the steps and ticked off her day: a three-and-a-half hour walk, then Good Friday services, the Stations of the Cross, late night and early morning, stress. It all added up. The stairs to Iggy's office rose before her, higher, longer.

Climbing, she thought of her friend Iggy. He had been nothing but a party animal in his home town. So, believing that he'd never be taken seriously as an attorney there, Iggy chose Taos. Well, he was doing just fine, thank you, after about two years of working here. They met not long after his arrival, a short time before Christy stopped lawyering full-time and began to restrict her practice to friends and family. She had realized, finally, that she couldn't change the world or the dark sides of her profession. Back then, when Christy met Iggy, she was taking on all comers to fight for those who had no one else. Iggy asked to sit in on one of her trials and their friendship began. Although now she wrote novels instead of briefs for the defense, Iggy still called periodically to ask for advice, but that was okay. Christy loved the law. Those who practiced it provided her reasons for quitting—well, one of the reasons for a burned-out idealist.

Finding the outer office empty, Christy called, "Iggy? You in there?"

"Come on in, Christy." Iggy reclined back in his chair. The only place for clients, his age-darkened leather couch, was cracked, his desk obviously second-hand, but Iggy took care of the essentials: a fine reclining leather desk chair for himself and a loaded new computer.

Iggy took care of his appearance, too. His black curls shone, his rat tail was neatly braided. A new emerald-green, jewel-tone, silk shirt and Levi's covered his considerable bulk.

"You look beat," he sympathized. "How were the services?"

With a sigh Christy sank down on the leather couch. "Moving. Subdued. Good Friday is always difficult for me, feeling the death of Jesus. Of course, today, I was thinking about Eusebio's murder and Los Hermanos' problems. Then we heard about the morada burning. What a bunch of tragedies, Iggy."

Iggy sat forward. "That's not all. Just wait til I tell—" The office door burst open, admitting La Doña Doris Jordan. Her elderly feet sported black, lace-up British walkers. Her battered, brown, bulging briefcase swung vigorously. Her ample frame wore a formless tweed suit. And, naturally, she had pulled back her gray hair in an uncompromising knot.

Damn! Christy thought. She was anxious to hear about Los Hermanos. The way La Doña was acting, one of her diatribes was coming.

"Chauvinist pig!"

Iggy's eyes widened in his plump face. He tugged on that rat tail trailing down his neck. "Not me, La Doña! You, Christy, all women I know, may know, and never even heard of—"

"Hush, Ignacio! This is not a time for levity! That blasted judge—" La Doña noticed Christy. "Hello, Christina. Out from behind the stove, eh?"

Christy shook her head. Best to ignore this baiting. Besides, her old mentor had so few trials now, she needed to milk the most out of them, and her friends cooperated. They also knew that at seventy-five, La Doña was lonely, though she would never admit it.

La Doña had paid her dues: going to law school back when it was almost unheard of for a woman to do so; taking on "unladylike" trial work; fighting for unpopular causes; and working the unpaid ones *pro bono*.

Standing, Doris Jordan addressed her tirade to both of them: "That blasted judge had the temerity to condescend, to turn to me in front of a jury, to turn to me and ask, butter melting in his mouth, 'To be p.c., shouldn't I refer to you as Miz, Miz Jordan?'"

Christy couldn't suppress a snort.

"Don't laugh at me, *Miz* Garcia y Grant! Not when I push you into college, shove *Feminine Mystique* in your face and down your throat, nag you go to law school when few women dared, and you end up chucking—"

"Now just a damn minute!"

Iggy intervened, "Please, girls—"

Those were fighting words for both, but La Doña jumped him first. "Don't *girl* me, young man. That only applies to young women who have not reached puberty. I believe we can safely assume Christina and I have. As to my earlier comment, sorry, Christina. It may have been, uh, below the belt, so to speak. But I'm so angry at that pantywaist judge!"

Swinging her jammed briefcase dangerously near Christy's head, La Doña indignantly proclaimed, "I stood right there in front of the jury and His Stupid Honor, telling him in no uncertain terms that I was *Miss* when I was the first woman in this god-forsaken state to practice law. I had to prove myself to become accepted and be called *La Doña Abogada*, Lady Lawyer, a badge of honor from the people here, before Taos was discovered by artists and hippies and who knows what. Before we even had electricity! And damned if I'm going to be a *Miz* now!"

Doris added more sedately, "Perhaps I over-react....I don't suppose you keep anything worth drinking in this hole of yours, do you, Ignacio?"

"No, ma'am, La Doña. Pepsi maybe?"

"I'll have that if it's cold....So what were you people discussing when I barged in?"

Christy exchanged relieved looks with Iggy. The storm had passed.

Iggy said, "I've been hired to defend the Hermano, Pat Salazaar, on the Eusebio Salazaar murder."

Christy stared at him in surprise. "You have? An arrest so soon? But why this other Salazaar? Is he related? And, for God's sake, what about the Hermanos you said were being hauled off?"

Ignoring half of this barrage, Iggy explained, "Pat is, was, a cousin of Eusebio's, Christy. And I don't think you listened. Pat *is* an Hermano."

Two dreadful hits against the penitentes: the tragedy of Eusebio's violent death and now a Brother was singled out for blame. Christy tried to compose herself and think, making her tone matter-of-fact. "There has to be more to it than his being an Hermano." Her heart beat faster. "Maybe racial."

Iggy shook his head. "Too early to think that, friend. Maybe innocent mistake. Appears that when they took the news to Eusebio's family, the parents assumed Eusebio had been hurt in a fight with his cousin Pat. Had no intention of accusing Pat, but it came out. Then the family tried to explain it away by saying Pat couldn't help having the evil eye, jealousy over Eusebio's success." Christy sat forward, ready to interrupt. La Doña snorted. Unfazed, Iggy continued his list: "A pretty girlfriend whom Pat admired. Money. Seems that Eusebio had been making a good salary as a scientist at Los Alamos."

"Los Alamos?" La Doña snapped at the words.

"Yes, Los Alamos. Top notch lab assistant, amazing computer skills. Then something happened. He stopped going up there in the last few months, but somehow began making even more money. No one knows where. Of course, all these motives made Pat Salazaar look really bad. Easier for the cops to settle on him than go after the entire Brotherhood."

Before Christie could speak, La Doña zeroed in, "The money? Was the victim working regular hours at this mystery place?"

"Apparently. But big secret—"

"He didn't do it!" Christy interrupted. "I don't know Pat, but I do know that an Hermano wouldn't kill a fellow Brother nor desecrate the morada with that death. Then the burning. Never!"

"There's more desecration than the murder, Christy," Iggy said.

"What could be worse?" she asked, her throat constricted.

"I mean in addition to the murder." Iggy gestured, sketching in the air. "The firemen found all sorts of Satanic symbols on the ruins of the morada. Someone painted pentagrams, upside-down crosses, and strangely shaped letters."

"Oh, Lord!" Christy jumped up. "That does it! Some psycho trying to pin the killing on an Hermano and then libel the whole Hermandad with Satanic crap! I'll defend Pat Salazaar myself!"

"The Hell you will!" Now Iggy was on his feet, too. "You've been a big help to me in the past, but I'm a perfectly competent attorney and I happen to be the one defending Pat!"

Deflated, Christy sat back down and lowered her voice. "I'm sorry, Iggy. That was out of order. Will you let me help with that defense?"

Iggy breathed heavily for a minute, then held up his hands, palms out, sinking into his chair. "You know it, counselor. Couldn't manage without you."

Christy sighed with relief, only to hear Iggy continue, "Wait. There's more. Seems like the police also received an anonymous call." He sat forward. "Big surprise. Just happened to name Pat as feuding with Eusebio and suggested drug peddling might be involved. Said this explained Eusebio's new improved income."

Christy and La Doña were speechless. Then La Doña commented dryly, "Between a drug motive and Satanists, I'd choose drugs. The other is rubbish."

"It's all rubbish!" Christy grew totally involved in planning the defense. Her mind raced ahead of her words. "Obviously the murder and the burning are connected and that lets Pat Salazaar out. Remember, he's an Hermano, almost certainly making the Good Friday walk with the others and away when the fire started and those filthy symbols painted on." Adrenaline pumped through her body. "That means Pat couldn't have done it. He wouldn't. Never!"

La Doña placed herself in front of Christy, preparing to examine the witness: "And upon what do you base this touching faith in one and all Hermanos?"

Meeting La Dona's look with a steady gaze of her own, Christy answered, "You've lived here more years than I've been alive, La Doña. You surely know all about La Hermandad, what it stands for."

Doris shot back, "And you surely know, missy, that I have no truck with any of that religious nonsense. Don't know and don't want to know."

Just as caustic, Christy retorted, "Whatever you think about religious nonsense, I know you care about injustice. Think back a second, years ago, before we were 'discovered.' A few Hermanos trusted a woman who wanted to know about their beliefs. She completely betrayed them, made up a sensational story, invented all sorts of lurid details."

La Doña nodded grudgingly.

"Well, I'm not going to let those insulting stories get started again."

The Lady wasn't going to admit defeat. "An earlier slander doesn't prove this Pat Salazaar's innocence."

"You'd know he couldn't have done it if you knew anything about La Hermandad."

"I presume you're going to educate me," La Doña retorted.

Accepting the challenge, Christy stood up to be on a level with this exasperating and beloved woman. She explained that St. Francis himself had begun a lay society that became known as La Hermandad de Nuestro Señor Jesus, the penitentes. It flourished in this northern territory of Spain where a few Franciscan priests, who had accompanied the Conquistadors, stayed to minister to the Spanish settlers, serving a vast area.

Christy took a deep breath. She expected an interruption any minute. "Next, Mexico took over the territory and ousted the Spanish priests in the early eighteen hundreds. Now, no priests up here, isolated devout communities...well, the Brotherhood had to take over.

"And they were the government in a way, the only ones to bury the dead. They still do that, you know, and chop wood for the elderly and disabled and help—"

"Here comes some east-side ignorance," Iggy broke in, "but there's no Brotherhood over there where I come from. And I don't understand your faith in them either. Didn't the penitentes get in big trouble with the Church?"

This was always the touchy part, trying to defend, explain..." Yes, when the Church was re-established, the Bishop felt that the penitentes went too far, using flagellation and types of crucifixions—tied, not *nailed,* to the cross—in their great devotion to Jesus. They wanted to suffer as He suffered. But the problems, politics and all, were eventually worked out. Los Hermanos are fully accepted now. Have been since nineteen fifty-seven." Christy sat back down on the cracked leather.

Seeing La Doña rising to cross-examine, Christy regretted not staying on her feet. "I don't believe you've proved your point as to the man in question."

The Lady may have been her mentor, Christy acknowledged to herself, but she was not in court now. Running one hand through her hair in exasperation, Christy replied, "My *point* is that during this holiest of all times and in their sacred space, the morada, an Hermano just could not kill!" She hit the sofa arm with her fist. "Especially when it's killing a *compadre*. No way. And I'll prove it in court!"

Iggy cleared his throat. Oh-oh. In her passion, she again forgot that it was his case. "Okay, Ignacio. *We* will prove it!"

"So, young man?" Doris snapped. "Why are you sitting here theorizing instead of getting the facts from your client?"

Iggy pulled at his rat tail, smiled, and said smugly, "I did."

"Oh." La Doña busied herself getting seated by Christy on the worn couch, briefcase at her feet. Once regrouped, she said, "Care to share with us, Ignacio?"

"Salazaar's story is about what you would imagine. 'No, he and Eusebio did not quarrel.' The woman in question is a Debbie Valdez and Pat claims they were all 'just friends.' 'No, never took drugs, never sold drugs.'" Iggy shrugged, then clasped his hands. "Pat got quite agitated explaining he could never, never, take a life in the morada. Never kill an Hermano, let alone a primo."

"Facts, Ignacio, facts," La Doña scolded.

"Fact. He made the Good Friday walk to Calvary. He was in the procession with the other Hermanos when they saw the smoke, rushed back and found the morada burning, Devil signs scrawled all over it."

"And what about the damned Satanists?" Christy asked, her expression growing troubled. She hesitated, reluctant to express her ambivalence as to Satan himself. Even priests she had known were in disagreement as to the existence of a personified Devil.

Modern priests, that is. Mama's generation wasn't about to give up its Devil.

Daring their ridicule, she added, "Maybe we should consider them, the Satanists, I mean. You know, the Devil attacks where there's good?"

This displeased La Doña. She made a face and shook her head. "For shame, Christina. You'd better distinguish between Satan and some pitiful misguided, muddle-headed cultists. Satanists would never call attention to themselves this way. It's some attempt to steer us that way. And on this you'd better agree. Otherwise, I'll think your brain's gone soft, cooking all those breakfasts. Next you'll be saying, 'The Devil made him do it!'"

The color rose in Christy's face. Iggy jumped in to head off another battle. "To answer your question, Christy, Salazaar doesn't know much about their signs and symbols. Just that they defaced the morada. One drawing was an upside-down cross in a circle. There were some kind of boxes painted, a pentagram, 'funny' letters written on the walls—" Not immune to the tragic waste, Iggy shook his head. He continued, "Mainly, Pat was distraught at the destruction of the morada, the center of life in La Mesa for centuries. That upset him more than being charged with murder."

Christy interrupted with, "Did he tell you about all the santos? That everybody takes their santos to the morada for Holy Week?" As its impact hit, she almost wailed, "Lost. All lost!"

"Yes, he did, Christy." Iggy answered. "Also, I quizzed him on the money angle. Confirmed that his cousin, who was apparently brilliant, had even more money than when he was working in the lab at Los Alamos, but wouldn't drop so much as a hint to anyone where he was getting it." Iggy paused. "Here's the downer. When the cops questioned Salazaar, he admitted sleeping on a mat next to Eusebio. Never heard a thing. Tough to explain away."

Eyes alight, La Doña leapt at the challenge. "I may be an old Anglo, but these are my people, too. We're all Taoseños. This case is going to require substantial investigation, and I'm going to be a part of it!"

Christy and Iggy exchanged a look unseen by The Lady in her excitement. Whatever they thought of her skills now, neither was willing to hurt the aging warrior. "So, what's the next step?" La Doña asked. "Someone's setting up that young man, and Christy's penitentes. Setting up the Satanists, too, bless their shriveled little hearts."

Iggy stood, stretched, shook his considerable weight. "How about we all go to dinner. We can figure who dunnit, and what we can do about it, over food."

Christy and La Doña smiled at one another. Iggy and food.

"Sorry, Iggy," Christy said. "But I am truly worn out. Not up to dinner. We'll get together tomorrow."

"Then you may escort me, Ignacio." La Doña was regal.

"Okay. Fine. Bueno."

"And bueno 'bye to you, Iggy and La Doña. See you." Exhausted, Christy slowly rose to head home.

Chapter VI

Christy crossed the flagstone courtyard. Here and there she had removed stones to make random flower beds. She peered down in the growing chill dusk to see if daffodils or narcissus might be coming up. Maybe a crocus or two? Christy then stepped up onto the brick floor of the portal. She ducked through the low doorway into the kitchen.

"Hey, there, peregrina." Mac lifted a slice of bacon from the frying pan. "I thought you might be ready for a bite to eat when you got home. I wasn't sure about Good Friday fare, so opted for bacon and eggs, the eggs being a nice mushroom omelet. Spinach salad."

"Sounds great and smells better, but skip the bacon for me. This is the super fast of all fast days. No meat."

Mac raised an eyebrow. Christy answered it. "Used to be no meat for all of Lent. It made for ingenious cooks. And Mama's generation even unplugged the radios."

"Sit," Mac directed, handing out a fragrant cup of the amaretto-blended coffee.

Christy flopped down on the cushioned banco near the kitchen fireplace.

"I want to hear all about your day, but rest yourself first."

"Yes, doctor." Christy was warmed by Mac's concern. They smiled, happy to see each other. "But I do have a lot to tell you. Bad stuff." Christy paused, remembering her duties. "Where are the guests?"

Mac's back was to her as he cooked. "Well, the trio are in their room, the honeymooners have left for a romantic dinner, and our good Duane Dobbs lurks somewhere unknown."

"So you don't like him either."

"Personable enough," Mac mused, "but I don't know. Something jars on me."

"You're just jealous," Christy teased. "You don't have a silk turtleneck."

"That's probably it."

While they were eating, Christy beginning to tell Mac about the ugly developments, the three from La Curandera's room came in with a flutter of apologies for interrupting.

"That's okay." Christy assured them. "Were you wanting restaurant recommendations?" They were and Christy gave them her preferred list.

Mac wanted to fix Christy another omelet, replacing her now cold portion, but she said, "You're too good to me, Mac. Almost too good to be true."

Mac didn't answer for a few beats, then said, "I wasn't there for Betty Anne. Too busy being the successful surgeon. I've tried to change."

Christy had no response to that, so simply offered, "Let's just relax in the living room and talk with a music background. I'm really too tired and upset to be hungry, but thank you, Mac."

He already had a fire going in La Sala's kiva fireplace. That small blaze added its happy glow to the lamplight, while the high ceiling absorbed the light and remained shadowy.

They each stretched out in comfortable chairs with their feet on footstools, Mac sitting on his spine, long legs looking even longer. The two friends sat together without talking because Christy didn't want to bring the day's ghastly happenings into the peace they were feeling. They drank their coffee and listened to the classical music station in Albuquerque.

The room was pleasing with its muted sunset colors in the upholstery, beloved, carefully chosen Indian pots and baskets, and colorful paintings by her friends. The wood on antique pieces gleamed softly as did the polished old-brick floor. Tipping her head back, Christy looked up at the high ceiling, high enough that in the old days a gallery ran around the room. It had been built to provide sleeping and storage space for guests and the occasional servant.

She tried to center herself, let in the feelings she had been keeping at bay.

"Thinking about your day?" Mac asked softly.

"No, not exactly. I've been thinking that I got so wound up in Pat's defense I almost overlooked the death of Eusebio. That made me think of when my John Paul died. We forget the families of victims, talk only about 'a murder,' not the consequences of that murder. A family loses a real person...." The words to explain the thought failed to come.

Mac stared at the fire. "I know. I saw too many grieving families before I became one of them."

"I'm sorry, Mac. I was thinking about myself, not you."

"And so you should. Now, tell me about the Hermanos."

Christy was surprised. The story had been developing all day, thoughts of it foremost in her mind. She had forgotten that Mac didn't even know about the arrest of Pat Salazaar. Sitting up straighter, emotions flooded back as Christy remembered. "When I got to Iggy's office, it turned out that the police had arrested one Hermano. He's Pat Salazaar, cousin of Eusebio, the man who was killed."

"Cousin of yours, too?" Mac leaned toward her, smiling

"No, but Mamacita was explaining I have a cousin who —" Oh, Mac was teasing. "Yeah, yeah, I know. Me and all my primos."

"Couldn't resist. Go on."

Christy thought a moment, running a hand through her hair as she did when thinking or nervous, and then summed up the police case. When she ended, Mac whistled. "Sounds pretty good for starters. Is this Pat Salazaar in jail?"

Christy rose to go poke the fire before she answered, "Yes, I suppose he is in jail and even here that's a frightening experience. Since he's not been arraigned yet, he probably won't be until Monday, what with the week-end. He'll plead not guilty and most likely be bound over for trial."

"Then what?"

Christy sighed, sitting back down, "Since the judge let him be represented by Iggy in his public defender capacity, it means

Pat doesn't have the money to hire an attorney or pay for his bail. He'll be held for trial, only released if we can prove he didn't do it."

"*We*, huh? I thought you were out of the lawyering business. Going to write full time."

"I am," Christy answered righteously, but then added honestly, "I'm torn, Mac. Things happen I can't turn down. Eusebio's murder and Pat's defense push all my buttons. I think of myself as modern as anyone, hate to say Anglo-cized, but these are my people, *la gente*, and they've been screwed over so many times. Now to drag Los Hermanos into it!"

"But—"

"But I'm sure Pat didn't do it. And Iggy needs help. He doesn't have the resources for the defense that the State has for investigating and making its case." The fire flared up, its light playing on Christy's face.

Mac paused, then ventured, "I understand your feelings, but I, for one, would like to see you stay out of it." Mac's laid-back style vanished as he sat forward, brisk and persuasive. "This is far worse than, say, a knifing in the heat of passion. Doctors are supposed to talk of psychosis and such, but I'd say this is evil, an evil mind involved here. Leave it alone. Stick to your writing."

Contrarily, Christy answered, "That's another reason I'm involved. If the State machine crushes the defense and Pat is convicted, that evil will still be roaming loose!"

Mac sighed. "Well, then...Who do you think burned the morada?"

Christy started to recite some of her reasoning since leaving Iggy, but she and the music were interrupted by "News from our neighbors in the North Country. In Taos, a member of the penitentes, a ritual torture society, has been arrested for the murder of a fellow penitente. The homicide is linked to Devil Worship."

CHAPTER VII

Saturday morning, and everyone descended on the dining room at the same time. Mac wore another pair of old jeans and a flannel shirt. Duane Dobbs again sported a soft tweed jacket over a silk turtleneck; it was dark brown this time. Lisa, Lolly, and Tama had dressed in hot pink nylon overalls for skiing. And the Raviolis had apparently purchased warmer clothes now that they saw they weren't in the desert. Christy had found no time to talk with Mac since last night, and now she prayed the guests hadn't heard the news of Devil Worship. Much as it upset her, Pat Salazaar's arrest would mean nothing more to them than just a sensational story. Determined not to show her distress, Christy served the hot spiced apples.

"Cinnamon apples," Lolly whispered in awe. "My grandmother used to make me cinnamon apples." She burst into tears, her red-head's complexion flushing to nearly the color of her hair.

Lisa and Tama tried to comfort Lolly, everyone else busied themselves not noticing, and Christy could recall none of the many stories she ordinarily told to entertain the guests.

Di, blushing and shy came through with a distraction. "When we were driving around Taos, I saw so many blue doors and window frames. Does blue have some special significance here?"

Enjoying the old legend, Christy answered, "That particular shade of blue is called Taos Blue for the color of the Blessed Virgin's robes."

Jack was taken aback. "What does that have to do with any-thing?"

Smiling despite Jack's tone, Christy said, "Because it is the color of Our Lady's gown, that blue is supposed to keep out evil spirits. So, paint it on openings, the doors and window frames, and you won't have any evil spirits in your house!"

Small laughs and giggles ran around the table, the usual response to mention of the supernatural. Mac cautioned, "Better not laugh. Christy takes these things seriously. It's not without reason that they call her Talpeña Bruja. Pass the butter, please."

Butter, toast, and today's homemade Danish went on their rounds as Christy replied to Mac's teasing. "I've told you that Talpa was known for its witches, and these days people make a joke of calling anyone from Talpa a bruja. But," she added gravely, "everyone knows there are no brujas in Talpa anymore."

She paused for the expected, "Why is that?"

"Because one day, a whole flock of witches had gathered here in Talpa. They were flying from hedge-row to hedge-row as witches are wont to do, when the people saw this big covey of brujas and were very frightened. But three brave men, good men, chased them all out to the highway. There they made a cross of themselves, so the brujas couldn't come back. Ever since, no witch has been seen in Talpa!"

"Coffee anyone?" Duane Dobbs asked, abruptly pushing back his chair.

Not comfortable with his attitude, Christy also rose, saying they needed more hot toast and Danish rolls from the kitchen. She really wanted a quick break from entertaining. She didn't feel like it this morning.

Christy was just sitting back down when Lisa asked, "While we're on the subject, was that walk you took yesterday the same as the Chimayo one I've heard about?"

Mac quickly corrected her by saying, "It's a different sub-ject, Lisa. Nothing to do with witches. The people who march to Chimayo on Good Friday do it for very spiritual reasons. It's a long walk by faithful peregrinos."

"Ooops."

"Never mind," Christy answered her. "Sometimes there's a fine line between faith and superstition. Chimayo is the Lourdes

of this country with its healing earth." Thinking of Duane
Dobbs' Department of Energy connection, Christy added,
"One year the pilgrims walked all the way from Chimayo to
Los Alamos, carrying some of the healing earth with them."

She paused and refrained from so much as a glance at the
man. "They were taking the healing earth to Los Alamos to try
to save the earth, to cure all those crazy scientists who are out
to destroy us!"

Silence. And a grin from Mac. The phone rang as Christy
watched her guests decide on their reactions. She ran into the
middle room to answer. "Casa Vieja Bed and Breakfast."

"¿Que pasa?"

"Breakfast's happening again, Iggy. And, no, I'm not doing
law. But just you wait 'til I get my hands on the person
responsible for that lying newscast last night!"

"What newscast?"

"Oh, never mind. I'll tell you later. What do you want?"

"Testy this morning, eh? I need your help. Many Hermanos,
that's many I say, tell me we cannot leave Brother Pat in jail
over the Easter Vigil tonight and Easter tomorrow. That it's
the climax of the whole year. That they will all, each and every
one of them, bond him out." Iggy's voice rose with each
declaration.

"Then why haven't you gotten it done?" Christy asked.

Iggy answered, "I'm not your staff, Miz Grant. And secondly,
have you happened to check on murder lately? I don't believe
you'll find it listed on that bond sheet there at the County Jail
along with three hundred bucks for a DWI. And there's no
magistrate til Monday to set bond if one's going to be allowed."

"Sorry, Mister Baca."

They both paused. Then, because he needed a favor, Iggy
put an end to the hostilities. "You don't happen to 'have a
cousin,' do you, Christy?"

Unhappy that she had forgotten about Pat sitting in jail,
Christy said, "Damn! Iggy. I didn't think. It just so happens I
do have a cousin. Judge George Fernandez. Hang up and I'll
give him a call."

"Great! Bueno 'bye." Click.

Quickly dialing, Christy found George at home, and explained the situation. The conversation concluded with his gleeful, "No, it's you I should thank, prima. I'm not a member of Los Hermanos or I wouldn't be home, si? But how this will please all the family!" He chuckled. "Also a few points toward re-election, no?"

Christy called Iggy with the good news. "He'll open court for you at eleven this morning," she concluded.

"You've saved my miserable hide, lady. Now, what can we do today?"

Christy recalled long hours of the night spent planning how the investigation should proceed. Now she sighed. "First I want to question the Salazaars, Eusebio's parents." Her stomach tightened in anticipation. "I hate to interrupt them while they're grieving, but we have to. We may discover clues to the killer by finding out all we can about the victim."

Christy arranged to meet Iggy at his office, then returned to the table. The guests still sat, meal finished, drinking coffee and chatting idly.

Tama leaned toward Christy. "I couldn't help hearing, you know? The man you're defending and Devil Worship? Does that have to do with the Roswell UFOs?"

Lolly looked up from her cinnamon apples, "Nope. Some cult. Satanic."

Christy forced a smile while trying to shut them up. "My fault. This really isn't breakfast conversation."

Whip-thin Lisa turned to her. "I'll change the subject. I bought you today's *Taos News* while I was out on my run this morning."

Mac laughed. "We appreciate the thought, but that's only today's paper on Thursdays when our weekly comes out."

"Oh. Well, I wanted to ask about these headlines on the Taos Hum. Crazy!"

Mac started to speak and Christy felt like hugging him for taking over the Hum. She commenced clearing the table unobtrusively.

In the dining room, Mac explained, "The Sound has been our other major mystery. By the way, people in Colorado are associating the cow mutilations with U.S. helicopters of some sort. Say they're often flying nearby. But back to the Hum. Seems to have started bothering people quite some time ago. A very low-pitched sort of noise, I guess. I can't hear it and neither can our hostess who has downright frightening hearing."

"Is it going on now?" Tama asked breathlessly.

Mac shrugged. "Who knows? Unless one of you...." He looked around the table. Head shakes. Tama's was reluctant. He bet she'd hear The Hum before nightfall. "Well, one couple disturbed by The Sound wrote about it in the *Taos News*. And that set off a flood of reaction. Letters. Meetings. Ridicule." Mac shrugged. "It is hard to take seriously when you can't hear it, but The Sound's a nightmare for many people. They suffer sleeplessness, headaches, nervousness and so on."

Lisa persisted, "But this headline in the paper....It says that your Congressman has tracked it down or something?"

"The Congressman is implicating the Department of Defense," Mac answered. "Some secret military project, I believe. Talk of submarines using it."

Duane Dobbs suddenly pushed back his chair and left the room, causing Mac to wonder whether it was talk of The Hum or something else that was eating the man. The Raviolis and the trio were also standing. Tama brimmed questions, but Lisa had apparently tired of The Sound. "C'mon, people," she urged. "We're supposed to be up here for the spring skiing. We're going to be last in the parking lot."

"But, Lisa?" Tama objected. "We were going to see if I could take a class at the Crystal Healing Institute?"

Mac cringed and excused himself. Taking the last of the dishes in to Christy, he said, "You did good, lady!"

"What?" Christy realized Mac was more perceptive than she'd thought.

"Putting on a happy face for your guests, considering how upset you were by that godawful distortion last night. So," he continued, "what's the drill for today and what can I do to help?"

"Well, I'm lacking a receptionist. There's no Desire today. No, no pun please, Mac. I'll let the machine answer the phone."

"That'll be an improvement."

Christy automatically shook her head at him, scarcely hearing the Desire crack, intent on what she planned to accomplish on the Salazaar case. She couldn't figure out how to stop that lie about ritual torture.

Mac offered to get the groceries, then return to take over the phone. "Despite the answering machine's superiority to some who shall go nameless, I know you're uncomfortable to leave reservations to it."

Christy managed a real smile. "You're a doll."

"I am many things, ma'am," Mac drawled. "Doll is not one of them."

"So how about finishing in here for me and I'll begin on the rest." Christy started to dash through the middle room when the phone rang. "Casa Vieja Bed and—"

"Why is Señor Salazaar still in the jail?"

Oh, not now! Christy prayed that Mama hadn't heard how the murder was being reported. But, even so, that demanding tone meant the third degree was coming. "Don't start on the lawyer business, please, Mama. I will help Iggy with the defense. Primo George will have the arraignment, the binding over, this morning. Then Iggy thinks Los Hermanos are going to put up the bond to get Mister Salazaar out. Okay?"

"No, not okay." Perfecta's gravelly voice accused, sinking Christy's hopes. "It is not right. He did not do the murder. And Los Hermanos have better to do this day. These accusations, these are the crime."

Fighting back irritation, Christy answered, "I agree, Mamacita, but if you want me to help Mister Salazaar, I can't talk now."

Perfecta ignored her. "They say it is the drugs. I say, No. Did I not tell you yesterday, I think it is the Devil worshipers who kill him. I have seen things—"

"Mama! Please don't add to those stupid rumors."

"Rumors? What have I not heard?" Mama's gruff voice grew even more so.

Lord, now she'd blown it. "Nothing, Mamacita. We just don't want people getting the wrong idea about Los Hermanos." Christy stood up from the desk. She was anxious to get moving.

"I speak not of them, but of El Diablo who attacks—"

"Mama!" Was there no hope?

"It is not the superstition, Christina." Perfecta lowered her voice significantly. "When we went last to Colorado for the hay and we were late at night returning, I saw a ring of fire on the mesa where they do their evil." Mama was in full swing now. Christy was held hostage by a black phone cord.

"And your prima Dorothy when she was in Wal-Mart? Now we meet there. The Plaza is no good since the hippies and *turistas* have taken it over. Prima Dorothy heard the Devil worshippers are making blood sacrifices. They are all over, these *malcriados*, evil ones."

Too cross to think, Christy snapped, "I know, Mama, and near Las Cruces they took over an abandoned church for their Black Mass abominations."

"Do not make light—"

"That's one thing I'm not doing." Christy then echoed La Doña. "Let's just say that I'd rather track down a drug ring than Devil worshippers."

Mama's voice deepened to a veritable growl. "Eusebio Salazaar did not involve himself with drugs. A good man. Hardworking. La gente say El Diablo wanted to kill Eusebio and other Hermanos because they are religious men and then the malcriados burned the morada to worship the Devil."

Christy tried to ignore a sudden chill. "Yes, Mama. But I have to say good-bye."

"Listen to your mama, Christina!" Perfecta demanded. "The Devil himself murdered Eusebio."

Christy respected the old stories, the old fears, but this was too much. "Some *man* killed Eusebio, Mama."

Snort. "Well, *no sera el Diablo, pero aspesta sufre.*"

"Mama!"

"Si, si. English," Perfecta sighed. "I say that this man may not be the Devil, but he certainly smells like sulphur!"

"I'm going to hang up now, Mamacita." Christy was firm, but to no avail.

"The rosary for Eusebio will be Monday because tonight is the Easter Vigil."

"Mama," Christy said. "Bueno 'bye."

"I'll pray for you, *m'hija.*" As usual, Mama had the last words.

Chapter VIII

The community of La Mesa began on the edge of a high, flat, table of land from which it took its name, then spilled down the sides toward the valley below. Mesa and valley were ringed by higher mountains, mountains that once held the gold that brought people here. But now the mines were abandoned, those new-comers they had attracted long gone.

Christy always felt a little surprise traveling north out of Taos: the scenery changed so quickly. Mountain grasses and ponderosa pine abruptly replaced sage, juniper, and piñon. The roller coaster road took them past the villages of Arroyo Hondo, San Christobel, and Questa.

Christy told Iggy about the newscast last night. Her new worry was whether a wire service might pick up the Devil-worship angle.

"It's lurid enough," Iggy said, not helping alleviate Christy's concern. "Add in Satanism? Well, guess it depends on whether it's a slow news day."

Rocking along in his boat of a car, approaching La Mesa, Iggy asked, "You haven't ridden in her before, have you?"

Christy tried to cooperate in the mood change. "*Her*, Iggy? This is a thing, a car."

"You wound us, Madam. She is a classic Chrysler Imperial that any self-respecting low-rider would kill for." At Christy's look, Iggy said in a normal tone, "Sorry, bad choice of words."

Christy dropped the joking to worry. "We're almost there, Iggy, and I think we should proceed systematically. Talk first to Eusebio's parents. Maybe view the crime scene—"

"I say hit up Eusebio's house," he argued. "See if we can find anything. You know we could get in somehow." Iggy was grinning with excitement, irritating Christy, who didn't like the role of older, more prudent counselor.

"If you're talking breaking and entering, Ignacio, you know I'm not some hotdogging new attorney."

Iggy turned facetious. "Another insult—"

The tone jarred on Christy. Eusebio was a real person now dead, those left behind mourning. "This is no game, Iggy." She cut him off. "Anyway, the police will have searched, will have secured the scene of the crime. We have better things to do with our time."

"Eusebio's house isn't the crime scene," he replied smugly. "The morada was. As for the police, you know that the State has only two cops for this whole area. And the Sheriff's deputies on a Saturday? And way up here in La Mesa? Forget it."

Iggy paused, then added sadly, "But since I'm so inexperienced, given to hotdogging, maybe this isn't what my client needs." He shook his curls. "We'll just visit the parents."

"Dammit, Ignacio, don't lay on the guilt." Christy's green eyes glinted dangerously. Taking charge, she said, "We'll see the parents and find out about Eusebio's house."

"And where might they be?" Iggy wondered innocently.

"Straight down there, off the side of the mesa, where you see all the pickups."

"Oh."

The small yard in front of the old adobe home was crowded with the vehicles of those who had come to bring food and condolences. Of course, some people had come calling last night, but more this morning. The *valorio*, the wake, would be tonight and then a reception follow the funeral.

The early spring sun wasn't that warm yet, but despite the chill, a number of men stood around outside smoking. Others leaned back against pickups, bare arms folded across their chests. Christy seemed right at home as she passed by them, exchanging greetings, murmuring sympathy. Ill at ease, Iggy followed.

They entered through a low doorway. The small living room was so crowded that they had to maneuver around people, too many people to get more than a glimpse of furniture and mixed bright orange-red-and-black carpet; of walls crowded with religious paintings and *retablos*; of santos and pictures of family nudging one another on those flat surfaces visible between visitors. Eusebio's graduation studio-portrait stood in a place of honor. A candle burned beside it.

Christy led the way to the kitchen. It was very white. Even the ceiling had white tiles covering the vigas that were so hard to clean. And what a crowd of bustling women! Many busied themselves arranging the plates, pans and dishes of enchilada casseroles, tamales, salads, tortillas, rolls, and desserts. Others stirred the big pots of chile, beans, and *posole* that covered the top of the combination wood and gas stove.

Instructing, "Be sure to ask the right questions," an abashed Iggy faded back out the door to join the men in the front room, muttering, "I hope I won't have to explain I'm the defendant's lawyer."

Christy stayed, feeling awkward and out of place. But when she could sort them out, she saw with relief that most of the faces were familiar. Without having to introduce herself, Christy was called by name as she and the women exchanged hugs and sympathy. Offers of food were pressed upon her. While she was trying to avoid one more command to sit and eat, Christy was approached by a familiar, small, heavy-set woman. She thought, "This is it. Please God I don't make her feel worse!"

"*¿Como 'sta?*"

"*Muy bien, gracias, Señora,* pero I regret...."

"You are the daughter of Edmundo and Perfecta Garcia, no?"

"Yes, Señora. And you are Señora Salazaar, the mother of Eusebio?"

"Si."

"I am so very sorry. ¡*Que lastima*! But I'm a lawyer. I have come with my friend to try to help, to find out who did this terrible thing."

"Not my *sobrino*, my nephew Patricio, no. We did not mean for him to take the blame. *No comprende* when the police come." Tears were close but held back.

"No, Señora, you did nothing wrong. A misunderstanding. We also do not think that Patricio is the one." Christy paused, then asked gently, "Perhaps you could help us?"

"I do not know. I will try."

The lurking ladies, many plump, some tiny-frail, all middle-aged or vigorous elderly, decided as one that this was a good break-in point. A veritable covey of grandmothers descended, bustled Señora Salazaar and Christy into seats at the kitchen table, and produced coffee and food from the condolence dishes which Christy had seen. Finally, the ladies began to reform in groups, Spanish swirling and dipping.

Christy placed her hand over la Señora's on the table top. "Please, if I may?" This was so hard! "Another question? I know it cannot be true, but the police say drugs, perhaps?"

The small figure shook indignantly. "Bah! Not my Eusebio! He has the steady job, important job. He makes good money, more than his father. He is a good son, sharing. Only last week he bought us a new freezer."

Intrigued, a tingle ran up Christy's arms, and she proceeded carefully, "But Señora, one hears that Eusebio no longer works at Los Alamos?"

"¡*Metotes*! They say what they do not know because it is secret and they are jealous." Señora Salazaar was indignant.

"Surely he works for Los Alamos. I know this thing. *La semana*, when my son buys the freezer, I say he cannot afford so much money. 'Mamacita,' he says. 'Look at my paycheck and see if there is not more money there.' And that paycheck? Bigger si, pero it looks the same as always, the ones I see before from the government. Si, he works for the lab. But where? ¿*Quien sabe*?"

Good Lord! Christy wondered. What was this? What had she uncovered? Her mouth going dry, she asked, "You mean Eusebio worked for the lab but not in Los Alamos?"

"He will not say. They tell him he must not speak. ¿*Donde*? Who knows? Pero, this I know. My son does not leave so early in the morning and it is not so late when he returns....Ai! What am I saying? Eusebio is no more!" Her face grimaced with the struggle to hold back the tears.

Christy's emotions were in conflict. True sorrow for this plump little person, who restrained her grief with such dignity, battled excitement over the discovery. So much opened up to investigate! First, one more question, "I regret, pero—something was said of the evil eye?"

The mother quickly made the gesture against the evil eye, thumb and forefinger of each hand circled and touching, but answered, "Bah. Nothing. Perhaps my son makes too much money to please his primo Pat. Perhaps they quarrel a little about the girl friend, no? Pero Pat is a good boy, and an Hermano. He would not kill my son! No, it is the Devil Worshipers who do this terrible thing and then burn our morada!"

Not about to argue with Señora Salazaar, Christy nodded and then framed her next questions the polite way, "May I ask where your son lived?"

"Right next door. See, there out the window?"

"Would it be possible for my friend and me to go in Eusebio's house?"

"But certainly, although I have not cleaned it as well as might be. The police came and went inside and then came out and put the yellow ribbon around it. But am I not the mother? I say what friends may visit my son's home now, no?"

In the front room, Iggy had found the father, a frail-looking gentleman, sitting erect in a big chair, cane in hand.

Desperately wishing he knew the Spanish ways up here, Iggy was suddenly too aware of his own unconventional curls and rat tail.

Leaning over to shake the old man's hand, rather like bowing over it, he said, "You don't know me, Señor. I'm Ignacio Baca. I'm sorry I didn't know your son, but I'm here to help."

Señor Salazaar nodded. Did he speak English?

"Uh, Señor, we want to find the person who...did this thing. Do you know of any enemies?"

"No enemies. A good son." The father stared straight ahead, the hand on his cane shaking.

Hard going. "Yes, sir. I'm sure he was. But if you knew of anyone...?"

Head shake.

"Uh, no? Well, what about where he was working?"

"Los Alamos."

"Yes, I know he used to work at the labs, but where was Eusebio working now?"

"Los Alamos." Firmly.

Defeated, Iggy let it go and also decided to forego all the questions on his mind: drugs, women. They would only insult this man. So, again expressing his condolences, Iggy turned away from the proud old gentleman. Maybe he could pick up something from what the men in the room were saying, luckily mainly in English. Mostly retelling the morada fire, each added a detail here, a side-bar there, the way of making any story grow to maximum size. Nor were tales of witchcraft neglected, as first one, then another, pointed out how the El Diablo lay in wait always, ready to strike down a good person, to do evil to a morada or to a church.

Then, hearing the voice of a true storyteller the others fell silent A fairly young man with a stocky build was saying, "So, you speak of what awaits even a good one. Pero I tell you my great uncle-by-marriage is not a good man, he drinks too much. And when he drinks he grows angry and beats his wife and children, no?"

Wise nods.

"And you must remember that this is in the old days, no cars, all horseback and wagons...."

"Mm-hum."

"So it is that one night my great uncle-by-marriage has been at the bar in Questa. Oh, a long time. He drinks too much...."

"Ah, si," and more nods.

"He is riding home through the night when what appears before him but a pig. Si, a pig!" The storyteller paused for emphasis.

"Being a cruel man, especially when drinking, this uncle-by-marriage decides he will run down the pig with his horse. Faster he rides, and faster. But no matter how fast he rides, he cannot catch that pig." A sip of beer.

"Then the pig turns around and smiles! Smiles at my uncle-by-marriage!" His eyes grew round. He shook his head. He spoke intensely. "At the same time, a great weight comes behind my uncle on the horse. It seizes him around the middle and is squeezing the life out of him!"

"Ahhh!"

"My uncle-by-marriage falls to the ground unconscious. When he comes to, he knows he has met the Devil! He drinks no more in his life!"

Eyes sparkled and there were grins at this good story. Then one of the listeners decided it was his turn and began, "Ah, but did you hear…?" just as Christy emerged from the kitchen. Her face was solemn but those green eyes! Something had happened.

Extricating himself from the men, Iggy joined Christy. They tried to shove their way outside politely. "Excuse me. Excuse…I'm sorry. Excuse me…."

Christy barely managed to contain her excitement until they were inside the Chrysler, then Iggy pounced. "What! What gives?"

"I don't know where to start! Eusebio lives next door. Right there. No breaking and entering, I have the key. And, Iggy! More money and…and he was still working for the lab, the D.O.E., anyway!"

"Thank you, Jesus! No irreverence intended, but I thought the father had it wrong, didn't understand."

Christy flushed. "Just a minute, Iggy. I know you don't mean to sound condescending, but I do get defensive. Remember our Spanish people here, especially the older ones, are speaking two languages, the Spanish they grew up with and English, so they're way ahead of us one-language types."

"No put-down meant," Iggy responded. "Lord knows I wish I had learned Spanish. So now." Deep breath. "Tell!"

She did, her mind swirling with ideas, excitement overriding sorrow and anger.

Eusebio's home was a carbon copy of his parents', a small low adobe tucked against a dun-colored slope that was sprinkled with skunk grass, flat mountain cacti, and stubby piñon trees.

Christy moved quickly, nervously. Even with a key, one was not supposed to cross police lines. And that was just what they were doing, stepping over the yellow tapes.

The house was very neat inside; Eusebio's mother would not have allowed it to be otherwise, cleaning in her sorrow, police or not. Christy uneasily glanced around the front room. "This was your idea, Iggy, so what are we looking for?"

Shrugging, tugging at his rat tail. "Well, actually....Hell, I don't know....Something to show where he really was working? Check stubs, maybe? Or dealing drugs? Shit, maybe a stash?"

Christy stood still in the center of the room. This was stupid. "Oh, Ignacio. You're sounding like a Nancy Drew mystery, amateur night. Between the police and Señora Salazaar's cleaning, you're not going to find anything important."

"We could go through drawers," he offered hopefully.

"No way! I'm very uncomfortable being here. I'm not going to ransack a dead man's things." Even in this mood, Christy still tried to think. What might clear their client? Or, unhappy thought, point to guilt? What if there actually was a dispute over drugs?

Iggy said, "All right. I know one place that shouldn't offend your sensibilities. Anyway, it was good for hiding before everyone and his brother decided to go for it, under the lid of the toilet tank."

Feeling like a trespasser, Christy still tried to scrutinize everything as she followed Iggy back toward the bedrooms. "Here, Christy," he called. "The bathroom's through the last bedroom."

Christy stumbled on the scrunched end of a small throw-rug as she stepped through the bathroom door, looked down, and saw a little mud ball and then another. A trail of them. A shiver shook her and sounded in her voice. "Iggy, Look here."

Ignacio was not impressed. "You've got a piece of dirt?"

Christy was revolted but intrigued. "No, look. It's shaped into a ball and there's a black hair wound into it."

"So?"

"So. It's an evil thing. Disgusting. Here's your witchcraft! I've heard about these all my life. It's one way to put a hex on a person, a strand of their hair in a clay ball. Then certain incantations, of course." Christy dropped one of the nasty things in her pocket. She needed to save it but had to get it out of her hand.

Iggy didn't seem interested, but Christy persisted, "This is important even if you don't believe in witchcraft. It means there's someone's around here who practices it. Not likely Eusebio dropped them under the edge of the rug. Most likely, the hex targeted Eusebio."

"I guess it worked. He's dead."

Christy's tone turned icy. "That's a crappy thing to say, Ignacio."

"Sorry," Iggy offered casually.

As Christy knelt on one knee to pick up two hex balls by the bathroom door jamb, that floor tile shifted under her weight. Curious, she got her fingers under the edge and lifted.

"Iggy, look!"

The dirt under the tile had been hollowed out. Several baggies lay there, each filled with a white substance looking like powdered sugar.

"Aw shit!" Iggy gingerly took out one little parcel. "A whole cache of dime bags."

"Dime?"

"Ten bucks a pop. Looks like our boy was dealing." Iggy's tone was discouraged.

"Did you check the toilet tank?"

"I was mostly joking. There's nothing there. Too obvious these days."

Knowing the bags must contain cocaine, Christy shook her head. "This could still be a plant, Iggy."

"That it could, counselor. That it could. Hold the thought, at least....But what about your hex balls?"

"I don't know. Maybe we *are* looking at witchcraft and Eusebio was making his money dealing."

Iggy slipped the small bags into his pocket, saying, "We'll decide what to do with these when we're in the car and on our way."

They casually walked out the front door. Christy knew that all the eyes in the nearby house were not really on them, that no one could see the baggie in Iggy's pocket, but she felt horribly conspicuous as they walked quickly, not too quickly, to the Chrysler.

Once in the car, Iggy drove sedately up the hill. "I don't like it," he said.

"I don't like it either," Christy fretted. "We have to take the stuff to the police. If Eusebio was dealing, that could involve all sorts of people as suspects."

"That's not what I meant." Iggy spoke crisply, all mannerisms gone. "Just think a minute before you keep on with the objections. The hex balls led you to the coke hiding place. I think a very clever mind is behind it." Iggy took a hand from steering to tug at his rat tail. "You were the one to defend Pat Salazaar, say that he wouldn't kill a brother Hermano, all the rest of it. Now these packages of dope at the dead man's house? It sets Pat up, adds to that phone call about drugs."

Christy was reflective, her thoughts flying. "Yes. The coke corroborates the tip. Eusebio's dealing, Pat's wiping out the competition." She spoke faster. "Now, I'll bet there's another phone call to the police to get them back here to find the coke. It's part of the frame—a good one. Satanic symbols on the morada, hex balls in the dead man's house...."

"Right. And these baggies are going into my office safe."

At these words, Christy's stomach clenched. "That's no solution. Concealing evidence, obstruction of justice. You have to turn the coke over to the police."

"Sure," he answered. "The State troopers are in charge out here in the county. No primo there. What do you think the good Sergeant Brown will make of drugs in Eusebio's house? He already showed what he thinks of your Brotherhood."

The question hung in the silent car as Iggy drove up the hill to the main road. Christy considered that Pat might be set up, and not necessarily by the killer. Sergeant Brown could be a racist. The next defense step should be to secure Pat's house, make sure they saw to it that there were no planted drugs or hex balls, whatever those foul things meant.

When Christy voiced these thoughts, Iggy informed her that the police had already searched Pat's place. "It's too late for second thoughts from the killer. Or the Devil."

"Don't joke about Satan, Iggy. We need to think seriously about what we're dealing with. Drugs, or Devil worship. This could be directed at my people, give the Hermandad a black eye."

Iggy couldn't resist, "Maybe spells go better with coke."

Other than giving the man one of her looks, Christy ignored that to ask, "Where are you going, Iggy?"

"Nowhere. Just driving while I think."

Christy looked around as Iggy's ancient Chrysler rocked along the dirt road. The sunlight lay warm on the grass that seemed to grow in clumps from the adobe earth. Not much sagebrush up here. Piñon. Juniper. And higher up on the mountain sides, solemn groves of dark green pine. The first pines framed an adobe capilla. "There's the chapel up there. The morada won't be far from it. Let's take a look before we go back."

"Good idea." Iggy turned the car down a rutted dirt road that wound downward and along the slope of the mesa, then up again toward where the two small square cupolas were visible atop the capilla.

"Ah!" The morada and cemetery jumped into view around a bend.

"Oh, shit!" Iggy exclaimed when they saw three rough wooden crosses standing alone next to the gutted morada. Ancient walls were jaggedly broken down and stained with black soot from the smoke. The remains of the roof had collapsed into the ruin. Most of the graves were marked with weathered crosses still showing bits of white paint. They were honored with plastic flowers in wreaths and bouquets, some still brightly jaunty in the sun, others faded from years in the elements. Saddest were those the firemen had trampled as they fought the fire. The yellow crime-scene tape stood out as a garish intrusion.

Christy was soundless. The lump in her throat dissolved. Tears ran down her cheeks.

Ignacio stopped the car. They sat.

Then Christy said softly, "All the years. All the love, the prayers...."

Finally they got out and walked toward the ruined morada, Christy crossing herself.

"Can you believe that!" Outraged, Iggy pointed. What remained of the walls were spray-painted, scrawls of black and red, signs and symbols. Christy was sickened by the obscenity.

"Looks like gang work."

"Not up here, Iggy."

"Well, you know some have even crept into Taos with their poison. Taos is getting its share of gangs, poverty, teen pregnancies—"

"No, that's not why I was disagreeing. Look at it, Iggy. There...and there. That's what Pat told you about and what some damned reporter's picked up on. Those figures and letters are Satanic. It's Devil worship or whatever you call it. Not gang graffiti. That hex ball I found is part of it." Again a frisson passed through Christy at the evil of it all.

"Yeah. I guess so." Iggy, close to the morada now, sounded distracted. "Look here, Christy. A step down into the building. The Hermanos stepped down as they went in."

"So?" What was his point?

"So, my friend. So! If someone knifed Eusebio outside, this step helped him fall inside!"

Skeptical, Christy asked, "What about all the other Hermanos? They wouldn't stand around and let someone calmly kill Eusebio."

"Well, no, but I think we're on to something. When we get the M.E. report.... Well, if Eusebio wasn't killed instantly. If he stumbled over that step down. It was dark, pitch black inside. They went to bed—lay down on their mats. Eusebio collapsed on his. Oh, hell! I don't know."

Christy was discouraged. "You still haven't explained the other Hermanos. Or the killer. How would he know Eusebio would stumble in? Lie down?"

"I said I didn't know!" Iggy snapped. Then, "Sorry, Christy, it's just..."

"I know. Let's go. This is so sad." Christy turned back to the car.

"Wait a minute. Come help me see if I can find any blood here on the step or inside."

There was nothing to be found. Iggy was first to give up and start back toward the car. He stopped. Christy followed Iggy's gaze. He was looking at a tan open area. It showed up against the still-bare aspen trees that replaced the dark pines higher up on the mountain. "What's that up there?" he asked.

"Used to be the old mine entrance. Looks as if there's a big clearing around it now. I never noticed it when the aspen had their leaves."

"Could be cleared for building," Iggy suggested.

"Could be, but I don't know what for. No one's worked that mine for generations." Christy lost interest. "I'm tired, Iggy. Let's go."

"'Say I'm weary, say I'm sad....'"

"Oh, don't be so flippant, Ignacio. Besides, wrong quote, wrong ending to the poem. Why not try a little Coleridge... *Like one that on a lonesome road doth walk in fear and dread...*da-dum, da-dum, *Because he knows a frightful fiend...Doth close behind him tread.*"

Suddenly Iggy exclaimed, "That's what I'll do!"

Startled from her reverie, Christy asked, "What?"

"The frightful fiend. I'll try to run down that drug dealer I defended a while back."

"You're not making sense, Iggy."

"Oh, yes, I am. I'll ask him what he's heard about Eusebio dealing. He'd know if a rival had set up shop, and if it's Pat. He'd even know if Eusebio was only doing drugs himself."

Christy didn't like it. "I don't know, Iggy. Poking around like that. You might get hurt."

As they walked toward the car, a wind came up, changing the soft spring breeze to cold. A tumbleweed blew across in front of them. Christy instinctively drew back. "My grandmother told me that's a bruja disguising herself as a tumbleweed....But don't be frightened, Iggy. She *might* have been making it up."

CHAPTER IX

Conversation in the car lapsed after Christy and Iggy left the desecrated Church. Each mulled over the discoveries. Finally, as they passed the cluster of Mexican import shops near town, Christy had a thought. "Drop me off on Padre Lane, Iggy. I want to check out that metaphysical bookstore. Then I'll walk to my car."

Iggy dutifully turned at the light but asked, "What now?"

"We don't know anything about Satanism. I want to see what I can find on it, and also check out those hex balls."

Iggy shook his head without comment.

When they pulled up in front of The Laughing Goat, Christy and Iggy exchanged a look. "Some name, considering," Iggy commented. "Sure you don't want to skip this? Just go on home?"

Christy slipped out of the car. "You're the one who needs to be careful, Ignacio." She lowered her voice, though no one was nearby. "Call me after your meeting with the pusher."

As Iggy drove off, Christy entered The Laughing Goat. The large room, smelling of incense, seemed rather empty. Sparsely filled book shelves stood on wide plank floors; a few glass counters displayed crystals, tarot decks, and magic miscellany; a satyr pranced on a large red and black wall poster; and a goat's head adorned the counter.

Christy took all this in, then noticed a plump man using a feather duster on shelves near the door. He wore a soiled, white, collarless outfit that reached to the floor but failed to hide his dirty bare feet.

Christy's greeting to the man seemed to hang in the air as he gave her a silent assessing stare. Uncomfortable, she moved into a second room to put distance between them. Skimming titles on the shelves, trying to determine where books on Satanism would be, a voice startled her. The proprietor's shoeless feet had made no sound.

"I don't think you'll find anything of interest here," he said

Christy didn't get the point. "Oh, no, these books have some intriguing titles. I'll just—"

Moving toward her, one hand reaching for her arm, the chubby character repeated, "Nothing of interest!"

Astounded, Christy realized she was being thrown out. Walking quickly to the front room, she saw a stack of fliers by the cash register. With barely time to scan the heading CALLING ALL WICCANS, she didn't get time or place. "A Coven Meeting?" she asked stubbornly. "Maybe you could tell me about hex balls?"

The man glared, then swished his dirty skirts over to the door. He held it open, gesturing to Christy. She left. She could, in time, have learned more, but at least she had found out that Taos did have an active chapter of witches.

Mac went to Furr's for the groceries. As he shopped, Mac remembered that when he and Betty Anne used to come to Taos, Furr's had been a lot smaller, located over where a new grocery and Big O now thrived. Betty Anne gone. And here in Taos, so much gone. Galleries taking over. Even where he had his hair cut one vacation—no more barber shop but instead another gallery in its place. More every day.

Mac shook his head. Cut the reminiscing and buy the groceries.

The fresh fruit picked out, Mac was pushing his cart down the frozen-food aisle, when he spotted La Doña Doris in conversation with some man. Tall, graying blonde hair cut short, lapis-blue eyes, middle-aged.

"Hello there, Mac," Doris boomed. "How fortunate. I want you to meet an old client of mine, Stephen Kramer. Dr. Kramer. Works at Los Alamos."

Mac wondered if this perfect Aryan type could be one of the scientists the government slipped in secretly during and after World War Two. No, not nearly that old and, to be fair, probably not even German.

"How do you do." An almost bow. No accent, but the careful diction made it likely the man spoke English as a second language. He was certainly handsome. No wonder Doris had a soft spot for him. Act friendly.

"Hey, Dr. Kramer. I'm Mac McCloud."

An imagined clicking of heels. The man must have come from Europe. "Delighted to meet you, Mr. McCloud." Dr. Kramer looked at Mac closely. He seemed the type who filed away faces, would not later fail to connect one with the right name and embarrass himself. Then La Doña managed it for him.

"Oh, it's Dr. McCloud, Stephen. Mac is a medical doctor."

"I'm so sorry, Dr. McCloud," came the apology, at the same time that Mac, smiling, said, "How could you know?"

"I want to show respect to a medical doctor," the scientist answered genially. "So many of us Ph.D.s on the ground. One has to be very special to be noticed."

"That's what I hear," Mac answered. "More Ph.D.s per square foot in Los Alamos than anywhere in the country."

Dr. Kramer continued to smile politely, but made no reply. La Doña, though clearly charmed by her client, couldn't pass up a chance to pull her weight with Christina and Ignacio investigating the Salazaar case. "Are you still working up at the lab, Stephen?"

"Oh, I keep busy." His eyes wandered. He seemed fascinated by the frozen waffles.

"Must be having some lay-offs up there. In fact, maybe you can tell us something. That young man who was killed, is it true he wasn't employed at Los Alamos any longer?"

Still taken up with the waffles, Stephen Kramer now stuck his head in the case, moving boxes about, as he gave a muffled reply. He emerged with a package which he placed in his basket, careful to avoid a black leather briefcase in the top section of the shopping cart.

Mac, amused, decided to follow La Doña's lead and asked, "Did you know him? Eusebio Salazaar?"

"Los Alamos is not large. I know most of the workers."

Undiscouraged, Mac persisted, "Then surely you knew him. Mr. Salazaar seems to have been highly skilled."

A glint of the blue eyes now. "Was he?" The precise voice softened. "I was sorry to learn he was killed. Such a death can only be a loss to all of us."

Mac, though naturally courteous, pushed a final time, knowing how much Christy needed to gather facts. "Our information is that Eusebio Salazar was no longer working at Los Alamos, but was still hard at some well paying project. We've ruled out drugs, so it must be that his professional skills were still in demand, although I suppose a hot-shot computer programmer could find work anywhere."

Dr. Kramer clamped his lips together, inhaled deeply through his nose, and spoke firmly. "I am not at liberty to discuss my work. No Los Alamos scientist may."

"Very true, Stephen," Doris Jordan cut in. "If we pry, it's because we are concerned about Eusebio's cousin, the young man accused of the murder. It is terrible for the family."

The man's face grew somber. "Yes, I am sorry for his parents. As for my work, I can't tell you much, but I can say that my team has attacked a difficult problem." His eyes began to sparkle. "From it comes new discoveries, undreamed of heights." La Doña started to speak, but he continued: "Test after test. One must replicate the results, analyze the data, take enormous care…." He trailed off, then began moving away.

"A pleasure, Dr. McCloud. And always, Doris. I mustn't keep you good people standing here. I know you have shopping to do." He pushed his cart off down the aisle.

Mac, somewhat uncomfortable, shrugged and looked a question at Doris. She sighed. "No, we went as far as we could. This is hard for Stephen. He's a friendly sort of chap, always polite, but very security conscious. I've always found him controlled, never indiscreet." She sounded a bit regretful.

After a moment, she added, "Stephen seemed very intense today, didn't he? Perhaps his dedication to science is why he never married. It's made his financial planning more difficult. No marital deduction. Only the one credit. Created trusts for him. Quite a bit of money, you know, made good investments. Very single minded our Stephen. Very."

Mac drove his Chevy pickup into the parking space across from the hacienda. No sign of Christy's Buick—or Duane Dobbs' big rental, for that matter. He was late and Christy should be here. Mac worried that it wasn't like Christy to leave the answering machine on all day, the hacienda unattended. And Duane Dobbs gone, too. Something about that fellow....

Mac carried the groceries into the house. Called out "Hello?" but didn't expect an answer, even from any of the guests. The house had that empty feel. He had learned empty too well since the death of Betty Anne.

The hacienda had proved to be a haven, plenty going on, happy people. Christy. He smiled, thinking about Christy, a mature woman. Able to share some memories, recall the big bands, for instance, without giving him a blank look. Sense of humor. Warm. Intelligent. Hmmm...

The uneasy feeling returned. Silly to make a production out of it simply because Duane Dobbs wasn't here either. Really no cause to think badly of the man. Just a personality thing. Probably a general disquiet because of the murder.

Christy had planned to meet with Iggy, okay. But not much they could do on a Saturday. Talk. How long could those two talk?

As Mac put the groceries away, he remembered that Christy had told him Father Joe blessed the animals at St. Francis Church today, Holy Saturday. It wouldn't hurt to run over to the church, check it out. Strolling, then walking briskly, Mac left the house.

CHAPTER X

Christy and Mac missed each other as Mac headed west on the road toward the church. Sometime later, Christy pulled in from the east end and parked by the garage. Tired from the strain of the day, she walked slowly as she entered the courtyard through the gate. Stillness held the space, the breeze quieted, the late afternoon sun sent shafts of gold here and there, picking out a flagstone's subdued shine, lighting a new-born daffodil into a yellow blaze. The scent of hyacinth was a heavy fragrance in the cool air.

The kitchen door stood open, so Christy slipped in. She heard a voice in the Middle Room and headed that way to see who was home, her moccasins soundless on the polished brick floor.

Duane Dobbs was sitting at the desk, facing toward La Sala, back to her, phone at his ear. He seemed angry. "I can't help it if the national media got on the story, found it so g.d. colorful—"

She paused to listen.

"Just because you said to secure the situation doesn't mean...!" Pause. "Goddammit! Don't blame me. I—"

Christy froze into place, frightened and fascinated.

Dobbs turned, saw her, dropping the receiver into its cradle. "What...!" Regaining his geniality with an effort, he added, "Sorry, Christy. You startled me. Trouble with the ex, I'm afraid."

It hadn't sounded like that kind of quarrel, but Christy didn't argue. "I'm the one to apologize. Didn't mean to intrude."

"Oh, you're not intruding at all. I've been wanting to chat with you." With a charming smile, Duane Dobbs took her by the arm to lead her over to a banco. Christy shrugged off the second arm of the day, went and sat on her own. She didn't like virtual strangers who took hold of the little woman. Nor could she tell if her guest was making a clumsy pass.

"Yes?" she asked.

Seeming unaware of the chill, exuding warm confidentiality, he began, "I couldn't help but notice you've been involved with this, er, unfortunate happening."

"You mean the murder?"

"Well, yes." Dobbs stood before her at parade rest, legs set apart, hands clasped behind his back. "I've had some experience with this sort of thing. Wanted, you know, to offer my help." He smiled down at her.

Christy felt the involuntary lift of her left eyebrow "You've had experience with murder?"

Dobbs chuckled. "Oh, no, nothing like that. Drugs. Drug investigation. I gather that seems to be the causal agent in the affair."

"Drugs?" Christy was startled. "What in the world does the Department of Energy have to do with drugs?"

Dobbs' smile grew fixed. "Now, I wonder how you got the D.O.E. into your head?"

Impatiently, Christy rose, walked over to the machine to check the messages, and said over her shoulder, "I understood you were from the D.O.E."

Another of those chuckles. "No, no, my dear. You misunderstood. It's the D.O.D., Department of Defense, not D.O.E. Rhymes, you see. And," Dobbs continued reasonably, "at the *D.O.D*, I work with security. In fact, although you'll have to promise to keep this quiet, I was sent out here because of drug-related problems at Los Alamos. Danger to national security and all that. Have to let a few people go, you know."

"Mmm. No, I didn't know." Feeling a cautionary tingle, Christy dropped it.

"Hey, Christy! Where are you, girl?" Mac yelled from the kitchen door as it slammed behind him.

Dobbs reacted by moving toward La Sala, pausing to warn, "You will keep our little chat quiet, won't you? Just remember, if you need any help with this drug problem, I'm your man."

That'll be the day!

As Mac came in from the kitchen, Christy stared bemused at the retreating tweed back, and then found herself wrapped in a bear hug. Scrunched against a flannel shoulder, her words were muffled. "What's this all about?" Sounding flustered, Mac said, "Uh, sorry. I'm just so damned glad to see you."

Christy laughed, "Well, I'm glad to see you, too, friend, but you're not usually so enthusiastic!"

"I was worried. Came home before. You not here. Gone too long. I went to look for you and ended up at the church."

She returned the hug. "I appreciate the concern."

Mac shuffled around, then said, "Come sit down in the kitchen. If you want, I'll make us a cup of coffee and tell you about it." Then, "Ooops, sorry, I keep taking over."

"*Mi casa es su casa*," she grinned, "or at least my kitchen is all yours—"

Relaxed, Mac poured the water through the coffee maker and cleared his throat. "I've been thinking about you getting involved in this case so quickly. You've explained why you felt you had to help out in this Salazaar mess, but not why you swore off the law in the first place."

Christy shifted mental gears, glad to leave the murder for a while. "Well, I guess I never expressed it all, even to myself, but there were a number of reasons....Of course the main one is how much I want to write, almost a compulsion. That's why I'm taking the risk of cutting my case load to nearly nil. But others? Well, simply being tired of the need to apologize for my colleagues. Some of their tactics. The up-front money. Losing sight of clients needs.

"Confrontation all the time. One of my last cases, a fairly new Albuquerque five-man firm on the other side. No negotiation. No attempt to work things out, not only for my client, but for their insurance client's good. Started right off with a scorched earth policy, baseless threats of sanctions just to set the mood. Probably called it playing hard ball and thought their bullying worked when we settled. I call it the *Jaws* mentality, the reason why there are so many lawyer-shark jokes." Christy sighed, "Sorry. Didn't mean to get on my soap box. It's been a day and a half. I needed to sound off about something, anything!"

Smiling at her, Mac brought the coffee, sat down opposite. "So finish the story," he demanded. "Tell me you didn't give in to the bully tactics."

Christy smiled back, said more calmly, "No way, but they'll never know it. My clients couldn't risk going to trial—for reasons that will remain confidential, sir. So we were delighted to get the settlement we did."

"Ha!"

"Thank you for your 'ha,' my friend." Christy sipped her coffee. She felt talked out, didn't want to organize any more thoughts "Mmm. I'm bushed. Let me put my feet up on this chair, undo the top button on my jeans, enjoy my coffee, and listen to you. Now. Tell me about your day."

"Well, there was that interesting bit....By the way, the best part of the day was the quick glimpse I had of Blessing of the Animals at Saint Francis. Worried you were so late coming home, I went by looking for you." He stopped abruptly, embarrassed at that admission, then continued, "Yes, well, some surprise to see the variety! Goats. Sheep. Rabbits."

Christy grinned. "I think that Blessing is the high point of Father Joe's Easter. So, what else?"

"Right. I stray. The interesting bit earlier was running into your lawyer friend, La Doña. Overwhelming lady. Well, she was in Furr's, talking to a client, a Dr. Kramer from Los Alamos...." Mac related the scene.

"Oh, boy!" Christy exclaimed, dropping her feet to the floor. "Los Alamos!"

Giving her a quizzical look, Mac continued. "Well, for all his poise, this guy was a strange bird. Very intense. Out to save the world. Even carried his briefcase in the grocery cart. He got vague when we tried to pin him down about his research, his lab team. The little he let slip sounded nothing like nuclear physics, more like biology or a medical field. So all we still know for sure is that Eusebio once worked up at Los Alamos."

Christy sat upright with excitement. "Does that ever tie in! No, no, go on with your story, then I'll explain."

"Not much more. Kramer is La Doña's client. She said he was always single-minded, never married, but she liked him. But it's made me wonder. If the good doctor is still working in

Los Alamos, what's he doing here shopping in Furr's?" Rising, Mac restlessly prowled into the kitchen and called back, "Want some more coffee? Or how about dinner?"

Her stomach revolting Christy answered, "Coffee, please. I can't bear the thought of food."

Returning with the cups, Mac insisted that Christy report on her day from the beginning.

Like a sculptor, she chipped away the extraneous, gave shape to the facts.

Mac stood as he listened, peered out the high dining room windows into the dark, paced around, and again ended up in the kitchen. "Mind if I turn on the radio to our local station? I think Saturday's the big band night."

Christy shook her head. "As long as I don't have to listen to any more news."

"Damn! Excuse me, ma'am, but I just remembered. Saw a couple of news vans in Furr's parking lot today."

"Oh, shit." The media would be after La Hermandad. Exploitation again!

The melody of "Deep Purple" laid velvet through the room. "Nice, hunh?" Mac held out his hand.

Christy let Mac pull her to her feet and they danced, fitting close together. But the music ended and the mood was lost when Mac asked, "So anything else in La Mesa?"

For reasons she couldn't understand, Christy left out the hex balls as she reported finding the coke. "But we couldn't decide if it were planted or not. Pretty good hiding place, not obvious."

"Yes, except," Mac observed, "the obvious can be right. Like someone can have an inferiority complex simply because he *is* inferior. But let's drop all this. Dance with me again, listen to the music, let yourself mellow."

"I can't mellow out," Christy answered crossly. "I'm too involved."

There was silence as Christy rubbed her forehead. "Duane Dobbs wants me to think drugs, too."

"Was that your little *tête-a-tête* when I came in?"

"Basically, yes." She stopped, remembered how uneasy the man made her, then recounted the scene. When she reached the part about Duane Dobbs' explanation of the D.O.D., Mac shook his head. "Wait a minute. Y'all are used to dealing with the alphabet soup here, what with Los Alamos and all. Which is what?"

"I'm not sure who does what. Basically, the D.O.E., the Department of Energy, runs Los Alamos though the University of California, I think. And I guess it was Mr. Dobbs' secretary made the reservations. Well, somebody told me that he was here from Oak Ridge."

"Oak Ridge was The Bomb," Mac interjected.

"Right, but he claimed that the Department of Defense sent him here to clean up a drug problem."

"Might actually be true. Cut the guy some slack. Our not liking him doesn't make him any kind of villain—unless, of course, he's making a play for you. Mmph, well... Scratch that. My point is assume drugs are obvious because they *are* the solution."

"Not the only possible solution." Christy hesitated, still curiously reluctant to bring up what was haunting her. "There's considerable evidence of Devil worship or witchcraft. I really don't know the difference. I went to a bookstore to research it, but was thrown out."

"From a bookstore?" Mac laughed incredulously.

"Not so funny," Christy answered crossly. "I *think* it was because I wasn't part of the in-group there, but even in Taos there's racism." Christy herself shook off that angle and continued, "Anyway, before this chubby character in a white dress pushed me out, I saw some really weird titles and a flyer on a coven meeting. It does all fit together."

She moved to look out at the dark courtyard, facing away from Mac as she broached the sticky topic of Satanism. Backtracking from The Laughing Goat's suggestive name, she somehow pulled up the energy to tell Mac about hex balls, the morada desecration, and that Devil worship might explain the mutilated cows making the news. Mac listened without comment, but she could feel his disapproval.

Conversation lapsed and they listened to "Sentimental Journey." Then, with a sudden thought and total change of mood, Mac grinned wickedly. "I've long thought that the C.I.A. is such a screw-up it must be the cover for the country's *real* intelligence unit. Dobbs is surely C.I.A. And, get this. Drugs are his cover. Mr. Dobbs is really here to investigate, ta-da!, the Taos Hum!"

Christy groaned.

Still enjoying his own humor, Mac kept at it with, "We'll call it 'Dobbs Does The Sound.'"

"Sorry, Mac. Too much has happened for me to joke around."

Mac sat down on the banco beside her. "I know. Just trying for some comic relief."

A KKIT announcer broke into the music: "Taos police are investigating the death of a man found behind Los Bailes on the north side. He was shot once in the back. No name has been released pending notification of next-of-kin. We resume our regular programming."

They exchanged a look.

Christy sighed, "We never used to have murders in Taos. The Crime Lab was a little baby blue van, always with four flat tires. And there was so little violence that the head man had the double title, Chief Investigative and Animal Control Officer. There was one murder seven years ago. Then that horrible stabbing. And now another body! How many killers are loose here?"

CHAPTER XI

The Church decreed that the sun had to set before Easter Vigil services could start. Then la gente, who had already sat down in the pews, left their seats in the warm church and came to stand in a cold circle around the carefully arranged wood *luminaria*. Father Joe touched the lighter to the bonfire and flames shot up into the moonlit dark, symbolizing God's pillar of fire that led the Israelites. The flames also consumed last year's palm fronds. Accompanied by prayer, Father Joe held the Easter candle to the fire to light it and inserted the pins that were its symbols. Next, after consecration of the new Holy Water, the people processed into the darkened church where tiny lights sprang up one-by-one as each person lit their candle from their neighbor's.

This was happening all over Taos, but Ignacio Baca was attending no church service. Instead, he tried to appear to be just hangin' at the bar of a well-known inn south of Taos, hoping his former client would walk in for a drink, or to do some business.

At least the bar was a comfortable friendly one, the patrons casual. Iggy thought that the Western music was kind of hard on an opera buff's ears, but he liked the atmosphere. Natural dark plank floors appeared almost soft from so many scrubbings, so many boots doing the two-step. Dim lighting, by contrast, made the flames in the big fireplace all the brighter.

Iggy nursed along his second Scotch and water and hoped he wouldn't have too long to wait. Just then he saw his quarry saunter in from the nearby door on the restaurant side. Clive

Castle was tall, lanky, a Taos mountain-man. He wore heavy Army pants tucked into calf-high laced boots, blue suspenders over a multi-colored flannel shirt, and topped it all off with a wide-brimmed, round-crowned Mounties-style hat. A heavy beard covered much of his face.

"Hey, Clive," Iggy called out softly.

Castle ignored him.

"Clive, Clive Castle," Iggy said more loudly.

The bearish figure ambled over casually, leaned past Iggy to order a drink, and hissed vehemently, "Leave me alone, man. The fuck you tryin' to do, set me up?"

"Chill out, Castle. Just need to talk," Iggy murmured.

"Get lost!"

"You want me to get real noisy about our business?" Iggy sounded grim and determined.

"Okay!" Castle muttered, "Bring your drink over to one of the back tables."

Being in such close proximity to the man, Iggy noticed how red and wet Castle's lips appeared peeping out from between his shaggy mustache and beard.

Silently he followed the tall figure, weaving between little tables to the far side from the bar and dance floor. It was even darker over here.

"The fuck you want?"

"You're not showing much respect for the lawyer who got you off," Iggy replied. "I just need some information."

"I'm not ratting on my clients! Anyway I'm not doin' that shit."

"Good. And I'm not asking you to hurt anyone. The man's dead."

"Who's that?" Castle was interested, and had calmed down enough to light a cigarette and take a drink of his beer.

"Eusebio Salazaar."

"Oh? The dude that got offed?"

"The one."

"Naw, Mister Baca. He was clean, man." Castle reflected, "Anyways so far as I know. Sure, I got my competition, see? Can't say nobody was dealing, lot going on all over town, but Salazaar? Naw."

Iggy was relieved, but one more question before he could relax, this one more ticklish. The mountain man was ready to rise, starting to push back his chair; Iggy held out his hand in a halting gesture.

"Now what? You said one question about the dead guy!"

"Take it easy, Clive. You surely want to keep an innocent man out of prison."

"Yeah? Who?" Castle asked.

"Eusebio's cousin, Pat Salazaar." Iggy watched Clive.

"Yeah, heard about that dude. Well, I'm not shaftin' him neither. Same answer. Far's I know....Well, not much anyhow. Hear he might buy a joint now and again. No heavy stuff. Not really doin' drugs. That it?" Standing. "I'm outta here. You fucked my night."

"That's it, Clive," Iggy said genially. "But how about you? Will I have to defend you any time soon?"

"Naw. I'm clean. Stayin' cool in my cabin up the mountain." The moist pink lips shaped a grin, showing brown teeth. "But spring's comin' on, and thar's a lot of mighty sweet gov'mint forest where a man might just grow him a patch of somethin' or other!"

Clive Castle was up and heading for the door as he finished his speech.

Iggy grinned at the retreating, suspendered back.

Chapter XII

Easter Sunday! The sun was out and the birds were singing! Well, cheeping, twirping, warbling. The magpies were quiet for once, not adding their raucous complaints to the concert. Christy woke to this joyous celebration, and the sense of relief that Lent was over. Christ had risen!

She had lain awake late into the night, wondering how, and if, the second killing fit in with that of Eusebio. Could there be a connection between shooting someone in an alley and stabbing an Hermano and desecrating the morada? That second killing fell within the town limits, so her cousin the Chief would probably handle it, but that might depend on the State Police who were investigating Eusebio's death. She'd have to see what information she could get out of each branch. Needed some expert advice on Devil Worship, too. Maybe find a brujo?

Christy tried to discipline her mind. Today's joy should override the evil events. And she should feel grateful for Mac, too. Christy smiled, feeling good about their growing closeness.

Glancing at the clock, she panicked at the time, then stretched comfortably. She remembered that Mac had said the guests were sleeping in this morning. He would deal with their breakfast so Christy could go to church. She could make the nine o'clock Mass, then go over to help Mamacita with Easter dinner.

Dinner! Oh, no! Christy groaned. She was supposed to bring the dessert. Damn. Totally forgotten in all that had been happening. Well, she'd just have to cheat and run over to Furr's after Mass. Pick up a sheet cake. Better shower and dress right now.

She used the shower to wash away stress, meditate a little. No dreams to recall this morning. Her regular Dream Class was Tuesday....Duane Dobbs jumped into her thoughts, the way he looked at her. Weird, sort of speculative. She hadn't realized that before, nor the feeling it gave her. Perhaps there had been a dream....

Christy dried off with a big towel, then got out astringent and moisturizer. The altitude and dryness gave the air the clarity, the sharp contrast of light and shadow that so challenged the artists, but it was hard on the complexion. A touch of shadow to make her eyes greener. She took more trouble than usual to celebrate Easter.

No jeans today. Easter finery, but comfortable. She chose an unstructured beige silk suit, full skirt, long-sleeved sheer pink blouse. In high heels, Christy struggled not to clomp noisily down the metal steps of the spiral staircase.

The house was quiet, a sleeping feel, La Sala still dim. Unconsciously Christy glanced back over her shoulder at the Don's Room. Creepy. She shouldn't be silly. The man had done nothing overt, except maybe make a tentative pass or two. But still, she couldn't shake her old conviction about the need to strike people with bad vibes from jury panels—or from her life....Pondering, Christy wandered into the dining room.

Oh! the dining room. A bouquet of spring flowers: elegant pale-blue Japanese iris and yellow daffodils. Surprise. Mac had already set the table, too. That dear face beamed proudly as he watched her reaction.

Touched, Christy cried, "Oh, Mac!" and gave him a big hug. If this was making up for Betty Anne....Well.

"And the Easter bunny came, too." He brought a basket from behind his back. Gay colors, ribbons, bows. A mega-basket of pastel jelly beans; bright, foil-wrapped, fat, chocolate eggs and yellow, sugar ones; candy white bunnies and yellow chicks; a large chocolate rabbit; all topped off with a plush, smirking pink out-of-place teddy bear!

Happiness bubbled up, displacing discomfort with so much caring. "This is the nicest surprise! And I was already impressed, you doing breakfast and all."

"Sorry. I guess I got carried away."

"No. It's beautiful. And I love those awful, too-sweet, colored eggs. Thank you!"

"So," Mac turned brisk. "How about a cup of coffee and a bite to eat before you go?"

"Coffee, please," Christy answered, still smiling. "Not supposed to eat an hour before Mass...Well, maybe just a piece of toast."

They settled at the end of the gleaming dark table, Christy admiring the flowers and the wonderful scent. "Ha. I hadn't seen the pink hyacinth lurking under the daffodils. Smelled it first."

Mac nodded, pleased with himself, if embarrassed. They drank their coffee in companionable quiet.

Christy said, "I wish you would come on over to Mamacita's for dinner."

"No, thank you. As a friend of mine used to say, 'Sounds like fun...but I just don't want to.'" Mac seemed about to say something, hesitated, and then ended rather weakly with, "You'll be all family today."

Christy wondered if Mac thought the family dinner might be some sort of commitment. Good. He hadn't abandoned his basic common sense. Just overdid it now and again.

He changed the subject. "You think I should light the dining room fire?"

Christy grinned. "Hey, man, it's spring!"

"Seems a little chilly."

They bantered, but then the dark in the back of Christy's mind overshadowed the bright day and she asked, "Any more news on that poor man we heard about last night?"

"No word on who it was. Just that he was shot in the back. Seems the police are going for a simple mugging."

Christy objected, "But Taos doesn't have muggings! Murders! I'm wondering if it has to do with Eusebio's killing."

"Now, Christy. Don't get started on that mess today. Enjoy your Easter. You even have my permission to eat the chocolate bunny from your basket."

"I'd better. I saved one once and it melted in the sun. Taught me to eat now or it may melt tomorrow!"

"You look very pretty in your Easter outfit."

"Thank you, sir. It's time I got to Mass. This nine o'clock is more packed, if possible, than the others today." Christy rose, found her purse and keys. "See you later. Good luck with breakfast. And, thanks again, Mac."

"My pleasure, ma'am."

So many vehicles jammed the church parking that Christy had to park near the highway across from Old Martinez Hall and Popular Video and Pawn. She remembered when that had been a dry goods next to a restaurant and her family still called the Santa Fe highway the "new" road.

The church rose from the earth, made of earth, to push against the tentative spring-blue sky. Huge buttresses, built of hundreds of adobe bricks, added more support to its bulk. Those, and the thousands of adobes in the church itself, had been made by many hands: young, still-soft hands; twisted arthritic hands; miner, sheepherder, school teacher hands; and women's hands reddened and roughened from lye soap and washings and tending babies, eight or ten living and more in tiny caskets lying in their hearts.

The men made the bricks from adobe clay and straw and sand and water, and put them in molds to dry in the sun. They needed many adobes to restore their church or the Archdiocese threatened to make it into a museum.

After the men rebuilt the walls, eight feet thick in places, the women moved in with their sheepskins to smooth on the skin of adobe mud. Their muscular arms worked the sheepskin in a curving motion, the circle of life. They covered the enclosing walls as well as the high reaching walls of the church itself which, like all the Franciscan churches opened itself to the shape of the cross.

A prayer was placed with each forty-pound adobe and each sweep of the sheepskins.

The church was so strong Christy could lean against its shadow.

Walking quickly, her heels giving a nice-feeling lift, Christy joined friends and family heading toward the church. Hordes of children crowded this Mass because Father Joe called the kids up front to bless their Easter baskets.

Martinez, Torres, Sandovals, Wilsons, Mondragons, Montoyas, primos John and Paul, Tia Betty. No Mama. She would have gone to the early Mass, and be at home in a flurry of cooking. But here, from all sides she heard, "Happy Easter! Happy Easter!"

As they all headed around the building toward the front, Christy suddenly saw a van with network letters on the side. It halted near the home of Señora Martinez. Feeling a chill, Christy stopped moving with the crowd to watch. A blond, pony-tailed young man in jeans got out, camera balanced on one shoulder.

Forgetting her growing dislike for confrontation, Christy crossed the little side road to pounce on the man. "Just what do you think you're doing!"

"Uh…" Christy's prey looked around. He was joined by a small woman who looked like a chipmunk in a business suit.

"Who are you?" Chipmunk asked, taking a steno pad and pen from her voluminous purse.

"None of your business." Christy's voice was ragged with anger. "I'm a parishioner and I'm asking what you people are doing here at our Easter Mass!"

"Afraid to give your name?" The tone was insinuating, the brown eyes protruding.

"Of course not," Christy took the bait. "It's Christina Garcia y Grant. Now," she bit off the words, "what are you doing?"

The voice implied untold secrets, "We heard the Devil Worshippers up here were Catholics, so, voila! we came to see."

Almost too irate to speak, Christy blurted, "That is absolutely absurd! No damned Devil Worshiper is Catholic!"

"Then, Miz…" the woman checked her notes. "Miz Grant, you state that these Devil Worshippers or Satanists are not Catholic?"

"Of course they're not." Christy replied. "You have totally confused the story. Some killer scrawled Satanic symbols on the morada in a nasty attempt to connect Los Hermanos with the murder."

Chipmunk was writing fast. Christy hoped that now she'd get her facts straight.

"Los Hermanos? Is that another name for the penitentes?"

"No. Yes. What I mean is that the penitentes are referred to as Los Hermanos, The Brothers, or La Hermandad de Nuestro Señor Jesus." Christy wasn't about to go into any more detail and, besides, the woman had stopped writing. "Excuse me," she said coldly. "I must go to Mass."

High heels tapping an angry rhythm, Christy walked quickly forward, then stopped abruptly. Cameras! Everywhere she looked, casually dressed men and women filmed the Easter crowd or focused on individuals. Some crews were accompanied by reporters, identified by their steno pads or handheld mikes.

Just beyond the walls near the main front entrance of San Francisco, a group of reporters clustered like ants. Camcorders and mikes were trained on someone. Oh, no! Christy groaned inwardly. It was her friend, elderly rancher Señor Archuleta, gesturing and obviously giving a statement. Christy hurried down the walk, barely aware of the smiles and greetings called to her from parishioners on their way into Mass.

"...mebbe three, four cows dead in the pasture. All the blood, not a drop left, all the blood taken from them. No blood on the ground, no blood to be found—"

"Señor Archuleta!" Christy cried, pushing a reporter out of the way. "Please don't tell these things!"

The old man looked at Christy, surprised, and hurt by her rudeness. Señor Archuleta was such a courteous old gentleman that Christy confused him by breaking in on a good story. Too polite to even chide her, Señor Archuleta said in a bewildered tone, "Buenos dias, Christina. Happy Easter. I am telling these visitors what happened to my cows."

He turned back to his audience, leaning forward to speak into the microphones already in his face. "And that is not all...."

Christy looked around for help and saw four or five news vans in the front parking lot. No way to stop them all. Other parishioners moved quickly to get the last seats and not have to stand outside. The people only gave the reporters passing glances of curiosity as they prepared to celebrate Easter. This bunch appeared commonplace to a parish accustomed to tourists and documentary makers, photographers and painters, all trying to capture the strength and beauty of the famed church.

Cold with foreboding, Christy turned away from Señor Archuleta and the reporters. She couldn't manage damage control alone. She joined the flow of parishioners. Soon the crowd would fill the nave and sacristy, spill out the front doors and back.

"Happy Easter!" the Mayordomos greeted her just inside the door, handing her the missal. Christy returned the greeting. Crossing herself with the holy water there, she determined to put all the ugliness out of her mind. She would think only of Jesus, Jesus risen from the dead this day.

Christy found a pew where they had room to scoot over. "Happy Easter!" was exchanged, smiles and hugs from another branch of the Martinez family, the three youngest clutching big Easter baskets. Some tourists were behind her, in shorts and cameras, and then Primo Claudino and his wife Dolores, holding the new baby. More friends in front of her. Reaching back, forward, touching, pats, smiles. "Happy Easter!" No sister Odelia. She must not have arrived from Española yet.

The decorations were a shout of joy, a contrast to the Lenten church, stripped and bare. The santos that had been draped in purple for mourning now wore white. Easter lilies vied in celebration with other seasonal flowers and multi-colored hand-stitched banners.

A commotion erupted behind Christy at the front doors, but she refused to turn around. She knew it must be the media people trying to push past the Mayordomos to take pictures and the Mayordomos, assisted by parishioners, attempting to keep them out. She would not let them intrude further on her Easter. A voice inside her said, "Be quiet, Christy."

Still, Christy looked at the front *reredo*, the altar screen, with new eyes. Would the vivid reds and greens, faithfully restored to their original brightness, seem garish to those eyes? These colors painted in swirls and curlicues on raised boards were an innocent contrast to the seven 15th century, age-darkened oils that they framed. No elaborate Renaissance frames for them. The medieval costumes, too, sharply differed from the primitive figures on the side reredo, still done in their original vegetable dye, softly faded now. The oil paintings were already three hundred years old when they were shipped to old Mexico, New Spain, in the 18th century, then brought up here by cart.

From where she sat, Christy couldn't see it, but she smiled anyway at the passing thought of the painting of St. Anthony. His santo was traditionally carved with him holding a separate Baby Jesus. We take our saints personally, she thought, remembering how Mamacita would take away the Santo Niño and hide him from St. Anthony, saying, "When I get my prayer, you get your Baby back!"

Christy turned forward again to look at the bottom left of the front reredo where a painting of Jesus being baptized by John the Baptist was proudly displayed. The painting was a family secret tourists never seemed to notice. It was unfinished; the head of Jesus had not been painted in at all! There were, however, four arms and four legs!

A finished painting of Jesus did stand out in the center of the reds and greens. Volunteers had finally stopped telling the tourists that it *might* be an El Greco.

Christy was touched to see that the decorating committee had made a little cave out of paper mache. Strips of gauze lay on the floor inside it representing the binding cloths Jesus left behind when he rose from the dead.

In sharp contrast to the Renaissance painting on the front reredo, the elongated, emaciated, carved Cristo hanging there on the wall, bleeding from his wounds, was as primitive as his pain.

Water flowed from a jug into a basin nearby, the living waters. And the tall pierced Easter candle was lit.

Lost in her reverie, Christy was startled as the big bells pealed, the guitars and voices began the processional, and the little bell clanged announcing the entry of the priest, preceded by the Cross and Bible raised high by the servers and lectors.

Sing praise. Cry joy. Hosanna! Christ lives! We are risen from the dead!

The celebration of Mass began.

When Mass ended Christy joined the people slowly moving out. She worried about who might be waiting, but the reporters seemed to have left. Thank heaven!

Much of the crowd lingered a bit, bright in their Easter clothes, moving, exchanging greetings, hugging. Mostly joyous but, as on Good Friday, here and there a dark spot at the mention of Eusebio's murder.

"Witchcraft!"

"Ah, si."

"Some say drugs?"

"No, no. The Satanists."

" Brujas?"

"No. Different."

"I say the same. Witchcraft."

Greetings for visiting friends and relatives mingled with these comments along with talk of dinners and the Easter egg hunt in Kit Carson Park. Then back to Eusebio and the new murder.

"And what of the one found yesterday?" "*¿Quien sabe?* Who knows?" "He was not from here, no?" She wanted to hear more of the gossip about that second body, but had to hurry to Furr's for the cake. She was stopped every few feet for hugs and "Happy Easter" and "We'll see you."

Mamacita's little adobe was tucked closely among its neighbors in Ranchos. Bright yellow bushes exploded with bells of forsythia in full bloom. Such a crowd of family rushed to the door to greet her that at first Christy had difficulty sorting them out. Embraces, kisses, laughter. "Happy Easter! Happy Easter!"

The house was too warm, especially with all these people whose faces were repeated in the family photos that crowded every surface, just like at the Salazaar's. Similar, too, were the many santos that shared the tops of tables and cabinets. Retablos hung on the white walls plastered with *tierra blanca*. But Mamacita wouldn't put up with vigas collecting dust, so the ceilings were covered with white acoustical tiles.

Petite, pretty Odelia and her husband Gabe were already here with three of their five children. Beer in hand, Tio Eli, who hadn't been to Mass with Tia Porfy, was moving back to his over-stuffed chair that sat squarely in front of the television. He brought his large, gnarled frame down with difficulty. Young Gabe, Jr. sat next to him on the floor. Tia Porfy headed back to the kitchen with Mamacita. Odelia and the girls returned to setting the table, now fully extended with a leaf under the white lace table cloth. Big Gabe wandered around looking lost.

Feeling a little ashamed of her cake, Christy carried it into the kitchen. Plants. Bright yellow walls. And the heat! Pans on every burner of the stove. Things in the oven. Mamacita still had a fire going in that part of her new combination wood and gas stove.

Mamacita bustled, and equally small, elderly Tia Porfy darted about. Odelia and the girls moved in and out carrying things. The daughters had obviously "made up" their mother: all three now had black liner around their beautiful dark eyes. With a little L'Oréal help, Big Odie no longer had any gray in her black hair, but it was still short and curly. So was Little Odie's, styled with new college sophistication. Mary had her peer group's high hair in front, long in back.

Mamacita's first words to Christy were, "Porfy said she saw you at the nine o'clock Mass. I was worried when you didn't come."

"I had to run to Furr's to get the cake." And she thanked God that Tia Porfy apparently hadn't seen either of her scenes with the reporters!

One scornful look at the cake from Mamacita. "*Muy bonita,*" she said coolly, "very pretty. Your sister Odelia brought this big ham. I was up at five o'clock this morning to cook the turkey. Then I dress and go to Mass. Then I come home and make the bread and pies."

"Yes, Mama." Making no excuses, Christy smiled and got to work.

Soon the confusion sorted itself out and they were all at the laden table, saying prayers for the repose of the soul of Papa (he would have been eighty-four), for the safety of brothers Juan and Patricio and their families in Colorado and California, for

Odelia's and Gabe's two sons away in the Navy, and the blessing over the food. Ham, turkey, dressing, red chile for the mashed potatoes, rolls, tortillas, tamales, salads. There was even *panocha*, the special baked Easter dish made from sprouted wheat ground into flour, flavored with caramelized sugar. Mamacita sighed as she looked over this banquet, "I hope there is enough food."

Naturally, everyone rushed to tell her it was a great feast.

Mamacita ruled one end of the table, Tio Eli sat at the other with another beer. In between were Tia Porfy, teen-age Mary, Gabe, and Big Odie next to Mama on that side. On this side, Christy was next to Mama, then Little Odie, Gabe, Jr., and back to Tio Eli.

There was a flurry of passing food. Tio Eli tried to slice the turkey, failed. Tia Porfy took over and, at the same time, accused Odie, "I didn't see you in Mass. And you wouldn't be here already if you went to the eleven-thirty."

Odie, conservative older sister, bristled. "We all went to the Easter Vigil in Española last night."

"Man, was it long!" from Gabe, Jr. He vigorously rubbed the shaved side of his head.

"It's a beautiful Mass," Tia Porfy corrected him sternly.

Odie, ready to make peace, said, "Beautiful and long. So many readings. What is it? Seven? Nine?"

Before anyone could answer, there was a sudden hoarse voice. "Too long!" Tio Eli pronounced. He seldom spoke.

Tia Porfy gave him a look. Wrinkles pursed her mouth.

"So how's Española?" Christy broke the silence.

Gabe grinned at his sister-in-law. "Now, no Española jokes. You know the Mayor has gone round the state asking everyone to stop telling Española jokes."

Brave from college, Little Odie said, "You mean like the tornado that hit Española? They say it did a million dollars worth—of improvements!"

Giggles.

"Now, Odelia," big Odie cautioned.

"Low rider capitol of the world!" Gabe, Jr. announced proudly. "Just wait 'til I'm big enough. Hydraulics to go up and down." He gestured with his hands. "Little rigid chain steering wheel." He mimicked steering. "Fifteen coats of lacquer and—"

"Sure," said his father. "I'd like to see you work that hard on something."

"Taos is the town having trouble," Odelia addressed Christy. "All those murders!"

Tia Porfy had been lying in wait to tell her news. "They say the new one was an Anglo from Los Alamos."

Surprise jolted Christy. She turned to her Tia. "Do they really know if he was from Los Alamos?"

Porfy shrugged her tiny shoulders. "So I hear. But why he was here? They say he was in the alley behind Los Bailes. *¿Que?* Why? *¿Quien sabe?*" she rattled off, then paused to pronounce, "I will tell you—"

Christy was shocked to hear verification of her thought that the second murder might be related to Eusebio's. She wanted to learn more from Tia Porfy about the Los Alamos angle, but Mamacita wasn't to be left out any longer. She took over with, "Aii! Witches, I say."

Normally Christy loved the old stories, and the old ways, but today felt as if she listened through a stranger's ears, wondering how they would sound to those avid reporters. Then, disciplining her mind, Christy told herself to stop it. These were her roots. She should relax and enjoy the *cuentos*. So she smiled as the young ones urged, "Tell us about witches, Grandma."

"Eh! What I could tell you!" Perfecta growled with menace. "Blue lights, blue balls of fire moving up and down above the Rio Grande in the gorge. And in Talpa, too, las brujas are seen again as in the old days."

"Witches? Blue fire balls?" the young ones asked.

"*Verdad.*" Mamacita nodded solemnly. "Blue lights. The brujas, they change themselves thus to fly by night. Then tumbleweeds by day. All this and a fire on the mesa where they do their wicked dances." Mama crossed herself.

"Did you see it, Grandma? Did you see them dance?"

"I see the blue balls of fire. And —"

Porfy had enough of her sister in the spotlight, so she interrupted, slicing the air with her knife. "No wonder the other man was killed at that bar. You know Los Bailes stays open on Good Friday. This year also." She lowered her voice.

"The Evil One himself was seen there. He thinks no one notices. He sits at a table with a coat on. But, ha! his tail is sticking out from under his coat."

The story was told often. The young people grinned at one another.

"Do not smile." Porfy scolded. "The Devil is no matter for laughing!"

Christy agreed but said nothing as she thought of the hideous blasphemy of it all.

Gabe interrupted her thoughts, but with more of the same. "Didn't I hear that the morada was covered with Satanic symbols?"

"Yes," Christy answered, "and I know people think that Devil Worshippers burned and desecrated the morada at Abiquiu. But here?" She paused. "I don't think so. And Gabe," Christy's voice grew passionate and she turned to look around the table. "You won't believe how the practices of La Hermandad are being distorted again! The other night, on the news, the reporter called the penitentes a ritual torture society!"

"Ai-ee!"— "No, no!" "*¡En el nombre del Señor!*" "In the name of the Lord!" the old ones exclaimed and crossed themselves.

Christy felt a sudden surge of love for Mamacita, Tia Porfy, Tio Eli and all the other *viejos* who had grown up in the more innocent years. At that time, Taos was so isolated most spoke Spanish only, and Anglos were referred to as "Americans."

Christy expressed only a little of this love that overwhelmed her as she tried to explain to Mama. "So today, at Mass, these viejos—not understanding this harsh, Anglo world—they were speaking to reporters who will probably twist what they say. That's why I was so sharp with you on the phone, Mamacita..." Christy stopped to get control of her voice, then continued, "Perhaps the Devil is involved—the crime is evil enough! And I even found hex balls with hair in them. But let's not allow outsiders to confuse these things with our Brothers."

Embarrassed by making such a speech, Christy stopped, but Gabe said gently, "I understand, sister-in-law." Even Odie nodded sympathetically and Little Odie and Gabe smiled at her. Mary seemed to have tears in her eyes. Nevertheless, Christy wondered how much los *ancianos* had understood.

Now Mama was saying, "*Su familia* did not join la morada but we were close with your tio and helping the auxiliary. No verdad, su tios and primos, many belong to La Hermandad. Good men who will receive many blessings in heaven. No. This desecration at the morada, this is not the old way of the brujas. No, it is like you say, some new Anglo —"

"Mama! I said no such thing. Now you're sounding prejudiced."

"Ha! Who is prejudiced? Did I not welcome your husband Jean Paul into the family like he was my own son?" Perfecta threw up her hands in supplication.

"Yes, Mama, but —"

"So Anglo, no?" Perfecta triumphed. "But now these killings and calling up El Diablo. And what of carving up the cows, eh?" She nodded regally to her audience around the table.

"Do you believe in the Devil, Tia Christy?" shy Mary asked of her hero.

"Well, I believe there is evil—" Christy began uncomfortably.

"There is the Devil, Christina Garcia!" Tia Porfy scolded.

"*Y* Grant, Tia Porfy." Christy corrected. "Christina Garcia *y* Grant."

"And you had better pray that you do not fall into his hands!" Porfy pointed her knife at Christy.

Big old Gabe to the rescue again: "Isn't your *La Llorona* story up here a Devil story, Christy? Down south she cries for another reason."

Christy smiled her thanks and made an effort to be her former self and join in, pushing the dark cloud from the family table, "You go first, Gabe. Tell the kids what you grew up with in Las Cruces."

Three sets of eyes were shining at their father although they had probably heard the story many times. Gabe refused the invitation, saying he wanted to hear the other version. Christy was still distracted, yet when the young people added their pleas, she laughed and said, "Okay, okay. I know that down south La Llorona wanders the banks of the Rio Grande sobbing. That's La Llorona, the crybaby, searching for the baby she threw in the river in a fit of desperation when a rich man deceived her."

Gabe couldn't resist adding, "Yes, she threw the baby when he laughed at marrying her, then she herself died from despair. And at the gates of heaven, the Archangel Michael told La Llorona that, yes, she was but a poor trusting young girl and she could come into heaven. Ah, but…But first she must find her baby and bring him with her!" Gabe looked sternly at them all.

"Now, forever, she walks up and down crying for her baby."

"Ahhhh."

"But up here in the north," Christy took up the tale. "La Llorona has a different story. She was a beautiful young girl who stayed home all the time to care for her aged mother."

Mamacita nodded firmly.

"Poor La Llorona never went anywhere…."

"As it should be."

"So one night, the neighbors came to tell her of a dance nearby. They asked her to go. 'No,' she said. 'I cannot leave my aged mother.' But the neighbors begged her to come for just a little while. To dance and have some fun.

"'No,' her mother said. 'I am a weak old woman. You must not leave me.'"

"'Come,' the neighbors beckoned. 'Come and dance!'"

"So La Llorona gave in. She went to the dance despite her mother's protests. And there she met a handsome stranger." Christy's eyes shone and her voice sparkled. "How they danced! How he whirled her about the floor! It grew late and La Llorona wanted to leave. But, no, the handsome stranger only danced her faster and faster!"

Christy dropped her voice. "Then, near dawn, the neighbors came running. La Llorona's poor mother had died!"

"*Pobrecita*! Poor little one!" The *ancianas* mourned.

"Yes, *la vieja*, the old one was dead. And the crowd turned to look for the handsome stranger—for it was he who had kept La Llorona dancing too long. But he was no longer at the dance. They rushed outside to find him. Gone." Christy paused and then continued quietly. "But they knew the handsome stranger had been the Devil. This was because there were chicken tracks in the earth—and everyone knows the Devil always leaves chicken tracks!"

The young ones clapped their hands. Tia Porfy pursed her lips. But Mamacita twinkled and said, "That is how we told stories in the old days, m'hija. You are truly a *cantadora*! A fine storyteller!"

Mama sighed. "And the riddles your padre could put! But now....Aii. We have all the things to make the work easier, yet no one tells the stories. And the riddles? Bah! They are forgotten!" Perfecta slapped her palms against the table.

Forgetting her new-found teen-age sophistication, Mary begged, "Tell us another story, Tia Christy!"

Christy laughed. "No, no, enough from me."

But Mary was not about to let her hero go. She thought she was asking the right thing with, "Will you tell us about the murders, Tia Christy?"

Tia Porfy had to show some spirit, so she rushed in with, "I say it is those crazy scientists from Los Alamos."

"You do?" Christy was totally surprised. She expected the witchcraft story.

"I do," Tia Porfy pronounced. "Poor Eusebio Salazaar worked at Los Alamos. Doing what, who can say? Scientist? Bah! The one at Los Bailes no one knows. But Eusebio? I say to you, why is it not something from Los Alamos? And this witchcraft? Bah! For show only!"

From the end of the table, a stern voice, rusty with disuse surprised everyone by announcing, "Time to go!" And Tio Eli began to struggle to his feet.

That signaled the end, although Mamacita said wistfully, "I wish your brothers could have been here. Patricio so far away in California, but Juan in Colorado. He could have brought the family. Pueblo is not that far away."

"But working, Mamacita," Christy spoke gently. "A long trip for one day when Juan has to go to work in the morning."

"I know," she sighed. "It is like the old days when Edmundo and the others went to Wyoming to herd the sheep in the winter. They had to make the money. But we were all alone here."

They crowded around to comfort her, and Easter dinner ended.

Although the adobe walls surrounding the courtyard were thick, Mac thought he heard the thunk of the Buick's door closing, and looked up from his weeding. Yes. Christy was coming in through the old wooden gate. She did look pretty standing there, smiling at him.

Christy shook her head. "What a way to spend an Easter Sunday—weeding my courtyard!"

"Good therapy. The sun is warm on my back. My hands are busy. Now the question is, can I stand up?"

Christy laughed, came over, and extended a hand. Mac refused it. "I think I can make it on my own." Rather stiffly, he stood up. "So, Easter lady, how about a beer?"

"You sit. I'll get it. You've been waiting on me all the time lately. Just give me a minute to slip into something comfortable."

Mac waggled his eyebrows. "The old slip-into-something-comfortable routine, eh?"

Grinning, Christy ordered, "Just sit."

Mac found a broom to sweep off the mud clods that had come up with the weeds, and was still at it when Christy returned. "Ha! Caught you! You're supposed to be sitting and here you are with a broom!" She handed him a cold beer. They sat.

"So tell me about your Easter," Mac prompted.

"Oh, Mac, " Christy cried. "I blew up at some reporters and insulted Señor Archuleta and came dragging a dark cloud with me to the family dinner!" She took an angry breath. "They say 'the shadow of the cross lies heavy on this land,' but I never believed it! No, it's this evil that is laying a shadow over everything!"

Mac's expression had mirrored Christy's emotions at each outburst. Now he took her hand, "Start from the beginning so I can understand."

Christy told him about the run-in with the first reporters and on into the rest of the story. Mac didn't brush it off, but said soberly, "You're right to worry. And prepare yourself for repercussions. But right now you're inside these thick walls and I'm here whenever a shoulder is needed....Look at the sky, the flowers, and tell me the good parts about your Easter."

Christy sighed. "Wonderful, Mac. There's so much warmth and love....I don't know...Seemed more so today. And, despite all, I really did feel a kind of, oh, maybe not rebirth, but renewal at least."

"And the family?"

Christy laughed, "Y su familia? We'll make a Spaniard out of you yet!"

"With a name like McCloud?"

"A challenge, Doctor!"

They smiled at one another, then looked around the courtyard. Christy felt the peace. Those old adobe walls really did keep out the ugly things. So old, they had seen it all and absorbed it away. That wonderful swamp willow, gnarled by the front gate. Mac's little house. The cherry trees on the far side, lightly beginning to bloom. Flagstones worn smooth by the feet of generations. The old wood beams supporting the portal....Yes, peace, but....

Mac asked, "What did your family say about the murders?"

"I was surprised. Aunt Porfy went with the Los Alamos connection instead of witchcraft".

Swinging his legs off the lounge chair, Mac sat up straight on the edge.

"Mac?"

"Seemed like quite a reach at first. We know nothing about the second body, right?"

"Nope. But—."

"Wait. Wait. I'm trying to tell you what I was flashing on. Los Alamos. Get this. I run into Dr. Kramer, a scientist wandering around loose in Taos and—"

"And," Christy broke in. "there's Eusebio, who worked for the lab, living up in that isolated community of La Mesa. A tight bunch. As Spanish as you can get."

"Gotcha!" Mac slapped his fist on the palm of the other hand. "And what's the connection?"

"Los Alamos!" they shouted at each other in unison. Laughed.

Christy pondered "We do know that Pat isn't involved with Los Alamos in any way. A Los Alamos connection would raise reasonable doubt, make it highly improbable for Pat..."

She slumped back in her chair. "Hate to think like a lawyer, but we don't know yet if there is a connection. It *could* be drugs, dammit."

"Or no connection. And here's a thought. What about the killing in the alley?"

"Right. But Taos just doesn't have random killings. Or didn't! Even those hateful gangs starting up here."

Mac stood, stretched, and changed the subject. "Right now I think it's gotten too cold out here to support life, ma'am."

Christy nodded. The light had gone out of the day. They wandered into the kitchen, as she asked, "So how did breakfast go? And thank you again."

Laying the Southern accent on thick, "Why jus' fine, thank you, ma'am. Purely scrumptious. Ah fixed them a fine low country breakfast, grits an' —"

Christy laughed. "Enough. I get the picture. Any calls?"

"Almost forgot. The honeymooners are checking out in the morning. Seems they're pining for that hot desert sun they thought they were promised. I can sympathize with that."

"Okay you cold-blooded reptile. You were saying?"

"Oh, yeah." Mac replied. "So the honeymooners are out but we had another reservation for their room: a single man for La Escondida."

"Where's this single man from?"

"Washington, D.C."

CHAPTER XIII

Murky evil shapes enveloped Christy in the dark pre-dawn hours Monday morning. Still pursued by the dream's bloody corpse of Eusebio, she woke trailing wisps of fear from her nightmare. She recalled a card game, poker with a dead man bleeding from stab wounds.

Christy sat up, seeing the room through the gray of her somber mood. The phone rang, sending shocks to her nerve ends. It was not Mama. "Surely you did not say those things, Christina!" said a voice made unfamiliar by anger.

"What?" Christy answered groggily. "What things?"

"That Los Hermanos are not Catholic!"

Her stomach balled up in apprehension. "No! I didn't! I—"

"Perhaps this Carlotta Garcia dash Grant is not you?"

"Carlotta? But I'm not...And 'dash'? You mean they hyphenated—"

"Then it was you? How could you say such a thing to be in the news? *Toda mi familia Hermanos estan.* That's 'my whole family' since you don't know your own language! We have been your friends always. No more!"

Hot blood rushed to Christy's face, adrenaline through her body. She was wide awake now, but the caller's phone had been banged in her ear. How in God's name? What? Those first reporters. Damn! She had said "Devil Worshippers." The Devil Worshippers weren't Catholic. Those media weasels had put that together with her speech about Los Hermanos.

That was the last time Christy had a moment to think. Every time she hung up, the phone rang again. Hurt. Angry. Bewildered. Sarcastic. The calls kept coming. Some said that the Lord God would curse her for saying such things. Others: "So, you must worship El Diablo yourself to slander the good men...." "...member of the Auxiliary. All of Holy Week Los Hermanos stay, praying. How can you say...?" "*Tu madre* should never have sent you away to school. You have forgotten where you came from!" "It is you who are no Catholic, not Los Hermanos!" "Never trust a lawyer!" "...always said you thought you were too good for us!" "More Anglo than the Anglos...!" "That one you are defending, they say is a Devil Worshiper!... Buckets of blood...!"

Through her pain, Christy realized that the callers would be attacking poor Mamacita too, for being the mother of such a person. Christy desperately wanted to warn her, but there was no space between the calls.

She didn't hear Mac knock on the outside door, didn't see Mac come in. Christy's whole world was reduced to the voices on the other end of that little blue receiver. She saw nothing. She was shaking deep inside a dark tunnel as vilifying words kept coming at her. Perhaps worst were the people that came out of the woodwork to agree with what they thought she'd said. They added their own nasty, ignorant thoughts about La Hermandad.

Mac gently took the phone from her rigid fingers and hung up on whoever was talking. It rang again. Mac held her hand. "Let it be," he said. "The answering machine will get it if you want to check later."

She hadn't broken down through all the ranting but Mac's kindness was too much. "Oh, Mac," Christy cried and, sitting on the edge of the bed, Mac rocked her in his arms. "I know, I know," he said, still holding her. "I saw the morning news on my contraband tv and came running up here to prepare you. Then I heard you trying to answer some of those...." He gestured in disgust.

Still muffled in Mac's flannel shoulder, Christy said, "They think I've betrayed them. Some couldn't believe I'd say such a thing. Others...." Christy again couldn't speak. And the phone kept ringing. Mac took it off the hook.

Finally Christy drew away. Stood up. Her anger was a cold flame now. "I have to get a kleenex, throw some water on my face. I had hurt feelings, but it's my own damn fault."

"What do you mean, 'your fault'?" Mac answered, ready to defend her from all comers, even herself.

"I came riding in on my white horse, ready to protect Los Hermanos. Involved in this damned case in the first place because I didn't want that Satanic crap dumped on them. Now I'm the one who...!" Fury and guilt garbled her words. "I really get the Brotherhood libeled!"

Suddenly another thought hit Christy. "Oh, Lord! Breakfast!"

"What can I do to help?" Mac asked quickly.

Christy managed a smile. "You can start by making me keep my big mouth shut. And thank you for standing by."

"Yeah," Mac didn't like compliments. "Actually I don't see what the big deal over the tv is."

"You'd have to have grown up here, see how deeply we're rooted in the Catholic faith. Then for me to supposedly say that Los Hermanos aren't Catholic....Well, it's like I reversed that old line and did say, the Pope's not Catholic!"

Mac grinned, "I get the picture. Just remember the people who love you will never believe it. Meanwhile, you're one smart lady, and my brain's not too shabby either. We'll figure out who dunnit. Prove each and every Hermano is innocent. Why, you'll be a hero, ma'm!"

Christy tried to smile at Mac, then said, "I'll do something about this awful face, so the guests won't know I've been crying. But if you could run over to Mama's? I can't get through to warn her."

"On my way." Leaving behind a grin, Mac ducked under the low doorway to the outside landing and disappeared. Christy doused her eyes with cold water, powdered her puffy lids, replaced the phone receiver, and then headed for her inside stairs. She almost bumped into Duane Dobbs as she maneuvered down them backwards. "Oops!" he caught her around the waist.

Christy yanked away involuntarily. She didn't have time for Mr. Dobbs, and didn't want his penetrating gaze on her swollen eyes. Just then Jack Ravioli staggered into them with his load of luggage. "Uh, sorry!"

"Some traffic jam!" Duane Dobbs said. Then to Christy, "Please excuse me from breakfast." Meaningful look. "Have to deal with that, uh, business I discussed with you."

Dobbs stepped down into La Sala, turned back to Jack. "You're checking out?"

"Yes, we...That is, Di...Di wants to try out her new bikini. Get some real sun in Scottsdale."

Didn't know our sun was fake, Christy muttered to herself, wanting to take her feelings out on someone. And why is Mr. Dobbs quizzing Mr. Ravioli? Now he looked at her. "You stay booked? Anyone new checking in?"

"Yes, as a matter of fact. Some man from Washington. Washington, D.C."

Hesitation. Then, "Well, must run."

Appearing with a load of her own, Di said, "I hope you don't think it's the hacienda or anything. It's just, well, Taos wasn't what we were expecting. And Jack. Well, you know, he..." She ran out of words.

As the two women reached the Middle Room, red-faced Jack was already back. "I think we're straight on the bill. I mean, my folks paid for everything?"

"All taken care of."

The Raviolis were gone, but Lisa came in. Skin-tight running shorts and tank top displayed great muscles.

"It's just gorgeous here! Neat getting to run on dirt roads, too. I ran toward the mountain. I guess it's Taos Mountain? Sun coming up, but I could see across the plains, some still in shadow. Glorious!"

Christy managed a smile. "Well, with all this mass exodus, I'm happy to hear your reaction!"

"Oh, we all love it here! I hate to see these last days go by. And Tama? She's in seventh heaven with all the spiritual stuff."

As the phone rang and rang again, Lisa gave Christy a curious look. "Say, you want me to get that for you? It's non-stop, hunh?"

"Some crank calls started this morning," Christy said in a tone of finality. Then, wanting to answer Lisa's obvious friendly concern, could only think of, "Thank you, Lisa. I'll cut off the ring and the machine speaker. We'll just hear a click."

Lisa lingered. "Well, if I can do anything?"

"No thanks. The coffee's on automatic, should be ready. Would you like a cup?"

"Not yet, thanks. Need to shower and wake up the gang."

Heading into the kitchen, Christy tried to take her mind off the hate calls by wondering about the new guest coming from Washington. Could the new man be D.O.E. or D.O.D.? Or, she told herself, just a vacationer, and your imagination is working overtime, Miz Grant....

Christy felt the pain returning and fought it back with thoughts of breakfast. With only the trio to cook for, she should fix something special, something she couldn't do for a crowd....Eggs Benedict. That should please them. Just happened to be her favorite, too. She needed a little spoiling.

Christy set the table and started preparations. Mac marched in. He was carrying an armful of the out-of-town newspapers. Dumping them on the counter by the door, Mac checked that they were alone, then said, "No need to worry about that little banty-hen mother of yours. She's hopping mad that anyone could think, let alone say bad things about her *hija*! Besides, she and your *padre* gave you the fine family name of Christina, not the Carlotta of the paper.

Mac placed his hands on Christy's shoulders. "From what your mama rattled off in Spanish, I got the distinct impression that the callers better repent their ways! She threw around El Diablo quite a bit, either consigning them to him or alleging they were already in league with him to be maligning you!"

Christy felt teary again, dropped the wooden spoon into the sauce and hugged that tall, lanky form. "Thank God for you and Mamacita, Mac!"

"Well, you're your Mama's daughter. Give 'em hell, tiger! But first, maybe you'd better go back to whatever's in that pan."

"Oh, Lord. My sauce! Damn! I have to be at one with the hollandaise when I add the lemon or it will curdle."

"Pretty mystic for what you've been through this morning, lady. A veritable symphony, eh?"

Christy nodded. She heard the women's voices but didn't want to leave the stove. She called out, "Is everyone here?" received Yeses, and directed, "Okay. Everyone sit down, please. It's Eggs Benedict today. Has to all happen at the same time, and hot."

Mac played host to relieve Christy, "Where are y'all off to today?"

Lisa and Lolly shook their heads. Tama said, happily, "I'm going to the Crystal Healing Workshop, you know? I wasn't sure I could get in?"

Christy served the food and Tama quickly took a bite. Eyes shining, she added, "Well, the planetary configuration was just right you know? And they say I can come!" She paused thoughtfully. "Of course I'll be on the beginner level, can't heal anyone til Master, you know?"

"Fine, fine," Mac said heartily and changed the subject to a run-down of tourist attractions. He concluded, "Of course, everything's strange in this part of the country. Another world."

"Is that why your license plates say NEW MEXICO, U.S.A..?" Lisa asked.

"Sure is. Many folks don't know they are still in the States."

A chorus of disbelieving "No."

"Yep. *New Mexico Magazine* carries a monthly feature on the missing fiftieth, New Mexico, that is. For instance, so many people ask where they can change their money, they have a standard answer at the Albuquerque airport: Right next to where you get your shots and buy the tequila!"

The trio were smiling but still looked skeptical, so Mac took one of Christy's stories. He hoped to see those now red-rimmed eyes sparkle again. "Christy shows the Saint Francis Church, the most photographed and painted Church in the country. She frequently asks visitors if they're from around here. One answer? 'Oh, no! I just crossed the border this morning.'"

Laughter.

Christy tried to smile but her thoughts were on the hate calls. Why did my people believe the worst? Believe I could have made such a statement when they've known me all my life? Where did all that anger come from? No more self pity. Get busy on the charges against Pat and resolve the trouble you brought to Los Hermanos. No, right now play the hostess.

Good old Mac was telling another of her stories, "...where the tour busses stop. He says that the most frequent questions are 'Do the natives speak English?' and 'Is it safe to talk to them?' Of course, we are all asked if we take American money!"

Everyone was giggling now and Mac, still trying to lift Christy's mood, prompted, "Tell them your English story."

Christy gave herself a shake and tried to be her cantadora self. "Well, every year we, the parishioners, strip off all the loose adobe and put new mud on the Church. We have to close it to visitors while we do. The cars circle watching us natives at play.

"So last year, I was working on the wall near the front, and a tourist comes up. Of course I'll be able to understand better if she shouts, so she yells at me, CAN–YOU–SPEAK–ENGLISH?"

"I tell her, Si."

Christy had to raise her voice over the laughing. "She grabs my arm, calls out to her friends, 'I got one! I got one!'"

Lolly was so tickled, she had tears running down her face. "More!"

"No, that's enough of my tourist stories today. If you want, I have a list of what type of paintings the different galleries show. Or anything else I can do to help?"

"No." "Fine, thanks." "Great breakfast." "We'll drop Tama off at her class."

They were gone in a flurry. And quiet drifted down on Mac and Christy. They smiled at one another, sensing new feelings. Then, regretfully, Mac asked, "Are you ready for the papers?"

Christy's stomach lurched, but she nodded.

Taking a load of dishes as he went, Mac brought the pile in from the kitchen and spread them out on the table. The first headline they saw read: TAOS MURDER RITUAL SACRIFICE?

Muttering, cursing, they read on together, starting with the lead sentence.

> Buckets of blood have been discovered in a
> search of the alleged slayer's home, according
> to one highly-placed police source.

"'Buckets of blood?!'" Christy and Mac looked up, looked at each other. "What the hell?!"

This as the tiny community of La Mesa in
northern New Mexico was rocked by the murder
of one member of a ritual torture society and
the arrest of another linked to Satanic practices.
Reports of cattle slaughtered and drained of
blood were cited by members of the nearby
famed St. Francis de Assis Church in Taos, NM.
The Catholic tie-in to Devil worshippers was
verified by Carlotta Garcia-Grant, prominent
parishioner and attorney. However, Ms Grant
stated categorically that the Brotherhood
entrenched in the state's rural north, known to
many as the penitentes, "are not Catholics."

Christy was too upset to speak. The hate calls hadn't
prepared her for this hideous linking of the Brothers and
Satanism. Garbled! All garbled! Christy was exploding with
anger. She needed to hit something, do something!

They grabbed at the rest of the papers. Some were more
subdued, but the gist of the stories were the same. Apparently
one service picked up from another. Some offered a confused
explanation that "Ms. Grant's statement" was disputed by
Church officials who "claimed" the Brotherhood was indeed a
reputable Catholic lay society. Frequently, the reporters then
added their own version of the penitentes' "troubled past." Most
went for the approach that the more sensation the better,
especially as to the "buckets of blood" found at Pat Salazaar's
home.

Christy's heart was beating too fast, her stomach cramping
badly. Then the "buckets of blood" comment sank in. That
overshadowed her personal fury. Where in the world did
"buckets of blood" come from? Did Iggy know this had come
out about his client? And she must clear up what had been
done to the reputation of Los Hermanos. That they had so
twisted her words!

"Earth to Christy. Hello? This is your doctor speaking," Mac
tried to lighten their mood with a sonorous voice. "Take some
deep breaths. In out, in out. Good. Now, what's on for today?"

"Lord, let me think! My housekeeper Ellie is coming today. I should help her clean the rooms, get ready for the new man. What a day to be tied down to a bed and breakfast! I need to be out working on these damned lies!"

They heard the click of the silenced answering machine, making them realize that the calls must have slowed for a while. "Let me," Mac said. He loped into the Middle Room. "We'll start answering the damn thing."

Mac picked up the phone and without waiting for a voice, barked, "Casa Vieja. Miz Grant was completely misquoted and plans to take action for libel. She will issue a statement later. Thank you for calling."

Mac heard squawking as he started to slam down the receiver, familiar squawking. Iggy. "For you, I believe." Mac handed it over with a grin.

"Iggy?"

"What the hell's going on Christy. The f...What's got into Mac?"

Still upset, Christy bit off her words, "Trying to protect me, thank you. And if you don't know what's going on, you must be the only person in Taos county who hasn't read a paper or watched the morning news."

"No, I slept late. Came straight here. So give!"

Christy summarized angrily, ending with, "No more questions, Iggy. Check the papers. You need to see what they're saying about Pat. Right now, you're the one I want to talk about. I've been worried—"

"Aww—"

"I'm in no mood, Ignacio," Christy cut in. "Did you see the drug dealer?"

Iggy described the meeting, then turned to his real reason for calling: with other business he had to take care of, would Christy take the task she had assigned him and talk to the girl friend? "It's Debbie Valdez," Iggy supplied. "And she's in one of the shops here on the Plaza. Let's see...Yuck. The Pink Coyote."

"Yuck is right." Christy said. "Terminal cute. We've caught it from Santa Fe. Speaking of which, Iggy. let's get together this afternoon. Go see Sergeant Brown."

"Good deal. And Christy? *Illigitimi non carborundum*...or some such. My Latin's lousy but my point about the bastards not getting you down is sound."

Mac was still sitting in the dining room drinking coffee.

He lifted a black eyebrow. "Change of plans?"

"Well, I can work with Ellie til the shops open. Then I'm going to interview the girl friend, one Debbie Valdez. That seems the most constructive thing I can do right now. Want to come along? Then have lunch on the Plaza? Oh, oh. What's going to happen if I make a public appearance before I straighten out this mess? Stoning on the public square?"

"Knowing you," Mac said, "you'll meet that head-on, all flags flying! Besides, I'll stand between you and the stone throwers."

There wasn't really any other business. What Iggy had to do was scratch an itch. Something, couldn't put a finger on it actually, was bothering him from the prior trip to La Mesa. He needed to return to Eusebio's house, go back to the morada, too.

Despite his bulk, Iggy had an easy stride up the alley toward the parking lot and was soon sailing down the highway in his great Chrysler Imperial. What a car!

Iggy slipped a cassette into the tape deck. It was *I Pagliacci* with Pavarotti. He loved to indulge his secret passion for opera and secret love for singing along.

By the time the trees had changed to ponderosa pine, Iggy's favorite aria was playing and, safely alone in the car, he was joyfully belting out the sorrowful *"Ridi, pagliacci"* down to the wonderful sobbing at the end to which he gave full throat.

Now it was time to figure out his approach to the Salazaars. Christy had done so well. He was uncomfortable with grief, didn't ever know what to say. No place for that humor he hid behind.

When Señora Salazaar opened the door, Iggy quickly reintroduced himself, thinking she had probably forgotten him. Then he said, "I'm sorry to intrude on your grief, but there is something I need to see in your son's house...Ah....Would it be possible for me to have the key again?"

"Si, si. Will you come in and have a cup of coffee?"

Iggy declined and Mrs. Salazaar gave him the key.

At Eusebio's place, Iggy ducked under the yellow Crime Scene tapes, unlocked the door. and stood gaping.

The house had been ransacked! Too much of a mess to take in. Chairs were over-turned, slashed. The floor was covered with stuff, books, papers. Not the police. Even the cops weren't this bad.

Overwhelmed and definitely uneasy, not frightened exactly, Iggy turned to go, then had a thought. He headed toward the bathroom.

The bathroom. He found the tile by the door, lifted it. Nothing. Well, it was a thought. Someone might have planted more coke.

Take the key back to Mrs. Salazaar. Be sure to ask—

She must have been watching. The door opened immediately.

Sharp black eyes looked up at him. "Did you find what you need in the home of my son?"

Iggy squirmed. "Uh, everything's fine, Señora. But, tell me, did the police come again to search?"

"No. No one comes. Is there a problem?" Soft face concerned.

"No, ma'm." He could feel the sweat on his face. Urged himself not to be a coward. She's going to go over there. You know it. "Well, yes, Señora, there is. I'm afraid someone has searched the house. Made a mess of it."

"¡Madre de Dios!" She crossed herself. "I go. I go right away this minute! Ai! *Y la policia*! What am I to do?"

"Please, ma'm. Don't go over there now. Don't do anything. And you don't have to worry about the police. I'll tell them about it. Let them come to see what someone has done."

"¿Si?" Her faced screwed up with uncertainty.

"Yes. Don't worry. Please wait. We'll take care of it. Okay?"

She agreed reluctantly.

Iggy scowled as he walked back to the car, thinking, she probably won't wait. Probably go over there as soon as I'm out of sight. He should call the cops, but still had that itch. Well, a few minutes wouldn't make any difference. He needed to see that morada.

Down the rutted dirt road. Back up again.

There it was. The morada. Forlorn. Gutted. Smelling of burnt wood, wet smoldering wood. Ugly scrawled circle, pentacles, strange letters with knobs on the ends. He could take in more detail now.

Iggy kicked at charred piece of wood, felt the breeze. The bright spring day seemed wrong. Wrong mood.

Eusebio's house. Then here. The only places he and Christy had been, but still that feeling of something overlooked...

As happened Saturday, Iggy's gaze was drawn to the cleared spot on the mountain side, the cut standing out in the midst of the thick trees. Now, that was something. Well, probably nothing. Wouldn't hurt to try to drive as close as possible. Maybe hike to that clearing, see where Christy said the old gold mine was. Los Pinoñes, she called it.

Concentrating on negotiating ruts and, at the same time, seeing if he was still heading toward the old mine, Iggy suddenly found himself on a virtually smooth road. Still dirt, yes, but it had been bladed, well kept. But, at the same time, he found himself facing a sign reading,

DANGER PELIGRO

RADIOACTIVE

KEEP OUT

It looked like he was heading right toward the old mine, so was this sign for it? Maybe somebody had found the old mine to be radioactive. Sure possible what with all the nuclear dump sites found around states like New Mexico. But if it were a radioactive old mine, why did it look recently cleared? There hadn't been anything on the news about an EPA cleanup here.

He sure as hell didn't want to risk radioactivity, but was this for real? Aw, shit! Maybe if he just drove slowly until he could see something....

Around this curve and.... Iggy stopped abruptly.

The clearing. A parking lot really. He could see the cars from this angle. A chain link fence around the perimeter concealed the interior with canvas camouflage covering. Geez! What kind of place was this? Was it something like that government site in Utah, was it? The one with all the weird shit? Workers bussed in so they wouldn't know where they were going. Military maintaining a perimeter. Aliens. Experiments.

And what about the marijuana farms in the woods. He knew from Clive and others that they existed. Had heard a person could get shot wandering into one.

It wasn't the huge stop sign in the middle of the road that got him. Or the familiar symbol for radioactivity.

It was the two blank-faced guards cradling shotguns!

They wore black uniforms with no insignia.

And here he was in the middle of nowhere! There were always guys going missing near Taos. Who was to know....Hadn't even told Christy....If they wanted to disappear him!

Iggy let down the window, commanded his voice not to squeak. "Hey, guys. I was just looking—"

One approached the car. "This is a government controlled area, sir."

"Guess I got lost up here. What are—"

The second one came up. "Back out of here, sir."

"Well, sure. I was just—"

The mood changed suddenly.

"Move it, Mister!"

"Could you tell me what this—"

Two steps closer. "Move it! Back, that's BACK outa here!"

Iggy moved it. Backed outa there.

The nearest guard turned to the intercom.

CHAPTER XIV

Iggy found a phone in a bar on the outskirts of La Mesa. Once inside, he thought it was good that he only wanted a phone, not a drink. His entrance had made conversation cease between the three patrons at the counter and the bartender. Four pairs of eyes looked him up and down, stopped at the curls. Looked at each other. Four pairs of eyes watched in silence as this stranger walked to the phone on the far side of the front door.

"Okay if I make a call?"

Short nod from the bartender.

Iggy gave thanks that the phone book still hung by its chain. He'd hate to ask that bunch for anything. Needed the Santa Fe Headquarters for the State Troopers, not the hot line. What the hell was he going to tell Sergeant Brown? Make it an anonymous call? No, no way for a member of the Bar to conduct himself. He punched in his credit card number.

"This is Attorney Baca in Taos. I'd like to speak to Sergeant Brown, please." Probably not there. Out cruising somewhere... .

"Sergeant Brown."

"Yes, Sergeant. This is Ignacio Baca in Taos."

"Good morning, Mr. Baca." The voice was cool but polite.

"If possible I'd like to arrange a meeting for this afternoon and—"

"You should see the D.A., Mr. Baca."

Iggy stood more erect, spoke crisply, "By law the State has to furnish me with all reports, evidence, lists of witnesses. I—"

"Tell that to the D.A. Nothing else?"

"Just one minute, Sergeant Brown." Iggy said with authority. "I am coming in to see you. Secondly, I'm reporting that the victim's house has been searched."

"Well, sure. We went through it already. What're you...?"

Iggy explained the situation to an irate state cop. "What were you doing out there. We still got our tapes up!"

Iggy wasn't about to answer that. "I'll see you this afternoon, Sergeant. We can share information. Good-bye."

Now, while he was still at the phone, he'd try Christy. He had to see her as soon as possible. After a couple of rings, a lilting voice answered, saying, "Good afternoon... Oh, it's still morning, isn't it? Good morning. Casa Vieja Bed and Breakfast. May I help you?"

Damn. It was Desire.

"This is Ignacio Baca, Desire. Is Miz Grant—"

"Yes, sir," Desire interrupted brightly. "Did you wish to make a reservation?

"This is Iggy, Desire! Iggy! I need to talk to Christy."

"I can take your reservation, sir. It is not necessary to speak to Miz Grant." There was a pause for sound to reach the brain at the other end. Giggle. "Oh, Iggy, hi. This is Desire."

Sigh. "Yes, Desire, I know it's you. Now let's start again. Is Miz Grant at home?"

"No, she sure isn't." Desire sighed, then brightened, "But you have a great day!"

She hung up. Damned if he was up to even a nice day. "Great day!" Shee-it!

Loping back to the car, Iggy thought he'd better see his client about those buckets of blood. Next, he might still find Christy on the Plaza after she interviewed Debbie Valdez.

"Let's park in the lot and walk around the Plaza 'til we find The Pink Coyote," Christy suggested, happy to get away from the phone.

Mac proffered an elbow. "Take my arm, ma'am, there's not a stone-thrower in sight. We'll have our own Easter parade." Smiling, Christy did so.

"Taos seems to be getting just a mite like Juarez," Mac commented. "A person can tell what's in each season by what the merchants are touting. Howling coyotes. Pueblo-style ladders...." Chatting, they strolled down the alley.

"Which way?" Mac asked at the corner.

"Let's try this North side. Meander toward Oglevie's. There's a neat shop near where the old jail used to be, specializes in silver."

"Look there, The Pink Coyote," Mac announced.

A bell tinkled as Mac opened the door and Christy took a deep breath, thinking, here goes.

Their senses were assaulted. Their eyes took in masses, crowds, groups, packs of coyotes! Floor. Counters. High shelves. Pink, yellow, blue, green. There was every color except for coyote-colored coyotes. Large, small, all sizes. Carved, wooden, painted coyotes wearing kerchiefs around their necks. Pink and blue kerchiefs, standard red and black patterned cowboy ones. Coyotes painted on metal. Almost every one of them with snouts lifted to howl. Many paired with poison green cactus. A stuffed cactus stood next to a bright plush coyote. And the scent! Overpowering. It came from candles, coyote shaped and others representing green cactus with pink flowers on top.

Overwhelmed, Christy congratulated herself that she had her wonderful Franzetti coyote. Had it back before it was even "in."

Christy had already prepared Iggy for this important witness, so she herself was ready for the lovely young Spanish woman behind the counter. Small and slim, thick black lashes set off her dark eyes. Her long black hair had the popular little short bunch of curls in front. Smiling, she asked "May I help you?"

Mac hung back politely. Christy looked around. No customers. "Well, yes. I need to talk to you for a minute. That is if you're Debbie Valdez?"

Looking puzzled, Debbie nodded.

"I'm Christina Garcia y Grant, an attorney working on the Pat Salazaar case."

"Oh." Big eyes got bigger.

Christy started off gently. "I grew up here, Debbie. I bet you did, too. Do you come from the Valdez valley?"

A tiny smile appeared, vanished. "No, I grew up in La Mesa but that's because my papa moved there when he married mama. All of his branch of my family are from Valdez.... Why do you want to talk to me? I don't know anything about the murder."

"Well, not the murder, Debbie. I just wondered what you could tell me about Eusebio Salazaar and his cousin Pat?"

Debbie was shaking her head before the question was out. "No. I don't know anything."

Christy soothed. "Of course you don't know anything about the crime itself, or why Pat was arrested. But what about those young men as people, their lives? I understand you, uh, dated both of them?"

Still shaking her head, Debbie answered in a small voice. "No, ma'am."

Smiling but intent, Christy looked directly into Debbie's eyes. Finally this, and the silence, elicited the reluctant answer, "Well, I went out a few times with each of them. It wasn't real dating, nothing serious, you know? Just being with friends, part of the crowd...."

Keeping her voice soft, Christy pressed, "But I hear that Eusebio and Pat got in a fight. Fought over you?" The silent negative came again, but there was more expression in Debbie's eyes. A flash of what? Anger? Christy waited.

"Not over me. They were both mad at me. I did start dating, and it was someone else. Steady, you know? So I couldn't hang out with Eusebio or Pat any more."

Thank God! What a break for Pat. But who was this other man? Better ease into it. "Well, I'm glad those two cousins weren't fighting, Debbie. And you started going steady? Are you still going steady?"

"I sure am!" Debbie declared proudly. "Maybe you know him. He's Stephen Kramer. Dr. Stephen Kramer, from the Los Alamos lab. He's very important there?"

Christy tried to keep a poker face and hide her excitement. "No, I don't believe we've met." Christy's trial training was to go carefully here, not frighten the witness. "How did you meet him, Debbie?"

"He came in here shopping. Oh, I know he's older and all, but right away, he liked being with me."

A trophy girlfriend? Debbie was pretty enough. No, make that beautiful. And Dr. Kramer might be the type whose ego demanded he feel superior.

Delighted with this unexpected discovery, Christy risked asking about drugs while praying she got the right answer. "There's been talk of drugs. Do you know if Eusebio or Pat were using?"

"Those two? Using?" Debbie crowed. "Give me a break. They were as squeaky clean as, well, whatever. No drugs. Me neither. That's for sure!"

Christy beamed on Debbie. "Well, thank you! I'm glad to hear it."

"Yes, ma'am. Would you like to look at anything?"

Christy shuddered inwardly. "Uh, not today. But thanks again."

"We'll see you."

"We'll see you. 'Bye."

As the pair left, Debbie stood very still. Then, looking thoughtful, she turned to the phone.

Scarcely out the door, Christy exploded, "Who-ee! Wow!" She punched Mac's arm. "Did hear that? Did you!"

"Stop beating on me, lady." Mac gave her hand a quick squeeze. "I heard! I heard!"

"No jealously motive for Pat! And no drugs! Coming from a straight person."

Mac interrupted. "Did you get the Dr. Kramer connection?!"

"And what might all this raucous public display be about?" a stern voice asked.

It was La Doña and Christy gave the ramrod hulk a hug. "Just wait til we tell you! Come on to lunch with us at Oglevie's. We need to talk."

Planting her lace-up brogues more firmly apart, La Doña appeared skeptical. "That we certainly must do in light of this morning's unfortunate publicity and the undoubtedly erroneous quotation attributed to you. But I don't know about your choice of restaurants. Ate in there not long ago. Bad service. Table of Texans got all the attention."

La Doña was caught up in her complaints. "Look around you. I don't know what the Plaza's coming to. I keep coming back, expecting to shop at Rexall and the general store. Gone. All gone. Instead, everything caters to tourists."

For a moment her face crumpled, showing all of her age. Then, her usual fierceness returned. "All right, young man. Give me your arm and we'll...what do they say? We'll 'do' lunch!"

They passed the stores in the downstairs foyer: hand-weavings in the artists' co-op; chile *ristras*, garlic, and wine from La Chiripada; great sweaters from the Andes. Then, starting up the stairs to the restaurant, La Doña gallantly tried not to show how heavily she leaned on Mac's arm, dared anyone to notice her shortness of breath.

As they reached the top and Oglevie's lobby, they heard, "Hey, guys. Christy. La Doña."

"Iggy!"

Simultaneously Iggy and Christy exclaimed, "Just wait til I tell you!"

"Children," La Doña addressed them firmly. "Contain yourselves until we find a table. Mac?"

"Yes, ma'am." He turned to the hostess. "Four for lunch, please."

Christy felt exposed to all eyes as the smiling woman escorted them to a good-sized corner table. Christy looked around. No need to be paranoid. This crowd wouldn't know what she had supposedly said about Los Hermanos. If they did, they wouldn't care.

The restaurant had a good atmosphere, popular, but quiet enough for conversation. And, despite the windows and doors to the outside balcony, the room had a kind of mellow dimness.

Smiling cordially at the hostess, Mac said, "Please tell the waitperson that The Lady here expects immediate service."

"Yes, sir."

La Doña bent over to tuck her big briefcase under the table. She looked up to command, "And Glenlivet with water, no ice."

They gave their orders, laughed when Iggy asked for just a salad. He righteously patted his round belly under today's new ruby silk shirt. Then, turning serious, Iggy demanded of Christy. "You first. Mine will take longer."

As all eyes turned to her, Christy began by addressing La Doña, "Thank you for believing I was misquoted." She explained what she had really said about Devil Worshippers and why the 'Catholic' comment had caused so much anger. La Doña scolded her for ever, not ever, making any sort of statement to reporters. This was the first Iggy had heard of the uproar. He swore in outrage.

Then, turning to the interview with Debbie, Christy built up to the climax with the news about Pat being squeaky clean, and then announced, "Debbie is dating one Stephen Kramer from Los Alamos. Steady."

"Impossible," La Doña bristled. "You describe a very young naive, shop girl. Not the type for Stephen at all."

Christy started to speak, but Mac interrupted. "I don't know why not, Miss Doris. You know Dr. Kramer well and I don't, but from the impression I had at Furr's I'd say he might like parading Debbie on his arm—and elsewhere."

Before La Doña and Christy could argue, Iggy exclaimed, "Geez! She's dating Los Alamos? Oh, Lord love us!" He stopped.

"What?" Christy and Mac asked in unison. "We are waiting, Ignacio," La Doña added sternly.

Iggy had to tell the whole story about Eusebio's place his way. He had just reached the part about Los Piñones mine when the waitress brought more coffee and conversation had to stop. Iggy asked about dessert.

"Just a minute, sir. I'll bring the tray."

When she returned, Iggy turned his most cherubic, saying, "Wee-ll, with that lunch, just a tiny salad, I guess I can have a bite of something sweet." He pointed at a dark concoction with whipped cream on top.

"The double fudge truffle, sir?"

"Uh, yes." Iggy glared defiance at the others. Then, turning very businesslike, he said, "Let's get back to the investigation, shall we? You said it was the old gold mine, Christy. Not anymore. I drove up there. Good road now. First I see radioactive warnings—"

The crew interrupted.

"Wait. Wait. First those signs and I thought of a variety of scenarios, but I went on—"

"Ignacio. That is not intelligent."

"I was met by a big stop sign and...Get this! Two guards carrying guns! I was told to, in effect, get the hell out of there!"

Iggy proudly surveyed the reactions of his friends.

"Well, my gawd!" La Doña was first to comment.

"Amen," Christy added, green eyes shining. This was worth pursuing.

Mac looked from one to another. "Appears this is going to take some thought. What are y'all up to this afternoon?"

"I told the good Sergeant we were coming to see him per Christy's orders. He's not too happy about that," Iggy responded.

Christy nodded. "For one thing, I'm hoping to find out if that body in the alley had anything to do with Eusebio's death."

"I sure don't see where it could tie in with Stephen Kramer," Mac added. "And Eusebio? Too bad Kramer was so close-mouthed."

La Doña nodded. "Yes. He's usually quite controlled, although he was unusually abrupt. I expect he's working under too much pressure." Brightening. "I have a proposal. Iggy and Christina will interview the Sergeant this afternoon. Then tomorrow morning, first thing, I will personally escort all of you to Los Alamos. By representing Stephen and his colleagues in years past, I surely have a little leverage to get some information to help our client."

"I can't go tomorrow. I have dream class," Christy objected. La Doña shook her head at this, her expression scornful. Before they could argue, Mac quickly suggested, "I'll sign on for Los Alamos. I could take the car home now, Christy, and you ride with Iggy, okay?"

"Hey!" Iggy said. "Being so pissed—excuse me, La Doña—at what the papers did to Christy, I almost forgot the big deal. I checked out the buckets-of-blood number they did on Pat."

Every eye turned towards him. Iggy strung out the drama for a minute, then said, "I ran over to the jail to see Pat."

He paused, took a large bite of chocolate truffle, received a stern "Ignacio!" from La Doña. Swallowing, he added: "You know Pat's a furniture maker? Into construction, too? Well, a pair of those rich commuting types are insistent on renovating the old way—being authentic. Want a new-old 'blood floor.' He has the farmers saving animal blood from slaughtering for it. Buckets of blood."

Christy smacked her forehead with her hand. "Stupid! Why didn't I think of that! I have a blood floor in my room upstairs! Blood really was used mixed with some kind of glue to seal dirt floors!"

"You were a mite distracted." Mac grinned. Christy didn't think it was funny.

Just as Mac returned to Casa Vieja, he saw a stranger going in the Middle Room door. The man struggled with his luggage. A long leather bag gave him the most trouble in his attempt to negotiate the narrow doorway.

"Here, let me help," Mac said, entering behind him and taking a garment bag.

"Thanks."

The stranger was compact and muscular. His blonde hair was clipped into a precise crew-cut. He headed toward Desire at the desk. "Fred Ritchie's the name. I have a reservation for a single."

Desire's vague gaze fastened on the long bag. "Are you a hunter? My brother's a hunter and he has a thing to carry his rifle in, looks like that. Well, of course, his isn't leather you know?"

"Golf clubs. A few favorite ones."

Desire giggled. "Oh, of course. Silly me. Why didn't I know it was a golf bag?"

"My reservation," the voice became rather sharp.

Not to be side-tracked, Desire gleefully nodded. "Oh ho! But it's silly you. That's a joke, see? Taos doesn't have a golf course."

Some wicked impulse kept Mac from helping Ritchie by reminding Desire of the new one on the south side.

Audible sigh. "If I could just check in, Miss?"

"Desire. My name's Desire." She prattled on while Ritchie's face turned a dark red.

Mac's better instincts prevailed. "Desire," he said firmly. "Please take this guest's credit card and get him signed in."

Tossing her long blonde hair, "Well, sure!" A little miffed. All business: "Name please."

Face still red, he carefully enunciated, "Fred Ritchie. That's R-i-t-c-h-i-e. Do you have my reservation for a single?"

Desire shook her head. To prevent an imminent explosion, Mac said, "The Escondida, Desire. Mr. Ritchie has a reservation for La Escondida." He smiled at the poor man, "Sorry."

Too exasperated to give Mac more than a brief, tight smile. "No problem."

Mac started to lift the long bag to help. "I'll take that," Ritchie said quickly. His abruptness surprised Mac. Desire couldn't have it right for once, could she?

CHAPTER XV

As soon as Christy and Iggy entered the State Police Headquarters, they found themselves in a tiny foyer, no more than ten by twelve feet. A receptionist sat behind bullet-proof glass. They gave their names, said they were there to meet with Sergeant Brown, and signed in. The receptionist gave them passes and then let them proceed through the double doors into a big hallway carpeted in gray, decorated with trophies, State Police uniforms, and badges.

Sergeant Brown strode down the hall to meet Iggy and Christy. Dark gray shirt stretched tight across his chest, buttons straining over his girth, thick leather belt and holster, tight gray pants. Apparently expecting only Iggy, his expression changed when he saw Christy walking a little behind in her casually expensive clothes. Was she money? Influence?

Iggy jumped in smoothly with, "Sergeant Brown, I'd like you to meet my associate, Miz Christina Garcia y Grant."

"Pleased to meet you, ma'am. If you'd come this way, we can use an interrogation room."

Christy winked at Iggy.

Once settled, Christy took the initiative. "Too bad you couldn't manage to meet us in your building at Taos, Sergeant."

"Uh, yes, ma'am." Leather creaked as Brown shifted in his chair.

She smiled at him. "That's all right. We're happy to accommodate you." Pause. "Have you received the medical examiner's report on Eusebio Salazaar?"

"No, ma'am. It usually takes five days. And with the holiday and all...." He turned to Iggy. "Now about you crossing police lines—"

But Christy intervened. "Yes, Sergeant. I understand you had made a prior search?"

"Yes we did," the sergeant sat up rigidly, "but—"

"And did you find drugs at that time?" Christy rapped out.

"No, ma'am." Sergeant Brown knew a cross-examination when he heard one. Again the leather protested as he moved, crossing his legs.

Christy made her voice more casual. "Did you search such places as, uh, the toilet tank, for instance."

The Sergeant was able to laugh at that one. "Well, yeah, sure. The toilet's as old a trick as the frozen-assets-in-the-freezer routine."

"True. On the other hand, you wouldn't go so far as to take up the floor?"

"No. The situation didn't call for it. Not in an open-and-shut case like this. The victim was stabbed, and stabbed by someone in his immediate vicinity. We didn't have far to look."

"And no drugs." Christy spoke with finality.

"No, but Salazaar's guilty as—"

Christy felt the adrenaline rush. This was the time. She'd laid a foundation. Both ethics and procedure demanded they produce the drugs now, but the risk was large. She sounded cool, however, as she said, "Then obviously the drugs we found were a plant." Christy prayed Iggy wouldn't react to this sudden admission.

Sergeant Brown's face showed the effort he was making to control himself. His voice choked as he responded, "You...You are telling me you have drugs from the victim's house?"

"We brought them directly to you," Iggy said to Christy's relief.

Christy chose the offensive. "And if the drugs were a plant, since Pat Salazaar was in jail, someone else came in with the drugs after your search."

"But you—"

Christy interrupted before Sergeant Brown could collect his thoughts about their violations. They'd destroyed any chain of evidence that could make the coke part of the defense, but that was ok, juries were funny about drugs. The point was to turn over the stash, and thereby to wake the Sergeant up to other possibilities.

She found herself enjoying the rush of the old trial routine, establishing the beat. "Yes, that brings us to our client Pat Salazaar's house. Has that been searched?"

"Yeah. But, okay, okay, now we're going back there to look for more drugs. Use a fine tooth comb!"

"And this time, Sergeant, let's hope there's no leak about buckets of blood!" Pushing her advantage over the startled sergeant, Christy continued. "You might have gone over this with Mr. Salazaar when Mr. Baca allowed you to interview him. That fine tooth comb would have found that the blood in question is animal blood used in refinishing dirt floors!"

"No shit?" He actually sounded human in his incredulity. "Excuse me, ma'am. This is one crazy country up north here."

"Not if you knew it, understood the old ways." Christy suppressed her annoyance, returned to her questioning. "You obviously found no drugs there either."

"No drugs." Reluctantly. Then, "But you bet your sweet... uh...bippy, that Salazaar's tied in with—"

"No drugs, Sergeant. And have you recovered the murder weapon?"

"We're looking. But you just hang on a minute on the drug angle. I could have you picked up for possession yourself."

"Surely you don't want to do that when we, two respected officers of the court, testify we found them in a dead man's house and brought them to the police at the earliest opportunity." Knowing it was best to move on quickly, she said, "Let's go back to your fruitless search for the murder weapon. A windowless morada? Two bare rooms? Plain dirt floor? I wonder where Pat Salazaar could have hidden it." Christy felt a ghostly jury behind her.

"We'll find it. I know he hid it somewhere before we took him in."

"Mm-hum. Are you pursuing any other leads?"

"Not at this time. We've got your client."

Christy smiled at Sergeant Brown sympathetically. "I don't think so, Sergeant. With no drug involvement and no murder weapon at the morada, and knowing that Pat Salazaar never left the building before your appearance at the crime scene....Also, did he exhibit any bloodstains?"

"The wound was very deep, just a slit, the blood wouldn't have splattered. In fact, it could take awhile for the victim to bleed to death internally."

"Yes? Isn't that another point in Mr. Salazaar's favor, Sergeant? Furthermore, have you pursued the Satanic angle?"

"Aw, cra—! We're after a murderer, not somebody wearing horns and tail."

"Hex balls were found," Christy announced calmly.

"The shit you say. By who?"

"By me, in Eusebio's house when we found the coke. Those tie in with the Satanic symbols painted on the morada, bring them into question."

"Look lady, I've seen graffiti before. And that's what the stuff was—just graffiti. And I haven't seen those hex balls you claim."

"It's our belief it was all done to mislead you. This is no ordinary graffiti. And Pat Salazaar was on the Good Friday march when the symbols were put on the morada and the morada burned. He could not have done it. There are witnesses. You need to find the person or persons who did."

Then, intent on discovering the State's knowledge of any other possible connections, Christy raised a last point. "What about the body in the alley?"

"What about it?"

"Are you investigating that death in connection with Eusebio Salazaar's?"

"Hell, no! Out of our jurisdiction. That's a simple mugging for the Town of Taos."

Now she shot quickly, hoping to surprise an honest response. "Did you check if the dead man also worked at Los Alamos?"

"Why would I ask? I don't care if he worked for the C.I.A. Nothing to do with my case."

"Do you even know his name?"

"Sure I know his name. Some guy name of Watkins. Bryce Watkins."

"And that's all you know? Just a name?"

"Hell, I know all I need to know—Bryce Watkins shot at close range in the back of the head in an alley behind Los Bailes."

So. That was the State's entire case on both murders. Christy stood up. "Thank you, Sergeant. We won't take any more of your time."

Leaving the Sergeant behind, a bemused Iggy followed Ms. Grant out the door.

CHAPTER XVI

Christy didn't get much sleep Monday night. The evening journal writing usually took the pressure off, but this time her mind squirrel-caged on penitentes and murder and what she should be doing. The newspapers printed nasty mixtures of lies and lurid distortions. Pat and La Hermandad both libeled. Her face felt hot and red in the dark as she thought of them. She ached with responsibility, as if all the wrongs done the Brotherhood in the past were on her shoulders now. She couldn't turn off her thinking.

Now Tuesday morning, her bed and breakfast duties done, Christy drove east out of Talpa, crossed the highway, and was on the road officially known as The Road Under the Hill, *El Camino Loma Baja*. To the right the land *did* rise sharply, supporting spindly cacti that soon would flourish intense fuschia flowers. This was the bottom of the Ranchos valley. No vistas of more sky than earth here. This was farm land with a river running through it and the mesas of Llano Quemado and Talpa rising above it. The fields were divided the old way, long and narrow, separated by hedge rows to which a few bedraggled puffs balls of milkweed still clung. Disked fields displayed dark, fertile furrows. Other fields, planted with alfalfa, had already made up their minds to come out brilliant green.

Willows edged close to acequias, irresistibly snaking roots toward the early spring runoff, their branches yellow, barely hazed with chartreuse. A big black old cottonwood, twisted like huge bonsai art, only allowed a glimpse of tremulous blue sky to the south. Christy looked at it while she pulled over to let an oncoming pickup come past. The road wasn't wide enough for two. The tree wore a menacing crow on one tortured branch. "Overdoing it a little, eh?" Christy asked the tree, trying to amuse herself—but she still felt a deep ache between her shoulder blades.

On the blacktop again, Christy turned down Valerio road where the small adobe houses snugged closer together until, near the mother church they nestled by each other like baby chicks, the houses and the church having once stood on a common where sheep grazed. Shops now.

Piñon smoke scented the air from stoves fired up to cook breakfast or to take off the morning chill.

Valerio Road ended at the highway which Christy drove across toward her destination, a dirt driveway. She was still in the community of Ranchos. Her Dream Class took place in a little adobe tucked into the fold of a slope that continued on down to an arroyo, wet now with snow melt.

Christy joined in the waves and hugs as other women drove into the parking lot, but yesterday's dream was uppermost in her mind. Eusebio's dead and bleeding figure still pursued her.

Chattering, happy to see one another, the dreamers straggled into the house and sat in a circle on the floor that was haphazardly covered with a variety of old oriental rugs. They had the look of longtime Anglo Taos: a variety of shapes but mostly on the thin side, clean faces innocent of makeup, wearing clothes in faded earth colors.

Sometimes the dreamers tossed dream fragments into the unseeable pot of images. Sometimes a dream evoked myths or fairy tales. Sometimes the dreamers simply told and interpreted the dream, helped by Andy, their leader, and the others.

Evolved into a tight women's group, the dreamers always took time to talk at the beginning. Today Christy's new notoriety took over. "Really put your foot in it, didn't you, girl?" "Old *Carlotta* here versus the media!" "Anybody try burning your house lately?" "How about a cross? Heh-heh, get it?" Christy was happy to hear the friendly teasing, although she'd never doubted their support.

Christy gave a quick explanation of the facts on the murders, but the group wanted more information.

"Are you involved with the case itself?"

"Do you know the attorney who's defending Pat Salazaar?"

"Do you think Salazaar did it?"

"Any truth in the witchcraft stories the papers carried? Was Satanism or some cult really involved in the murder?"

"What's your reading on this mess?"

"And that other guy who was murdered, uh, Watson? Watkins? Are the two killings connected?"

Christy answered as best she could without breaking any attorney-client privilege. At the end, she admitted that she had thoughts, suspicions, questions swirling in her head, and maybe a pertinent dream. Perhaps her psyche held the answers.

While the session got started, Christy anxiously considered the dream that the hate calls had almost overshadowed, remembered that it had, in fact, visited her just before they started. The dream was strange, frightening. Was it informative?

With the beginning ritual completed, Sandra immediately spoke up from across the circle. "I have a dream that's stayed with me. Anybody mind if I go first?"

Christy was disappointed, almost choking on the need to express her nightmare, but she made no objection.

"Well," Sandra began, "it starts with the shot of just a baby, out in nowhere....like in the 2001 movie? Then I'm with a couple who're fighting and throwing the baby back and forth. When I can get hold of the baby, it's immediately happy and waving its arms and legs. Then the couple go at it again and I'm crying, 'Can't you see I can't do anything when you act like this?' This keeps on—the couple and the baby and me, saying the same thing. Finally, the camera zooms out and there's the baby again out in nowhere and it's laughing and cooing."

"Ohh, wow."

"Some dream!"

"That's a huge one."

Eyes were shining with excitement around the group, but Andy sat very still, looking serious.

Slowly, gently, the other dreamers began to ask questions. No one wanted to lay an interpretation on Sandra.

"How did you feel?"

"Were you the baby?"

"That couple fighting—are you in conflict over something."

Like a fragile balloon, the dream was carefully batted about, helping Sandra center on its meaning.

Andy said, "That's very existential. The baby is who you can be," and the discussion went on from there until there was no more to be said about Sandra's dream.

They were all silent a moment or two. Christy's heart pounded as she could not dislodge her dream of a pursuing corpse and bloody card players. Andy must have sensed her discomfort. "Christy? Do you have a dream you'd like to share with us?"

CHAPTER XVII

Iggy picked up Mac for the trip to Los Alamos. La Doña sat regally upright in the Imperial's passenger seat.

Mac got in back, for once finding room for his long legs, and the big car moved off.

Conversation gave way to desultory chatting until they reached Española.

"Good time of day to come through Española," Mac commented. "Most of the low riders are in school."

Unveiling a surprising streak of romanticism, La Doña said, "I like to think of the low-riders and their cars as comparable to the *caballeros* of old, the young horsemen showing off their prancing steeds, parading for the pretty *Señoritas*." She cleared her throat. Neither man dared a word.

Iggy cut across the edge of town to take the grass-bordered road through Santa Clara Indian lands. They passed a right-hand turn. La Doña raised her window-side arm to point. "That's the Puye site, a partially-restored cliff dwelling, probably abandoned about 800 years ago by the Santa Clara Indians when the terrible drought sent them down to live by the Rio Grande. Now it's a tourist attraction operated by the Pueblo for those who like to wander around ruins. If you go on up that BIA road, you get to Santa Clara Canyon and its lakes. It's a beautiful picnic spot. And there are bears....Another day, it's well worth a stop."

Mac smiled at her quick reversion to lecturer.

The terrain began to change. Black Rock Mesa jumped up on their left, rising vertically out of the dun-colored earth. On their right, weather-carved sandstone buttes lifted curves and pinnacles which continued to dominate the view as Iggy turned the car right to begin the steep grade towards Los Alamos.

La Doña turned her head slightly to address Mac in the back seat, "So, young man, you've not been to Los Alamos before?"

"No, ma'am. That's one reason I'm tagging along. And, of course to look for something new to deliver to those state cops, Sergeant Brown in particular." Then, to tease her. "Why not your Dr. Kramer? He's so exactly the picture of the obsessed scientist—the movies might have typecast him in the part."

Seeing her stiffen, Mac hastily continued: "Yes, yes, I'm just joking. But," suddenly thoughtful, "maybe I just revealed something unfunny about myself. Perhaps I'm a bit of a chauvinist—as well as anxious to help your client."

The Lady relaxed. "Yes, you might be, Dr. McCloud, but you have made an accurate deduction. Dr. Kramer's father was one of the scientists our government slipped out of Nazi Germany. Sent first to work on missiles in Alabama, probably at Redstone, then here to Los Alamos where Stephen grew up."

"I knew quite of few of these scientists when I was young. That was after they came, secretly, to try to split the atom. The researchers are still wrapped in heavy security up here, of course. They keep their secrets, but not like when the Manhattan Project began in forty-three."

Iggy chortled, "I hear that even now those Ph.D.s wash their cars when they get back on 'the hill' if they have to go over to Santa Fe or Albuquerque."

"Ignacio. No idle gossip, please," La Doña chided. She added, "In the days of the Project, everyone living in barracks and Quonset huts for dormitories, gas rationing was severe and it wasn't so easy to leave this isolated spot. Feynman, I believe it was, hitchhiked to Albuquerque almost weekly to visit his ailing wife in the hospital. When he and other scientists went off site, they avoided using their actual names. And, I add, very few outsiders were allowed to enter. Oak Ridge was the same. That tradition has persisted and is taken very seriously. I often wonder if the scientists at the labs talk even to each other."

The big car smoothly negotiated the steep climb, the switchbacks. "Fantastic view," Mac said, peering out over the deep canyon, looking back toward a panorama of flatlands and mountains. The near view was equally spectacular. Long, near-vertical drop-offs fell to piñon and juniper strewn lower elevations. Across from them, the trees climbed partway up mesas of varying shades of brown volcanic tuff which marched off into the distance. Near the jagged tops of the formations, the trees gave up the struggle, leaving bare rock in shades of ocher and sienna bleached to near white farther up. The other side of the road butted up against the striated peach-colored cliff, which still showed the marks of having been blasted out of the rock.

"It is beautiful, but sort of chilling," Iggy commented. "When you think that this was the only road in." He shivered. "Kind of like those men with guns up there in La Mesa. Here, only one road and guards and the atom bomb!"

"Sinister," Mac answered. "Too bad in a place of such natural grandeur."

"Robert Oppenheimer didn't come up here for the view," La Doña said sternly. "He'd been to the Los Alamos boys' school as a child. Remembered its total isolation. Nothing else here. He was a brilliant administrator, came back to pull the physicists, Fermi, Feynman, and others that General Groves called 'those prima donnas,' into the team that developed the bomb. Oppenheimer was a first-class nuclear scientist in his own right as well, but misguided."

"You mean the stuff I've read about his troubles?" Iggy asked.

"I do not!" La Doña corrected. "Robert has been honored as a fine citizen. No I mean that his brilliance helped lead us to the atom bomb. Something this world could have done without. Robert knew that. When they exploded the first one, he quoted from the *Bhagavad Gita*: 'I am become death, the destroyer of worlds.'"

They fell silent.

The car topped the mountain, moved past the airport on the right. A small forest of piñon, blue spruce, and ponderosa bordered the left side of the road as it stretched along the Parjarito Plateau at the eastern edge of the Jemez Mountains and the rim of a gigantic volcanic caldera. They entered the town of Los Alamos, sitting high on a mesa amid vistas of pine-clad slopes.

"Where to now?" Iggy asked, looking around at the town, a clean and pretty place, as they drove through.

"Turn left here over the bridge, and then, just before the light, bear right."

Following La Doña's directions, Iggy soon had them across to the south side of the canyon and onto the road leading to the Bandelier turnoff, and heading further west, across the Jemez to Cuba.

"Make a left into that big parking lot for Tech Area 3." La Doña turned to Mac. "We want the Administration Building. I don't know how many facilities and high-security laboratories make up the whole Los Alamos National Laboratory. The Department of Energy has also, from time to time, opened a facility elsewhere like its Nevada test site."

Iggy pulled into one of the few vacant spaces, stopped the engine, as Mac asked, "Why would Dr. Kramer be working on HIV in a place like this?"

"If I remember right, D.O.E. has an Office of Health and Environmental Research. There have been health issues raised by radiation damage since the fifties, and scientists here have done world-class research. I can't remember how long the Human Genome project has been in place." She paused a moment.

"We need to try that building over there, behind the fence. The security station is that small structure just to the outside. They can call Stephen."

"I thought his secretary told you he wasn't in," Iggy commented as they got out of the car.

"We'll see about that."

"I'll wander around awhile outside," Mac offered. "I need to stretch my legs, and we don't want to look like a committee."

In the small security facility, high-tech equipment screened those with badges and let them through. Visitors had to approach courteous but firm guards who immediately asked La Doña and Iggy to state their business. "I am Attorney Doris Jordan and this is my associate, Ignacio Baca," she demoted Iggy. "We are here to see Dr. Stephen Kramer."

"I'll put a call through," one guard answered. "It could take awhile. Why don't you go over there," pointing out a building, "wait at the cafeteria up on the second floor. It has a splendid view, much better than the coffee. I'll notify Dr. Kramer where you are." He picked up the phone.

"How shall we approach this?" Iggy asked as, back outside, they looked around for Mac. He had disappeared.

"Well, I certainly hope this isn't a wild goose chase. And I wish we could confirm that the man shot in the alley ties in to Eusebio's murder. That could be what we need to get Sergeant Brown to consider some other suspect than Pat Salazaar."

"Right. The state's just handed that killing over to the town. It won't be easy to get them to pull it back, or work the cases together."

By now they had reached the cafeteria, were finding a vacant table. The coffee smelled burned. They fell silent, turning over what little they knew. Eventually a woman entered and approached. She looked about fifty, wearing her suspiciously auburn hair pulled back in an elaborate French twist. Her charcoal business suit was tailored to allow for wide hips.

La Doña stiffly rose to her feet. "Why Vern. How nice to see you, my dear. But I asked for Dr. Kramer."

Tone and posture tinged with annoyance, Vern answered, "I told you on the phone that he's not here this morning."

"Then we will simply wait."

"Well, I can't stop you, but I don't know when Dr. Kramer will be back!"

Iggy, who had also risen, just stood there, looking from one to the other.

It was going to be up to The Lady. "Vern, my dear, I've known you since you arrived here twenty-five years ago, right out of secretarial school. Won't you join us in a cup of coffee and see if Stephen returns?"

Slightly mollified, Vern shook her head. "I have a great deal of work to do. "

"We'll stay here ourselves, then."

Vern almost wailed, "There's no point! And, besides, he's not—" She bit down hard on her lip.

La Doña didn't miss the implication, but gave no sign. She simply said, "Then give us five minutes and we'll be off." Sitting down firmly, she waved to the third chair. Iggy had already reseated himself. He thought: La Doña versus Vern. No contest. Vern sat.

There was an uncomfortable pause. Vern, wriggling, was the first to break it. "Why have you come all the way up here to see Dr. Kramer? Doesn't he come to you when he needs your professional help?"

"Yes, yes he does. But this time, we need to consult him. A young man has been killed, Eusebio Salazaar. He apparently was employed here in Los Alamos. We hoped that Stephen could—or rather, would—tell us something about the work, see if it suggests any reason someone might kill him."

Vern's annoyance faded to sadness. She also looked nervous. "Eusebio was a good man, very skilled with computers. That's all I can say."

Iggy asked quietly. "Did he work for Dr. Kramer? Were they on a project together when he died?"

The secretary shook her head vigorously, dislocating a pin or two from the French twist. "I told you, I've said all I can. I can't discuss any aspect of Dr. Kramer's position. He's a very senior scientist. He's often away."

"You mean Dr. Kramer is on a project elsewhere?" La Doña bored in. "I saw him shopping at Furr's in Taos."

Vern merely stabbed the errant pins back into the twist of auburn hair and pressed her lips together.

La Doña, sensing they had the answer they wanted, moved to get one further fact. "Bryce Watkins," she rapped out, "Does he work here, in this lab, work for Stephen?"

Face paling, Vern burst out, "Don't you know? He's dead—"

Standing quickly, straightening her skirt over those broad hips. "I must go back to my desk. Dr. Kramer will call you, I'll leave him a note....*give* him a note. Now, please excuse me."

La Doña rose majestically, turned to Iggy. "Will you escort me to where the car is parked? I believe we have sufficient information with which to proceed." Then smiling kindly, she made her exit line. "And I would suggest, my dear, that you take every possible precaution towards your personal safety. Two men have died."

Iggy and La Doña found Mac by the car. As they were driving back down "the hill," Mac found himself overwhelmed with the view, so different from that going up. He could see beyond nearby sculpted sandstone cliffs and buttes some thirty miles to the blue-gray mountains at the Santa Fe end of the Rockies. These great rock creations rose suddenly from flat gray-green high desert. Santa Fe's Sangre de Cristos were southeast. Snow-covered Truchas peak was thirty miles northeast. The Rio Grande was marked by a border of still-bare cottonwoods as the Great River wound its way south.

Enraptured by this breath-taking scenery, Mac tried to focus on the reason for the trip. "How did you do?"

Iggy spoke up. "I believe we did well. We didn't get direct answers, but Stephen Kramer's secretary let slip that Eusebio was likely still part of a project team. And get this, she certainly recognized the name Bryce Watkins, and knew he was dead."

"Yes," Doris Jordan sighed. To quote Shakespeare: 'The lady doth protest too much.' And, I may add, too quickly. She gave away that Stephen isn't working regularly around his office as well."

Iggy and Mac kept quiet. They knew she was trying to look at her old acquaintance in light of these facts. "I remember Stephen's specialty was DNA, some kind of genetic engineering," she went on. "He's more than a biologist, he's a computer wiz. Applies the lab's super computers to the research of field workers, experimenters. He hinted he was working on eradicating some scourge. It could be cancer, it could be AIDS, maybe Alzheimer's. I know they're working on HIV up there. I wonder if he is working on some discovery in Taos. It seems clear that his work—whatever—and wherever—is highly secret."

"How could he be working in Taos?" Mac was puzzled.

"Well, I've learned over the years from various clients that you can start with something D.O.E. is fundamentally interested in and branch off. They sometimes support research they don't have a direct interest in if it falls under the 'for the public good' umbrella. And if security is a greater concern than usual, as I pointed out earlier, D.O.E. might open a new facility off campus.

Iggy looked over at her with a grin. "You're no slouch on examining witnesses and building conclusions, La Doña. But what was that warning about Vern's 'safety' and 'two men have died'? We don't know that Kramer's research has a thing to do with either death!"

"I believe in rattling the cages, Ignacio. One never knows what will cause the beast to misstep."

CHAPTER XVIII

Having gathered her thoughts, Christy shared with her dream class. "It was strange. I'm not sure what to make of it. The dream has haunted me through all this other mess." She paused, thoughts darkened by the hate calls.

"The dream began with Eusebio Salazaar. Still dead, he chased me, calling my name. He was bloody. Blood was coming out all over his body, not only where he was stabbed."

Shudders and: "God." "What an image." "You must have had really bad feelings!"

"Yes, bad. I ran from Eusebio. His bloody corpse. And it was dark. Very dark. I could see nothing but the two of us. Frightening! Then, as dreams can go, it was still dark, but I was playing cards, poker, with some men I didn't know. That is except for Eusebio."

Someone said, "My Lord," the others were intently silent.

Christy shivered. "He was gray-white from being dead, oozing from his wounds. I looked at my poker hand and Eusebio said, 'Don't bet on the full house, king high. Forget the king, go with the double deuce.'"

Now everyone listened, holding in speech. Christy continued, "Of course that's all wrong for poker. I didn't know what he meant, but I saw I could choose between two hands. I said, 'Double deuce? You mean bet on a pair?' She took a breath.

"He was impatient that I was so stupid. 'Double deuce,' he said again. I studied my hand and could only see the two of diamonds. It wasn't red, but black like clubs or spades. Still staring at the two of diamonds, I woke up."

They all made supportive noises. Christy looked around the circle, the friendly faces, and then they turned toward Andy, who said briskly. "Remember a 'bad' dream isn't necessarily bad. This one is certainly trying to tell you something. You're in the dark, a fact in your waking life. And think about Eusebio. He's showing you that he's been murdered, is bleeding. You say that was bad, but what if Eusebio is not chasing you? What if he's simply trying to catch up to you to tell you something?"

The tight ball in her stomach loosened. "Yes! That feels right. And the last part, I wasn't frightened at the poker game...." Christy went silent.

"Stay with it," Andy said. "Stay with what's coming to you about the card game."

"Well," Christy answered slowly, "I see it begin to make sense from what you were just saying. I'm in the dark. Eusebio's trying to tell me something. Then, the poker game, giving instruction. Men are playing with me."

The other women nodded.

"But what does it mean? 'Don't bet on the full house, king high. Go with the double deuce.' And a black two of diamonds?"

"Remember how dreams can pun, speak indirectly," Andy urged.

"Yes, I know...." Christy thought as she spoke, but shuddered when she returned to her feelings of last night. "Eusebio may have had good intentions—but he made such a bloody corpse!"

The Dream Class ran over its casually set time and now she was late for her massage from the curandera in Pilar. She would never make it by one o'clock. Had no time for lunch. Well, a Pepsi and Hershey bar had been lunch many trial days. Have to make do now. She had the Pepsi in the car holder and the candy bar in the glove compartment. And to think people made fun of her for carrying supplies everywhere.

Off to Pilar and a massage from Señora Santissima Avila.

Soon Christy was negotiating the horseshoe curve. The Buick handled the well-banked road nicely, but still....She especially didn't like this southbound side with the low cement barrier. Too many cars had crashed through. A long drop-off....

Christy wondered if she'd meet the crew coming back from Los Alamos as she sped down the long hill.

The turn-off to Pilar was by the Yacht Club hostel, gathering place for the rafters. This year's snow-melt in the mountains meant lots of white water thundering through the Rio Grande, bringing crowds of rafters and creating unhappy residents of what had once been a quiet village.

Christy took the Pilar turn-off, then swung left down the narrow lane to the small adobe near the Rio Grande. Señora Avila lived there long before rafting caught on big. Curandera, healer. Her little house by the river adjoined fields that would soon bloom rich with herbs. How special those youthful jaunts had been, gathering herbs with Santissima Avila.

The curandera came to the door, smiling as Christy got out of the car. The large woman wore pink scuffies and her hair was in curlers covered with a white chiffon scarf. Not exactly a spooky image!

"Welcome, welcome. God bless you," Señora Avila greeted Christy in a hoarse voice.

Christy felt herself open to safety in the presence of the healer and the atmosphere of her home. "And you, also, Señora."

"Please excuse the voice," the Señora croaked, "I cured a man of bronchitis today and must take it on myself."

Christy nodded.

"Come in. Come in."

She ushered Christy through the front room with its slightly dingy, pink sectional furniture, into the dim back room. It was heavily scented with the smell of some unknown herb. "Before the massage, we pray, si?"

"Yes."

After lighting candles, Santissima Avila led the two of them through one "Our Father" and a "Hail Mary," and then murmured, "The clothes, please."

Christy stripped and lay on the padded aluminum massage table that seemed so out of place in this atmosphere. The Señora draped her with a light blanket and soon strong hands kneaded her back. Santos and softly burning religious candles crowded this ancient-feeling room. Relaxing, Christy felt warmth enveloping her.

"Aii! You should have come to me sooner. The muscles! You are tight, tight. Too much stress, eh?"

"Si, Señora. Too much."

"You worry yourself with the death of poor Eusebio, si?" Feeling Christy's startled jerk, the healer murmured, "Ah, ah, lie still. Do not jump about."

"How did you know?"

"I am a curandera," Santissima answered simply, but with pride.

Christy took this opening to ask about one of her worries, but she had to word her question carefully not to insult the Señora. "I know you have nothing to do with brujos or brujas, but I wonder if one was involved in the murder?"

Señora Avila spoke slowly. "To get their power the brujos often band together and—¿como se dice?—project, project as on a television screen. I hear what was done to the morada, that was wicked, very wicked, yes, but not the work of brujos. The hex balls you found—"

Christy jumped again at more unexpected knowledge, and Santissima paused, noting, "You do not expect me to know that either, eh?" She continued. "They could be part of a brujo's spell. But the rest? The signs and symbols? No."

Stretching Christy's arm, the curandera added, "Nor do brujos murder. I know you worry about the Devil."

Christy started to frame a question, but again was answered before she could get the words out. "Yes, I do know a brujo, but only because he also lives here in Pilar. I can give you a telephone number to help you reach him, so that you may ask yourself. Me, I have nothing to do with them! I and the other curanderas we are healers, not like those others in any way! Now be silent and breathe. Let prayer do its work through my hands."

Relaxing, consciously willing her mind to let go of all thoughts, Christy grew sleepy. She was vaguely aware of the curandera murmuring prayers, more aware of the powerful hands working out the knots. Then she felt her relaxation go deeper than that, and then down another layer of consciousness.

She slept.

Whop! With the Señora's brisk slap on her fanny, Christy sat up. She reached for her blue sweatshirt and jeans. "Beautiful, Señora. I feel so much better. Thank you."

"Bueno. Now, we will pray before you go."

Santissima took Christy's hand and they prayed together. Christy was at peace.

Walking Christy to the front door, Santissima made the sign of the cross over her, and pressed the paper with the phone number into her hand.

Christy repressed a shudder. All her legal training and experience was no match for growing up with her *abuela* and the evil she taught brujos brought.

Reluctantly, Christy closed her hand around the paper. If anything could help solve the greater evil....

Then, as Christy was about to leave, the curandera said, "Stop. I must warn you. Do not be led astray by false presumptions. You must stay on guard and obey your instincts."

"What?"

Firmly. "Danger is near. Be alert. That is all."

"Uh, thank you."

Santissima Avila beamed at her. "We'll see you."

"We'll see you," Christy answered, still feeling a chill at the unexpected warning.

Back on the highway, Christy pondered the curandera's words. False presumptions indeed. Did that relate to her questions about the brujos? Satanists? Constant surprises from that woman. Was there a real meaning to this warning? It certainly tied in with her Eusebio dream.

Christy drove up the straight-away, the double lane heading north to Taos.

Now, the first splendid view as she popped out of the canyon. Like coming out of a tunnel: the world was alight and the whole valley spread out under the sapphire sky. A glimpse of the deep blue cut of the gorge. Taos in the far distance, backed by the gray-blue looming Sangre de Cristo mountains, streaked with white snow.

The next view would be the best, the one after the horseshoe.

Her thoughts returned to Santissima's warning. Maybe she'd been taking this too lightly. Maybe the Devil was involved. Whatever, one didn't mess around with murder. It—

The sight in the rearview mirror took all of Christy's attention. A heavy dark car sped around the lower curve behind her. It accelerated, fast approaching her Buick, then started past on the wrong side. As the dark vehicle's hood drew even with the mid-section of the Buick, Christy wrenched the wheel left, trying to get away, horrified that the car was sharply veering toward her.

Slam!

Metal screamed as the front end of the assailant's vehicle hit the passenger side of Christy's Buick, violently shoving Christy against the seat belt.

The impact knocked her car into the southbound lane. She hurtled toward the cliff. Worst point! Worst! Fatal drop down! Slammed over to the wrong lane. Wrong lane. She could wreck with another car. Forget it. Going over would be more deadly. Cement barrier coming up! Huge drop-off. Out of control! Heart lurching with the car.

"Help me, Jesus." Her mouth was dry, hands wet on the wheel, but she gripped it, cutting back, determined not to panic, not to over-correct.

She made it! She was again on the highway.

Expecting her to go over the edge, the other driver overshot, slammed on the brakes. The tires of the bigger automobile squealed as they bit into the cement, then were shoved into reverse. That car backed up then leapt forward attacking her again.

Christy gunned the Buick, trying to race ahead. No good.

With a crash of metal, the dark vehicle hit her again! Christy's head jerked. She bit her cheek. The deadly void came at her in slow motion while she desperately tried to wrestle her car back from the brink.

The void kept coming. She was going to die.

Fear paralyzed Christy for an instant. Then she screamed to herself, "No! Fight!"

Out of control, the Buick shrieked toward the drop-off. "Turn!" she commanded. "Don't skid. Turn into the skid."

The loud groaning noise of metal grinding against cement. Christy's Buick slid along the cement protective wall as she fought death. She tried to breathe, ordering herself, "Easy. Easy. Can't! Can't! You can. Hang on. You know snow and fish-tailing. Go with it. In the name of the Father and the Son and the Holy—"

Christy turned into the swerving brought about by the impact. She didn't brake. She held on to it...."Thank you, Jesus!"

Dripping wet with sweat, shaking violently, Christy slowly drove the car the few hundred yards north to the turn-out on the east side. She looked for her attacker. The dark car had disappeared down the road.

Tourists were photographing the view of the gorge where she had shuddered to a stop. My God, she couldn't believe it! Didn't they know she had nearly died? How could they be taking pictures? Everything was in sharp focus and, at the same time, unreal.

Christy shook. Gasped. Lord! but it felt good to suck air into her lungs! She must have held her breath the whole time.

And how did she get here? The Taos end of the horseshoe? It had all seemed slow motion: the barrier coming up; the look of the highway as she fishtailed; the impact, hit again. But she had somehow kept the road, progressed through the rest of the horseshoe.

Thank you, Jesus. Oh, Mary, Mother of God!

Finally, Christy calmed enough to think. Who was it? Who tried to run her off the road? She hadn't had a chance to identify the vehicle; her concentration fixed on driving for her life. No license plate; it had been all front end and flashes of cement and drop-off while she fought to stay on the road. No driver visible, the windows were tinted glass.

She could remember nothing but glimpses of a dark car, dark door, dark hood.

Dark dream. Nightmare. But she was awake. And someone wanted her dead.

CHAPTER XIX

When Christy felt she could manage, she drove straight home, shaking all the way. She concentrated on the road, each mile a struggle, the residue of terror moving sluggish through her body.

Mac took one look at her. "What…?"

Christy's fiercely maintained composure collapsed. She let Mac wrap his arms around her. "Someone tried to kill me!"

"Oh, my God! Are you hurt? In a wreck? Let me look at you!" He pulled away to see better, his hands gripping her arms. Christy wanted to pour out her story. On his part, Mac, the doctor, was determined to find out if she needed medical attention. "Let me tell you," she complained.

Mac's concern mixed with fury as Christy told him about being slammed and slammed again. Fright buzzed in her head as she relived it, pouring out the whole terrifying incident. "And it was the one stretch, the one stretch of the horseshoe that's the terrible drop-off!"

"But you were heading north."

"That's what I'm trying to explain, Mac. He cut in from the outside, then hit me. Shoved me into the southbound lane!"

"Was there traffic?"

"No, thank God!"

Mac raged, made her sit down right there in the kitchen, got her a cup of strong sweet tea. "Listen, sweetheart, you're not thinking straight. You should have gone straight to the police to report this. We have to get them out here, let them check out your car, find any paint from the other car, any clue. This must be connected to the murders. The police can look at other cars for damage, find out where everyone was who might be involved."

"Every who?" Christy's words dragged. "We don't even know who we suspect."

"True. And a local investigation may be fruitless. I'm becoming convinced the killings—both of them—connect to Los Alamos, not Taos. You don't know about my day yet."

Her voice still ragged from the ordeal. "Why would...Why would anyone want to kill me? I don't know anything. We've only been poking around."

"Maybe one poke too many, but all this can wait." He patted her shoulder, careful not to jar her. "Let me make the call." Soothing voice, and Christy was in no mood to be soothed. But Mac was not to be deterred. He headed to the phone, dialed the Sheriff's office, then returned to sit close to Christy to try to get her to tell him if she had pain anywhere. Slightly reassured by her answers, Mac let her sip her tea and rest while they sat waiting.

Christy knew the young sheriff's deputies who came out, Louis Rael and Alex Romo. They seemed sympathetic and courteous as she told her story again, this time more coherently. Mac listened intently, his arm now around her. It seemed to be a permanent fixture.

"Can you describe the car or driver, Miz Grant? Louis asked.

"Only that it was dark. A dark-colored car. I never really saw the driver. Tinted glass, and he came up behind me so fast. Then, after he hit me, I was trying so hard to stay on the road..." Christy shuddered, remembering. "Not go over the cliff."

Alex stood silent as Louis continued the questions. "Are you sure it wasn't an accident? Maybe some drunk?"

"No, no. No accident! I might have thought so if it had been just once. But I told you, he crashed into me a second time when I was fighting for control!"

Christy wanted to get this done, get some rest, but patiently answered their standard questions. Then Alex asked, "What about that crack you made about Los Hermanos?" The coldly spoken words hurt and shocked her. "Someone want to get you for that?"

Christy's throat closed up, making her speechless for a moment. She stood up. "Get out. Just get out of this house now! You *know* the papers lied. Just forget about investigating this!"

Mac was mad, too, "That's a damn fool thing for you to say! You don't believe that garbage!"

Undeterred, Alex continued, "You think of anyone else?"

"Cut that crap!" Christy turned to the other deputy. "Louis, listen. I'm working with Ignacio Baca on the Eusebio Salazaar homicide. Whoever tried to kill me has to be connected with that."

The deputies exchanged a look, then Louis said, "We're on that case, ma'am, along with the State Police. Joint jurisdiction. Guess we'd better see what Pat Salazaar's been up to."

"Hey, that wasn't Salazaar!" Alex objected. "Miz Grant said 'big car'. You know Salazaar drives a pick-up. One of those little ones, an Isuzu, I think."

Louis argued that didn't prove it wasn't Salazaar, then, turning back to Christy, "Have you come up with something? Gotten too close for somebody's comfort? Like Salazaar, maybe?"

Christy didn't want to answer any more questions, didn't want to have to use her mind in any way. "No. I don't know. I'm no threat to anyone. Look, just let me make a complaint to Sheriff Manor in the morning, okay?"

Louis had one more question, "What about this, uh, Inn, what is it? Bed and Breakfast you run? Who's staying here now and are they here?"

"Good question." Mac fielded that one. "Let's check the parking lot, officers. There's one particular car—well, maybe two—that could show some damage."

He stood, but hesitated now that he was about to leave Christy alone. "You look mighty rocky. I'd like to take your blood pressure when I get back, see about shock. Could do that with what I have with me, but there might be internal injury. I don't have the equipment for a full look-see. Maybe I should take you to the emergency room?"

Christy couldn't bear to hear any more words from anyone, even Mac. She sat slumped, her voice slow. "No, I'm sure that I'm not really hurt. In shock, yes, but not the kind you're talking about, Mac. I'm just bruised from banging up against the door and steering wheel…. Anyway the letdown from all that adrenaline has me so worn out, I'm too tired to see any other doctor."

"What about a muscle relaxant?"

"Mac!" Embarrassed by the fuss, Christy turned to the deputies, ignoring Alex' former crack as she said, "Thank you Louis and Alex. I appreciate you coming out. And letting me make a formal statement, a complaint, tomorrow."

Louis smiled, happy to forget the penitente business. "Well, we're neighbors, Miz Grant. Right? You take care now!" Alex added, "See you."

It took effort to smile at them.

Now if she could manage the stairs, then a hot bath and bed….

Christy switched on the space heater in the upstairs bathroom and turned on the hot water full blast. Almost too weary to bother, she made herself find some Epsom salts and dumped in a lot. Her muscles would be glad tomorrow. She threw her clothes on the floor, wondering if she'd ever be willing to wear them again. She climbed into the tub.

After soaking in the mineral bath, Christy put on her comforting, ancient, purple velvet robe. She barely had the energy to turn back the down comforter, but was too chilly to flop down on top. Now, bed!

Heart pounding, Christy woke in the dark. She felt someone's presence! "Who's there!"

"Sorry, Christy." Mac apologized.

"Oh, Mac! You frightened me!" Her breathing was still ragged.

"I tried not to make a sound, wanted to let you sleep…" Mac trailed off as Christy switched on the bedside light, looked at the clock radio. Eight p.m. She turned back to Mac and saw that he looked chagrined and only half-way visible. He peered up at her from the stairwell, his bottom half hidden as he stood on the stairs below.

"Forgive me, Christy. I know we don't invade one another's privacy, but that's normal times. This evening I've been sneaking up ever so often, uh, just to check." Sheepish voice. "Well, after today, I had to make sure you were still breathing!"

Christy simply gazed at him, face blank. She had been in an exhausted sleep, then awakened in fear.

Mac scowled in embarrassment. "No way for a physician to behave, knew you didn't have any life-threatening problems, but, well....Sorry. Should have let you sleep."

More awake now, her mood improving, Christy answered, "Don't apologize, Mac. I appreciate it. And I'm ravenous! What did you have for dinner?"

More of Mac appeared. He sat on the floor, legs still down the stairwell. "Well, uh...Well, I didn't exactly eat. Thought you might wake up, want something. I thawed that green chile stew you had in the freezer. Been keeping it warm, so if you woke up...had the idea maybe green chile stew and tortillas would perk you up."

"Sounds just right! Just a minute and I'll be right down."

Mac disappeared.

Christy made her way slowly and carefully down the same stairwell. She felt like an invalid, it was so hard to move on legs made shaky from the aftermath of tension. She hurt in unexpected places.

The hacienda was friendly, familiar, quiet.

The dining room glowed with candlelight from the wrought-iron chandelier. The room held the piquant scent of green chile stew.

"There you are!" Mac called from the kitchen. "Now, you just sit down and I'll dish it up. I kept it hot on the stove."

Christy sat, drained and limp.

Mac forgot about serving, strode back into the dining room. "Now. Let me look at you," Taking her face in his big hands, he looked carefully into her eyes. "Damn candlelight," he grumbled. Then, stepping back, still looking at Christy intently, Mac demanded, "Tell me exactly how you feel. Really."

She smiled. "Really," mimicking his stern tone, "I am really all right. I soaked in Epsom salts, slept."

"On a scale of one to ten?"

"Oh, stop, Mac. I am not one hundred per cent, okay? But I promise you I'll survive. Did you give all your patients this much care and concern?"

"I'll get the stew."

Christy asked his retreating back, "Are all the guests out?" Mac answered from the kitchen. "Yep. No cars when I took the deputies out to look. And no one's come in since, that I know of."

"What about the new guest? Ritchie? Yes, Fred Ritchie?"

"You mean Mister Golf Clubs? Don't know. He's been the invisible man," Mac said as he carried in the steaming bowls and warm tortillas.

"Thank you. You're great, Mac, when you lay off the doctor-mother hen routine."

"Is that what they call a back-handed compliment?"

Christy persisted. "So you haven't seen Mr. Ritchie all day?"

"Nope," Mac answered casually. "Of course, we were all off to Los Alamos this morning."

"But he didn't come in for breakfast and is still out." Christy worried the Ritchie question, chewing at it. Her nerves jangled. She suspected everyone.

"Maybe I should check his room for you, see if his bags are still there."

Just then, La Doña and Iggy came barging in through the Middle Room.

"Oh, oh." Mac muttered to Christy. "I had to call to tell them what happened. I didn't know they'd come rushing over."

Christy sighed. She wasn't up to guests, not even these beloved people.

La Doña had exchanged her big, bulging battered briefcase for a big, bulging black leather purse. It must have been a good serviceable model many years ago. With her face drawn up in worry, La Doña looked her age. "Child! Child! I called Ignacio, made him bring me straight over. I can't see to drive at night, you know. I had to find out for myself if you were hurt. Can't trust a man to tell you anything! Let me look at you."

Now it was La Doña who carefully took Christy's face in a hand twisted by arthritis, smoothed Christy's hair back with the other. Looked intently into her eyes. "Hrumph!" Gruffly.

"Appear to be all right. Pale. Dark circles. How do you feel? Any parts damaged?"

Tears came to Christy's eyes. What a fierce old softy. "No, I'm fine. Just knocked about and sore." She hesitated, then added, "Frightened, too. No one's ever tried to kill me before."

"We'll speak about that. But for right now, you'll do," giving Christy's shoulders a gentle shake.

Iggy hung back, trying to act above all this sentiment, but his tugs on his rat tail were a giveaway. Now, he took his turn, needing to touch Christy, too. "You're sure?" Iggy asked. "You're really sure you're okay?"

Christy grinned. "Cross my heart and hope to…Well, I won't finish that one, but I swear everything's in working order. Even the car. Drove it home. But," She turned to Mac, "I didn't stop to see. What does my poor Buick look like?"

Shaking his head, Mac said, "Not so hot, I'm afraid. Went over it pretty carefully with the deputies. You can see where he hit you on the right hand side to knock you over into the southbound lane. Would have taken a big, heavy car to do that to your Buick." Mac swallowed and shuddered. "Uh, then there are long deep scrapes where you were grating along the barrier, a dent towards the back that you got when you were fishtailing.…That's enough of that, okay?

"Can you tell where he hit me the second time?" Christy was recovering, her mind at work.

Mac sighed. "The car's really messed up, Christy. But, yeah, bashed in closer to the front, too."

"Jeez!" Iggy's black eyes were round with shock. He hadn't heard the details before. La Doña was, for once, speechless. She went a sickly white, fumbled for a chair, sat down shakily.

Christy started to rise. "Mac!"

Mac had already jumped up. "Don't faint, Doris. Put your head down between your legs. Let me—"

"I'll do no such thing, young man!" she snapped, pride injured by her display of weakness. "Is one supposed to stand endlessly? I simply felt like taking a seat—uninvited, I might add."

They all smiled with relief. Ferocity was back.

"Then may I get y'all something? Something to eat? A drink?"

"Please join...," Christy began, when Duane Dobbs appeared in the doorway.

"Excuse me," he said. "But I need to speak to you, Miz Grant."

Taken totally by surprise, Christy stared at him for a moment, then, "Yes? What is it?" She heard an echo of her cold tone and softened it, "Excuse me, won't you come on in?"

"No, no. Didn't mean to disturb the, ah, gathering. It was just about my reservations..."

Christy didn't feel like being courteous. She continued to sit. "Oh, that's right. I forgot. You're checking out in the morning, aren't you."

"Well, that's just it," Duane Dobbs answered. "My, ah...The business we talked about? Well, as regards it, I need to stay over a day or two. Of course, if my room is booked already—"

Christy didn't want him to stay. Didn't want the man around. But her mind wasn't sharp tonight, so she said only, "No, I don't believe your room is taken tomorrow. I'll have to check beyond that."

"Good deal!" he answered. "Afraid I'd run into the same trouble as at the car rental place. Made me return the Lincoln. They said that it was already reserved for a family coming in, needed the size." He chuckled, "I guess, this being Taos, you understand that.

Christy held back a gasp. He had turned in his big black car! Was the man taunting her now? Had he tried to kill her?

CHAPTER XX

Christy lay in bed barely waking, her eyes still shut. Before she opened them, a sense of doom washed over her. A darkness filled her mind where sleep had been. A nightmare? she wondered. No, something worse. Something bad has happened. Then she remembered: someone tried to kill her.

Christy opened her eyes and looked wildly around the room. Not here. The car. Oh God, that black car had tried to smash her over the cliff.

Her mind had worried it the night before, questions running around and around. In a calmer state she had thought that If she could figure out why someone wanted her dead, she would know who killed Eusebio.

Last night, all of the crew felt shock and upset at the thought of Duane Dobbs' involvement but were unable to talk for fear he might be lurking, listening. Low-voiced conversation conveyed that no one wanted him in the house with her. By then she was too drained to care; had crossly told them Mr. Dobbs wouldn't do anything so obvious, wouldn't try to harm her in her own house.

Now Christy said, "Well, thank you, God. I made it through the night." She stretched, testing her muscles, and found them not too bad, considering. Starting for the bathroom, Christy glanced through the French doors to the outside landing. A sleeping bag lay on the landing; a familiar head of white hair barely visible; a shotgun within arms' reach. What? Laugh? Yell?

She moved closer. The early sun was shining lightly on his sleeping face, character lines smoothed into a younger, more innocent Mac.

Both touched and irritated, Christy demanded, "Mac, Mac. Wake up!"

The eyes squinched more tightly shut. "Oh-oh."

"'Oh-oh,' is right! What in the world do you think you're doing?"

"Sleeping?" Mac's blue eyes peered up at Christy.

"Up here on the landing." Exasperating man. "You know what I mean. And with a gun!"

"This wasn't the plan," Mac explained as he sat up. His hair was a mess. "The plan was I would watch...Well, kind of sit shotgun. Then sneak off before you woke up."

"Mac!"

"Yeah, well." Mac fumbled an explanation. "I got cold, thought I'd sort of slip into the sleeping bag for a while—" He stood, shook out the sleeping bag, began folding it.

Christy grinned.

Mac tucked the sleeping bag under one arm, picked up the shotgun with his other hand. "Well, uh...See you downstairs." And he started down the steps.

Christy smiled all through her shower. Mac had changed her mood, pushed the dark menace into the background a little. Ready to dress she examined her face in the mirror. It wasn't too bad, a little pale but no real signs of a brush with death. *Doña Sebastiani*, Lady Death, with her arrows, would have to wait a while yet. Better add some blusher, though.

Clean jeans. New coral-colored velvet sweatshirt. That should brighten the complexion.

Unh. Muscles hurt as she descended the spiral stairs. Oh no! She could hear voices in the dining room. She was late! No bread risen, ready for the oven. What to fix? No time to bake. Pancakes. She could whip up pancakes and bacon in no time.

What was this? The large backside of a body on the banco! It was wrapped cocoon-like in an old blanket.

Christy slipped over for a closer look. Peered over the body. "Iggy! Ignacio Baca!"

No movement.

She shook his shoulder. "Iggy! Iggy, wake up!"

He rolled over. The banco wasn't that wide. The cocoon landed on the floor. Iggy yelped, attempted to disentangle himself.

"This is ridiculous!" Christy hissed, aware of the people in the dining room. "First Mac upstairs, now you! Another bodyguard, I assume?"

"Good morning, Christy." Iggy tried for sweetness.

"Don't good morning me!"

Iggy was on his feet by now, black curls awry. "May I have a cup of coffee?"

"Certainly," Christy snapped. "I'm going to have to explain you to the guests anyway. Just don't get imaginative on me!" She lowered her voice. "And make yourself presentable first."

"Yes, ma'am, Miz Grant, ma'am."

"Oh, hush!" A thought. She turned back. "What did you do with La Doña? Am I going to fall over her on the floor somewhere?"

"Took her home and came back. Mac and I were worried about you."

"Well I was just fine, thank you." Christy relented. "And, seriously, I do thank you."

Moving on through the Middle Room, into the dining room, she wondered what to tell the guests? How to explain Iggy?

Sure enough, they were all gathered. Damn. It was a pain to start breakfast when guests were there ahead of her. Thank God for the automatic coffee maker. Yes, thank God. Must go by the church this morning and really thank Him. Last night's prayers weren't enough gratitude for getting through the horseshoe alive. And for friends like Mac and Iggy.

Naturally she saw Duane Dobbs before anyone else. His back was turned toward her as he stood alone, drinking coffee. Fred Ritchie was over near the coffee stand. Neither was speaking to the other. Christy felt her heart lurch, stomach start that panicky feel at the sight of Dobbs. She told herself to forget about everything: fix breakfast.

The three from the Curandera's Room were chattering together happily. All turned as Christy came in. "Good morning. Sorry I'm late. Pancakes and bacon in a minute."

Directing her little speech to her men guests, Christy said, "You all may have noticed an extra guest in La Sala. It's my friend, Ignacio Baca. He'll be joining us shortly." Puzzled looks, but no one asked the obvious questions: why the man was sleeping on the banco, for instance.

The trio all followed her into the kitchen. "Can we help?"

"No thanks, that's all right." Christy declined with real appreciation for the offer.

"We mean it, you know?" Tama said earnestly.

So Christy took them at their word and all three went to work happily while Christy put the bacon in the microwave. The phone rang. Oh, no. No time to talk to anyone now, especially if that anyone were Mama. Lisa asked, "Shall I get it?"

"Please."

In a moment, Lisa was back, saying, "It's your mother."

Winding up tighter, Christy was tempted to ask Lisa to say she'd call later. No. She had to give Mama a brief report. Christy walked quickly past Duane Dobbs into the Middle Room. Without bothering with "Hello," taking a deep breath, she said firmly, "Look, Mamacita, I have something important to tell you, but I'm right in the middle of fixing breakfast."

"Buenos dias, Christina. Where are your manners?" Perfecta asked gruffly.

"Please, Mamacita. I—"

"All day I spend on the telephone for m'hija, trying to explain to *todo le mundo*, everyone, that no daughter of mine would say such a terrible thing about Los Hermanos, but not one word from you," Perfecta rattled off in outrage. "Worse, not one word since Easter. You did not like your Easter dinner? Odelia, she called—"

"Mama, Mama," Christy interrupted now, close to desperate. "Just let me tell you something right away. We'll talk later, okay?"

"What is this thing you cannot stop and explain presently or what I saw yesterday on the tv to your own Mother?"

Christy had to be tough. "Just don't worry, okay? If you hear anything, well, please just remember that I'm perfectly fine. I'm not hurt."

"Christina Garcia! You expect me—?"

"I have to hang up now, Mamacita. I'm sorry. Don't be unhappy with me. I'll call you later."

"Christina!"

"Good-bye, Mama." She hung up, then headed back to the kitchen, feeling more out of sorts for having upset Mama.

Mac's long form, clad in worn jeans and work shirt with the sleeves rolled up, was somewhat bent over the electric skillet. Happily flipping pancakes, he tried out a hesitant smile. Christy shook her head at him. With Lolly there slicing honeydew she couldn't voice her new complaint to Mac: his failure to tell her about Iggy acting as the second bodyguard.

From the dining room, Christy heard, "Hello, Mr. Dobbs. We met last night." As she looked in, Iggy turned to Mr. Ritchie and stuck out his hand to shake. "Good morning. I'm a friend of Miz Grant's, Ignacio Baca." Good. He didn't try anything fancy.

Christy told Lolly, "Please have everyone sit down when you take in the honeydew. And, thanks a lot."

She and Mac finished up and soon all were being served. Mr. Dobbs and Mr. Ritchie, of necessity seated next to one another, were exchanging "Please pass" and "Thank you" only. There was tension between them that made Christy wonder if they had met before.

Too distracted by all that had happened, Christy had no entertaining stories to go with the meal, but Lisa once more came to the rescue. "I was wondering about a place to exercise. With the ski slopes closed, my morning run just doesn't cut it. I'm feeling fuggy."

"There's the Taos Spa just a little way from here. It has about everything you could want."

"Nautilus?" Lisa asked.

"Hot tub? Jacuzzi?" Lolly asked.

Christy smiled. "Yes to both. And, if you like, I'll call about a guest membership. You can pay by the day, I believe."

"Not for me, I'm going to my Crystal Healing Workshop, you know?"

Lisa sighed. "We know, Tama. But you really need to work out."

"I have muscles, they just don't show like yours, Lisa," Tama defended herself without a question mark. And plump, red-haired Lolly had to join in for her own defense. "I may be round, but I'm not soft either!"

Mac's blue shirt made his eyes appear even bluer than usual as he tried to change the subject diplomatically. "More news on The Taos Hum!" he announced. "Some fellow from the University of New Mexico is heading up a so-called federal task force. The government's going to isolate The Hum with UNM scientists, ones from the Los Alamos and Sandia labs, and folks from the Air Force. Going to get to the bottom of this, by God!"

The women laughed at Mac's dramatics, but Christy still felt withdrawn, abstracted.

Conversation lapsed again, then Lisa turned to Christy to ask, "Would you mind checking the Spa for us, Miz Grant? I'd like to get that workout before we start the tourist bit today."

"Of course. I'll be happy to." Christy pushed back her chair. As if on cue, everyone else left the table.

Christy met Desire coming in the Middle Room door. "Good morning, Desire. I'll be with you in a minute. Need to make a call first."

"Hi, Miz Grant." Today Desire was a vision in white: lace-edged white ruffles on her peasant blouse set off rounds of breast, full broomstick-pleated white fiesta skirt, white high-heel boots. "You mean you want me to call someone for you?"

"No, Desire. I'm making a phone call. See?"

"Oh, okay."

Lisa grinned, looking from one to the other. She waited while Christy phoned the Spa and then thanked her when it was all set up. At the same time Mac came in to remind her of the meeting at Ricky's and that Iggy had already left. Mac added firmly, "I'll drive. Neither you nor your car are in any shape..."

Revitalized by her morning innkeeper routine, Christy was able to finish up and they were on their way. Last night, when Christy was too drained and Duane Dobbs too close, the group had agreed to confer at the restaurant this morning. Driving only a short way past the Talpa Y, they were soon at the popular Mexican cafe.

Seeing Iggy and La Doña seated at the big, curved, black leatherette booth at the far end, Christy started toward them, but was stopped by the cold looks directed her way from a number of old acquaintances. Oh, Lord! Still trailing wisps of yesterday's nightmare, Christy had forgotten the fury focused on her from her supposed attack on the Brotherhood. She would have to run the gauntlet at Ricky's, explain herself to friends and neighbors offended and hurt by her reported comments to the media.

Tempted to say, "To Hell with them!" Christy stopped at one table after another, forcing a smile, and tossing out casual lines like, "Can you believe how I was misquoted? Those reporters can't get anything right, can they?" Then she would segue into "And have you met my new neighbor? This is Dr. Mac McCloud." Christy hoped that their anger would turn to curiosity. A new man for Christina Garcia, eh?

Finally, Christy and Mac were seated with Iggy and La Doña, Christy still flushed from the effort of facing all that hostility. Mac, beamed on her and said, "Good show, m'dear. Made me proud, even if you did throw me to the wolves."

At both Iggy's and La Doña's curious looks, Christy snapped, "Don't ask! Okay?" Then, "Sorry. It's that Hermandad business." Trying to lighten the mood, she peered at the remains on Iggy's plate and added, "What in the world did you eat? A second breakfast?"

"Just a couple of pork chops with eggs and biscuits and gravy."

"Iggy, Iggy," she said mournfully. "Your poor heart. You already had pancakes and bacon at the hacienda this morning!"

"My heart's in fine shape. Don't you know Americans are returning to good food in droves?"

La Doña had grown restless. "Please. We came here to discuss serious matters."

"I know," Christy sighed. "There's so damn much to think about!"

Mac turned to La Doña. "You were there for Duane Dobbs' bombshell last night, that he had gotten rid of a car that might have rammed Christy, but I haven't had a chance to fill her in on our Los Alamos trip."

La Doña seated her tweed-suited bulk more comfortably and summed up the interview.

Christy felt the group was out of sync, concentrating on Dr. Kramer now. She objected. After what Dobbs said last night, he had to be the one who tried to kill her.

"You know better than that, Missy," La Doña spoke with asperity, hiding last night's show of sentiment. "Mr. Dobbs' tale created a suspicion only, adding to our superfluity of suspects. However, I admit I fail to see a motive for Stephen Kramer whatever his secret activities may be."

"Profit," Mac stated, surprising them all after his silence.

He answered their questioning looks in his low-pitched drawl. "I've been thinking about it. As a doctor myself, I dealt with pharmaceutical companies frequently. I can't estimate what a patent on an important new drug would be worth, but have seen the enormous profits drawn from charges to the patient." A pause. "What if Dr. Kramer were, for instance, actually working on the HIV virus? We know someone at LANL is."

Iggy nodded. "It would be worth a fortune to a pharmaceutical house that develops either a cure or an immunization."

"Wait," Christy said. "Kramer's not working in the private sector. He's working for the government. No patent money for him."

"True," from La Dona, although she was looking uneasy.

"Moreover," Mac continued, "it might not be a breakthrough in AIDS research at all. Think about his DNA work. What if, in the process of looking at the HIV virus, Kramer's research led him into something even more profitable? Some kind of genetic engineering. Say isolating some gene controlling the immune system?"

Mac's deprecating grin embraced La Doña and Iggy. "Actually, while you two were going *mano a mano* with Vern, my walk had taken me towards the Oppenheimer Study Center. I was curious after our conversation and went in to discover LANL's Research Library. So I used one of their terminals. A quick check at the Human Genome site got me thinking. It puts the D.O.E. right into this discusssion. Their own mission statement is that the HGP is sponsored by the D.O.E. and the N.I.H. with a goal of mapping all the genes on every chromosome in the human body and to determine their biochemical nature."

"Now you're doing the alphabet soup, Mac," Christy smiled.

"What in the world is a genome?"

Mac's excitement was revealed in his brisk reply. "Genome is the name given the complete set of instructions for making an organism. That blueprint is replicated in every bit of your body, earlobe, liver, skin on your thumb—"

Iggy had been twitching in impatience. Now he interrupted. "All this speculation may be fun but—"

"Being run off the road is not exactly fun," Christy snapped.

"Sorry, Christy, that's not what I mean," Iggy responded mildly. "What I'm getting at is we still haven't come up with a good solid defense for Pat."

Still testy, Christy countered, "It will be one helluva defense if we find the real killer! And it might just help me stay alive!"

"Calm down, Christina," La Doña admonished. "We're doing our best."

Mac tried to lighten the atmosphere. "Will you look there! Ricky has an Elvis clock. White cloak and all with a clock at his feet. Right next to the ship in full sail on velvet!"

Refusing to be distracted, Christy demanded, "Well, what about Duane Dobbs? Are you three saying that you think he might be telling the truth?"

"That should be easy to check," Iggy answered. "I can run over to the rental company. See if old Dobbs turned in a wreck."

La Doña took charge again. "You do that, Ignacio. We need to obtain some hard evidence. Dobbs or Dr. Kramer. I just may be able to look into the latter in more detail."

"La Doña! What are you up to?" Christy exclaimed. Her concern was met by silence and a smug look from The Lady. That led Iggy to object the loudest. "I saw those thugs with guns," he said. "Something's going on up there and it just might have to do with Kramer. So, I don't want you messing around with him, La Doña.

A look. "I intend no messing around, Ignacio. Just a few additional discreet inquiries. Now, for the rest of you?"

"Hold on a second," Mac drawled. "Y'all seem ready to break up this little meeting and I want to bring up another subject. We've got Mr. Ritchie with his mysterious golf clubs. What with a new golf course that few outsiders know about yet—"

Mac was interrupted by La Doña's questions and had to explain Ritchie and the suspicious locked rifle or golf case. "Also, Christy and I both noticed a seeming hostility between him and Duane Dobbs this morning."

La Doña returned to cross-examination mode. "Why this morning? Why not earlier?"

Mac sighed. "Because Fred Ritchie has also been the invisible man. No breakfast Tuesday. No apparent contact with Dobbs. But, who knows? My knowledge of how professional killers work is limited to reading thrillers."

"Still," Christy argued, "there's the same problem as we had with Stephen Kramer. What's his motive? Why would either man try to run me off the road? Kill Eusebio? Or shoot Watkins in the alley?"

"How do you propose we investigate?" La Doña asked.

"I have some ideas," Christy answered. "But first I need to give a statement to Sheriff Manor. I intend to get some facts into the record there."

La Doña nodded. "Try that. And then, would you have time to see the Chief of Police?"

"Chief Garcia? He's my primo."

They laughed at hearing of another of Christy's cousins, but she added, "The town of Taos has jurisdiction over the shooting. Thank God I can finally deal with Barnabe Garcia even if you all think it's funny."

Iggy returned to, "What do you have in mind, La Doña? Dobbs? Ritchie? The other homicide?"

"All the above, Ignacio. Now that Christy reminds us that Chief Garcia is her cousin, there's hope he will be forthcoming. That is if anything's known about these men. Further, we need to find out if the local police are connecting the deaths now that the point's been raised with the troopers."

Christy spoke slowly, pondering, "What if we could also get my primo to check out your discovery at Los Piñones, Iggy? The old mine which is suddenly being guarded."

"Yes!" Iggy gave her a high five. "That's it! Let's see if you can sic the Chief on finding out what's up there."

"He has no probable cause to search," La Doña squelched their enthusiasm.

Iggy came right back with, "Then let's give him one! We can borrow from our own case. What about suspected drugs? Last year they raided a drug manufacturing operation."

"And what about the underground marijuana farm?" Christy added. "That was up north wasn't it?"

"Do it!" Iggy commanded with excitement.

More thoughtful, Christy said, "Well, I'll see. Feel out primo Barnabe. There's a question of jurisdiction, too. He'd have to stretch to find it out at that mine. That's county and state."

"If you got the Chief interested, he could take along the Sheriff's people. They work together sometimes." Iggy was not about to give up the drug raid.

La Doña hefted her heavy briefcase from the floor at her feet. This was the signal. Meeting concluded.

Christy had purposely failed to mention the brujo angle to the crew. In fact, she wanted to set up a meeting with that brujo without Mac knowing, so she said, "Before we go to the Sheriff's, Mac, I need to run home, see how it's going with the acequia."

In answer to Mac's puzzled look, Christy explained, "If you irrigate with water from the ditch, this is the day you have to help clean it. We do it every year before irrigating starts. That's really the big sign that spring is here."

"Do you want me?"

"No thanks, Mac. I already arranged with my primo Octavio. It takes all day and quite a few beers. I just need to see if he showed up." She felt some guilt for deceiving Mac, but she had to follow up on this, see what a brujo said about Satanists. Someone out there wanted her dead.

La Doña had scarcely returned home when she received a phone call. "Jordan Law Office."

"Yes, Doris. Stephen here." His voice was charming. "Stephen Kramer."

She kept her own voice light. "Yes, Stephen, I was just thinking of you. I've heard felicitations might be in order."

"Thank you. And what a coincidence! After our chance meeting in the grocery, I realized it was time I saw you about redoing some of financial picture, my future having taken on new possibilities."

With a little, shy hesitation, he added, "We just may be able to use that marital deduction you were wishing for."

Something seemed a little off key in all this brightness, he was usually a somber man, La Doña thought. Still, marriage could take a middle-aged man hard, and he did require a total revision of his will.

"I went to Los Alamos yesterday to see you on another matter," she said. "I gather you are spending a lot of time with us, in Taos. I should have remembered your bride works on the Plaza."

"My secretary did mention that I missed your visit." He paused. "I am here a good deal these days. We could easily meet. Why don't we make it soon? Make a social occasion of it." He paused again. "What about dinner tonight? Are you free?"

"I believe so."

"Then let's say eight o'clock. Oh, and let me pick you up."

"That will be fine. See you at eight." He hung up, but La Doña held on to the receiver, lost in thought.

CHAPTER XXI

Iggy said his good-byes to the group at Ricky's and headed across the parking lot. The crew. A far cry from the University gang, a bunch of party animals there, for sure. Lucky the good Lord gave him the brain that He did, never would have gotten by otherwise.

Now here he was with a major murder case and the motley crew that had developed to help him: one retired Southern doctor, one sharp old lady lawyer, and one skilled defender who'd rather be writing books. What an odd combination, but how effective!

Better get some relief from all those mental gymnastics. Try to mellow out so he could do some deep thinking himself.

Sorting through his cassette case. Wagner? No, no heavy romantic today. *I Pagliacci*? No, wrong mood. *Barber of Seville*? No. Too comic. Ah, *The Magic Flute* with Blochwitz, a great tenor. Mozart, light but radiant, sometimes melancholy.

Ought to go back to the office. After all, he did have some cases besides Pat Salazaar's. Well, only take a minute to run over to the north side, check out that rental now.

Christy was right: Dobbs seemed like their boy last night, turning in his car when they knew the car that hit Christy had to show visible damage. He had his aching back from that damned banco to prove he thought Dobbs was the danger. But now, on reflection...Shit. Why would Dobbs try to kill Christy? What could she have on him that she didn't even know she knew?

D.O.E.? Well, they were the prime contractor at Los Alamos, but last heard the U.S. government wasn't into bumping off its citizens. Yeah, maybe *heard* was the operative word.

Mozart's music soared and sparkled. Iggy drummed along with it on the steering wheel at the red light where the road split by Lo Fino. Ah, here came the good part! Hard to sing-along with Mozart. Not for Blochwitz, the lead tenor, it wasn't!

Green light at the Plaza intersection but you always had to inch along here anyway.

Finally, the car popped free of traffic, the music surged, and Iggy was away to the rental place. He parked and walked briskly to the door, reached for the handle. Whoa! Sign on the door.

"CLOSED. WE'RE OUT OF CARS! COME BACK TOMORROW."

Shit! Talk about typical Taos. Where else would they just close up? Not too surprising though. He knew how high tourist traffic was in Taos. Hope the other guys had better luck with their assignments.

Two of Iggy's motley crew leaned against the counter in the warren of minuscule rooms that constituted the Taos County Sheriff's department, part of the Courthouse complex.

Having written out her complaint, Christy waited for Sheriff Manor with Mac, using the time to outline what she wanted to say in her mind. The event seemed too bizarre to be believed. Apprehension constricted her lungs.

Christy and Mac watched khaki-uniformed deputies and office personnel pass by, intent upon their tasks. They listened to clacking office machinery and unintelligible static voices over radios. Odd how all personal conversation stopped in waiting places: hospital waiting rooms, doctor's offices, airport lounges, even this tiny office. The mind went blank. Or privacy screens went up. Well, she could stop rehearsing her speech to Aaron Manor and worry instead about her up-coming meeting with the brujo. She pondered the run-around she'd gotten from his people. Surely more difficult to see the brujo than to get an audience with the Pope. During the last call she had been told she would be given an appointment after a background check on her! Never should have called in the first place.

Christy was lost in thought and off-guard when Sheriff Manor approached. He was a rather scholarly looking man in glasses, tall as Mac. "Sorry to keep you waiting, Miz Grant and ah…?

"This is my friend, Dr. McCloud, Aaron. He has to chauffeur me today until we can check out the damage to my car."

The Sheriff stuck out his hand, "Glad to meet you, Dr. McCloud."

"Call me Mac, Sheriff," Mac said with a smile.

"If you'll just come this way. My office." Bare bones utilitarian. Stuffy. Spring didn't have much chance in here. Sheriff Manor waved them to hard visitors' seats. "So," he said. "I understand you had some difficulty yesterday. An accident?"

Christy knew this was going to be hard. "I was run off the road. It was no accident!"

"You've given your statement? Signed the complaint?"

Keep calm. More effective that way. "Yes, I have, Aaron. And I think this must be connected to the Eusebio Salazaar case."

The Sheriff widened his eyes behind his round glasses. "What leads you to that conclusion?"

"I've been working with Ignacio Baca, the attorney defending Pat Salazaar. It's the only thing going on in my life." Sheriff Manor smiled. Bastard. Christy corrected, "I mean the only thing that would lead to any sort of violence. And when the other driver came at me, forced me towards the drop, it definitely was intentional."

The Sheriff echoed her. "Intentional? But that's certainly a clumsy way to attempt murder. The car would show the damage."

"Murder is a stupid way for anyone to try to solve their problems, " Christy shot back. "Maybe this shows Eusebio's killer is losing it, becoming rattled as we investigate."

"Suppose you tell me exactly what happened."

Christy described the attack, trying to sound matter-of-fact, but her heart beat faster and her hands felt wet as her body remembered the terror.

As she ended, the Sheriff asked, "Where were you coming from?"

"From Señora Avila's home."

Mock surprise. "The curandera?"

Damn!

The crisp questions and answers continued until a final, "Yes, well, we'll do everything we can to track down the car." Then he unexpectedly added, "You say that you're assisting on the Salazaar case. Have you been concentrating on anyone in particular?" The pale blue eyes showed no real curiosity.

Hesitating, Christy glanced at Mac. She was trained to look for evidence, not make false accusations, but the Sheriff's disinterest made her stubborn. She pointed out why Pat made a poor suspect, voiced her suspicions. They sounded weak, very weak, but Sheriff Manor heard her through, was polite. "Yes, Miz Grant, although I do think the right man's been picked up. And investigation should be left to law officers. But still, you have to look at everyone, every possibility in planning your defense. If you bring us anything factual, we will take a look."

And that was it.

"Thank you, Aaron," Christy said with dignity. She walked quickly to the door. Mac followed.

Through the little anteroom. Cheeks hot.

Barely out the door, still on the Courthouse courtyard, "Dammit, Mac. I felt like an idiot!"

"I know. But what else could you do? It's hard to convey all the little things that add up, the feelings and impressions."

"That's exactly what I'm supposed to be able to do, as a writer and an attorney," Christy retorted, nerves still thrumming. "But the Sheriff didn't ask for any details, any more description of Duane Dobbs. Cold, called me Miz Grant after years on a first-name basis. He doesn't plan to do a damn thing!"

Mac didn't need to alter his long strides for Christy now. She was practically racing down the extended shallow steps.

"It's not as bad as that," he said. Christy glared at him. "No, no, I'm not trying to smooth your ruffled feathers. Just think. Sheriff Manor can't ignore the fact that some bastard nearly ran you off the road. Your car is damaged. You're a prominent member of the community. A lawyer, even if semi-retired. He'll be forced to do something."

Christy thought about it. Wasn't quite as angry as she climbed into Mac's pick-up. "Let's go see Chief Garcia. Maybe my primo will be more receptive."

"Right," Mac said, then paused. "Wait. It's past twelve. They're probably closed. How about some lunch first?"

Christy smiled at him. "Okay. And I'll cool down, maybe?"

"The thought had crossed my mind."

It wasn't hard to decide on Monte's Chow Cart for lunch. It was close by and one of Christy's favorite eating places—a beat-up brown van attracting shoulder-to-shoulder pickups in its often-muddy lot.

Afterwards, Mac drove them a few streets past the Plaza, directly to the Police Station in the old branch bank building. They entered a pleasant but fairly bare open area: a few chairs, a wall decorated with what seemed to be every police shoulder patch in the country, and a counter part way across the back. Christy reminded herself that this was just her cousin, Chief Barnabe Garcia, but the interview with the Sheriff made her anxious.

A smiling, Spanish woman greeted them. She was young and pretty.

"'Como 'sta, Miz Grant?"

"Bien, gracias, Louisa. 'Y su familia?"

"Bien, bien, gracias. I bet you're here to see your primo?"

"Yes, I am. Is Chief Garcia in right now?"

"Sure is. Just a minute and I'll tell him you're here." Louisa disappeared down the hall to the left of the counter.

Mac grinned at Christy, whispered, "See? It's going to be better here. You'll get somewhere."

Louisa popped back out. "The Chief says, 'Fine. Come on back.'" They followed Louisa down the hall past small offices.

At the sight of Christy, Chief Barnabe Garcia rose to greet them, and then came around from behind his desk. He was a heavyset man who still appeared muscular.

"Ah, Prima Christy!" he said, giving her a bear hug and reaching out to shake Mac's hand. Christy explained why Mac accompanied her.

"Sit! Sit!" Chief Garcia said, waving at the leather armchairs.

"Ah, you're looking good, Prima! *Muy bonita!*" He beamed at her.

"Gracias. And so are you, Barnabe...considering your age!"

The Chief laughed. Mac looked puzzled. Relaxed now, Christy explained, "My cousin here is three days older than I. We often celebrate our birthdays together."

She turned back to Chief Garcia. "You probably know why we're here."

Throwing up his hands, he answered, "Yes, yes, I've heard about that terrible thing that happened to you, Prima. We can't afford to lose you! You're too valuable to all of us."

"Thank you, Barnabe. It did seem like a close call."

The Chief shook his head. "What can you tell me, Prima Christy? What you said about La Hermandad, that mistaken news business? It made anger, si, but surely not murderous anger?" As Christy nodded, the Chief was already answering, "No, we're not that kind of people, not your friends and neighbors, however strongly they might support La Hermandad and believe you insulted them. I was a member myself before I became so busy and important." The Chief smiled at his self-mockery. "No, many involved, educated men take the time to remain Hermanos...Ai-ee! What kind of a fool would do this thing?"

"That's just it. I don't think it was just a foolish driver or some drunk, Barnabe. I think someone seriously tried to run me off the road!"

The big swivel chair creaked as Chief Garcia leaned back in it, laced his fingers over his belly. "Tell me exactly what happened, Christina."

When Christy finished her story, the Chief's big face was settled into grooves of concern. "But do you have any idea who might want you dead?"

Whew! That was putting it more baldly than any of them had, causing a heavy chill in the pit of her stomach. "No, Barnabe. But maybe you can help."

The Chief looked quizzical. Christy continued, "Ignacio Baca and I have been working together on the Eusebio Salazaar killing. You could help by telling us if Watkins ties in."

Chief Garcia lifted his hands, palms up, shrugged. "What can I say? I do not know. I can tell you that Watkins was not killed in a simple mugging. He carried a lot of cash, still in his wallet. He wore an expensive watch, still on his wrist. We checked with Social

Security, have now discovered he worked at Los Alamos, but I talked to them today and got nothing. Naturally they claim national security's involved."

"I knew it!" Christy exclaimed. "Taos just doesn't have muggings. "

Barnabe went on, "I've been doing other investigating, interrogated the bartender at Los Bailes among others. He knew Watkins. Seems he was living in our vicinity which is odd, it's a long commute to LANL."

Christy leaned forward. "We've been looking at two, actually three, suspects other than Pat Salazaar. The State Police don't seem to have anything on Pat except that he was the man closest to Eusebio at the morada. No blood, no knife, nowhere to hide it. Motives, like drugs or a woman, don't hold up. A motive associated with his work might. Maybe our case links with yours, given that two men who worked at the Los Alamos facility are dead. We should look at Dr. Kramer."

The Chief nodded. "I see." Spreading his hands. "What has this Kramer done to make him a suspect?"

Christy's mouth was dry from all this talking, the strain of trying to make a believable case for all their thoughts. "Mac and I talked to the young woman who was supposed to be the cause of jealousy between Eusebio and Pat. Turns out that, instead, she's this Stephen Kramer's girlfriend!"

"Is that all?"

Christy refused to be deflated. "No. We know that Eusebio had worked with Dr. Kramer, and that both were up to something secret here in Taos, separately if not together. And Dr. Kramer's secretary knew Bryce Watkins, seemed upset he was dead. Mac went up to Los Alamos yesterday with Iggy, that's Ignacio Baca, and La Doña Doris Jordan—"

Grinning widely, Chief Garcia interrupted. "How many citizens are conducting this investigation, Prima?"

Flustered, "Well, that's all. Just Mac and Iggy and La Doña."

Shaking his head, "That appears to be more than enough, Christina!" Pause. "But where are my manners? Would you and the doctor like a cup of coffee? A Pepsi?"

"Oh, yes, please. A Pepsi?"

Mac finally spoke. "May I get it? Chief, would you like one?"

"Yes, Doctor. Just straight down the hall there."

As he started out, Christy said, "Wait, Mac, please. Tell Chief Garcia about a possible motive."

Mac paused near the doorway. "We've learned that Kramer is absent from his lab, but deeply involved, we think, in some medical research." Raising an eyebrow. "I think we've run into some sort of top secret project that might originally have been sanctioned by the government, probably funded by D.O.E., but now has slipped out of their control…. Back in a minute." He disappeared out the door.

Chief Garcia turned back to Christy. "I admit that you and your, ah, group, give me food for thought. And you've thought carefully about these matters which seem confusing yourselves. However, you mentioned three suspects. Who else do you have in mind?"

Under her cousin's sympathetic gaze, Christy presented what little they had on Duane Dobbs and then added, "There's a Fred Ritchie. Oh, it sounds silly, but he came—his timing was remarkably pat—carrying a long leather case that he *claims* holds golf clubs and, well, he doesn't act like any tourist."

As Mac returned with the cold Pepsis, Chief Garcia spoke: "You know, jurisdiction is tricky here. Eusebio Salazaar belongs to the Sheriff and State Police who must take on a homicide outside the town, say at your morada. Watkins was inside city limits."

He smiled wickedly, "However, I would not be unhappy if we happened to solve both cases for the State Police." He turned serious, "Especially Eusebio's. I did not know him well, but he was a good man and, as I said, I used to be a Brother. I want to do all I can to find his killer."

The Chief became very businesslike. "You have given me a little information I can work with. Who does this Dobbs truly work for? Where is Kramer? Did he have some relationship to both Eusebio and Watkins, maybe even something outside their work? Perhaps this will lead us somewhere." He paused and grinned, "But I don't know that I can investigate the one you say acts funny."

Then sternly. "Investigate, but by us, Prima Christy, I mean the Police Department. I do not mean you and your friends!"

He pointed a large, blunt finger at her. "You have already made yourself dangerous to some person. Do no more!"

Unruffled by her cousin's scolding, Christy said slyly, "Then if you must work alone, Primo, maybe you'd consider something else."

Not so genial now. "What is that?"

"When Ignacio was properly looking into places in La Mesa important to his defense of Pat Salazaar—" she wasn't putting anything over on Primo Garcia, he was grinning at her again— well, he came upon strange activity at Los Piñones, the old mine. You know where I mean?"

The Chief nodded. "I know it."

"It seems to have changed drastically. Now there's a new road. A large camouflaged cleared area. Men with guns."

"Yes?"

Careful now with the zinger. "It might be some drug operation, might it not? One that needs investigating? And if one happened to find Dr. Kramer on site, well—"

Chief Garcia seemed to be pondering. Christy didn't risk looking at Mac, didn't breathe.

Silence.

Finally, the Chief said, "You have a point, Prima Christy. Guns and drugs. But I have no authority in La Mesa."

Gently persuasive, Christy suggested, "What of that raid on Ski Valley Road? Men with dogs stopping motorists, looking for drugs. Wasn't that a joint operation? Deputies, National Guard. Who knows who all was involved?"

"And some hornet's nest we created, Prima!" Barnabe expostulated. "You know of the law suits?"

Don't press too hard. "Wouldn't this be different, Primo?"

The Chief smiled, nodded. "And perhaps with all these letters of the alphabet—D.O.E, D.O.D—well, perhaps the D.E.A. could be of assistance to our problems."

The Gambler's advice sang in Christy's head: "Know when to hold the cards, know when to fold…" Also, quit when you're ahead. She rose. "Thank you for listening to me, Primo."

He shook his head, ruefully. "Next time, Prima Christy, we shall speak of my daughter Carmelita's wedding. It will be soon, you know."

Better not count your money. "I know, Primo Barnabe. And I'll look forward to the dancing."

They left.

CHAPTER XXII

La Doña Doris Jordan closed up her home office and moved to the other side of her house. At her age, she could allow herself the luxury of early hours now and then. Ah, but she was bored. So much probate work. The spice had been missing.

Convenient to be in the old part of Taos, so near the Plaza. Not that it was the meeting place it used to be, but she was still able to walk there when she felt like it, thank God. The old legs holding up well, much better than her eyes. Clean living and lots of exercise. Hardly ever found it necessary to consult a doctor. Good thing, too: nowadays boys and girls passed themselves off as doctors when they didn't look old enough for college.

Doris walked smartly through the house toward the bedroom. The rooms of the old adobe were clean and bright. No one could accuse her of keeping an untidy house at her age. What a parade of young women helpers there had been through the years. Some from town, some from the Pueblo. All encouraged to go on with their education, nagged as they shook out the wonderful old Navajo rugs, dusted the pots representing the best potters from most of the Pueblos (even a couple of Maria's from San Ildefonso), shined those gleaming hardwood floors. And the paintings! Back then, many of these now-famous artists lacked money for legal fees, bless their hearts. So, she bartered and now look! Handsome, handmade furniture, too.

In the bedroom, Doris took off her business clothes. She had long ago decided that a serious nap-taker undressed and put on a robe before a lie down.

She wanted to be rested, have a sharp mind for discussion with Stephen Kramer. And she looked forward to matching wits. How good it felt to anticipate some excitement once again.

Perhaps she should tell Christina or that young man of hers that dinner with Stephen was scheduled? No. It would serve no purpose to alarm Christina. They would confront her with this ridiculous age thing. Try to protect her from herself. And whatever they said, she would nonetheless meet with her client. She would, however, take precautions.

At peace with herself, La Doña lay down to sleep.

It was dusk when La Doña saw Stephen Kramer drive up. She watched from the window as he locked the car, then stood a moment staring at her adobe wall. She was pleasurably excited. It was good to feel this alive again. To have an escort for dinner. All gussied up, too, in her good black silk. She had also exchanged her briefcase for a purse, equally large and maybe a mite unshapely.

As he approached, La Doña saw strain, perhaps pain, on Stephen's clean-etched face. My but the man had aged since she began representing him. In fact, in the last few days. She opened the door. "Good evening. What's this you're driving, Stephen? Where's that fancy car of yours?"

"Good evening, Doris." Leading her out. "Ah, you mean the Lexus? I was traveling about on government business today, so I am entitled to the use of a government vehicle. Saves driving my own so much."

He unlocked the door for Doris and went around to the driver's side, picked up a soft, black leather briefcase from the seat before getting in.

La Doña settled herself, fastened her safety belt. "So, Stephen, did you bring your old will with you?"

"Mmm? Oh yes, and some other rather important papers," he answered. "We can look at it in light of new developments. I expect we'll need to review, look at any changes my marriage will cause. And you've mentioned the tax laws have changed anyway." He tucked the slim case between himself and the door.

La Doña placed her purse comfortably on her lap.

"Would you like me to put that in the back seat out of your way?"

"No, Stephen. This is just fine. I might need a tissue."

After driving down a few streets, they turned right and soon passed the Lilac Shop. La Doña was hungry. "So. Where are you taking me to dinner?" Left onto the highway, and heading into the little community of El Prado.

"I thought that new restaurant on the north side would be acceptable. Excellent food there," Kramer answered. He was driving a bit too fast. The Mexican import shops were speeding past.

It was completely dark.

Where were they? She so seldom got out at night, it was disorienting. "I don't think so, Stephen. I believe I would prefer somewhere right in town, ah, say The Apple Tree?"

"Humor me, counselor," he said, slowing the car. "You will enjoy something new.

"Of course, Stephen. If that's your preference."

There was no more conversation at the car sped north, soon reaching Le Petit Gourmet. Stephen came quickly around the car to open the door. Inside, the restaurant tried for a continental ambiance that wasn't really Taos. La Doña eyed the maitre d' in his tux. The seating diagram lay under a small spotlight in the dim room.

"Dr. Stephen Kramer. We have reservations."

The man agreed in accented English and showed them to a table, seated them, then flicked out napkins on their laps.

So, Stephen," La Doña wasted no time. "This news of yours is true?"

"Yes," he answered, smiling. "A lovely young lady, Debbie Valdez."

He looked closely at La Doña and added, "You don't seem surprised at who she is."

He knew Christy had gone to The Pink Coyote, she thought. Why didn't he say so? "No, a friend of mine mentioned Debbie was seeing you."

"What else did she mention?" Stephen asked sharply.

"Oh, nothing of any importance." Bad choice of words, she must encourage him to say more. But a waiter appeared. They ordered, Stephen making a show over the wine. When the waiter left, La Doña turned to conversation to finance, making the discussion last until the waiter returned with the wine, filled a glass.

Stephen sniffed the cork, lifted the table's candle and wine glass together to observe its color, and then swirled a taste around in his mouth until he finally nodded. He ruined the effect of all this, however, by gulping down most of the Saint Emilion, pouring out more.

"I would, of course, want an ante-nuptial agreement."

Very sensible of you, Stephen, to consider at the beginning that divorce could enter the picture."

"I always consider all eventualities," Stephen answered quietly. "She is, as you must know, considerably younger. And very pretty."

Better not to comment. She moved on. "Will you and Miss Valdez be living in Taos?"

"It's too soon to say." Stephen smiled, but sweat glistened on his top lip. The food arrived just then and, before Doris could pick up her cutlery, he stabbed quickly at the beautifully arranged meat on his plate. Stopped. Waved to the waiter as he wiped his forehead with his napkin.

"Yes, sir?"

"Would you turn on the overhead fans, please. It's much too warm in here."

"I'd be happy to, sir. But it is a cool evening, and the other patrons—"

"The other patrons can allow me a little comfort!"

Where was this man's usual courtesy? Growing agitated herself, La Doña began to eat her broiled salmon. She watched her companion, whose face had acquired a pasty look under its sheen of perspiration. Was he ill?

In silence, Stephen moved the food around his plate with his fork, took a few more small bites of his Steak Diane, then threw down his napkin.

Something was clearly wrong. "You've hardly eaten, Stephen. Are you feeling ill? If not, may I finish my meal? We can postpone business to another time."

"Yes." He twisted in his seat. "Ill. That must be it. I'd like to leave now. Waiter! Check please."

Perhaps he needed to get to a doctor. She thought of calling for the one cab in town, or even Iggy or Christina. No, no need to make a fuss; he could hardly drive off and leave her here alone to wait. She hoped he wasn't feeling too sick to drive back.

Stephen rushed though signing for his credit card and soon had them outside, walking quickly through the chill night.

Once in the car, Stephen turned right, heading north. What was this? Home lay south.

This situation is deteriorating, La Doña thought. Keep it calm. Get yourself home. "Ah, Stephen," she tried speaking kindly. "I believe you should have turned left, back to Taos."

Kramer turned his face toward La Doña. His smile was not pleasant. He did look sick, but sick with anger. He seemed to be choking on words held back like a need to vomit. They burst out, "You silly old cow! Sitting there, pretending to be helping me."

Shock racked La Doña. Out of the blue, the words hit like body blows. She hadn't expected his total loss of control, hadn't expected irrationality.

"I've been wanting to call you that all evening. Think you're so smart? You and that bitch and that fat slob out at the project!

He must be referring to the mine. So, it was all true. Iggy had been right about the presence of the guards. It was a high-security facility run by D.O.E. And their case, the murder, did connect to Stephen's research. But why? And what to do about the man himself? And where in God's name was he going?

"You people think you're moving in on me. I know it. I thought about killing you—I was clumsy, spur of the moment when I saw the Grant woman driving in front of me—realized I can't simply eliminate everyone. Just knew, since the calls, that something had to be done...."

What was he reaching for in that briefcase? A gun? No, a bottle of Maalox for God's sake!

Doris Jordan wouldn't admit to herself that she was frightened. The man had gone out of his mind, true, and she might have gotten herself in over her head, but she'd try to reconnect with his rational side. She couldn't just leap from the car, and if she did, what then, in the dark? She couldn't even talk him into letting her drive them to town, maybe to the hospital, not with her hopeless night vision.

"Stephen, Stephen. Lord love us! You call me names and swig Maalox! Let's calm ourselves, get something stronger to soothe your stomach?"

Eyes on the road at least. His voice now seemed tightly controlled. "I've been reviewing all my options since your trip to Los Alamos. I thought things would move quicker, your looking closer wouldn't matter. But it's all become too much!"

La Doña spoke carefully, "What's too much, Stephen?"

"You people. You damned interfering people. I planned it meticulously. I was far cleverer than this backwater place could ever understand. Then the bunch of you! Prying, blundering about, destroying my design. Forcing me to improvise...."

He had fallen apart. She must bring him back. "Yes, Stephen. You planned beautifully."

"Don't sneer at me, bitch," Kramer hissed, silencing Doris. She realized sadly she had fooled herself into thinking she'd had a relationship of trust, that he valued her. And, equally foolish, that she thought herself a tough old bird, could handle anything. She'd never been verbally abused before, let alone in physical danger. Combat in the courtroom could be brutal, but its rules kept things more or less civil. Not important now. So much she hadn't expected. Unwise not to have told Christy.

She tried appeasement. "I'm sorry I interfered, Stephen. I—"

"You are on your way to the airport. I thought it out quickly at dinner when you gave yourself away. I've devoted years to pure research, to discovery, to advancement, living like a monk, only my computer for a companion. My rewards came from advancing science. So much can be done with super computers, years compressed." He drank again from the bottle.

"Then a great breakthrough came, just a by-product of the AIDS research. I was filled with elation. Then I realized, given the policies, who would know of my work? Would recognize the genius?"

They had gotten the AIDS right, but not completely. "What have you discovered that's so important?"

Stephen Kramer laughed, a great, wild, choking laugh. "What have I discovered that's so important? Immortality, that's all. How's that for so important?"

La Doña was intrigued despite her danger. "How can you 'discover' immortality?"

"Through the Human Genome Project. Planned to succeed in mapping around 2003, figure the sequencing. Thirty four million chemical letters spell a single chromosome, three trillion units of genetic code! Eusebio and I pushed that ahead with our supercomputers, far enough ahead to discover that aging is a disease—a discovery that grew directly out of looking at the immune system. We can withdraw the slow-down gene and insert a young, healthy gene to reverse the process. We can live forever!"

"But the government—"

"Oh, yes, by dinner I knew you knew. Your questions gave it away. I have to get out of this country before they steal my work—*mine*—and claim it belongs to them."

He drew a deep breath. "I'm planning a new life with Debbie. Such a beautiful girl. I met her on the day of my final breakthrough." Speeding up. "For a moment, I considered killing you, throwing your friends off balance, the police, give myself a little more time. Then I realized you would have told people about dinner. It would bring me into the spotlight at once."

Kill! Oh, my God! He had shown hysteria, but kill? And this little outing was only supposed to be for some subtle probing— on both sides, it seemed. What should she do? Such an explosion! "Let's not talk of killing, Stephen Kramer. We've know each other....You don't mean—"

"I do mean. But I'm still ahead of you! They won't make a move on me if I have you as hostage."

"Hostage? Where, Stephen? There's nowhere to go."

"The airport, you old fool. I didn't grow up in Los Alamos without learning to fly, and on instruments. I have what I need, a portable hard drive off my workstation, some CD-Roms I've burned for backup. The Los Piñones location was ideal for keeping people away from my work. The guards weren't so well trained as those at LANL—one reason I pushed to open a work area away from there." He paused. "I've run a high security disk erase on my workstation hard drive, overwriting all the critical data with a random pattern of zeroes and ones. If they're closing in, I have you."

Now he looked pleased. "Dinner, a leisurely dinner, not very suspicious. And this late, we should have a good start if their limited intelligence makes them slow in figuring it out."

Stephen drove wildly now, racing through the new red stop light, reciting the frustrations that had apparently tipped him over the edge. "My plans had gone perfectly. No one suspected. But then, Vern told me....And Debbie....That Grant woman hot on my trail. Eusebio was dead. Necessary. He knew, but if suspicion turned away from his cousin, it would strike me. Then somebody kills Watkins. And you head to Los Alamo...."

What was this? No time to think about it. She was in real danger. If not from Stephen, from the car. An accident seemed likely at any moment. And her heart! It seemed to be squeezing the breath right out of her. Stupid. Stupid not to foresee the possibilities.

She had said nothing but Stephen moved further out of control, his voice high and loud, beating on the wheel with his Maalox bottle. "Shut up! Just shut up! You think my plans were faulty? Well, let me tell you this. They were a model of precision thinking. Of simplicity."

La Doña was taking deep breaths, trying desperately to stay calm. "Yes, Stephen, I'm sure they were."

As she talked, La Doña slowly pulled her hand out of her purse, drew out her father's pistol from the World War One. "Stephen." He didn't hear. "Stephen!"

He looked over at her. She had him. "This is a pistol, Stephen. I will shoot you unless you slow down and turn this car around. At once."

Lord, La Doña prayed, this is a time for Christina's God to make an appearance. Was Kramer too crazed to care whether he was shot? Would he call her bluff? Yes.

"Stupid old woman!" he screamed "You can't shoot me at this speed! No woman, especially an old woman, is going to—"

Use your courtroom voice, Doris, she ordered herself. Convince him. "Stephen." Slowly, word by word. "You must slow down and turn around. I - will - kill - us - both, if need be. I would prefer, prefer, Stephen, to die now, rather than let you kill me later, when you're safe. SLOW DOWN!"

Kramer did. And La Doña thanked God.

Sternly. "Turn the car around."

Kramer did. He suddenly deflated.

"That's a sensible man. Now proceed directly back to Taos. You can tell me how brilliant you are on the way."

Using all her will power, La Doña held the gun steady. It pointed unwaveringly, held up high where he could see it. This was ridiculous, but what could she do. She couldn't drive the car. Why had she been so stubborn refusing a cell phone? Even if her eyes were so bad, she could have punched in 911. Wryly, Doris Jordan acknowledged she had closed her mind, refused to accept her limitations, forgotten that others—Stephen!— had vulnerabilities.

They drove at a slower pace, the man now mumbling. She could understand occasional bits. "Kill Salazaar, the only assistant who knew what I - I! - had accomplished. He was such a talented programmer, I needed his help, had to let him too close. Do it at the morada. A knife in the back. He inside. All of them, all of them lying down to sleep near the body. Everyone a suspect. Then, to send them flailing further, return during one of their peculiar marches, add a new element...."

They passed back through El Prado. "Such Promising results. Further gene research indicated. Now, no one knows where to go with it but me. A king. I'll be a king! It's sold for millions!"

Kramer squirmed, tilted up the bottle, dropped it on the floor. She wondered nervously if he was up to something, or just fidgeting. Obviously in pain....must be ulcers with that Maalox. Now he was clawing at the black case at his side.

La Doña tried to ignore her heart palpitations. She must keep him calm, talking. "And what did you do that was worth millions, Stephen?"

"I identified the gene!" he cried. "The gene, you old woman! Too late for you. We can tag it. Start gene therapy. Stop aging!"

They were approaching the light and right turn onto Placitas. He had the briefcase open, had pulled out a new bottle, opened it. "It's what the alchemists philosophized about centuries ago, the universal cure. The cure—" He whipped the car around the corner, simultaneously flipping the full bottle of Maalox on her lap. Doris glanced down at the spreading liquid.

Stephen pulled a knife from the briefcase. He lunged toward her.

Car almost stopped. Can't kill the man. Keep him from killing me. Shoot once just across his prow, just to his right. Noise! Enormous noise of the shot in the car! And following so close as to be almost simultaneous, the car accelerated, crashed up into the railroad ties on the embankment of the Lilac Shop. The driver's side smashed hard against it.

The recoil of the ancient gun, the wreck, all the noise so loud as to be truly deafening. Thrown violently against the door, La Doña was stunned.

Passenger door swinging wildly. Out door. Stumble. Don't fall My God! The horn was sounding. Was he alive? Dead? Coming after her with that knife?

She couldn't wait to find out, couldn't risk that knife to check. She'd call 911 from home…if she made it home. If Stephen didn't catch her first.

Get away! Get away from here. Head for home and the phone. Feet don't fail me now!

CHAPTER XXIII

The ringing telephone in the dark jerked Christy awake. Frightened as usual when the phone rang at this hour, her mind raced through who could be in trouble, sick, dead.

Recorded voice: "This is the Taos County Jail. You have a collect call from" pause for new voice "Doris Jordan." Back to recording: "If you wish to accept the call, press one now..." Christy, trying to get the light on, heard the voice still speaking, "...hang up."

Dark. It was too dark to see. Light. Quick, press one. Doris Jordan? La Doña? What!

"They tell me I've killed a man." No preamble. Just stark words. Think.

"La Doña?" Could this old, quavery voice be La Doña? What was she saying?

"Yes, Christina. This is my one call to my attorney."

"You've killed...Who have you killed? Where are you?" Dry mouth. Could hardly get the words out.

"In jail. The police say that I shot Stephen, but I didn't, Christina. I did not! He attacked me, but I—"

"Hush, La Doña," Christy interrupted as her mind began to work. "Don't say anything else. I'm on my way."

La Doña's voice broke, "Thank you, my dear" She hung up.

Oh, God! What had happened? La Doña in jail! Shooting. It made no sense, no sense at all.

She looked at the clock: twelve-twenty in the morning.

Grabbed jeans and a shirt, any shirt. Ran a brush through her hair.

Down the stairs. Too much clatter.

Christy tried to quell her worry for her old friend and marshal her thoughts. The first thing to do was get to the jail, hear La Doña's story, see if she could get her released on her own recognizance. It must be a mistake. No. La Doña said….What had she said exactly? That she killed Kramer or the police claimed she had?

Oh, dammit! Christy swore, realizing she and Mac never did get around to checking out the car. First the angry call from Mama, "worried sick" that Christy told her not to worry. Angry to be, as she claimed, "hung up on." After appeasing her, checked the reservations, visited with the trio, dinner, talking. Phone call setting up brujo appointment. Writing a little in both her journal and book.

So now it still wasn't safe to drive the wrecked car, especially late at night. She'd have to wake poor Mac.

Christy ran through the kitchen out the door to the courtyard. It appeared unfriendly under the waning moon. Pounding on the door to the tiny guest house, she called, "Mac! Wake up, Mac!" Probably woke Dobbs, too. A moment passed. The door opened. Mac stood there in tailored blue pajamas, feet bare, hair rumpled. "Christy! What's the matter? Are you all right?"

"It's La Doña, Mac. She's in jail! She called from there."

"Just a minute. I'll dress." Wonderful Mac. No questions. No fooling around.

"I forgot to get a jacket," Christy explained, "and I'm freezing. I'll meet you at the Chevy." Mac disappeared. Christy ran to the kitchen, grabbed her wind breaker off the hook by the door.

Very soon they were off down the single-lane dirt road, Mac driving it as fast as he dared. Now onto the Talpa Highway, down to the Y, around the corner, north on Santa Fe. Worry and tension prevented more than short spurts of conversation.

"Did La Doña tell you why on earth she's in jail?

"She was very upset. I wouldn't let her talk. I only got that the police say she shot Dr. Kramer." Now that Christy's mind was working better, she took that in. Kramer must be dead. Then her thoughts careened back to how best to help La Doña. Christy barely heard Mac's exclamations as she considered.

They drove in silence, speeding on a nearly empty road, just a stray car now and then. Lonely street lights emphasized the feeling that they were the only ones awake, making an emergency journey in a sleeping Taos. Past motels, businesses. Green light at the old bus station. Furr's big parking lot lit, the grocery itself nearly dark. Another green light.

Tendrils of anxiety fanned out, like snakes, from a lump in Christy's stomach. The courthouse complex was coming up, the jail in one side of it. Mac took the corner into the side street too fast. He pulled into the courthouse parking lot. Christy was out and running. She didn't look back to check Mac.

She pressed the jail buzzer. The door opened. Gray. Gray and cold. Institutional. White lights drained out any color.

Christy's steps sounded as she walked quickly into the area where the two jailers watched television. Its noise was isolated in the late-night quiet of the jail. Christy felt like she was seeing through water, walking under water, so dim was her vision. One jailer looked over at her. Stood up. Thank God! She knew him. Benny.

"Benito! Is it true? Do you really have La Doña, uh, Miss Doris Jordan, locked up in here?"

"Afraid so. Hold on now. You have to sign in, Christy. This a friend of yours?" He was looking at Mac who had caught up with her. Christy signed in, answering "Yes. He's a doctor. We have to see Miss Jordan."

"Okay. We don't have many guests tonight. I'll just take you on back."

Benny led them through the door into the cell area. More cold gray walls, cold cement floor. A double cell for women. Oh, God no! There she was, lying on a bunk, black shoes toward them.

La Doña slowly pushed up to a sitting position and awkwardly arranged herself on the edge of the bunk. She looked old, frail, her bulk diminished somehow. Ludicrously dressed in a fluorescent orange jump suit, The Lady seemed vulnerable with neither her bulging briefcase nor big, black purse.

Benny opened the cell door.

Christy rushed over to hug her old friend, then pulled back a bit, only a gentle squeeze.

"I never was one for fashion," La Doña indicated the orange jump suit. "Left me my shoes, though." She stuck out her feet, showing her sensible black lace-up brogues, incongruous against the fluorescent orange pants of the jump suit.

"Oh, La Doña!" Christy choked up, had to turn away from the pathetic sight of her fierce old mentor, critic, friend.

Some kind of padding covered the walls of the cell. A naked, lidless stainless steel toilet crouched in the corner. Plastic spread over the bunk beds. A thin strip of foam rubber acted as a mattress. One blanket.

Christy heard Mac ask, "May I?" She turned to see him holding La Doña's wrist, looking at his watch. He was taking her pulse. In a professional voice new to Christy, Mac said, "You can't stay here. I want you in the hospital."

Ignoring him, La Doña looked at Christy with old eyes. "They brought me in and I was processed. Took all my things and inventoried them. Finger printed me. Made me put on this absurd outfit. Only call had to be collect. Sorry."

Christy tried to console her while considering options.

La Doña kept on talking. "My tidy little practice of law failed to prepare me for this. Never realized how demeaning.... One loses one's soul a bit."

Christy fought back tears. They wouldn't help her friend.

"They claim I shot Stephen!" La Doña announced angrily.

Christy focused on getting the facts of the story, commencing with why La Doña was with Kramer in the first place. Mac interrupted, insisting on her need for medical care. And, though her voice often slowed and wavered, the formidable lady pushed aside his objections to fill them in.

Sighing with fatigue, La Doña ended it. "Well, to cut to the chase as they say now, he turned at the Lilac Shop, brought a knife from somewhere, maybe that briefcase. I fired once, across his prow, not at him. Don't know if I blacked out then or right after as the car crashed. Hit my head. Then I was out the door and running. Went home. Meant to call 911. I know I should have checked his condition but, well, I must admit I was frightened, Christina. He was ready to kidnap me, kill me. I expected him to chase me."

"Oh, La Doña!" Christy risked a quick hug. "Why didn't you call me? Call the police?"

La Doña glanced guiltily at Mac. "I, ah, I am afraid that I rather collapsed. The police roused me by banging on the door some hours later. Must have had to wake up the magistrate to get a bench warrant."

"That does it!" Mac exclaimed. "A woman your age under that kind of stress. Then running. Now you admit you collapsed. You are going to the hospital for heart, blood pressure, shock, and anything else I can think of! You hear?" Mac turned and snapped, "Christy, make arrangements!"

For some peculiar reason this made the two women smile at one another.

"Yes, sir, Doctor," Christy answered, realizing this was the quickest way to get her friend out of this awful place. She turned to shake the bars and yell, "Benny! Benito, come back here!"

The stocky jailer came into view with maddening slowness.

"La Doña needs medical attention. Dr. McCloud says she must go to the hospital."

"Can't do."

Damn! Of course not. Christy was irritated with herself. Benito had no such authority. "Well if you can't, who can?"

"The Chief mebbe."

"Where is Primo Garcia?" Christy asked through gritted teeth.

"Hospital. Said he had to have the body ID-ed."

Christy controlled her tone. "Then let me out so I can phone him."

He opened the cell door, but said, "No phone 'cept the collect one."

Her patience was gone. "Come on, Benny. Show me your phone."

He did.

With Christy's urgent persuasion, the hospital quickly had Chief Garcia on the line.

"This is your cousin Christy, Barnabe. I'm here at the jail with La Doña Abogada Doris Jordan. Dr. McCloud is here, too, and says she needs to be hospitalized. Will you please tell Benito to let her out of here?"

"Sorry, Christina," the Chief rumbled. "I wish I could, but I can't do that."

Frustration, worry and strain got to Christy. "Why in hell not? She shouldn't be in here! She shot that damned Kramer in self defense! That's if she shot him at all. She says not."

Chief Garcia's tone was soothing, "Hold on, Prima. It's not that simple. There's no knife at the scene. Nothing to support her claim that Kramer attacked her. She simply shot him."

"What?" Christy was startled, sick, but struggled to hide it. "Shot *past*, Barnabe. She does not admit to shooting *at* him, much less hitting him."

"Please, Prima. Whatever she says, the victim has a bullet hole in his brain. And La Doña claims she fired at Dr. Kramer when he lunged at her with a knife. Uses some odd phrase, shot across his prow. Says he had it in some kind of briefcase. No knife. No briefcase. Nothing but her billfold, how we knew she was the shooter by the way, and that antique gun of hers. A bullet through the head and no other gun!"

Christy struggled to keep her dismay from her voice, regain some composure. "We can discuss all that later, Barnabe. Must be some mistake. Right now, we need to get La Doña under medical care before she has a heart attack or something. She's very stressed, and too old to withstand it."

Silence. Then, "All right. I'll have them send an ambulance."

"We can just take—"

"No, Prima. La Doña is in custody on an open charge of murder. It has to be the ambulance with one of my boys guarding the prisoner."

"All right. Whatever you say." Christy hid her relief.

"Now, let me speak to Benny. I'll okay her release, arrange for a guard."

Christy felt she'd put all her energy into persuasion but managed a good front as Benny hung up and escorted her back to the cell.

She smiled at La Doña and Mac. "Okay. Ambulance on its way."

"Ambulance!" La Doña snorted. "I have no need for any ambulance, Christina."

"Sorry. I guess they have to go by some silly procedure," Christy answered casually. "Mac and I will follow in Mac's Chevy. We'll be right there with you."

Yes, a little ferocity was returning. "I do not need my hand held, Missy."

"Of course, you don't. You—"

"Nor any condescending either!"

Smiling in relief at La Doña's attitude, Christy said, "While we're waiting, tell me the details, how it all happened. You only hit the bare bones before."

Mac said, "I'd rather she didn't. Just sit quietly til we can get her checked out."

La Doña snorted again.

"Just a little, Mac," Christy said and turned to La Doña, "You're sure Dr. Kramer had a knife?"

"Of course, I'm sure. I was holding the pistol on the man, but then he made the turn, threw his bottle of Maalox—"

"Maalox?"

"Maalox," La Doña repeated firmly. "Spilled on my good black silk. I reacted like an idiot, looked down, and that's when he managed to drag the knife from his briefcase." Sadly. "I am getting old. I should have expected it, knowing how Eusebio died."

Christy wasn't about to upset La Doña by saying there was no knife, but the lady herself added, "Boys in blue claim no knife. Sloppy police work is what I say."

Christy refrained from looking at Mac. "I'm sure they'll find it," she answered.

The ambulance arrived. They heard its wail and dying hiccup.

With shaky effort, La Doña got to her feet. "I did not shoot the man, Christina. I told you, Just a warning shot. Across his prow, just like they do to halt ships at sea. The image came to me. That's all! However, it appears I may need a defense." She reached out and gripped Christy's hand. "You will promise to defend me, won't you, Christy? None of this silly business about having retired. You will do it, won't you, child?"

Christy could not refuse her friend. "Yes, La Doña. I'll defend you." Realizing her sadness showed, Christy quickly added, "If it's necessary, that is. We're going to get this all straightened out."

The ambulance crew reached the cell.

Once in the Chevy on the way to the hospital, Christy was able to drop the cheery pose.

"What was that last routine all about?" Mac asked as the siren of the ambulance wailed in front of them. Christy looked ahead at the dark, deserted street. "It looks bad, Mac," she said and explained the police position. The siren still cried but was pulling away from them. Fast.

With too much and too little to say, they were still quiet when they reached Holy Cross. The ambulance was already parked alongside the emergency room entrance. A man and woman wheeled La Doña in on a gurney. Unprotesting, she lay frighteningly still.

Mac sensed Christy's alarm. "It's okay. I think she's just exhausted. Doris is a tough old bird. She'll make it. Do just fine."

"Thanks, Mac."

A shock of bright ceiling light reflected on shining floors when Christy came in from the dark night. She was comforted to see Barnabe just inside the doors, standing at parade rest, arms behind his bulky torso. He might be her courtroom adversary eventually, but for now it was good to have him around. He seemed so solid in this wispy hospital world of nearly three in the morning.

Chief Garcia greeted her. "They took your friend into a cubicle in there in the E.R., Prima. Now the doctor and nurses care for her."

"Where?" Christy started past him.

The Chief gently took her arm. "Patience, Christina, patience. She is being examined. We must stay out here in the waiting room." Christy followed Barnabe, but peered back trying to see which one of the cubicles he meant. They were all curtained off. She couldn't see La Doña but belatedly realized where she must be. A uniformed man sat uncomfortably on a stool across from the first cubicle.

Chief Garcia was about to speak to Christy, when a woman with long curly red hair approached. She began the whole maddening admitting ritual. Christy filled in all she could on the papers but, naturally, more was needed.

Returning to the E.R. door, she saw with relief that her friend Linda was on duty. "May I just speak to La Doña? Get the information for admitting?"

Linda smiled, said, "Sure thing." and led Christy toward the first cubicle, saying in a whisper, "It's not the usual routine but I put Miss Jordan in a gown already. Wanted to get her out of that awful jail thing."

Christy appreciated that.

Mac was already there. He must have come in while she was trying to fill in the forms. He told a white-coated man, "No, I'm not licensed in New Mexico. Mine's in Florida, and it has the most stringent requirements in the country. Afraid we try to keep out the snow-birds, retiring doctors from the North. Now, for Miss Jordan..."

As Christy came up to them, Mac broke off to say, "This is Doctor Site," introducing the slight, sandy-haired man. But Christy was only interested in La Doña. Her friend lay passively on the narrow black gurney, her face as gray as her hair. It was frightening to see her so quiet, somehow intrusive to see her with her hair loose. It lay thin against the flat hospital pillow.

The sight of Christy brought some light to La Doña's sunken eyes.

Mac said reassuringly, "She's doing fine, Christy. Blood pressure, heart. Want to do more checking, but—"

"Don't 'she' me, young man. I have a name." La Doña's grumpy attempt to assert herself relieved Christy as did the next bit, "You should be in bed, Christina. Rising so early with that bed and breakfast folly of yours."

Christy squeezed La Doña's hand and explained what she needed. Then Dr. Site politely but firmly excused her. Following after Christy, Mac explained, "Mainly, she's simply exhausted. Let me see that they do all the testing I want, get her back to a room, settled in. Then you can say good night to her before we leave." He disappeared back into the cubicle, then popped his head out. "I'll be with you in a minute."

Chief Garcia was still in the hallway, pacing the floor, grumbling. "I have to wait around here—hate hospitals—until

I can get a positive ID on the victim. I have his address book. Some names back East but no apparent relatives. Los Alamos names, too."

The Chief glared at Christy. "You know, if it weren't for *that* damned town—sorry, Prima—I wouldn't have any murders in *my* town! Eusebio working at Los Alamos. That Watkins guy. Now this Kramer character."

Christy pushed aside her feelings for her friend to think as her attorney. She began meekly, "Did you try his secretary, ah, Vern something?"

"Yes, I tried her! No answer."

"What about the fiancée, Debbie? Debbie Valdez. I interviewed her. She lives here in Taos."

"She does, does she? Right. I saw that name and phone number in Kramer's address book." He pushed open the E.R. doors and yelled, "Hey, Bobby! Get out here!"

"Yes, sir!" The guard rose from his seat and trotted over to them.

"Go find one Debbie Valdez. She's the girl friend. Break it to her gentle. Then bring her in for an ID."

"Yes, sir!" Bobby was off, again at a trot.

Mac joined them in the waiting room. "La Doña will be all right. We're keeping her overnight for observation. Rest mostly. They'll have her settled in her room shortly."

Christy smiled and gave his arm a quick squeeze, then had a thought: La Doña must not go back to that jail. She squeezed Mac's arm again much harder, trying to convey the message. Mac seemed to understand because he quickly added, "However, one never knows about these things. Especially with a woman of La Doña's age. I will have to see how she is tomorrow before she could possibly be released."

"Oh, right." The Chief appeared more interested in grumbling. "Well, we may get somewhere with identifying the body, but this place! Can't get anything out of them about the victim's wound, except that he's dead. I knew that!"

The Chief stopped speaking as two nurses came wheeling La Doña out on a gurney.

Mac put a hand on Christy's shoulder. "Wait a little minute and we'll go on back." Chief Garcia looked at his watch, already impatient for Bobby to bring in Debbie Valdez. "Then I'll have to get the body sent to Albuquerque to the medical examiner. They always say at least five working days and this is Thursday, so then there'll be the week-end…"

Christy eased in with, "But you said you know Kramer was shot in the head."

"Any fool could see that. We still have to have an official autopsy by the medical examiner. I'll tell you one thing. Even though her Luger is a small-bore gun and Kramer's wounds seem made by a small-bore, well, if we can find the bullet, we'll know right away if it came from that antique La Señora was carrying. A World War One souvenir. The 'War to end all Wars' and it was the next one yet that sent all our Taos boys to the Philippines and the Bataan Death March."

Christy seized the opportunity to press, "Then you'll release her? When you find that the bullet doesn't match?"

"You know better than that, Christina. We have to send it to ballistics. That's what will show if it was fired from an old Luger."

Christy wanted to argue but restrained herself. She needed cousin Barnabe to work *with* her, not become stubborn or antagonistic. "How can we get all this speeded up? Get La Doña cleared. Call it self defense if the bullets match? Justifiable homicide?"

Chief Garcia raised his eyebrows. "Justifiable? I hope! But you know, Prima, that you must first explain why La Doña was carrying a gun with her. I'm as anxious as you are to see that lady free. Have known her all my life. A good woman….At first light my boys are going to search that car of Kramer's. I'm hoping to find the bullet buried in the door, maybe. Maybe outside. Victim was slumped over the steering wheel. See if there's evidence of anything, anything at all."

Christy tried to nudge gently, "Then you could send the bullet to Albuquerque some kind of express?"

"Yes, Prima, I could." The Chief was grinning at her. "Ought to be getting word from ballistics on the gun that shot Watkins, too."

Overlooking Watkins for the moment, Christy added, "And the government car? Have you thought about Dr. Kramer's own car? That it might have been the one that hit me?"

"Mm-hum."

Once again, Christy heard The Gambler singing in her head and pressured a little bit more, "I guess you'll want to locate that black leather briefcase. Kramer told La Doña he had all his disks and research papers in it, had sold it for a fortune."

Chief Garcia was looking as if she'd gone too far but before he could speak, Debbie came rushing in. She was crying. Her face without the skillful make-up looked very young, vulnerable. Christy and Mac were familiar figures, so Debbie turned to them. "Now he's dead and we were going away together." Crying hard. "Not now. How can he be gone? I did love him! All my friends are gone! Eusebio killed, Pat arrested—"

Uncomfortable, Mac excused them, "I think we can go see La Doña now."

Wondering if there were any more information to be had from Debbie, Christy walked after Mac through to the hospital patient area. The nurses' station curved to the right of them. The few nurses there did the ever-present paper work.

Looking up, Loretta said, "Room 109, doctor," to Mac, and they went on down the hall, looking at numbers.

Mac eased open the door to 109. La Doña was waiting for them, but seemed to be having trouble keeping her eyes open. "Ridiculous," she mumbled. "Never go to the hospital. Better off at home."

Christy took her hand. "Just for now, friend. Sleep and you can go home soon."

"Must have given me something." The fierce old eyes closed.

Christy leaned over and kissed La Doña's forehead. She and Mac looked at one another, then slipped out of the room.

It was cold outside, cold in the Chevy. Mac turned on the heater and suggested they go for a cup of coffee. "In fact," he said, "We could stop by Daylight Donuts, have one, and buy some for breakfast."

Shivering Christy said, "I never cheat like that on my guests' breakfast."

"Ma'am, there's surely a time and a place for everything under God's sun—and cheatin's one of 'em."

Shaking from cold and fatigue, Christy felt depressed but smiled at this. "Okay. I'll do it. And right now I could do with hot coffee and one of John's donuts, freshly baked."

"Good deal. He gets in at three or four. If John sees us, he'll surely let us in."

Mac drove the few blocks to the donut shop where John did let them in, and was soon serving his friends hot coffee and hot donuts, beaming all the while.

When John had returned to his cooking, Mac said, "Don't be so down. La Doña's going to come out of this just fine."

"Her health, yes. Come out of the rest of it? I don't know....By the way, thank you for catching on so quickly about keeping her in the hospital. I don't want her going back to that jail."

"Sure. What are you worried about, then?"

Christy sighed. "I'm so afraid. La Doña is old and shaky, was being attacked, never shot at a person before. How can she be sure she missed him?"

"But it was still self-defense."

"I don't even know about that, Mac. There's no knife...." Christy's voice was dragging.

"Eat your donut. Doesn't that do it anyway? If she thought he was attacking her, I mean."

"A prosecutor could say that Kramer was the victim, that he just lunged at her to take the gun. She's old. Her eyesight's not so good."

"Well then, tell me about self defense. If the man frightened her so badly?"

"To use deadly force she had to have had a reasonable belief that her life was in danger, or that she would suffer great bodily harm. In some states, you can only use deadly force to counter deadly force, and with your back to the wall. Her age will make it hard to believe this was the script."

Quiet a few moments, Mac said, "Christy? I don't want to hurt your feelings or get you all riled up, but you've used *old* several times now. Uh, you don't suppose you're questioning La Doña's story for that reason? It could all be absolutely true, you know."

She rejected the idea she could be guilty of ageism. "I know that! I'm just pointing out the problems!

Mac held up his hands. "Okay, okay. Let's drop that. Sorry I made the suggestion. So tell me something: the Chief tossed out a comment about La Doña carrying a gun. Would that make it premeditated murder?"

"Depends. If we can show she always did for protection, or that she had reason to fear Stephen Kramer....Lord, Mac! Have you thought? We haven't even talked about the fact that Kramer's dead! And that he told La Doña he killed Eusebio. Just wait til I tell Iggy!"

Mac grinned, "Sounds like you're back in the ring."

Christy grinned back. "Another old fire horse hearing the bell clang." Her face fell, "But think of poor Duane Dobbs, I picked on him just because I didn't like him, decided that he was the one who tried to run me off the road. Now we'll likely find Stephen Kramer's own car bashed up instead. Went after me because of Debbie. And our sinister Mr. Ritchie with his golf clubs! I've been such a fool!"

Mac shook his head. "If fool there be, it's we, not thee. I was number one bodyguard. And as for Ritchie, why, he probably heard about that new golf course south of town."

Christy added, "Or thought he was going to New Mexico's version of Scottsdale like our honeymooners."

Silence as they both pondered. Then a shudder ran through Christy. "If La Doña's story is accurate, who took the briefcase and the knife? Who really shot Kramer? And why?"

Finally home and in bed, Christy said her prayers. "Watch, O Lord, those who wake or watch or weep tonight, and give your angels and saints charge over those who sleep." She added to St. Augustine's prayer, "Please God, especially La Doña, Mac, too," then finished that prayer and said her others, asking that God guide her in finding Kramer's killer. "...and deliver us from evil."

The sky was gray with the coming morning.

Maybe, since Mac had bought the donuts, she would have a couple of hours sleep before breakfast. Christy began to relax, started to doze.

The phone rang.

Chapter XXIV

The phone call was from Mama.

Christy groaned, "Oh, Mama! I've been up all night and was just about asleep."

Pobrecita," she sympathized, "What worries you so that you cannot sleep?" Then in a sharper tone, "You did not stay out all night, did you? Did you go to the jail in the dark?"

Oh, no. If Mama knew that, this would be a full interrogation. In preparation, Christy pulled the pillows up to lean against.

"I hear the early Hometown News. That is why I call."

Christy groaned again. "Oh, no! I'm going to have to ask Stuart to cancel that early news on KKIT. He's ruining my sleep!"

"So. Are you going to tell me the story? Why has La Doña Abogada been arrested? They say that, see. And the death of this other one from Los Alamos, it is reported—"

Christy tried to shorten the quiz. "Please, Mamacita, I must get some rest!"

"Then tell me why la vieja is in the jail on an open charge of murder."

Maybe if she summarized the whole thing? "They say La Doña killed the Los Alamos man, a Stephen Kramer. And this you'll be happy to hear, he said to her that he had killed Eusebio Salazaar!"

"El Diablo did it and burned the morada." Firmly.

"No, Mamacita, I told you, Dr. Kramer *said* that he killed Eusebio."

"Hah! Then La Doña Abogada killed El Diablo and that is a good thing, muy bueno! She will be blessed."

"Yes, Mama. Now you know everything. So, may I hang up and go to sleep?"

"What of the dead one in the alley behind Los Bailes?" Perfecta asked, making Christy realize that she *had* forgotten that Watkins might be a loose end. Barnabe had mentioned that he'd soon be getting the ballistics' report back on that shooting. Her subconscious must have filed it away as taken care of: Kramer also killed Watkins. Important to ask La Doña tomorrow, no today, already Thursday.

After a little sparring, Christy thought she was going to get to hang up, but had to check a sore spot of her own. "Mama?"

¿Si?"

"Why do you speak with such respect of La Doña Abogada when you never wanted me to be a lawyer?"

"I speak thus because she is la vieja, the old one, and you are my daughter, Christina."

They hung up and Christy thought, almost six. Maybe just a short nap?

Christy managed to sleep an hour and made her apologies to the guests for the donuts, adding a choice of healthy cereals, extra fruit, and ginger pears that she'd put up last fall. While she did her chores on automatic pilot, Christy thought out her plans to see La Doña and interview the lady. She needed to get this mess straightened out before La Doña was dragged down into the quicksand of the formal legal process.

It seemed no time before the guests were all at the table, even Fred Ritchie. Duane Dobbs looked a bit haggard, but naturally, Kramer's confession had changed Christy's view of her guest. Could he feel that her animosity to him, if not gone, had lessened? She hadn't liked him before he ever became a suspect in her mind. She still didn't.

Mac with almost as little sleep as she, was quite lively. Good thing. She was in no mood to entertain the guests. In fact Mac was in the middle of explaining "the Taos shuffle"—apparently having used the phrase to someone—" a name I gave it, our hostess never having noticed the shuffle that goes on here. The reason is she's a champion shuffler herself."

"Then what I was talking about was a shuffle?" Lolly asked.

"Yes, indeedy. For instance, when we were converting the sheep shed to a guest house, I needed a part, a small coupling for some plumbing and went to the hardware store. The clerk showed me where the coupling would be on the shelf if they had it. But they didn't. 'Mm-hum,' I agreed. But if they did have it, that was where it would be. 'Mm-hum.' And if they had had it, it would have cost a dollar ninety-five—"

Giggling, Lolly joyfully put in, "But they didn't have it! So—"

"Right! You get the picture. I call it the shuffle because you stand on one foot, then kind of shuffle to the other."

Dobbs and Ritchie didn't seem amused, but Christy had to explain, "I guess I never noticed, growing up here, but the reason for what Mac calls the shuffle is probably that we are so isolated, not much happening. Any event becomes a big deal and needs to be told right. You add a little here, put on a bit there, turn the whole thing for another perspective, stand back and admire it—"

"Voilà!" Mac exclaimed, "The shuffle."

Whereupon, with all but the two men guests laughing, Christy felt forced to say, "But it's sad really."

Round-eyed, Tama asked, "What? Why sad?"

"I see new people coming in and they're still living in such a rush. They get an unspoken invitation to shuffle, though I never thought of it that way before, and blast on by without noticing. Lose some of the richness of life here." Memories flooded over Christy: neighbors waving, riding her bike on quiet country dirt roads....

Way to go, Christy. You managed to put a damper on that conversation. Now what? Better hope they haven't heard Mama's early Hometown News about La Doña shooting Kramer.

End of hope. Lisa was speaking: "...earphones when I was running. So what's going on with these murders and Satanic bull? I thought Taos was a haven of peace."

Mac came through, answering smoothly, "Oh, it seems wrapped up now. Back to our peaceful life. Our friend Doris Jordan accidentally shot a Stephen Kramer when he attacked her. He, in turn, admitted to having killed the poor man you heard about last week. End of story."

Thank God for Mac. The subject closed neatly.

No one said more. Duane Dobbs openly scrutinized her. Fred Ritchie, however, seemed oddly intent on his empty plate.

Christy's thoughts returned to last night and the need to get on with La Doña's problems. She pushed her chair back. "If you'll excuse me, I have a phone call to make." Christy stood up abruptly and left the room.

She dressed in jeans that were soft and pale blue from wear, a downy turquoise blue sweatshirt, and a flowered scarf containing the same shade of blue. Lucky even an attorney didn't have to dress up in Taos since she'd be seeing a variety of people professionally. First, arrange for Iggy at the hospital.

"Law office."

"Hi, Iggy. You beat the secretary in for once?"

"Not her day." He sounded grumpy, too.

Slightly uncomfortable, Christy offered, "I know I should have called you sooner, but no excuses. I guess you've heard the news?"

"Which news?" Iggy asked caustically. "Your client, La Doña, on national tv? Or my client calling me at home with reports of the shooting? About six this morning."

Damn! Now she'd have to smooth his feathers. "Pat Salazaar called you?"

He had, having heard the news of La Doña's escapade through Mama's grapevine. Christy apologized, then asked, "Tell me first what's on tv."

Iggy's tone returned to normal. "Lead off with desecrated morada ruins. Fade into old picture of The Lady accepting an award. Story is elderly attorney shoots Taos Satanic cult leader during wild midnight ride."

Christy's "Oh, Lord!" came out choked. Worse than she thought.

"Cool it, Christy," Iggy responded briskly. "Could have been worse, much worse. And think: if they're calling Kramer the Satanic leader, that clears your Brotherhood. Then, too, it makes La Doña look like a hero. But either the Chief or hospital sure has some answering to do. They leaketh. Now, do you want to give me the facts?"

She did.

"Then," Christy ended, "when Kramer lunged with a knife, she fired once across his prow and—"

"His what?"

"Prow, Iggy. Like a boat. Prow. The car crashed and she ran home. I got the call after midnight."

Disbelieving. "Damn! That wasn't on the news. Our seventy-five-year-old friend was sprinting through Taos at midnight? Oh, my God! How is she?"

"Not so good," Christy worried. "Mac got them to put her in the hospital. He says she'll be okay though. And you know how she brags about keeping fit, exercising."

"This is not a good presentation, counselor. You're leaving out essential parts. Your story sounds like that old shaggy dog joke that begins, 'The dogs are dead. Why? Well, they ate the burned horse meat.' Etcetera."

Christy was in no mood for this. "I'd have the story straight if you didn't keep interrupting! Now, listen." Christy summed up the case against La Doña as told by Chief Garcia. "So they say was no knife and La Doña simply shot the man."

"Ridiculous!"

Iggy's immediate response made Christy feel ashamed for lingering doubts. "You don't think she might have made a mistake?"

"One mistake, maybe. But if La Doña says that Kramer attacked her with a knife and that she did not shoot the man— well, then, that's what happened. Anything else?"

"The Chief was waiting for daylight to search the car thoroughly. Try to find the bullet that killed Kramer. Says he should be able to tell by looking if it came from La Dona's Luger. She still had the same ammunition her father had in it. I know because she told me one time when lecturing on the danger of hand guns."

"Looks like we have a lot to do. What are your plans?"

Christy explained she had to take the car to the shop and then wanted him to meet her at the hospital. Iggy agreed but asked if there would be any conflict in working together now that Christy represented La Doña.

Having already thought through this ethical question, Christy explained, "You want to prove Pat Salazaar didn't kill Eusebio. I need to prove La Dona's telling the truth, that Kramer did it. We're not likely to get into any ethical gray areas."

Feeling rushed, Christy asked Iggy to buy some papers on his way to the hospital.

Christy descended by way of the outside stairs to see if Mac had returned to the guest house after breakfast. She went slowly, enjoying the feel of the adobe stair wall under her hand, cold from the night before mixed with warming from the early sun.

The courtyard had drastically changed mood from this morning's chill wee hours. The flowers hadn't suffered from the cold, but were sprightly and bright. The cherry trees were beginning to lose their pale-pink blossoms to freshly green leaves. The deeper pink blooms of the ancient swamp willow looked very nice.

Her hunch was right. Mac answered her knock quickly. "I've been a grouch. Sorry, Mac."

"No problem. Any more news after Lisa's Satanic bombshell?"

Christy told Mac what she'd heard from Iggy wondering how the national news got on the story so quickly. He answered, "Probably hanging around hoping for more buckets of blood. You know this case has all the stuff the tabloids love and the networks report with regret."

Mac offered to take her to drop off the car, so Christy was soon slipping behind the wheel of the Buick with remembered fear. Someone had wanted her dead. Pray God that someone was Kramer.

Dan's Body Shop was only a short way down the Talpa Highway.

Dan himself, a slim young adult, came out to meet them; depressing to think he was the son of a high school friend. Talk about age! Aging. Ageism.

"Jeez! Miz Grant. What did you do to your Buick?"

"Some creep tried to run me off the road. This is what happens when you fight the horseshoe curve."

They both stood gazing at the poor Buick in the soft, early sun, and discussed repairs. As that conversational ball was batted back and forth and she shifted her weight from one foot to the other, Christy grinned. *This* was the norm and *this* was "the shuffle," but now, she was the one with no time. Iggy would be waiting at the hospital and she was anxious to see La Doña, so she had to end it with, "How long 'til you can check everything out?"

After another discussion, Christy joined Mac in the pick-up, smiling as she shared "the shuffle".

What a different drive at ten in the morning. Now the sun was out and Taos was wide awake. Taos bright and innocent was the reality. Dark and fearful journeys to jails and hospitals were the dream. That was it! The dream. The King was in her dream—

"We're here," Mac announced. No time to pursue the thought of kings. They were already in the parking lot in front of the new one-story hospital. A gaggle of people, obviously news crews, had video cams trained on the front of Holy Cross or each other. Reporters spoke into mikes. Others wandered about with their cellulars. The sight made her nervous. Would they pounce?

Apparently Christy was unrecognized. She and Mac were simply live bodies as news crews approached nonchalantly. Mac firmly pushed Christy through the jam and into the hospital.

Chipper little Mrs. Maestes was on duty as a volunteer receptionist, but showed no signs of resentment toward Christy's supposed penitente comment. She was quite pink with excitement. "Oh, Christy," she bubbled. "All these reporters! They wanted to see your friend, La Doña Abogada, but the nurses and doctors, you know, Doctor Site from the E.R. and La Dona's own Doctor Woods? They wouldn't let them in and had me call the police! The police, Christy. And Chief—"

Mac's hand was still pressing firmly on her back, so Christy said, "I'm sorry, I—"

"¡*Que lastima*! La Doña Abogada chased by a killer with a knife!" She brightened. "But I went back to see her and she seems just fine. Maybe a little grumpy? Ah, but who wouldn't be?"

Down the hall at the patients' wing, Bobby, the guard from last night, was on duty again, his stern mask relaxing as he recognized Christy and Mac. He moved aside and pushed open the doors for them. Once through, Mac strode ahead of her to the nurses' station. Talk about a difference, Christy thought. Mac was in his element here, courteous but commanding: the doctor on duty. Mac went behind the nurses' station, stood reading La Dona's chart. The nurses were taking the attitude that nothing exceptional was happening.

Christy asked, "Okay to go on back?" and received permission.

She had to check the doors again to find the right number, saw a group of elderly ladies surrounding a bed, too many to see the person on the bed. She stepped back to look at the number once more. 109. Right. She went on in.

Oh, Lord! From the door she had seen mainly backs. Now her eyes picked out one woman even smaller than the rest of the crowd. "Mama! What are you doing here?"

Looking only slightly flustered, a little pink, Mama said, "Buenos dias, Christina. We came to pay a visit to La Doña Abogada." Looking up at the television set mounted on the wall, she added, all innocence, "Now we see the news. Our Doña Abogada Señora Jordan is famous already!"

Christy looked around the circle of beaming faces. How could she be angry at them? Mama would be truly concerned about her friend but also guilty for having come sneaking over here to get all the details first hand. She obviously hadn't expected the tv bonus.

The other ladies had taken over the remote. Switching channels, they squealed with delight every time they saw a picture of their new hero. Although Christy herself was anxious to see how the story was being handled, hopefully with no repeat of her alleged "Catholic comment," her first concern was her friend.

La Doña was sitting much too erect but looking good. Her eyes were snapping, whether in anger or amusement Christy couldn't tell, but they were no longer dull.

"And good morning to you, Christina. How do you like my gown? The ladies brought it, and some other things I needed." La Doña was fully covered in a high-necked, long-sleeved blue flannel gown. It even sported a few ruffles. Her hair was back in its tidy bun. Both the bulging briefcase and big black purse rested beside her on the bed. Her hand held a newspaper. "Our town seldom makes the state news, never this. Take a look."

Apparently having had time for only a short item below the fold, the national paper still carried a small front-page story headlined: ATTORNEY SLAYS SATANIC MASTER!

As Christy tried to read the rest, Mac appeared at the door, stopped in mid-stride at the sight of the ladies. "What the...?"

"Good morning, Dr. McCloud. I'm entertaining."

"I see," he said wryly. "I know the Chief kept out the reporters, so what's all this? I thought I saw a sign limiting the number of visitors to a room."

Mama's circle of friends made little leaving noises, gathered up purses, began patting La Dona's hand, hugging Christy. "We'll see you." "I'll pray for you." "Take care." "We'll see you." And soon they were gone.

Mac was already taking La Dona's pulse, scolding. "Over-excited, eh?"

She gestured toward the television set, "Rather too many references to the attorney being elderly but after the unfortunate actions of the police last night, it is rather gratifying to hear one's self being described as an avenging angel."

Ignoring this, Mac fussed, "And that bed is wound up too high. I want you down and resting." Lowering the bed as he spoke, Mac asked, "Has Dr. Woods been by?"

"Yes, the old fool was in this morning. On his high horse. Lectured me. Said the E.R. called him last night. I suppose you put them up to that?"

"Dr. Site wanted the name of your family doctor. Christy supplied it. Your pulse is steady, a little rapid. Color's good. I don't like your eyes, though. Over-tired. Too much exertion."

"My eyes are just fine, thank you. And before you start some silly speech, I want to tell you that I have decided to remain a guest of Holy Cross for a while."

La Doña glared first at Mac, then at Christy who was looking concerned at this admission of weakness. The Lady held up a hand. "No. Not what you're thinking. I am perfectly fit. Always have been. I have simply determined that until Christina has all charges against me dismissed, Holy Cross is preferable to the Taos County Jail."

"Sensible lady!" Mac smiled at her. "I will be happy to oblige, tell the police that in my best medical judgment—"

"And you can wind me right back up, young man!"

Iggy rushed in, apologized for being late, explained that he'd picked up the papers, been waylaid by reporters, and finally came to a halt at the side of La Dona's bed. He looked at her carefully, then smiled in relief. "Well, you look fine to me, Miss Doris."

"I'm happy to hear that you approve, Ignacio. Have I called a meeting? What is all this?"

Mac squeezed the hand he'd been holding for her pulse. Christy came around the other side of the bed. Iggy stood at the end.

Mac explained he was here as her doctor, if unofficial in New Mexico, while Christy and Iggy told La Doña of their concern for her. They were all answered with a snort. Then, as usual, La Doña took command, demanding to know who had leaked the news. "Must have come from that cousin of yours, Christina!"

"Not Barnabe! Anyone could have overheard your story before I got to the jail."

"Humph. Not satisfactory. Now what have you accomplished on my behalf?"

Despite La Dona's testy comments, Christy told her the Chief's investigative plans. "If the thorough search of Kramer's car and the vicinity doesn't turn up the knife, I'll push finding it and the briefcase when we see the Chief later on."

"You're going with Ignacio? Is he assisting in my defense?"

Iggy answered for himself, "Yes, I am. Christy and I don't see any conflict in working together. But I'm not going to the Police Station. That will be Christy and Mac."

Christy pulled over a straight-backed hospital chair, metal with a gray plastic seat. She settled herself by the bed with her yellow legal pad and pen. "While last night is fresh in your mind, I need you to start at the beginning and give me all the details."

La Doña pushed herself more erect, away from the propping bed. Her eyes glinted, "You are taking my statement?"

"I certainly am," Christy answered crisply. "You've got yourself a defense lawyer."

Mac said, "I'm not sure," which made the contrary Lady immediately want to give a statement. "First, Dr. Kramer called to inquire about changes in the estate tax laws—"

"Now wait," Christy interrupted as the first of her planned questions came up. "I let it go last night, but why in the world would you go out with him? You already considered him a suspect!"

Looking just a touch embarrassed, La Doña explained, "You and Ignacio each had parts of the investigation to handle. I was...I, well...I determined that I could be a part of it by questioning Stephen. Draw the man out. See if he was involved or gave himself away. I never expected that I would provoke him into trying to run, and taking me with him."

Iggy interrupted. "Is that where the media got the Satanic crap, er, excuse me, La Doña."

She nodded regally. "In a later portion of my story, I mentioned to the boys in blue that Stephen Kramer was quite proud of himself for sneaking back to burn and desecrate the morada. One assumes a leak—"

Christy broke in impatiently, "A hostage? But why? I need your statement from the beginning."

"Christy!" La Doña said crossly, unaccustomed to being treated as a client.

"It's important, my friend. I can't have any holes in your story. There's a lot of explaining to be done."

La Doña sighed dramatically, but cooperated in giving a cohesive account until Christy stopped her with, "Wait. Why were you carrying a gun? And why not a cell phone?"

"Because I despise those self-important gadgets." She was not going to admit she couldn't really see to use the damn thing after dark. "And as for the gun, I put my father's pistol in my purse for the same reason that I often do—for protection."

"Not good enough. How frequently do you carry a gun when you're going out to dinner with a client?"

"As frequently as one is a suspect in a murder investigation!" La Doña snapped.

Mac noticed that La Doña was leaning back against the pillows now. "Is this too much? Should Christy wait until you're more rested?"

La Doña answered with a glare and turned back to Christy. "Go on."

Bit by bit they went through La Dona's account until they came to Kramer's pulling a knife. At this point, Christy asked for his exact words.

Sitting bolt upright again, The Lady spoke precisely. "I do not know his exact words, Missy. The man was driving like a lunatic, threatening to kill me as he did Eusebio. 'Bitch' and 'silly old cow' come to mind. I was not taking notes on his conversation!"

Mac said, "Maybe you should take a break, Doris. I don't want you tiring yourself out."

"I am not tired. I am angry."

Christy and Iggy exchanged a look and it was he who asked, "Can you remember any reasons Kramer gave for killing Eusebio? That will help Pat's case enormously, La Doña."

Mollified, La Doña repeated Kramer's murderous story, then commented, "The Satanic symbols were only a smoke screen devised after the stabbing. He appeared to find it quite clever. Apparently, my comments on the latter were what aroused the media.

"Stephen himself only made up his mind to kidnap me at dinner. His prior choice had been murder! But he decided we, our team, were getting too close, safest to take me hostage. Besides, he thought I'd told you of the meeting, and he could buy no time by killing me."

Christy had written as fast as possible. Now she shook her aching hand. "Is that when you brought out the gun? And again I'm asking you to remember what Stephen said or did to provoke that response."

La Doña explained the sequence, but Iggy couldn't restrain himself. "So, if by then you had a gun on him and he was heading back to Taos, how did he come to threaten you with a knife?"

"The Maalox you people found so amusing. I was dealing with a madman, mumbling, carrying on. He turned at the Placitas light. Not sedately. Then he suddenly threw the open Maalox on my lap. Christy, will you see about the cleaners? I don't want that stain to set in my good silk suit."

La Doña waited for Christy's nod. "I glanced down, the knife came out, and you know the rest."

Leaning back complacently, she clasped her hands on top of the covers.

Mac had been watching his patient anxiously. "That's fine, Doris. We'll leave you now." He walked over to Christy.

Iggy risked another question, "You didn't take his briefcase with you when you ran?"

"I took nothing but my own purse and gun, both of which I was holding. Apparently, in the, uh, excitement, I had never properly closed my purse. The police found my billfold. They commandeered the gun when they came to the house. And, once again, the rest you know. If not, read the papers!" She lay back against the bed, this time closing her eyes.

Christy said gently, "Something else, La Doña, and then we'll let you rest. I need to tell Chief Garcia where you were when Eusebio was killed, and also the Saturday that Watkins was shot."

Eyes open and angry. "Do they think I'm some mass murderer, roaming Taos with knife and gun?"

Christy refused to be irritated. "La Doña, please."

Heavy sigh. "Very well. Thursday night I attended a gallery opening in Santa Fe. It had some typically ridiculous name, ah, the Laughing Frog, I believe. Wouldn't have gone but a young friend of mine, Paul Alvarez, was the featured artist."

"And Saturday?"

La Doña was lying back, eyes closed again. "Saturday? Um, let me think. Dinner with friends. The Delaneys. I am sure they will substantiate my presence. Alibi, I believe you call it."

Christy felt too sorry for her friend to react to the sarcasm. "Thank you, La Doña. We'll talk to the Chief. Have this cleared up in no time."

Worried that the session had taken too much energy, Mac turned to caution his patient, but said nothing. The old warrior was asleep.

CHAPTER XXV

Leaving La Dona's hospital room, Christy's and Mac's first concern was to make it past the remaining bored reporters. Their numbers had dwindled, many rushing off to find a new twist, maybe another Satan slayer.

Once in the pick-up, Mac saw how tired Christy looked. Normally he liked that turquoise top on her, made her eyes look greener. But these weren't normal times and her eyes were blood-shot, her usually golden skin, sallow.

If La Doña was to be believed, an unknown assailant had shot Kramer. Was Christy a danger to someone else? Didn't bear thinking about. Lucky Christy's car was going to be in the shop a while. That meant he could stick close driving her around.

He'd used his medical credentials last night to see the body. Kramer had been shot behind the ear, not a logical place for Doris Jordan's bullet even if she had aimed at the man.

Christy watched Mac as he became lost in thought. She was lucky to have him in her life, despite his becoming a little overprotective at times.

First she wanted to find out how far the Chief had progressed, and, most importantly, that La Doña's gun had not killed Kramer. Next, clear the underbrush by proving La Doña's whereabouts at the times of the two murders. The pressure was on.

At the police station, Louisa again greeted them at the counter. They did the routine, then Louisa said, "The Chief's a little grouchy, just threw out some reporters, but said he thought you'd be coming in, Miz Grant. Told me to bring you straight on back."

Christy's stomach roiled around in nervousness even though she reminded herself it was just primo Barnabe she was seeing. However, Barnabus himself didn't help by acting more officially The Chief as he rose and came around his desk to meet them.

Christy sensed that each of them was eager to get past the minuet of greetings required in Taos, but they still went through it. Finally everyone was seated, coffee had been offered and refused, and it was time for business.

"Just want you to know there were no leaks from this office," Chief Garcia announced grimly.

Christy nodded, all business, too, and asked bluntly, "Did you find the bullet?"

The Chief's expression was solemn, "I'm afraid so, Christina."

Oh-oh. Her heart began to beat faster. "And?"

"We first had to tow the government car to our lot. This my men did as soon as possible. They could not search until we had it here."

He didn't want to tell her bad news. "Please, Primo!"

Chief Garcia was not to be hurried. "When they had good light, the officers commenced a thorough search. They began where the likely trajectory would have taken a bullet."

Restrain yourself, Christy. Don't yell at the man.

"Therefore, they looked first at the driver's door. It had been crushed when Doctor Kramer hit the railroad tie on the embankment of the Lilac Shop."

Now! Now!

"Officer Marks was successful. He found a bullet embedded in the door on the driver's side." The Chief sighed. "I have already explained to you that one cannot be positive without ballistics, but ballistics will do no good for this one. The bullet, passing through the victim's head, struck hard metal on the door, then buried itself in the upholstery, having spent itself by then. No other bullet."

"Barnabe!"

"Yes, Prima. I know. Your friend. And I like to call her mine, also. I am sorry to say that this bullet could well be a nine millimeter, the size for the Luger, but it's unidentifiable in its flattened condition." He sighed and leaned back in the creaking chair.

Christy's hands were wet, her heart beating heavily in her chest, but she focused sharply. "There must be more! Are they still searching? If this was the bullet from the Luger, then there's another bullet in that car. Or outside, in the bank, maybe."

The Chief shook his head sadly. "I'm sorry. The driver's window was broken, but in place. And raised. No bullet passed through it." Before Christy could voice her challenge, the Chief continued, "They search still, but we have found the bullet. La Doña Abogada is old. She was frightened. I am sure she thinks she is telling us the truth, but no—"

Mac, an outsider, risked breaking in. "You know I'm a physician, Chief Garcia. No expert in guns. But I wonder two things. First, if the bullet passed through Kramer's head, it surely had blood and brains on it. Secondly, if it didn't and was in the condition you say, how can you be so close to certain it killed Kramer? Why not assume that it was the one La Doña shot and missed?"

Christy looked at Mac gratefully. He was taking the position of "second chair" in a trial, allowing her to regroup.

The Chief shook his head again. "The trajectory was right. A nine millimeter does not make a large exit wound. The door and window were bloody."

"The bullet, Chief?" Mac pressured.

The chair creaked forward. Chief Garcia shifted position. "Ah. We are uncertain as to the matter on the bullet, but remember, it had passed through the upholstery on the door. Small and crushed, there's no reason the bullet should have more than a minuscule amount of blood on it. The crime lab in Albuquerque can tell us."

Christy had grown angry at her favorite cousin. She felt as she did when she had a hostile witness on the stand. She spoke sharply. "What kind of door is it?"

"What kind?" The Chief sounded puzzled, frowned at Christy.

"Yes," Christy responded quickly. "Is it fabric, leather, what?"

"A soft fabric. Stitched in rows, you know?" Chief Garcia responded slowly.

"And the condition of the door at present?"

"Christina, Christina," the Chief complained.

"Condition," Christy rapped out.

"Well, I told you that side of the car hit the railroad tie. The door is what you might call buckled up, bent."

"On the inside also?"

"Yes, yes, of course," the Chief grew grumpy at all these questions fired at him from his beloved prima.

"Then," Christy's trial self had taken over, "I suggest that your men may well have overlooked the second bullet which, unlike La Doña's bullet, did pass through Kramer's head. If the second bullet was also a small caliber, it stands to reason it would leave a small hole burying itself in the fabric."

Christy continued to bore in. "You gestured, indicating the stitching was up and down, something like a quilted pattern?"

Beginning to look disturbed, Chief Garcia simply nodded.

"All the more likely that the bullet hole is out of sight in crumpled, quilted folds. And that other bullet is bloody!"

"Have you completed your cross- examination, Counselor?"

Christy could feel Mac trying to catch her eye, slow her down. She refused to look at him, "No, I have not finished, Primo Barnabe. The life of a fine, respected attorney, a Taos treasure, is at stake here. You find one bullet and take the easy out. Blame it on La Doña Abogada, say that she's just a poor vieja. I say it's time to tell those officers of yours to bust ass finding a second bullet, one that does have blood and brains on it. And you get that first one down to Albuquerque pronto!"

Chief Garcia was breathing heavily. He controlled himself as he asked, "Have you finished giving directions to my men? And me? Is there anything else mi prima bonita would care to tell the Taos Police Department to do?"

Before Christy could reply, Mac spoke up. "What about that place up there at La Mesa? I think you said it's an old gold mine?"

Both combatants glared at him.

Mac forged ahead. "I think we kicked around the notion that it might be a secret laboratory? Well, Chief, I don't want to interfere—"

"Hah!"

"But here you have three Los Alamos people, all scientists. All needing a place to work. Stephan Kramer told La Doña that he had made advanced discoveries in his lab, a top secret lab. Could it be at the old gold mine? Would you think it was a good idea to proceed with your previous plans? The raid on the mine?"

Gruff but cooling down, the Chief muttered, "Kramer's dead."

"Well, yes, Chief Garcia, but what would you have to lose? If La Dona's story is accurate as to Kramer's confession, that's where they've all been working. You just might find what you need to help everyone close the files on Salazaar and Watkins!"

"But, she—"

Mac kept right on talking persuasively. "Right! And if she's not telling it straight—" He heard an objection from Christy, ignored it—"you might actually make a big drug bust anyway."

He sat back beaming.

Christy raised her eyebrows at the Chief.

Both she and Mac held their breaths.

"Whatever my cousin thinks, nothing would make me happier than proof Miss Jordan is telling the truth. I think you've made a good point, doctor. I will look into proceeding with the raid. As I explained before, it will take coordination with other law enforcement. That will take time." He braced, expecting an outburst from Christy.

Instead, although still quite pink on the cheeks, Christy beamed upon Chief Garcia and said, "Thank you, Primo."

The chief stood up. Christy and Mac rose, too. Christy had something to add but hesitated for fear of causing another flare-up, "I believe Stephen Kramer may have been living in Taos? Near here anyway."

"Yes?"

"Has his place been found?"

"Yes, he had one of those new condominiums out past the old blinking light on the way to La Mesa." He added gently, "We did find that out, Cousin."

Christy didn't rise to the bait. "I wonder if that condo has been searched. We do know he always carried his briefcase." She swallowed. "Whether or not it was in the car."

"I'll keep that in mind."

Christy kept smiling. "Thanks again, Primo Barnabe."

They left.

Silence across the parking lot and as they got into Mac's pick-up.

Silence as he made the turn and started back down Pueblo Norte.

As usual, Christy was drained after the adrenaline rush she got from cross-examining.

"Was that your courtroom style back there?" he asked. "I've never seen it, you know."

"Only partly. I was angry and it never helps to actually lose your temper in court, although the pretense may aid the cause. But it gives the other attorney an advantage if you really lose your cool." Pause. "And I did lose mine, didn't I?"

"Just a mite. But I think the Chief will follow through. You made your point and I think Chief Garcia will institute a more thorough search."

"And the raid on Los Piñones?" she wondered aloud.

"Yep. Think he'll do that, too. Now, try to stop thinking about all this. We'll have a bite to eat, take a nap...."

"And tomorrow is another day." She grinned at him.

"Home, Miss Scarlet?"

"Home."

Christy didn't want to eat out anywhere and have to speak to people, preferring to go straight home, check on Desire and the status of her guests, and then take some time for herself.

She came on through from the kitchen and stopped short at the sight that met her eyes.

Desire was a Western vision from high-heeled white boots up to the calf, to a white felt cowboy hat. It hung down her back from the white leather throng around her neck, leaving her long blonde hair to tumble at will.

Desire beamed at Christy. "You're looking at my outfit, Miz Grant, aren't you? Don't I look good?"

"You look very pretty, Desire. Any new reservations?"

"Well, in a way. That nice Mr. Dobbs, he goes, I look good enough to eat...he says he planned to check out this morning."

"Damn! I forgot to ask," Christy grumbled.

"Yes, ma'am. Well, Mr. Dobbs says business has forced him to stay over.' I got that right, hunh? He goes be sure and tell you exactly."

No end to Dobbs. "Yes, Desire. Any other messages?" Christy asked, feeling rushed. She wanted to take a quick nap and then get some writing done.

Nothing crucial in the way of calls; just a reminder of the Chamber dinner.

Gratefully, Christy headed through La Sala toward the spiral stairs. Oh, to get to sleep!

Just before Christy drifted off to sleep, she tried to empty her mind of all the squirrel-caging concerns by focusing on the brilliant cloudless blue sky. She woke to the dark grayness of a heavy rain storm. New Mexico's typical quick-change weather.

Perfect weather for writing and she was fresh enough to make the chapter changes on the computer before dressing for the Chamber dinner and still have time to visit with any guests who might happen to be at home. Felt guilty about the trio. She hadn't been here to give them the attention she usually gave guests. Fred Ritchie, too, although he probably wouldn't have been around anyway. He and Duane Dobbs remained nearly invisible.

No jeans and sneakers tonight. What about the slim blue silk? That and her 'liquid silver' necklace, and the earrings from Zuni, tiny copies of the rainbow man.

Downstairs, the trio came into the Middle Room just as Christy reached it. They were laughing from running through the downpour, Lolly struggling to lower her giant red umbrella to get through the door.

"Where should I put this dripping thing?"

"Just stick it there in the corner, Lolly. Your umbrella won't hurt the floor." Then Christy included all of them as she asked, "Would you like to come into La Sala and sit for a while? Have a drink. Tell me about your day."

That seemed to please them and soon all were in La Sala. Christy squatted down to light the fire against the chill. As the fire caught, Christy stood and looked around the room. Soft lamp light and firelight reflected on polished wood. Homey. Comfortable.

Mac came in, stopped a moment at the sight of Christy, then moved quickly to her side. "Killer dress! Beautiful," he murmured for her alone to hear.

She answered, "Pretty fine yourself, sir." And he was looking handsome in a soft tan jacket over a blue shirt that made his eyes bluer still. Mac also wore a bolo inset with obsidian, coral, and mother of pearl, made in the Zuni way like her earrings.

Mac smiled at the others, asked if he could get anyone anything. At their "No thank you," he folded himself onto the low banco by the fireplace.

Christy joined Tama on the plump love seat. Lolly and Lisa had relaxed in the cushiony armchairs, their feet up on the ottomans.

"We went to Chimayo, like you suggested?" Tama said. "It was so spiritual, you know?"

"Such a gorgeous day! Well, to start with," Lisa added wryly. "We decided to make the drive, rather than wait til the trip back to Albuquerque."

It seemed strange to hear guests going about the ordinary tourist things while so much else was happening. Christy couldn't shake the shadows that overlay their casual chatting.

Thunder boomed dramatically.

Lisa's rather brusque voice was wondering as she commented, "You have so much here in New Mexico! No wonder your license tags say land of enchantment!"

Christy liked that. "It's a lot of things. Our immense sky, somehow a different ratio than elsewhere, more sky than earth. The stars so bright and close at night.

"It's the Indians praying the sun up and praying to keep the earth alive. It's them still walking this earth, both dead and alive. And their sacred Blue Lake in Taos Mountain.

"It's the shadow of the cross, not just in paintings but a shadow on the land. And our smells and bells.

"It's joy and anger, too. The anger of both Indian and Spanish activists. And rocks called Apache Tears. And the clarity of the light...." Embarrassed now, Christy looked around the group. "Excuse me. Sometimes I get carried away."

They all made little supportive noises and Mac eased her tension by saying, "No one faults you, even if we don't fully understand." He stood and offered Christy his arm, "And now, my lady, I think it's time we said our good-byes. The Chamber awaits us."

Christy took Mac's proffered arm, but couldn't shake the premonition that with Stephen Kramer's death the waking nightmare, begun Good Friday, was reaching its crisis like an illness.

Chapter XXVI

Christy spent a restless night, her thoughts gnawing at the deaths: Eusebio Salazaar, Bryce Watkins, Stephen Kramer. She was especially bothered by questions. Who had killed Dr. Kramer since La Doña surely didn't? Was she, Christy, still a threat to someone?

At least nothing impeded her plans for a trip to Santa Fe. Breakfast passed quickly, no story telling today! And this was one of the days for her housekeeper, Ellie, so she could leave the phone to Desire—along with a lot of hope!

Christy dressed for Santa Fe in a favorite longish full skirt from Taos' own Desert Designs. It was patterned in unusual desert shades of browns and blues. She wore the matching shirt like a jacket over a cool short-sleeved cream knit, slipped on sandals, and was ready to interview the gallery owner. She could wait until later, here in Taos, to run down the featured artist, Paul Alvarez, along with La Dona's dinner hosts. Right now it was best to confirm La Dona's alibi with the impartial owner of the Laughing Frog.

The morning sun lay warmly on the landing and picked out bits of glitter in the adobe of the staircase. Lower down, most of the courtyard was still in shadow. The sun wasn't yet high enough for its rays to reach over Casa Vieja.

Mac didn't seem to be in his little guest house, so Christy checked the kitchen. Her helper Ellie was already busy. Ellie's flat Slavic face beamed as she came in. "Now don't you look nice! Where are you going?"

"Thank you, Ellie. I'm off to Santa Fe today." Christy smiled at the compliment and question. Typical Taos. If she happened to be dressed in something other than jeans and a sweatshirt when she went to the grocery, the friendly check-out clerks always wanted to know where she was going.

Christy asked about Ellie's large extended family, just as Mac came through from the Middle Room.

"Doesn't she just look pretty as a picture, Doctor?" Ellie asked proudly.

"That she does," Mac answered. Then, "Ready?"

"Let me grab a Pepsi and ice and we're off."

Once they were outside, Mac looked at the hacienda's small parking lot and commented, "All guest cars gone. I wonder what those two gentlemen really do all day. Maybe they have a secret rendezvous somewhere every morning."

As she settled into the pick-up, Christy answered, "According to Dobbs' second version of the facts, he's out chasing druggies in Los Alamos for the D.O.D."

"Do you believe that?" Mac asked as he pulled into the narrow dirt road.

"Oh, Mac, I don't know. And then there's Fred Ritchie. He really has me baffled."

"The invisible man. Bland. No personality."

Christy nodded in agreement, then changed the subject so they'd head the right way. "If it's okay with you, I'd like to stop by Holy Cross and see La Doña before we go to Santa Fe." She hesitated. "And something else on the way. I'll tell you later." She could just imagine Mac's reaction when she said they had an appointment with a brujo!

The reporters had deserted the hospital, so Christy and Mac were able to breeze in with no interruptions. At the nurses' station, Mac stopped, as before, to check La Dona's chart while Christy went on ahead.

La Doña called out from a chair by the bed, "No need to be peeking in Christina, no reporters and your mama and the ladies have already come and gone. And look here. They brought me lovely bouquets from their gardens."

Only slightly ashamed to be flowerless, Christy entered. "You're looking great!"

"Back to my old self," La Doña replied. "However, I am unaccustomed to receiving guests in gown and robe."

"That elegant outfit deserves a fancier name." Christy admired the heavy satin Chinese kimono: deep red with an embroidered gold dragon on the back. Her old mentor had unexpected aspects to her personality.

Mac and Iggy entered at the same time, Iggy in a rush as usual. "Wanted to catch you guys all together," he said breathlessly. "I tried to see Kramer's girlfriend, Debbie Valdez, yesterday but of course she didn't go to work, Kramer having been shot. Probably a good thing I couldn't call either. From what you said, the poor kid was awfully broken up."

"You're right, Iggy. It's better for you to see Debbie today," Christy agreed.

La Doña wasn't to be left out. "I assume you intend to confirm my story that Stephen said he had sold his research for millions?"

Iggy answered apologetically, "Well, yes, La Doña. We believe you, but if he let anything slip to Debbie, why, all the better."

Mac took La Dona's pulse, listened to her heart, looked her over. "I saw Doctor Woods' entry for this morning on your chart. He thinks you're in good shape."

"Too good," La Doña snapped. "I had to convince Henry that I needed continued bed rest. Eventually he seemed to understand that jail was bad for my health! And now that I also have notoriety," she added sourly, "it's best that I conceal myself behind the hospital wardens."

"Treating you all right here?" Mac asked in his professional voice.

"Nursing good. Food bad."

"Otherwise?"

"Otherwise, young man, I am bored out of my socks. There's only so much I can accomplish from a hospital bed."

"You need to rest. You've been through a stressful experience. Take some time off. Enjoy yourself."

"Humph! Well...I do have my secretary coming over. She'll bring my docket list and calendar. I'll make a few calls."

Mac shook his head and grinned at her, then turned to Christy. "Isn't it about time we headed for Santa Fe?"

La Doña gave her a steely look. "My alibi?"

"Your alibi," Christy answered firmly.

Iggy drove his Chrysler Imperial directly from Holy Cross to the Plaza. No time to start an opera. Have to make do with a spot of chamber music.

At not yet ten o'clock, the tourists weren't out in force. There were a few of the usual disappointed early birds, peering wistfully in windows, wondering why no one was around to take their money. That left a parking place in front of his second floor office.

Iggy walked across the end of the central square, aiming toward where Christy had told him she found the Pink Coyote. Sure enough, there was the too-cute sign and a very attractive young woman just unlocking the door. Her beauty was slightly marred by the puffiness of her eyes. This must be Debbie.

"Hi, there. I'm Ignacio Baca," he said, putting on an enthusiastic front.

Debbie's smile was not a happy one. She greeted Iggy automatically, then became suspicious. "Are you the police? They've already taken my statement. That was after they made me identify...." Her lip quivered and she choked up.

"Oh, please don't cry," Iggy wailed, flapping his hands, wishing he could make that pretty face smile.

His reaction surprised Debbie out of her tears. "Well, are you?"

"Police? No, I'm a lawyer representing your friend Pat Salazaar. Can we go inside the shop?"

Debbie looked at him doubtfully, taking in not only the bulk of him inside an extra-large crimson silk shirt, but the huge jeans that would look like a tent if hung out to dry.

Iggy had thought maybe Debbie's look was because he was defending Salazaar. But, once inside, he understood it was because of his size. The place was so tiny, so filled with every imaginable sort of coyote that Iggy was afraid to move from where he stood just inside the door.

Debbie walked behind the counter. Iggy sidled over, hoping his backside wouldn't knock over a coyote.

"I know that Stephen, Dr. Kramer, did not kill Eusebio. I couldn't love a man who would do that," she announced belligerently.

"No, of course not," Iggy soothed. "I'm so sorry this happened to you."

Slightly mollified, Debbie asked, "Then what do you want?"

Iggy held up his yellow pad with one hand, "Just to have you tell me a little bit about Stephen Kramer..." Debbie started to protest, but Iggy overrode her. "Now don't get upset. You see a friend of mine was arrested—"

"The old lady who shot Stephen," Debbie said angrily. "It was even on the tv!"

Tugging nervously at his rat tail, Iggy explained, "Well, that's the problem, Debbie. We think someone else shot him and you can help us find out who it was." Stay away from Kramer's confession.

Debbie's dark eyes examined him intently. "The cop said—"

"Let's not worry about what the cops believe. Let's just see what we can figure out, okay?"

Debbie was looking at him dubiously, but Iggy proceeded. "First, tell me how you met Stephen." Iggy spoke gently and was soon leading Debbie through the questions. Luckily, every time she began to get tearful remembering Stephen, a tourist or two would wander in, making Debbie force control on herself. The trouble was that these interruptions extended the time it took to get her statement. A lot of weight on Iggy's feet. And still no admission from Debbie as to any of Dr. Kramer's plans.

At nearly eleven, he said, "Look, we're about done and I'm awfully tired of standing. Couldn't we have a cup of coffee or something?"

Debbie polished a smudge off the glass counter. "I can't leave the shop."

"Surely the owner wouldn't mind if you took just a little break. Please? My feet?" Iggy looked pitiful.

Debbie smiled. "Well, maybe five minutes." She turned the sign to CLOSED and set the other one to BACK IN FIVE MINUTES.

They walked the short way to the Apple Tree Restaurant and entered its pleasant dimness leading to the outside patio down the hall. It was a little chilly this early. Plastered walls were hung with original paintings. Since the booths were too tight for Iggy, they sat at a table. When the waitress came, Iggy decided one of their pastries wouldn't be out of order. Debbie only wanted coffee despite his urging to have something more.

"Now." He spoke around the first scrumptious mouthful, while, at the same time he tried to make room for his yellow pad amid the cup, plate, glass and utensils. "You were telling me that Stephen said you would take a vacation?"

She nodded, the tears welling in her eyes again.

"Do you know where the money was coming from?"

She looked away.

"Debbie?" Iggy cajoled.

"Well," Debbie ran her finger around the rim of her cup. "He made a lot working for Los Alamos. Stephen was a doctor, a Ph.D., you know. He was thinking of retiring, not just a vacation."

"Yes, I know. But most scientist don't make huge incomes." Now Debbie watched her spoon as she stirred her black coffee. "Debbie?" Iggy gently urged. "Did Stephen have money of his own? Come into an inheritance?"

She shook her head, still looking down.

"Did you suspect he was making extra money?"

"Stephen was such a brilliant man!" she answered fiercely. "They didn't appreciate him at Los Alamos! They let him set up a secret lab but that was just for their project. AIDS something." She clamped her lips shut.

Iggy tried gentle persuasion. "If Stephen told you not to tell anyone, he wouldn't care now, would he?" Shaking her head, she wouldn't look at him. "A genius. Did he discover something very special?"

Debbie exclaimed, "I *tell* you I don't know! He didn't tell me anything! All I know is that we went out that first night and was he ever excited! About to explode! He couldn't even tell me, it was so secret. But later, he said it was all his! He did all the work! He was the one with the brains! It was his, and he was going to sell his own research."

Thank God! At least close to confirming La Dona's story! "Debbie?" Iggy asked. "Do you like opera?"

Mac was aware of the tension in the Chevy as they headed down into the first curve of the horseshoe. Reading Christy's mind he said, "It's only natural that you feel nightmarish seeing this place again. Anyone would. I do."

"Thanks, Mac," she said, gritting her teeth as they drove past the low metal railing barricading the drop-off. Her body remembered gripping the wheel, wrenching, alternatively braking and accelerating, the awful impact of the big car against hers, the sound of the long grinding screech. And the evil behind it. Someone trying to kill her.

Farther on, Mac's voice brought her out of it: "Now how do you like that?" Mac read the sign. YACHT CLUB? Is that for the rafters?"

Mac was trying, but, caught up in anxiety, Christy answered shortly, "Yes, I think so. Down below here is one of the major put-in points. They ride the white water from Pilar through what's called the box."

She abruptly added, "We have to turn off here." As Mac braked and glanced over at her in surprise, she explained with some embarrassment, "We, uh, I have an appointment with a brujo." Mac stopped the car on the shoulder. He gazed incredulously at her, then reacted as expected: a torrent of words to the effect that he wouldn't be a party to any such thing, was disappointed in her, and no way was he driving to any witch's house!

Christy let Mac object strenuously, then said, "No, please, Mac. Keep on down this road. It's okay. I haven't flipped out. I'm just getting what you could call an expert opinion."

"But La Doña said…"

"I know," Christy answered. "But I have to check."

Having had his say, Mac shook his head, but followed Christy's directions to a small pink house tucked in a fold of the hill away from the river. They pulled up on the dirt road in front.

Feeling sharp electric nerve charges, Christy got out of the car and opened the little slatted wooden gate. Her apprehension built as she walked up the white gravel path, Mac behind her.

The front door opened. A short balding man stood there. He was dressed in a three-piece brown business suit, the vest tight across his medicine-ball belly.

"I am Señor Andelmo Ortiz," he announced formally. "And you are?"

Talk about misconceptions! Astounded, Christy formally introduced herself and Mac, and Señor Ortiz ushered them inside. Looking like a pouter pigeon, he bustled ahead of them down a short hall. Already more relaxed, Christy and Mac were shown into the brujo's office where he took a seat behind a lovely old carved wooden desk. Ortiz gestured for Christy and Mac to take the clients' chairs in front of the desk. Mac perched his lanky frame on the very edge, ready to bolt.

"Now," Señor Ortiz addressed Christy briskly, "I understand you do not want to know if someone has put a hex on you, nor do you seek the name of your enemy."

Christy was still dumbstruck. Finally, she managed to get out a "No. I—"

"I wouldn't tell you anyway," the man said with a sharp look. "If you knew, you might seek revenge. There are, however, many ways to find out if you have been hexed."

"Yes, Mr. Ortiz. But I wanted your advice only."

He made a clicking sound with his tongue, disapproving of this departure from convention. "The advice you seek is not one of my usual services." He held up a hand as Christy was about to speak. "I will answer, however. The signs on the morada were not done by a brujo or even a group of brujos. We do not do that sort of thing. The hex balls?" He smiled tightly. "The ones you found are worthless."

How did he know about the little clay balls? That was one of many questions jamming Christy's mind, but she found that she was already being told the fee. She fumbled for the money and was hustled out. As they started down the path, Señor Ortiz called after them, "Come back and we will discuss more important personal matters. I have clients to see now."

Once in the car, Christy and Mac looked at one another and shook their heads. Mac whistled softly and said, "Never in all my born days would I have guessed that's what a witch looks like. Or that *anyone* would ever get me in spittin' distance of one!"

Laughing from a combination of relief, let-down and surprise, Christy answered, "Nor I, Doctor, nor I. And I'm a native."

"Will this put to rest any lingering doubts you had about Satanism?" Mac asked.

Christy considered. "I set it up before La Doña's escapade. Now we know the witchcraft wasn't traditional." Christy felt the menace return and fell silent.

They were in the part of the canyon where the rock on one side was a pink that edged from darker shades of rose to rust and sienna. Pinon, juniper, and red cedar found every stray pocket of soil in which to grow, sometimes singly, sometimes clumped. Across the river, above the old Chile Line railroad bed, there was an occasional gentle slope in the steepness. Still-bare deciduous trees took advantage of these places, and also grew on the few visible little beaches. At this hour of the morning, the sun only found that side, highlighting the spring-fed green meadows, and seeming to pick out each individual rock. Only here, in the canyon, was the vast New Mexico sky not a presence.

Taking the curves of the canyon smoothly and obviously wanting to stay clear of any brujo discussion, Mac asked about the flower-decked crosses they had passed. "I think that's three I've seen," he said. "I've always wondered about them, but never remembered when I was with someone who could tell me."

"They're called *descansos* and that means a stopping or resting place, like a cemetery. Someone died there in a traffic accident, so family and friends put up the crosses to mark the spot where the soul left the body. They bring flowers." And thanks to God there wasn't going to be a descanso in memory of where she went off the horseshoe.

Christy continued, preferring this kind of memory. "In the old days the men carried the coffin from the church to the camposanto. They would have to stop to rest now and then and would mark where they put the casket down. Like I said, descanso, a stopping or resting place."

The road took them near the Rio Grande, the river beginning to swell now with the annual run-off. Christy mentally ticked off the next melodious towns: Rinconada where the view opened up, Embudo with its cross high on a crag...

The cottonwoods grew close, branching green across the road. With the river up, light rose swamp willows had their feet in the water. Pink apple blossom and white pear bloomed in the orchards. Christy smiled in delight. They had met late spring coming north up the river valley.

Mac broke the comfortable silence. "Despite all the hassles we won't discuss, you do seem to enjoy getting back in harness again."

"Yes," Christy answered slowly. "Oh, not the death of poor Eusebio or Watkins. I'm even sorry about Kramer. But I like putting a case together, piecing the puzzle."

"Why quit the law then?"

"Writing is my first love now. The rest? I told you when I jumped on my soap box the other night."

"Really? Surely it's more than that Albuquerque five that I recall pissed you off?"

"Yes, it's more," Christy answered. "They're just part of the attitude, maybe worse than some, the hired guns primed to beat out the other side, no matter what's fair or right. Or how it's done. Intimidate. Throw an avalanche of paper work. Wear down plaintiffs already broke from medical bills and loss of jobs." Christy could hear her voice growing angry, but couldn't stop. "They justify their actions as doing their best for their client, but that's not it. They take pride in a win at any cost and care nothing for an equitable resolution!"

Turning on the radio to a mellow Albuquerque FM station, Mac said, "I didn't mean to upset you."

Recognizing, and a little irritated by the attempt to soothe her, Christy controlled her voice. "There's more. I've represented so many people who couldn't afford a lawyer. They had been wronged and I couldn't just turn them away. Like the poor character who kicks in a cigarette machine and gets sent up for two-to-ten with an appointed attorney. Compare him to the white-collar executive who steals millions and gets off with the best of defense lawyers.

"I've stood next to the desperate ones, Mac, and smelled, really smelled, the fear. And there are so many hurt by the system! I can't represent them all and I'm worn out. I'd rather write."

Mac took one hand from the wheel to give her shoulder a squeeze.

"Sorry," Christy said. "I wasn't yelling at you, just upset. I keep apologizing to you. It seems like my buttons get pushed too easily these days."

"Medicine's the same," Mac answered. "I wasn't able to help everyone who needed me. I can understand your feelings." Mac's voice tightened as he had to slow down for an out-of-state car constantly braking ahead of them. He could see a procession behind him in the rearview mirror.

Christy grinned. "You can take him in Velarde. That's always been our theme song through the canyon, 'Take him in Velarde.'"

Before Velarde, Christy gazed at flat high mesas stretched against the vast blue sky and imagined looking up to see rows of Indian hunters, warriors, outlined there. To the left the canyon walls held huge tumbled volcanic rocks, so dark as to be nearly black.

Velarde was a tiny town of fruit stands and wonderful apple orchards. They were already pinker, touched with more of the season than Rinconada had been. Distant catalpas showed off with a green so vivid as to be electric. Globe willows showed chartreuse.

Noting tourist shops, Mac said, "Will you look at that orange job!" Then added, "Oh-oh! Did I push another button?"

Christy grinned at him. "Nope. I'm ambivalent like so many in Ranchos and Taos. I'm in the tourist business after all. I guess I just wish we were back to barter. You shoe my horse and I'll cut your hay. The Anglos brought in cash and the system crashed."

Mac sounded a little testy as he asked, "Then I should just quietly fade away?"

Christy smiled, shaking her head at him. "No. No, Mac. I'm not against new people. Not at all. I just don't want everything to cost so much, including taxes. It's awful for our old ones and driving our young people away. Look at Santa Fe. The joke is, 'If

you have to work in Santa Fe, you can't afford to live there.'
That's not very funny."

Miles of beautiful, mostly open land stretched between
Española and Santa Fe. The skin of the desert showed through
its skimpy covering of blue grama and sage-green buffalo grasses.
Richer, darker greens dotted the pointillist painting created
from the vegetation. Sandstone buttes, carved by wind and
erosion, shaped into castles and spires and organ pipes, rose
into the blue sky, so much sky!

As they neared Santa Fe, Christy suggested, "You're going
to need to turn left up ahead, take the cut-off to downtown,"

Glancing right, Mac said, "Always planned to come out here to
the opera, but we never did."

"I always do, too," Christy answered. "And look at me, a
lifetime resident…Do you know what they call this flea market
here next to the opera? Der Flieder Market!"

Soon Mac needed directions in Santa Fe. He had been there
before, but wasn't sure about Marcy Street or the Laughing
Frog. Mac struggled with Santa Fe traffic and tourists who
wandered into the road willy-nilly.

A fat, grotesque, dark green frog cut from wood constituted
the gallery sign, swinging from the front porch of a bungalow
painted dark green to match and trimmed in hot pink. The
frog's grin was rather menacing.

As they entered the Laughing Frog, Mac exclaimed, "Great
Jehozaphat! Will you look at this!"

Color exploded at them from the walls. Wild. Bold. Gaudy.
Garish. The right adjective depended on a person's taste. Paint
was splashed, thrown, on very large canvasses. There was impact.
You had to give the artist that.

A svelte woman glided toward them across the plush gray
carpeting. Christy took in the Santa Fe look: straight fair hair
pulled back into a turquoise and silver clip low on her neck;
tan, obviously natural-fiber top; long dull-purple broomstick
skirt; high fawn-colored moccasins with silver clasps. This must
be the owner.

Mac seemed to be the object of the woman's greeting and
"Help you?" but Christy introduced them both and explained
her errand. The woman smiled politely. "You want to know if I

remember a patron at the Paul Alvarez Opening? Such a dear boy. His innocent and exuberant use of color. His primitive relating to the forces which—"

"Yes," Christy attempted to interrupt the patter politely. "Miss Doris Jordan was here. I forgot to ask her, but if you had a Guest Book to sign that evening...?"

"But, of course. It's right here," gesturing toward a delicate old pecan table, too delicate for the overwhelming swirls of color on the walls.

She glanced through the names as Christy said, "A large woman. Hair in a bun. Wearing a black silk suit."

Memory returned and the gallery owner smiled with more warmth. "Oh, yes! But darling Paul called her something—?"

"La Doña Jordan?"

"Of course. And," she added triumphantly. "Here's the name! Right here in our register!"

Christy felt relief, like she could stand up straight after being burdened down, though she told herself she had never, never doubted La Doña.

"If I could just quickly write a statement for you to sign?"

The woman stiffened. "I don't know that I could sign—"

"Please." Christy's voice was friendly as she continued to scrawl rapidly on her yellow pad. "Won't be anything to it. Just a little note saying that you recall seeing La Doña Jordan at the opening as well as finding her name in the register."

As the woman hesitated, Mac joined the conversation. "Then if you have the time, I'd appreciate it if you could explain these paintings to me."

Eager to get to Mac, the gallery owner quickly signed the brief statement.

Trying to maintain a solemn expression, Christy watched Mac earnestly appreciate the spiel.

"Powerful," he murmured. "Powerful." And her favorite, "Now *that's* a painting!"

Christy directed Mac to Bagelmania for a great combination of food and Santa Fe's New York atmosphere. They shared the satisfied feeling of a mission accomplished.

"Does this automatically get the case against Doris dismissed?" Mac asked.

"Dismissed? Not automatically, no, and this is just the underbrush," Christy answered after they ordered. "The District Attorney will want to check it out himself, my taking the gallery owner's signed statement was to keep her from changing her mind later. But when we bolster La Dona's alibi with that of the artist, Paul Alvarez, I won't have to do much persuading to get the D.A. to see that she had nothing to do with Eusebio's and Watkins' murders." Christy's tone turned somber as she added, "Of course, that leaves the big problem, proving either self defense or that she just plain didn't shoot Kramer."

Mac tried to try to give Christy a break with banter all through lunch. But as they sat over coffee, neither wanting dessert, Christy could no longer fight off her foreboding. The evil hadn't ended with Dr. Kramer. "I feel uneasy, Mac. I'm left with all sorts of questions."

"Like?"

"Like first of all the brujo. He left a lot unanswered. Did Dr. Kramer burn the morada and paint the symbols by himself? Are others involved?"

"He offered to find out who tried to kill you."

Thinking he was being facetious, Christy gave Mac a look, but saw his expression was somber. She went on, "And can we say that Kramer killed Watkins, too?"

Mac took a sip of coffee. "Well, La Doña didn't mention Kramer's confession to that, and shooting Watkins was a different m.o. than knifing Eusebio." Mac pondered, then added, "But still, maybe Watkins was in Kramer's way and killed by him."

Christy nodded, still musing, while Mac signaled for the check.

"We still have another player," Mac said as he thought. "The person who bought Kramer's research."

"Not Watkins," Christy said slowly. "He wouldn't have been working if he were someone with millions available to pay Kramer. But, what if? Maybe he was hired to spy on Kramer by the buyer with the deep pockets, easy enough if he worked at LANL, killed when no longer needed."

They left and Mac was quiet, negotiating Santa Fe traffic. As they started back up the hill, he said, "We've been forgetting the briefcase that surely held his research data. The Lady described it. I saw it in the store. We can surely assume that whoever shot the doctor stole the briefcase."

There was another pause, then Mac smacked the steering wheel. "That could be it! Whoever was buying the research from Kramer decided it was a helluva lot cheaper to just do away with the good doctor and take the damn stuff!"

"So he, she, wasn't following Kramer so much as following the briefcase?"

"Right!"

They grinned proudly at each other.

Growing serious again, Christy said, "That still leaves me feeling very uncomfortable. Someone wanted me dead! I try not to think about it, but the cloud is always there in the back of my mind. It could be anyone from anywhere. Someone never seen in Taos. I don't know whom to suspect."

"Who prowls at night?" Mac asked, then answered his own question, "Duane Dobbs and Fred Ritchie."

"Now you're scaring me," Christy said.

"Hush, now or I'll go back to the old body-guard-in-a-sleeping-bag routine."

Mac was trying to lighten the mood. He didn't succeed.

CHAPTER XXVII

True to his word that he would raid Los Piñones mine, Chief Garcia called the Sheriff, his counterpart at the State Police, and the National Guard. Since this was supposed to be a drug bust, the Chief also brought in the D.E.A. He spent time Friday convincing a judge that he had probable cause for a search warrant. This whole fandango did rest on Baca's word as to the armed guards and set-up so, despite personal preference to the contrary, Chief Garcia included him.

Before dawn on Saturday, the law enforcement forces gathered at the Taos Police Station. Their squad cars overflowed the parking lot and lined both sides of Civic Plaza Drive.

The personnel might have grumbled at being called out for a dawn raid on a Saturday morning, but they enjoyed the excitement. Taos County usually didn't offer much.

The street lights shone on silent, empty streets as the Chief's patrol car pulled out first, leading the cavalcade out of town. They went the back way, out Placitas, past the Lilac Shop, turned left and were on the highway, heading north, going fast. El Prado was quickly left behind, through the Old Blinking Light, and soon the signs for other small communities flashed past. Down the long sweeping hill into Arroyo Hondo, up again and past San Christobel and the D.H. Lawrence shrine and ranch.

The rare driver at this hour gaped at the seemingly endless procession of light-flashing police, sheriff, and government cars.

The vegetation changed from the high desert piñon and juniper to the higher-altitude pines, black against a sky becoming gray with dawn.

Down another long hill and into the town of Questa where only the stray light showed here and there in a home or little business. Miners would have been up, getting ready for work, but the mine was closed now.

The silent procession rushed into the final run to La Mesa and beyond.

Almost all of the residents of La Mesa still slept in this gray dawn, but a few ailing and elderly were restlessly awake. From their windows, they watched with astonishment as patrol cars—black, black and white, brown, blue, blue and silver—rushed by soundlessly, red and yellow lights flashing. An ominous sight.

The convoy arrived at the point where the dirt road started another ascent up to Los Piñones. The conglomerate of law enforcement parked every which way at the base of the mountain below the old gold mine.

Iggy thought this was about the most fun he'd ever had. Lord! What a ride! He watched Chief Garcia instruct some representatives of the various agencies to stay at their patrol cars. They drew their guns, placing them on hoods and roofs of the vehicles, leaned there, and prepared to wait.

From the remaining posse, the Chief pointed to those appearing most fit and said, "Take a hike. A real hike. I want you up in those trees on the far side of the mine before we get to the front. Need you men to seal off the back way. If this is a drug lab, they'll be scattering every which way."

Most of the selected "volunteers" grinned happily. They were country men, accustomed to tracking through the mountains to hunt for elk and deer.

"The rest of you come along with me. You, too, Baca. We'll surround the front. Don't let anyone out, cars or on foot."

"I'm going with you," Sergeant Brown demanded.

The Chief lifted his shaggy eyebrows. "Thought you had your man. You been saying Pat Salazaar like a broken record.

Sergeant Brown grinned at him. "Thought you showed probable cause for a drug raid in order to get the search warrant. That's what this is, isn't it, Chief? A drug raid?"

Scowl. "Don't get cute with me, Sergeant."

"Wouldn't think of it, Chief Garcia."

They walked directly up the new road toward the cleared area and the dark gash that was the old mine. That many men could not move silently but, surrounding them, the great old forest imposed its own silence, that of thick blue spruce and huge, high-reaching ponderosa pine.

The quiet was broken by the angry screech of mountain jays. Iggy tried to control his panting. He jumped as a nearby deer was startled and ran off, loudly snapping and rustling the underbrush.

The sun popped over the top of the mountain, leaving the mine and La Mesa below still in shadow, but lighting the lower plains that stretched away in the distance.

As Iggy and the others approached the camouflaged fence and guardhouse, Chief Garcia saw a wave from higher up the mountain above the old gold mine. The rear echelon was in place.

"This is where the guards were, Chief," Iggy murmured, wiping sweat from his eyes.

Silence in the protected area. But then Iggy saw two men stumble out of the guardhouse. "Yes!" he mouthed and Chief Garcia gave him a relieved look. After all, he'd exposed himself to a lot of ridicule on the strength of Iggy's report.

It was obvious that the men had just been awakened, but were unaware of the cause. They had grabbed up their clothes in bundles. Still in undershirts, the two were sticking arms through sleeves of uniform jackets.

Still oblivious, the bigger was trying to scratch an itch on his belly as he dressed. He had a protuberant red nose. The other, wiry and weasel-faced dressed more quickly.

All at once, the two guards took in the large contingent of uniforms—blue, black, and khaki. "What the hell?" They reached for shotguns.

Chief Garcia stepped forward. "Hold it right there. I have a warrant to search these premises."

"No, sir!" Weasel stood firm. "You're Taos Police, right?"

The Chief nodded.

"Got no authority to come in here. This is posted U.S. Government Property." Pause. "Yeah, and I recognize the fat guy. Already told him get his ass outa here!"

Sergeant Brown stood alongside the Chief. "Look, buddy, Attorney Baca's none of your business. I'm here with the New Mexico State Police. We're coming in."

Men reached for their guns, raised their weapons.

Iggy held his breath.

Weasel and Nose didn't budge.

Weasel mimicked Sergeant Brown, "The State Police ain't worth shit where the federal government's involved."

Red-faced, the trooper looked at Chief Garcia. "Let's take the bastards!"

Aware of the tension in the fire power behind him, Chief Garcia said, "Hold on everybody!" He turned back to the guards. "I can't take your word for it. I've seen marijuana plantations with guards like you fellows. Where's your authority?"

Weasel told Nose, "Get the papers."

"Stop! You're not going into that guardhouse alone. Go with him Sergeant."

Hand on his holster, the Sergeant joined Nose as they entered the guardhouse.

The Chief addressed Weasel, "Whose authority are you planning to show us?"

"The Department of Energy, that's what! This is a top-secret installation. You have to have security clearance to get in here. And your warrant doesn't give you that."

Iggy and the Chief exchanged looks of glee, hearing D.O.E. They had their Los Alamos connection! But Chief Garcia presented a stony face to the guard. "What's going on in there?"

Weasel smirked. "Not a damn thing! Kramer and Salazaar, his number two man, are dead and we're Closed Until Further Notice!"

"Then what are you two guards doing here?"

"Supposed to protect government property 'til some fucker in Los Alamos or D.C. tells us different. That's why we been sleeping here since the top honcho died."

Sergeant Brown returned and offered a document to Chief Garcia. He saw that this was indeed a licensed facility of the United States Department of Energy and addressed both guards, "Well, maybe we can resolve this without having to take you boys in. One thing we're looking for is Dr. Kramer's briefcase. Evidence in a case. You two see that around?"

Nose actually spoke, "Took it with him when he left in a government car Wednesday. Always takes it."

"Ain't been back because he got himself shot" Weasel said.

"Where is Dr. Kramer's own car?"

Iggy held his breath again. Lord, let it be the one that hit Christy. End all this.

Sergeant Brown elbowed the Chief, muttered, "I sent some men to look over the fence in back. They saw a black Lexus. Say it's got some dents."

Thank you, Jesus!

Chief Garcia nodded, saying casually to Nose, "I guess that's Kramer's car round back, hunh?"

"You got no right!"

"I take it that's a Yes."

One of the Taos Police officers, who had been left behind with the patrol cars, came huffing up from below. "Radio, Chief. We just heard from Washington on that background check you asked for. Some top dog wants to talk to you. Says what are we doing screwing around an on-going federal investigation?"

"That's just the man I need to talk to!"

He turned to the D.E.A. agent, "I think you'll want to go back to the station with me. It appears you federal boys have a case of your left hand....

"Don't any of you dismiss your men. We're making a quick stop at my office. If it turns out I like I'm guessing it will, we have to get to a Talpa hacienda pronto!"

Dobbs! Iggy thought. The information is on Dobbs and the Chief's going to...Oh, God! Christy!

In his room at Casa Vieja, an angry man was packing. He would have been out of here Thursday morning if he'd had his way. Now, damn fuck-up, thanks to his man following the usual Washington stupidity. Have to find another room.

He had made the call before midnight Wednesday. Told Washington mission accomplished! But the voice instructed, "You know you have to have the results checked out by a qualified scientist, someone who can at least screen the data and make sure what we have is what we want."

"No problem," the man in Talpa answered. "The contact is already in place here."

"The fuck you're saying?" Washington lost its cool.

Sinking feeling. "But I was sure….Bastard checked into Casa Vieja last week."

Wrong goddamnit! Wrong. Now he had to connect. Wouldn't let him leave until Washington was sure he had all the necessary proof. Make certain nothing was left, nothing in someone else's hands.

He swore non-stop as he slammed shut the case.

The other guests of Casa Vieja were in their rooms. Mac worked on the courtyard, getting an early start on weeding.

In the dining room, Christy slowly cleared the table, her mind on other things.

She had dreamed of Eusebio again—a bloody, dead Eusebio. But not the same dream. No, this one began with a Doberman stalking her. She ran but, snarling, it grabbed her hand, its teeth tearing into her flesh.

Then the dream flashed to the card table as before, the one she had told her dream group about. She held the same cards. Eusebio was again telling her, "Don't bet on the full house, king high. Bet on the double deuce." The king…King-Kramer. But if she didn't bet on the king, went for the double deuce….

The phone rang, startling Christy because she was so deep in her reverie.

Mama.

"What are you doing?"

Christy was still in the dream world. "What? Oh, clearing the table, Mamacita."

"You will get too tired, cooking, taking care of those guests, cleaning…."

Christy's mind wandered. The dream was unraveling. Eusebio who wants to tell her something in the dream. What does he know? Who killed him, of course! King-Kramer admitted killing

Eusebio to La Doña....Wait! She's to bet on the double deuce—
D.D.—Duane Dobbs!

"Christina! Answer me, Christina."

Christy's mind was making connections. Reasoning. Her tone
was vague, "I'm sorry, Mamacita. I was thinking about a dream."

"What dream is it that is so important that you can't listen..."

Christy gazed blankly out the window near the Middle Room
door as she talked. She heard footsteps through la Sala and looked
that way. Duane Dobbs was approaching, each hand gripping
luggage handles, a raincoat draped over the big garment carrier
and something else in his right hand.... Suddenly it all fell into
place. Oh, God! Dobbs was able to check on Kramer from his
position with the D.O.E. Dobbs killed Kramer. And in the dream
they were all "playing" with her...

Christy stared. She heard Mama's voice, suddenly wanted her
to get help. But she mustn't precipitate a showdown while alone.
"Yes, Mamacita..." Maybe he wouldn't notice, "La polizía! Rapído!"

Dobbs hit his head on the low arch between La Sala and the
Middle Room, stumbled, juggled the bags. They dropped. The
raincoat slithered part way off the pieces it covered, the garment
carrier and a black briefcase. Smooth, soft-looking leather. A black
briefcase!

He noticed Christy's gaze, looked down. And then Christy
seemed to see in slow motion. Dobbs' movements checked for
a moment. His hand plunged into the side pocket of the
suitcase, emerged with a knife.

Christy dropped the phone. It hung dangling. Mama's voice
squawking, "Christina! Christina Garcia! Answer me! What is
the matter?"

Christy froze in silence.

"Just shut up!" Dobbs hissed. "Don't make a sound. Put it
all together, haven't you? Just now?...But I caught you
eavesdropping before. Heard you talking."

The words were hard to take in. His fury hit her like a physical
blow. Fear made her blood surge, her chest cramp.

Duane Dobbs talked on, the sounds like stones against her
body.

"Kramer used this knife on Salazaar. It was in his car. And I have a gun in my pocket. I used it before, but the knife is better, won't make a sound."

Christy stood up slowly. She could not speak. Terror. This was absolute terror. She could do nothing. Her mind a white nothing.

Still speaking in that deadly whisper, Dobbs said, "We're going to walk out that door to my car with this knife against your back. You will drive us—"

She heard no more. Her terrified brain began to work. This is what she'd thought about in calmer times. Go with him and there's no hope. He'll kill you where there are no witnesses. Remember the self-defense class. Surprise the attacker. Shout! Shout bloody murder! Dobbs jumped back in astonishment. Christy's pointed fingers jammed at his eyes.

Hearing Christy, Lisa, Lolly and Tama raced out of their room. They saw Dobbs raising a knife clenched in a raised fist. The knife was coming at Christy!

Without thought of the knife, Lisa made a flying tackle from behind.

Tama looked around for a weapon, saw the umbrella in the corner, and came poking violently at Dobbs with the point.

Between Christy, the tackle and the umbrella jabs, Dobbs lost his balance and went down, hitting his head on the desk. Blood flowed. The knife flew out of his hand.

Lolly threw her considerable weight into a jump onto Dobbs' chest as he lay prone.

Lisa, still on the floor from her tackle, crawled over and retrieved the knife.

"His pocket!" Christy yelled. "He has a gun in his pocket!"

Dobbs was too stunned to reach for the gun before Lisa had the knife at his throat and Tama had given Dobbs' arm a mighty jab with the umbrella.

Hearing the commotion, Mac ran in from the courtyard through the kitchen and dining room. He stopped just inside the Middle Room, stunned at the sight before him. Christy was staring down at Duane Dobbs who lay on the floor at her feet. Lolly sat complacently on his chest, offering a gun up toward Christy. Lisa knelt by the motionless Dobbs, holding a knife at his throat.

Tama stood menacingly above him, an umbrella gripped in both hands like a weapon.

The frozen tableau returned to motion. Mac saw nothing left to do except hold Christy and call 911. He saw the dangling phone, lifted it with one hand while gripping Christy with the other. No sound on the line.

The sound of many sirens ripped into the silence. They seemed to be speeding closer down the dirt road.

The sirens wailed and hiccuped to a stop. Someone shouted, "Police! Don't move! We're coming in!"

The women smiled at each other. A little late, fellows.

Two large men, Chief Garcia and Sergeant Brown, elbowed each other and Iggy's big belly through the narrow door. But a tiny figure skipped under their arms and was first inside.

Mama!

Mama hurtled her little body across the room to join Mac in wrapping her arms around Christy.

"Christina Garcia! I heard you wanted the police. The noise. You shout. I knew you needed your Mamacita!"

Chapter XXVIII

Duane Dobbs had been taken away in handcuffs.

Lisa, Lolly, and Tama had been thanked profusely by everyone.

A happy but red-faced Iggy ostensibly had to go see his client, although Christy suspected he also had to recover from overexertion. He would be back.

Chief Garcia was leaving, too, but had also promised to return. "I want to get all my ducks in a row."

"And you'll see to La Doña? Be sure she's released?" Christy asked anxiously.

"No problem. I'll take care of the paperwork, call the district attorney. He owes me a few."

Mac said, "There's no reason...uh, by now, that is, for her to stay in the hospital. I'll call Holy Cross."

Chief Garcia beamed, "I will personally escort La Doña Abogada back here this afternoon. Right now I have to inform the State of New Mexico, the Sheriff's Department, and the government of the United States that it was my arrest."

Everyone insisted that Christy needed to rest after her ordeal. "What about you guys?" she said to the trio. "You did all the work!" That brought back fear to tinge her elation. Lord, Lord, it was over!

"Good thing, too," Mac hugged her again.

"Anyway," Christy added, "I'm way too hyper to rest. Besides, I want to call La Doña before she hears the big news anywhere else!"

Mama had been torn. She had to choose: go home and call all her friends with the big story of Christina's heroism and knife attacks and captured killers and FBI, or stay to hover over Christina and hear all the details first hand. It was a terrible choice, but finally maternal love, and being in at the finish, won out. "I stay," she announced. "Christina must rest, then eat."

Starting for the kitchen, Mama returned to hug Lisa, Lolly and Tama. "Thank you," she said with dignity. "I understand from what is said here that you have been brave in protecting my daughter. You will stay and eat and tell me all the story. I left the telephone to come to the rescue." She turned again toward the kitchen.

Christy protested, "No, Mamacita. There's no need for you to fix lunch."

"There is need," Mama answered firmly and briskly removed herself to the kitchen. The last heard was, "A large meal..."

Lisa was the spokesperson for herself, Lolly and Tama after they had exchanged looks: "Will that be all right, Miz Grant? We're supposed to be checking out, but we sure want to hear what's been going on! We sort of came in at the climax!"

"Then please stay for the big wrap-up," Christy said, almost giddy now.

Mac called Holy Cross to organize La Doña's dismissal, then asked the head nurse to switch the call to Doris Jordan's room and handed the receiver to Christy. La Doña answered with a curt, "Yes?"

"It's Christy, La Doña." Her voice was excited. "Have you heard the news?"

"What news?"

"You're completely cleared!" Elation.

"That's not news. It's been obvious from the beginning of this farce."

"No, no, La Doña. Just now. This morning. Duane Dobbs has been arrested after attacking me." There was so much to say that she had trouble sorting out the words, and her turbulent emotions.

"You're not making a bit of sense, Christina," La Doña grumbled, but Christy could hear the smile in her voice.

"I know I'm not. Just hear this: Chief Garcia will pick you up and bring you here. Everything's beautiful!"

Silence, then, "One could debate such an extravagant statement, Christina, but I'm happy the matter is resolved. I will expect a detailed account. I assume Pat Salazaar is also in the clear?"

"Yes, yes. Iggy has gone to tell him and bring him back. You, all of us, we'll put the whole story together. Who did what. We'll all get together here. Lunch, too."

"Thank you, my dear." Finally a bit of emotion in the firm old voice.

"What did she say?" Mac was smiling, still standing close to Christy as she sat at the desk.

"Not much, but she was pleased. And just think. Pat proved innocent. And those blasted reporters will have to admit Los Hermanos had no involvement!"

"Come and sit in the sun on the courtyard. Take a few minutes to relax. Calm down while the trio are packing and before the mob arrives. This is your doctor speaking," Mac ended with a loving smile. Lord! He could have lost this woman.

The bright sun on the courtyard was a surprise. Until it hit her eyes, Christy hadn't realized how dark it had seemed inside, dark with violence, dark with the presence of a killer.

Mac pulled a lounge chair into a spot of full sunshine in the middle of the courtyard and Christy stretched out in it, seeing the happy colors of the tulips and hyacinths. The blossoms of the cherry trees were fully out now and the huge old cottonwood spread its new green leaves over the wall. The wall. Its thick, solid adobe surrounded her in protection. And the olive tree, just coming into bloom, laid its fragrance on her, the incomparable scent of New Mexico.

They all arrived and were at the table. What a difference! and what a sameness! To her right as they had been for two weeks of breakfasts, were Lisa, Lolly and Tama, with Mac at the end, but Pat Salazaar now sat next to Tama on that side. And a total difference down the other side: from Mac, it was Iggy, La Doña,

Chief Garcia, and Mama happily ensconced next to her favorite nephew, the Chief, and at Christy's left hand.

Christy looked lovingly at little Mama, Mamacita, pink from her exertions in the kitchen and the excitement. I've left her out so much, Christy thought and look how happy she is in the midst of it all.

Smiles turned to laughter as Chief Garcia asked, "Which one of you ladies tackled Dobbs?" and they began their story that's been told many times by now: "I tackled..." "I jumped on his chest. I told you I'm round but not soft..." "Poor Duane Dobbs knows just how round!"...."Don't forget me and Lolly's umbrella, you know? When Lisa had a knife at his throat... ("I did! I did!") I kept him down, poking him with the umbrella, didn't I?"

Chortling (the Chief) and giggling (Iggy's falsetto), those two shook their heads and asked to hear the story straight through. Pat Salazaar was round-eyed. Stern La Doña gave up her dignity, wiping tears of laughter from her face.

Quiet Pat turned to Tama next to him, regarding her ethereal prettiness in astonishment, "You were poking a killer with an umbrella?"

This started them all off again and La Doña gasped, "Tell it! Please tell us exactly what happened!"

Christy sobered, thinking of the terror, and began the explanation for her guests , some knowing bits and pieces, some hardly anything at all.

When La Doña took over to tell her part, Chief Garcia had the courage to interject, "Stephen Kramer's own car has proved to be the one that repeatedly struck my Prima Christy on the horseshoe curve."

A gasp from Christy. "Barnabe! You've got the car? It was Kramer, not Dobbs who tried to kill me?"

Looking smug, Chief Garcia said, "Apparently there was no damage to Dobbs' first car. He really did turn it into the rental place, but for reasons of his own. Maybe wanted something more inconspicuous to tail Kramer in. But after our raid this morning—"

"Raid?" a chorus from around the table.

"That's my story," the Chief said with some importance. Iggy cleared his throat loudly. "And Mr. Baca's," Barnabe amended, then became even more magnanimous. "I have to give it to you, Ignacio. You did better than I expected.

"But first, in answer to my prima. We've made a sight match, not official, between the damage to Kramer's Lexus and the paint scraped off Prima Christy's Buick. And that's not all I have to tell you. I—"

La Doña was not about to have her jury speech taken from her. "I have not completed my account, Barnabe Garcia." Shoulder to shoulder, she glared at him.

"Sorry, La Doña."

"Yes." La Doña accepted his apology, then added grandly, "You have a great deal for which to be sorry."

"I know, La Doña. But under the circumstances—"

"Under the circumstances of my practicing here for well nigh one half of a century?"

This could be an endless argument, so Christy urged La Doña to continue. She did, summing up her terrifying ordeal in her usual dry fashion. La Doña never had a more satisfying jury response than that from the four across the table who are staring at her in awe.

Chief Garcia gave La Doña a sitting bow. "If I may add?"

She nodded her head graciously.

"The Albuquerque O.M.I....medical examiner's office," he explained for the uninitiated, "has been so rushed, they're working weekends down there. Sent me a fax just before I came over here." The Chief paused for effect. "Kramer was shot by the same gun as Watkins. It was not La Doña's Luger."

"Hot dog!" from Iggy. Applause from all the others.

The Chief continued, "Watkins was evidently Dobbs' informant on Kramer's progress, maybe turned to blackmail. Verdad. In addition to the ballistics' evidence, we also have a witness to Dobbs' presence in the alley behind Los Bailes. The bartender."

"How come you're just now getting that information?" Iggy asked.

"The witness was waiting to provide a description until the Crimestoppers offered an award." The Chief grinned wickedly. "Too bad we already had our man."

"But my cousin Eusebio?" Pat finally asked timidly.

"As La Doña just said, Dr. Kramer told her he had killed your cousin. And Dobbs' claims it is indeed Kramer who committed that homicide."

Iggy proudly brought up the raid at Los Piñones, then magnanimously let the Chief have center stage.

The Chief had changed from the morning's uniform to a casual blue sports shirt and jeans, but they somehow saw a uniform expand as his chest swelled. "We wrapped the whole thing up," he reported, "the site was indeed being run by the D.O.E., Department of Energy. But now closed."

"You mean the Department of Energy is the villain in all this?" Lisa asks.

"No, ma'am. Well, not exactly. They've been on the tail of Kramer, using Dobbs as their agent, but Dobbs was playing a double game, hoping to steal from Kramer in turn and sell the work himself."

"Well, Dobbs must have picked Casa Vieja because it was so out of the way. How could he have imagined the direct link to Salazaar and Kramer through its hostess?" Iggy smiled.

"And you can bet your sweet a...I had a thing or two to say to Washington." Chief Garcia sounded angry. "I hit a stone wall on Dobbs when I ordered that record you asked for. Mr. Baca had the same problem. This morning I talked with the D.O.E. who were screaming about an on-going investigation. They had caught on to Dobbs' dual dealing, nailed his Washington contact, and sent a man to the scene to get the goods on both Dobbs and Kramer."

"Hey, you guys?" Tama looked from one to another. "I sure am confused, you know?"

The Chief explained, "Dr. Kramer and his team were doing authorized research into HIV and AIDS. The doc here would understand it better, but listen. D.O.E. told me that some months ago, the group were sent up here to the gold mine where a bacterium deep underground was recently discovered. Kramer and his microbiologists went to remove samples for study. Los Alamos scientists were closer to the spot than researchers from the Center for Disease Control in Atlanta or the National Institutes of Health in Washington. And Kramer could quite easily move the final stages on his immune system work to the new site.

There was a bit of a rush because D.O.E. thought it possible that there would be a commercial use for this new bug, that it might clean up some problems by eating and processing industrial waste—making itself benign." The Chief sighed. "Ironically, Kramer's immune system work had already given him a shot at selling immensely valuable results to a private pharmaceutical house, but of course D.O.E. didn't know about his breakthrough, tagging the gene that controls aging. Moving off site to Los Piñones made it easier for him."

Mac spoke with excitement, "If that's true, if Kramer's research pans out, it is the magic bullet! But I just don't believe immortality is that easy to achieve—or possible!"

La Doña scolded. "Let's stick to the facts."

"Fact is," Chief Garcia responded, "Dobbs was kept here by his buyer until that very thing could be checked out: was Kramer's research worth a damn, or rather, worth the millions he claimed to have sold it for."

Mama grew restless. It seemed the good part was over and she had phone calls to make. So much to tell the ladies!

La Doña complained, "All this speculation may be quite entertaining, but a small matter concerns me. Has this Duane Dobbs confessed to shooting Stephen? And how in the world did he appear on the scene so quickly? I was there, remember!"

"Yes, he has, La Doña," the Chief answered. "First of all you weren't here when Prima Christy told us what Dobbs said when he was threatening her with the knife. He bragged that the gun in his pocket was the one he used on Watkins and Kramer. In the second place, while he was all shaken up from his encounter with these fine citizens," a nod to the trio, "Dobbs was babbling, 'The briefcase, keep your eye on the briefcase.' And, La Doña, Dobbs thought it pretty clever that he was right behind you, tailing Kramer when he tried to kidnap you."

"And then seized the moment and shot Kramer?" Christy asked.

"Sure. The perfect crime. He may or may not have heard La Doña's shot, but he saw the wreck, saw Kramer slumped over the steering wheel, and La Doña Abogada running away.

"The autopsy shows Kramer was shot behind the ear, through the head. Apparently Dobbs leaned in the passenger door, shot

Kramer, found and grabbed the briefcase. Now he had what he came for: all the research worth millions and no one to tell the tale."

"And Watkins?" Mac asked. "Why did Dobbs kill Watkins?"

"We know Dobbs had to have someone here to monitor Kramer inside LANL. In his official D.O.E. capacity, Dobbs knew when Kramer's original research took the surprise turn, but he needed a spy. He knew when Kramer had succeeded in isolating the gene. We can only guess that Watkins kept him informed. When Watkins was no longer needed—bang! Dobbs didn't want a witness."

Mac shuddered. "Dobbs may well have thought Christy was a witness, too. It wasn't only that she saw the briefcase."

Mama jumped up to hug Christy at the same time that Desire floated in.

"Hi, everybody," she says. "I heard the news and thought I better come over to help out."

"What news?" Mama asks sharply. She wanted to be the first to tell her friends the story.

Desire stood behind Christy's chair, radiant in a gauzy, floaty baby blue dress. Darker blue short shorts were visible through the translucent, jaggedly cut skirt. "Oh, you know? My boy friend told me about the raid out at La Mesa? And my other boy friend said there was a police car parked over here? So, here I am!"

La Doña, with her own opinions of Desire, spoke sharply to Pat Salazaar, "I notice you have surreptitiously looked at your watch a number of times, young man. Are we keeping you from a more important appointment?"

"Uh, no, ma'am."

Mama was eager to leave. So many to call! She hugged Christy's neck again. "You be careful. Go to bed early. I pray for you." Then she formally thanked Lisa, Lolly and Tama once more.

Chief Garcia stood and stretched. "Not used to sitting so long....Well, I better be going, too. There's a lot of paperwork to be done. Loose ends. And I mustn't neglect our Mister Dobbs!"

Christy also rose so she could give her cousin a mighty bear hug. "Thank you, Barnabe," she whispered.

Lisa said abruptly to her friends, "Better get our bags and get going," hoping there would be no more thanks, but there were from Christy and Mac.

As the trio left the dining room, Tama got the last word, "Look for me? I'll be back, you know? I was out of body when I found Taos in the first place, wasn't I?"

All these imminent departures brought everyone into the Middle Room, Pat Salazaar seeming particularly fidgety. Looking at his watch again, Pat said, "If you good people could just...." His sentence was never finished as he cocked his head, his ears almost seeming to prick, like a dog listening

"Yes, ma'am!" Pat announced happily to La Doña. "I do have an appointment!" Then racing to the door, he called back to Mama, "Thanks for dinner, Señora!" And was gone, leaving everyone puzzled and questioning.

"Shhh!" Christy's whisper cut through the confusion. "Listen!" And she, too, ran outside followed by the others.

Then, they could all hear faint, but audible down the road, men's voices chanting strange, plaintive alabados.

Mac, Lisa, Lolly and Tama looked totally bewildered, but La Doña appeared delighted, and Barnabe and Mama Garcia were beaming at one another, Mamacita doing little hops to try to see better, stopping now and then to hug Christy

Christy looked like a child radiant over a Christmas present she's about to open, but a little fearful this may not be the *one*.

The singing grew louder. They could see the beginning of the ragged line of Los Hermanos coming around the curve east of the hacienda.

Pat Salazaar was in front. And, as more and more Hermanos gathered, filling the small dirt lane and the lot across the way, Pat lifted the little piece of white paper in his hand. The singing stopped.

Clearly his throat nervously, Pat read in a near shout, "La Hermandad de Nuestro Señor Jesus of La Mesa morada, and those of our neighbors there, and many here around Talpa, Ranchos, and Taos, have come to thank you and praise God..."

Christy lost the rest of Pat's words. She could only absorb the sight before her as Mamacita alternately crossed herself and hugged Christy's arm in speechless excitement.

The awesome group of Spanish men of all ages and backgrounds, even an Anglo or two, some stooped, some upright, limping, sturdy, fierce and gentle, began to move.

A whisper entered Christy's mind.

Come quickly, m'hijas, her abuela calls. Count how many Hermanos you see. Count them carefully.

Eyes bright, Christy murmured aloud, "Oh, Grandmama, this time I see twenty, thirty, forty...Maybe fifty?"

Ah, m'hija, count again. More and more...and not only the living march!

The long, long line from La Mesa and all the moradas of the North Country passed by.

Not in the shadows, but in the bright new spring sunshine, the chanting was jubilant, giving thanks to God.